ALSO BY JESS

12/14/23
10.99

The Magnolia Parks Universe
Magnolia Parks
Daisy Haites
Magnolia Parks: The Long Way Home
Daisy Haites: The Great Undoing

Never
Never

NEVER

JESSA HASTINGS

Bloom *books*

Published by Bloom Books, an imprint of Sourcebooks
P.O. Box 4410, Naperville, Illinois 60567-4410
(630) 961-3900
sourcebooks.com

Cataloging-in-Publication data is on file with the Library of Congress.

Printed and bound in the United States of America.
VP 10 9 8 7 6 5 4 3 2 1

To that very first lost boy who I loved so much when I was so little.
You went to a faraway place that none of us could follow, and you are probably the
reason I first fell in love with the story about the forever young, forever free boy.
You were youth, you were joy, you were the little bird that had broken out of its
egg, and you are, to this day, time-locked in my mind all golden and laughing.
I hope you found what you were looking for. I hope that you are free.

DISCOVER
NEVERLAND

CHAPTER ONE

THERE IS A BOY OF LEGEND IN THE TALES PASSED DOWN IN MY FAMILY. HE glides on the coattails of the sun, rides the wind, and freedom runs through his veins. His heart, they say, is wild, but in every version of any story I've ever been told about him, never did I hear that his heart was untamable.

A captor of the imagination and a liberator of the soul, they say about him. My grandmother, she knew him, and her mother before her. My own mother as well. Our family's legacy is laced with tales of him and who he is and the adventures they had with him…some terrifying, others exhilarating, but always, always beautiful.

Beauty is funny though, don't you think? Because beautiful doesn't necessarily always mean good, and just because something doesn't make you happy doesn't preclude it from being beautiful either. An impertinent lesson I won't realize for quite some time though.

My grandmother, Wendy, she would tell me stories of her and this boy, how he came to her one quiet night in 1910 when her little brothers were being particularly boisterous. He tapped on her window—as she always knew he would because her mother's mother said so and she believed her—he sprinkled gold dust on her, and away they went. Happy thoughts and all that.

You know the story.

The boy, he took her to a faraway land tucked behind a star, where pirates were still true, mermaids didn't hide, and fairies flew through the air like autumn leaves on a windy day. He took my mother there, just like he took my grandmother and my great-grandmother.

Just as he would come for me.

I've been told these stories since before I could remember. They were embedded into my brain without my consent, actually. Magic was all around me whether I liked it or not, and I did not. Like my mother before me, I consider myself a learned woman and far too old for bedtime stories.

That boy, the one from their stories, they say he came for my great-grandmother Mary when she was twelve; he came for Wendy when she was thirteen, my mother when she was thirteen. I should be the same, so they thought.

And that was the story they'd tell me as they tucked me in at night all through my younger youth.

Sometimes my grandmother, sometimes my great-grandmother (but never my mother, because she said the stories would rot my mind).

"He'll be on his way for you soon, I imagine, Daphne." My grandmother would smile at me every night of my childhood as she'd leave the window unlatched for me so that he could enter.

But see, the boy never came.

Ten, eleven, twelve, thirteen—the years trickled by like rain on windows, and yet my windows, which remained unlatched, also remained unfilled.

The older I grew, the more I began to wonder if the legend in my family was just a strange bedtime story. A weird practical joke, perhaps, that everyone got carried away with and took too far for too many years.

By the time I was fifteen, I could see it on the faces of my grandmothers—this fear that maybe something had happened. Maybe that man with the hook had gotten the better of the boy finally. Or the great battle he'd always spoken of, maybe he died in it. I'd watch that thought fly across their faces the same way they said he'd fly across the sky, but eventually they'd always resolve he could never. It was impossible for him to die because he was the Never Boy, and he might say that death would be an awfully big adventure but it was also absolutely not his lot, or so they reasoned.

If you were to bring him up to my grandmothers to this day, still arriving on their faces would be a tickling blush and a dreamy, far-off look in their eyes. All youth and sunsets, adventures and wonder, mistakes and a magic that I'm quite sure I don't think really exists, but it does, for them at least. It's as though the boy lives in their memories and so do they, young and immortal, the clock hand rolling backwards, unwinding time and loosing its chains on them, and they are, once again, unbound by the cages of age.

Not my mother, it's worth noting, though she too lives in a certain past. However, it's the ancient kind, somehow much harder to reach.

Wendy said my mother had visited Peter. Mary, my great-grandmother, said my mother stayed a long while. I don't know what's true and what's not about my mother's past and her alleged life in Neverland. I do know that these days, she spends most of her time in the Yucatán Peninsula on a "very important dig"—those are her words. She's an archaeologist, see? A "matter of life and death," she calls this dig of hers. I doubt that that's true though. I can't fathom possibly how it could be, seeing as everything she's digging up hasn't been alive for quite some time now. I suspect quietly within myself that the death of which she speaks might more be her own. That she wasn't made to be a mother and that being one, were she to act like it—even just once in her lifetime—that it might kill her.

By the time I was fourteen, I was well done with the entire facade. I had started by then at Roedean and—with good reason— my dorm mate* was uncomfortable with my tendency to leave the windows unlocked at nighttime. That aside, I was past the age of bedtime stories, and I was tired of the fairy tales. The mystical boy I'd been told my entire life was truth had morphed into myth, though Nanna Wendy and Grandma Mary still swore up and down and inside out that he was real and on his way to find me from some corner in the universe.

The truth is I don't need him to come and find me anymore.

It's 1967, and I'm seventeen (soon to be eighteen) years old. I don't want to spend my summer with a strange thirteen-year-old boy. Aside from the concept of the aforementioned residing within a status of questionable legality, it also just happens to sound rather terrible. I've far more pressing matters on my mind than an imaginary boy who crows at himself and all the things he does.

This summer is all that's standing between myself and the start of my real life.

---

* Charlotte.

I was always young for my year at school. My mother enrolled me early. She said once it was because I was smart, but I think it was because she wanted to be in Belize. But it's worked rather well for me because I'm quite ready to grow up. I've been a grown-up all my life, I think. I've had to be.

The most responsible adult I know is obsessed entirely with ninth century Mesoamerica, and my grandmothers are completely off with the fairies,* though not literally (much to their dismay).

They are lovely though. Please don't for a second think that they aren't.

Wendy and Mary are my favorite people in the world, bereft of reality though they may be.

It makes them both sad—Wendy especially, I can tell—that he's forgotten me. "He forgets things sometimes, see?" she'd say with a grimace, as though that makes it sting less. That I'm either forgettable or raised by lunatics.

They are, at least, profiteering lunatics. Wendy wrote and illustrated all her stories into a great big one; you've probably read it. She wrote it under a man's name because it's a man's world. More so then than now, maybe.

The sexual revolution is upon us (or so they tell us), but I'm not vastly interested in sex as it is. I'm interested in intelligence and the pursuit of it.

I like geology. That's strange, my friend told me. It's a weird thing to like. But I like this planet. I'm happy to be on it, happy to be grounded by it. It's beautiful here, so why wouldn't I be? I don't need a silly star with mermaids on it. I've got this one, with all its strange and peculiar variants of life busting out all over. Manatees and hummingbirds and fireflies. What a world.

Another thing on this planet that I love? Cambridge. And I got in. I start in the autumn. I made Wendy lie on tables in the library with me while no one was looking and breathe in the wisdom of those who'd gone before me, and I felt for the billionth time in my life a great urgency to learn absolutely everything I can, to know it all. Sometimes Mary says she can see it on me, aging me, all the knowledge I try to get growing me up, but then Wendy's always said it's strange how love can undo you. Time unravels in its presence, she says. It pierces the veil of our understanding.

It's not an overly spectacular night. Quite regular, actually.

---

* Or with Arthur. I used to hear a lot about Avalon.

Brisk, even.

The air's cool, our street in our little corner of Chelsea by the park is, as usual, blissfully quiet, and the sky is all clear, peppered with stars that, upon closer inspection, were perhaps unusually bright.[†]

And it is on this night of no great or particular significance that my story really begins.

You know how you grow accustomed to the sounds of your own home?

With the exception of my time away from school, I've lived at number 14 all my life. It's the house my mother grew up in, and hers—the Darling home[‡]—three generations. I know the sounds of my house in the depths of me—blood memories, maybe. Embedded in my DNA.

I suppose it's important to pause here and let you know that there was a constant and unspoken battle that raged within the walls of my bedroom: one of windows up and windows down.

The unlatching I could deal with. As I mentioned before, at my grandmothers' insistence, my bedroom windows were always unlatched,[§] despite exponentially rising crime in this city. And who was I to argue with them? They wanted to see me mauled to death by a gang of youths who scaled the wall of a Chelsea home looking for an easy window to open and climb through for drug money? That's fine. My death could be their burden to bear. Less fine by me, however, was the flagrant invitation for trouble by leaving said window flung wide open.

"He mightn't know to come in otherwise," Wendy would say.

"Then he's not very bright," I'd tell her, and she'd roll her eyes.

"Well…" Mary would interrupt. "He can hardly go around opening the windows of everyone around town, can he? He'd be charged with a home invasion."

"And perhaps he should be!" I'd tell them in insolence.

"Daphne!" Wendy would sigh before opening it again.

I mentioned before that it was brisk and oddly so for the time of year.

---

† One in particular, I daresay, but that's all you'll hear from me about it.

‡ The one from the stories.

§ Sorry, Charlotte.

Every night since I'd returned home from the library, I'd close my windows, fearful I'd catch my death if I didn't, but without fail, every night, one of my grandmothers would creep in and open them back up again, almost as though it were a nervous tic they had. We'd argue about it in the mornings, but secretly, I'd grown accustomed to the breeze on my face, and on the occasional nights they themselves fell asleep before they had a chance to open it, I found myself having a considerably worse sleep because I liked how the cold gave me an excuse to sleep with something heavy on me.

It's rather late on this brisk, starry, quite regular evening, around midnight or perhaps just a smidge before. I'm asleep when I hear my window open.

I'm a light sleeper. I always have been.

I smile at the sound of the window pulling up as it always does. I wonder which grandmother it is, those sweet pests. I'd know in a minute because I know their sounds too. Wendy always steps on the same floorboard that creaks, and Mary, no matter how many times we've played this game, her walking cane hits the door on the way out.

I wait, brows up, listening for my clue so I can complain to the right one in the morning about them minding their own business and how they'd rather me have pneumonia than risk their imaginary boyfriend seeing a closed window.

But I hear none.

No floorboard creaks.

No cane hits.

I wait.

They've opened my window all my life. I know the sound of my window opening, so I know for certain that it is open…that and I can feel the breeze I wait for.

I bolt upright, and it takes only a second for my eyes to adjust, but even before they do, I can make out a figure standing there.

Tall. Broad. A man.

In a split second, I think "Shit! It's finally happened! The youths and the drug money!" However, I decide I won't take my imminent death lying down, so I smack on the lamp that's next to me and sit up as quickly and tall as I can.

"Who are you?" I ask him quickly, sharply. I hope he doesn't catch my nervous breathing.

His face screws up. "You don't know who I am?"

And that is when I notice his face.

Golden hair. Interesting eyes that stick out on his face, but I can't tell the color from here. He's just in a pair of faded, ragged olive linen trousers that tie at the front. Shirtless.

Distractingly so, if I'm honest.

You don't see a lot of shirtless men around London, I suppose is the thing. And it's barely summer anymore, and there aren't beaches here anyway, and who's swimming in the Thames, and I'm just staring at his chest, dazed, mouth a little ajar. His skin is so tan that he looks dirty. I tilt my head because maybe that is literally just dirt? His feet are definitely dirty.

Though, admittedly, quite large.

I look up again at his face.

Heavy brow, head tilted as he watches me, eyes dancing over me, and possibly, if I were to dissect the moment, he might look as confused as I do.

I jump out of bed and glare over at him, and I'm not scared anymore, though perhaps maybe I should have been? Maybe, in retrospect, one day I will be.

Instead, I raise my eyebrows to his question.

"Am I supposed to?"

"Yes." He scowls. "Bit embarrassing for you that you don't."

I fold my arms delicately over my chest.

"Is it not perhaps more embarrassing for you that you've broken into my bedroom expecting to be known and yet you are not?"

He gets a look in his eye. "You must know who I am a bit, or else why aren't you afraid?"

"I could be incredibly brave," I tell him, nose in the air.

He rolls his eyes. "Or stupid."

I huff a bit, cross my arms over my chest, and peer over at him through the light that the moon's throwing on him. "Are you"—I blink twice—"Peter Pan?"

"I knew you knew who I was!" He points at me, victorious.

I squint over at him, shaking my head. "You can't be." I frown as I take a careful step closer to him. He's about six foot one. Maybe bigger. Tall, for certain. "You're…" I blink a few times, face nearly scrunched. "Big?"

He looks down at his bare chest and puffs it up a little, flicks his eyes up at me, and does this thing with his eyebrows that might make my heart go weak at the knees. "I know."

"But you're supposed to be…" I look for the right words. "A boy?"

He looks annoyed. "I am a boy."

I tilt my head at him again. He doesn't look like a boy. He looks my age, maybe even a tiny bit older.

My eyes pinch. "Well, so how old are you then?"

"Bigger than you," he tells me quickly.

"I didn't ask how big you are." Though he is indisputably bigger than me. I stand a mere five foot six. "I asked how old you are."

"Older than you," he tells me, and it's then that I notice he has an American accent. Evasive answer. No surprises there…damn Yanks.

"Which is how old?" I put my hands on my hips, beginning to feel cross.

"The perfect kind."

I stomp my foot. "Which is what?"

He takes a step towards me, and now I can see his eyes.

Green. Unmistakably green.

Peter Pan looks me up and down. His head is cocked to the side.

"You're the perfect kind of old too."

I blush. I don't know why.

I swallow quickly, shake my head, and refocus.

"Come on, Wendy." The boy reaches for my hand, and I snatch it away.

"I'm not Wendy."

He rolls his eyes and groans, a bit impatient and rude.

"Well, what are you then?"

"Do you mean 'who am I'?"

He rolls his eyes and says nothing.

"I'm Daphne."

His face pulls. "That's a weird name."

I pull one back. "No weirder than Peter Pan."

"My name's the best name." He shrugs proudly.

I squint over at him. "Why Pan?"

"Why Daphne?" he shoots back in a dumb voice, and I think he's a terrible pest.

I take a big breath and sigh at him to make sure he knows I'm displeased, but as I do, I accidentally smell him. You know how the air gets when summertime's close? Like frangipani and the ocean. He smells how the air feels right before the storm. He smells like freedom, and I don't mean to, but I breathe him in. And once I feel him inside my chest, there's this peculiar sinking—it's rather distinct—that the feeling of him being there might not ever quite leave.

Do you ever get a feeling like that? A foreboding? A grave permanence to whatever's about to come next?

That's how breathing Peter Pan in feels. Like taking the first step on a carpet rolled out in front of you.

His eyes flicker around my face with a curious intensity I don't understand, and I wonder whether he'll kiss me, he's leaning in so close. Does he even know about kisses? My cheeks feel hot, and I swallow nervously before I shake my head at myself.

I mustn't forget—because it's undeniably a woman's strength—that I'm dreadfully stroppy at him for, off the cuff, calling me stupid, getting my name wrong, and then calling it weird. I turn from him, arms folded across my chest and my brows high with indignation.

"Wendy, girl." He cranes his head around my shoulder. "Why are you angry?"

"Wendy isn't my name." I move away from him and sit on my bed. I don't think I much like him, if I'm honest. He's not making me feel good inside myself, yet I so desperately want his approval, and I've never wanted the approval of a man before.

I've had boyfriends before. Lots of boys like me. I'm attractive enough in a conventional way, and I'm clever. I'm from a well-to-do (albeit considered eccentric*) family. I'm mysterious and aloof. I don't care about the things some other girls care about. When Jasper England asked me to his family's manor for dinner, every girl in my dormitory screamed, but I didn't.

I went. I had a fun time. We kissed. He was good at it. He asked me what I wanted to do after I finished school, and I said I wanted to go to university.

---

* But perhaps less so than previously thought, as it appears what I considered to be their primary eccentricity is evidently real.

He asked if I wanted to get my MRS, because if I did, he could save me a lot of time.

When I said I wanted to get a degree in mineralogy, he stared at me like I told him I wanted to stick a fork in a power socket.

We dated for the entire summer,[*] because he actually really was a very good kisser, and at the end of it, Jasper asked if I was joking about "the geology thing," and I said no, and then he dropped me home shortly after, and we've not spoken since.[†]

I don't know what it is about Peter Pan that's made me feel instantly disheartened, but I do. I don't know why. I obviously don't know this boy, except that I do, I think. I know him how you know him and we all know him…from once upon a dream.

And no one likes it when a dream is fractured.

"But you are a girl." Peter kneels in front of me, and he puts his hands on my knees, and this is the first time we touch. My brain makes a note of it because I know my heart will want to remember it later. I'm wearing quite short bloomers and a white, cotton camisole, and he's staring up at me, smiling.

Peter's brows furrow, and his smile is confused but present.

"The best girl I've ever seen," he tells me matter-of-factly, and my cheeks go pink.

This pleases him, my pink cheeks. I can tell because his chest puffs up a little and he jumps up off the ground, shoving a hand through his blond hair.

He walks around my room, looking at the posters on the wall.

"Who's that?" He points to a poster on my wall.

I glance over at the poster and then give Peter a confused look. "That's Mick Jagger."

"Do you know him?" He frowns.

"No, but—"

"Why's there this picture of Mick Jagger on your wall then?"

"Well, because he's rather sexy, don't you think?"

Peter pulls a face. "What's sexy?"

---

[*] The one before this one.

[†] I believe he's just gotten engaged.

I purse my lips. "Handsome," I tell him. "Or pleasant to look a—" I barely get the words out before he pulls a dagger from his belt and slices my poster in two.

It all happens so quickly—a blink-and-you-miss-it sort of change in him—but Peter's face goes like a flash from inquisitive to dark. The poster flits to the ground, our eyes following it.

"Hey!" I growl. "That was my favorite!"

"I'm your favorite now." He gives me a curt smile.

I frown at him.

"I don't like to share," he says, inspecting his dagger before pocketing it again.

"Share what?" I cross my arms again.

He frowns at me. "You."

And I wish that didn't win me over, but it does in the slightest. Perhaps it's because I've never really known the approval of a man before.

"Fatherless girls who are left unchecked are a danger to society and themselves," I once heard one of my grandmothers' more judgmental friends say. I'm unsure what she meant by that, but it may have been pertaining to an instance such as this one.

The thrill of pleasing him, even if it means losing a thing I loved before.[‡]

It's just a poster, I tell myself as I stare down at it and sidestep anything it may imply.

"Why are you an American?" I ask him, tilting my head.

"What's an American?" he asks suspiciously before adding quickly, "I know what it is but I just want to make sure you do."

I give him a look. "An American is someone from the Americas."

"Right." He nods. "Which is…?"

"A continent?" I frown. "And a country."

"On…?" he says, eyebrows up.

I frown more. "Earth."

"Oh." He nods again. "Right. No, I know—good. Do Americans know everything?"

---

‡ Loved might be a stretch.

I roll my eyes. "I mean, they think they do."

He shrugs. "That's probably why I am one then, because I do know everything."

I roll my eyes again as I look up at him.

He really is rather tall.

"Is anything that they said about you true?" I look up at him as I collect the remains of my poster and fold them up, putting them into a drawer.

"Don't know." He leans casually against the wall, folding his arms over his barrel chest. "What'd they say?"

"Well…" I stand up, walking over to him. "For one, they said that you were a boy."

"I am a boy," he tells me, proud.

"Barely." My eyes fall down him and snag.

My grandfather,* before he died, he'd spend all his time in the garden. Ours was the best garden on the street, wildly beautiful, and I loved his hands when he'd come inside. I'd make him a cup of tea and pass him a Jaffa cake, and he'd eat it without washing up first, and it made me happy. Peter's hands remind me of them, so I suppose he makes me happy too.

We're toe-to-toe now, and I take his hand in mine, turning it over, inspecting those giant paws of his, and I love how rough they are. Instantly, I do. I know that's a strange thing to say—there's dirt under the nails—but still there's something beautiful about his hands.

"These are not boy's hands," I tell him, and he grips mine back, inspecting them closely.

"These look like girl's hands to me." His eyes peer down at me, and he doesn't let go of my hand. "What else do they say about me, girl?"

"That you fight pirates?"

"I do." His chin sticks out in pride.

"That you fly?"

And then he grins at me ever so dashingly. It makes my heart feel as though it's taken flight itself.

"I do." He nods solemnly.

---

* Wendy's husband, of course. Alfred Beaumont.

"Will you show me?" I find myself batting my eyes at him.

His chest puffs up again and he nods.

And then he's flying.

It's not zippy, how you might think it would be. It's…if you imagine a feather falling slowly and gracefully to the ground, play it in your mind in reverse, and that's how it looks when he floats up.

I wish my face weren't alive with delight, but I know it is.

"How do you do it?" I marvel up at him, and listen to me when I say this: he is a marvel.

"Happy thoughts." Peter Pan shrugs like it's nothing.

"What are you thinking about?"

"You." He grins and then he reaches down, offering me his hand like a gentleman. I peer up at him, my lips pursed.

"Now, girl." He gives me a look. "Think of me."

As though I needed that specific instruction, as though I wasn't already partially if not somewhat completely enamored by the golden flying boy in my room. As though I wouldn't—from now on, for the rest of my stupid life—be in one way or another either enraptured or tortured by him. And then my head (and maybe just ever so quietly my heart) clunks the roof—without my permission, I suppose, in more ways than one—with a dull thud as I float up and away.

"Peter!" Grandma Mary cries, her tiny, frail self barely filling half the doorframe. "I thought you'd died."

Peter floats down, eyeing her, suspicious.

"No one could kill me." He frowns a little, tilting his head at her as he did to me, and it makes me feel unspecial. "Who are you?"

I look from him to her, and the weight of my great-grandmother's sadness brings me back down to earth.

"You don't remember me?" she asks him.

His eyes pinch. "I remember everyone."

"I'm Mary," she tells him, and Peter takes a fearful step back.

"Liar."

"It's true, Peter. I'm old now." She gives him a sad smile. "Ever so much more than twenty."

"But you promised." He cranes his head so he can see into her eyes.

"Peter," she says gently, stepping towards him, but he takes another step back. "We've had this conversation before."

"When?" His chest looks huffy.

"A thousand times in this same room."

Peter shakes his head, and the way he's frowning is breaking my heart. His tender face, how he doesn't understand how someone might break a promise they made to him. I can't imagine that happens all too often if one could help it…

"But I was only gone for—"

"I'm ninety, Peter," Mary tells him, and Peter Pan falls to the floor like a stone.

He looks up at us—first her, then me—and his eyes are brimmed with feelings that, as I'm staring down at him, I'm quite sure he can't quite understand.

I don't think to do it—it happens quite involuntarily—but I find myself dropping to my knees next to him. There's something so desperate about him, so in need of all my focus and all my attention, and I feel him lifting out from my pocket the keys to my inhibitions.

I touch his face like I have no control of my hands anymore, as though they're already his, as though they're magnets to his face. "You don't have to cry."

He smacks my hand away and jumps up from the ground, wiping his face briskly with the bend in his elbow. "I wasn't crying." He glowers at me.

"Besides, Peter," Mary says, and I know she's trying to distract him. She does the same things to my snot-nosed little neighbor. "You too have grown."

Peter Pan straightens himself up, and all unpleasant emotions seem to have evaporated as he grins at her.

"I know! Aren't I so tall and handsome?"

"And insufferable," I tack on the end.

"What'd you say?" He glances over at me, blinking and obviously not listening to me, which makes me angry and also (regrettably) a little bit more attracted to him.

"Daphne, darling." Mary swats her hand at me. "Don't be so piddling. He's a dish."

"Yes, girl." Peter grins at me. "I'm a dish," he tells me proudly.

Mary looks over at him, her old eyes all young again in wonder.

"Peter, why did you grow up?"

"I'm not all the way up." He drifts up in the air, reclining back into it as though he's on an inflatable lounger in a pool.

"But somewhat." She eyes him the way only an old friend can.

Peter cracks his shoulders, then shrugs, conceding. "Had to."

"Why?" I frown.

"So I could win the fights I have to."

"And which fights are those?" I ask nosily.

Peter Pan glances at me with a look in his eyes that ought to alarm me but doesn't.

"All of them," he tells me, then breathes out his nose. "You'll see."

"Perhaps I don't want to see," I tell him for no real reason at all.

He floats down to me, and his eyes lock with mine. "You want to see." he tells me, and I do. Then Peter claps his hands, eyes brightening. "Should we go?"

"Go where?" I blink.

Peter and my great-grandmother laugh.

"To Neverland, dear," Mary tells me, like I'm the silly one.

My brow furrows, and I look at her like she's mad. Which she is. I'm seventeen! God willing, I start university in a few months. I have my life planned. I can't run away with a boy I don't know.

I shake my head at her, and Peter rolls his eyes, impatient.

"Darling." Mary touches my arm gently. "You must go with him."

"Why must I?" I ask her quietly.

"You know why," she tells me, and then she gives me this strange smile. It's one I'll think on for days and years and hours to come. When all time blends together into nothingness and the memories of my old life start to morph and fade like clouds being blown away across the sky, I will still think of that smile.

A blessing? Permission? A warning? The edges of her smile that may have told me which of the aforementioned it truly was will fade eventually, and I will wonder forever whether she was implying this is nothing more than a rite of passage or, actually, a birthright.

I glance over at him, and a sliver of me is relieved, I don't know why. Like going with him is a pull towards destiny. And I don't even believe in destiny! I believe in science and facts, not boys who are supposedly some peculiar part of my fate.

But here he is. Like they always said he'd be...

"What about my education?" I ask in a small voice.

"Your education will always be here." She gives me a small smile.

I reach out and touch her. "And what about you?"

She gives me a sad, tired smile. "Soon I'll be gone."

"Where?" asks Peter.

Mary looks at over him solemnly and then back at me. I don't think he understands, but probably it's better this way—there are just some things you don't want the sunshine to know.

"You must go, Daphne," she tells me, her hand on my face. "Like I went and my mother before me...and Wendy after me and your mother after her. This"—and then she lowers his voice so that he cannot hear this part—"he is your fate, darling. That he's here for you now, like this." She gives me a strange and weighty look. "It is fate."

My shoulders slump under the weight of it all, and she laughs.

She glances between Peter Pan and I. "Sweetheart," she sighs. "There's a universe waiting for you out there."

"Yeah, girl." Peter gives me a proud little smirk. "Come on."

He grabs my hand, and I want to be able to say that it annoys me—I pretend that it does—but it feels like static electricity. Our eyes catch, and the way he's looking at me, I know that he feels it too, because rather suddenly, he looks a bit frightened, and then he snatches his hand back.

"Do you even know my name?" I ask, eyebrows high.

"Course I know your name."

"Go on then." I shrug, petulant. "What is it?"

"D...D...r...agon."

"Dragon." I blink once. "You think my name is Dragon?"

He scoffs. "No. It's...D...ais...Daphne! Daphne. Ha! I was right. I knew it."

I look at Mary. "Absolutely not."

Mary smiles, amused. "Darling, you are too old here already."

"No, I'm not. I'm only seventeen!"

"Ever so barely." She gives me a look. "Soon you will be eighteen, and even now, you already need to grow down. You always have."

"I've only just finished school. What would people say, me disappearing in the middle of the night with a strange boy?"

"It doesn't matter what they say, Daphne. It matters that you're happy and that you're free."

"It's 1967!" I throw my hands in the air, exasperated. "We live in London, not Benghazi! I'm very free, and I'm very happy!"

She touches my face with a maternal tenderness.

"My pet, that is because you're yet to truly know either." She gives me a small smile that looks edged with sadness, and a thought I hate rustles through the air of me that maybe I'll never see her again. "Go," she tells me. She takes my face in her hands and kisses my cheek.

She reaches for Peter's hand. He looks scared at first to be touched by an old person, as though it's something that perhaps you might catch if you weren't to wash your hands thoroughly straight after, but then he gives her a smile, and I watch pass between them a moment that feels like I shouldn't have witnessed it, but I do: a silent goodbye. The last time they'll see each other. The end of the road for their great adventure.

"I'll fly you to the stars when it happens," he tells her quite solemnly.

"I'll be young again when you do." She smiles ever so sadly. "Remember me as I was, Peter," she tells him, and he nods obediently. "And you…" She turns to me, smiling gently at the door. "Remember me as you will be."

And then she slips out of my room, closing the door behind her. I stare after her, and I don't know when I started crying, but I am.

Peter looks down at me and takes a step closer. He tilts his head again, and with his giant paws he has for hands he wipes my face clean with the heels of them.

"Just happy thoughts now, okay, girl?" he tells me.

I nod.

"Are you ready?"

And the question is perhaps more loaded than I want it to be. Am I ready to never see Mary Evangeline Darling again in this lifetime? Am I ready to leave everything I've ever known for a magical boy? Am I ready to have my heart completely shattered? Everyone's stories with him are filled to the brim with adventures too wonderful to explain on paper, but there's always a common thread, and that thread is something about which we do not speak. It's something I've watched them skirt around all my life and never look directly in the eye. A strange dance the women of my family seem to innately know the steps to, and soon I'd see that I'd join them. Without much time or conscious thought or effort, I too would fall in step and also skirt the edge of the common thread.

So then, the answer is no, actually, I'm not ready for any of that, and even still, my heart begins to float away, like a kite trapped in the sky that is his eyes, and I can feel that none of that matters. It's not a choice, is it? It's what Mary said it was. It's the fate of my family; we're tied to him. "And thus, it will go on," Wendy always said. It is our burden to love him. Which I don't, and I shan't. But I could see how one might.

"Right." I clear my throat. "Well, what do I need?" I glance around the room.

He gives me a playful look. "Me."

I roll my eyes. "No, but what do I actually need, in a practical sense?"

He floats over to me and tilts my face gently so it mirrors his. "Just me."

I smack his hand away, feeling flustered because my cheeks are pink, and they didn't go pink for Jasper England's Icelandic-blue eyes, and they won't go pink for Peter's even if they already are.

"What a ridiculous thing to say!" I shake my head at him as I rummage around my room for a rucksack.

"I'll look after you, girl," he tells me, his face quite serious, then he reaches for my hand. "Come away with me." He pulls me towards the window, eyes bright like the stars that are calling us. "You'll never have to worry about grown-up things again."

He floats backwards, pulling me up onto the edge of the windowsill, and I eye him carefully.

"Never really is such an awfully long time…"

In that moment, teetering on the border of everything I knew and everything I could know—standing on the cliff's edge that would ultimately be the sharp drop-off into the rest of my life—I want to be able say that you could have swayed me either way, that if you promised me a life of safety and security and happiness that it would have been enough for me to bar that stupid window closed for all my days, but there is something so sweet about the unknown and something so thrilling about tumbling into something and someplace new, and even though I haven't yet been, I suppose a part of me could tell that one day, Neverland would be both the great landmark and landslide of my life.

You might think I'm foolish for jumping out my window in the dead of night with a boy whose hair is as messy as his heart, but then, if you don't understand the lure and pull of the boy in question, I'm terribly sorry to inform you, but you've never met Peter Pan.

CHAPTER
TWO

I DON'T KNOW HOW IT HAPPENS OR HOW HE EVEN DOES IT, BUT I'M QUITE sure that Peter can fold time and space as though it were a piece of paper in his back pocket, because that bloody second star to the right that I've stared at all my life, in the scheme of things, really only took a moment or three to get to. Black holes are real, by the way, though it is my belief that you won't have conclusive confirmation of that on Earth for a good few more years. He might be in cahoots with the black holes, actually. He told me that crossing the event horizon usually stings but that he asked it not to sting me, and to his credit, it didn't. There is, however, much to be said about the inside of a black hole— far less ominous than one might think, what with its name and all, and I do insist that, in this particular scenario, its bark is worse than its bite. A swirling hot mess of everything in the universe that has existed or will ever exist sort of swimming above you and around you and maybe (I'm not totally sure but) possibly through you—quite the sight to behold.

Watching Peter Pan fly feels like watching a dolphin swim out in the open ocean.

He glides in the sky and skims the stars, and I've never seen anything like him, like a stone skipping across the sky, weaving through comets like a beam of light. He's all the parts of the electromagnetic spectrum we can see and even parts of it that we can't, all bound in wonderful flesh to the freest of souls. You couldn't even try to tell me in this moment (because no matter what you'd say, I wouldn't have believed you anyway), but there is a steep and formidable price paid for this boy to have his freedom, and he is rarely, if ever, the one to foot the bill.

As we are flying through the inky black of the night right on the edge of our atmosphere, out of the corner of my eye, I see Peter watching me.

I peer over at him.

"Girl." He squints.

I raise my eyebrows, waiting.

"You really are very pretty."

My heart swells more than I'd like it to, but I try to keep a level head. "But do you think I'm clever?"

"We'll see." He gives me a sly smile, and I frown a bit.

All I've wanted in my life is to be clever. Cleverness has been my raison d'être since I was ranked first in my class in year seven and my mother happened to be there. She was quite pleased. I've been ranked first ever since.

"Now, girl."

I huff, annoyed. "Have you forgotten my name again already?"

"Daphne, girl." He gives me a smug look. "Have you ever held hands with a boy before?"

I don't mean to laugh, but I do. Just a small one. More of a sniff than a laugh actually, so I turn it into a cough.

"Yes."

Peter Pan's entire face darkens. "Who?"

"Um…" I purse my lips, trailing.

"You've forgotten his name?" Peter asks, hopeful and gleeful.

Jasper. And Steffan. A Welsh boy I dated last spring. We also kissed, but I don't think Peter would care for that specific detail.

"Sure," I lie.

Peter swoops over and takes my hand in his. "You will remember forever the day you held hands with Peter Pan."

He throws me a devil-may-care smile.

And he's right, I will. But I do wonder how he's already forgotten that we held hands in my bedroom not an hour ago. I think it's better not to say it; he seems not to like being corrected. Who does though, to be fair. I hardly think it's a commentary on him as a person. At least no more than it is one of me that I won't say to Peter something that he won't like because I want him to like me.

How terribly silly of me. How terribly like the kind of girl I'm not. Imagine it, me, not saying the true thing to spare a man his feelings. Ridiculous.

And yet, it would be the first of many such occasions.

It would take me a very long time to learn that there are many different kinds of men in this world (and all the other worlds like ours) but a surefire, quick, and easy way to discern a true man among men is how much of yourself he allows you to be in his presence. A real man will allow you to be your whole entire self, with breathing room and space to change your mind and even evolve it. A mere boy might let you be yourself just an eighth of the way, if you're lucky.

Peter squeezes my hand.

"Now, you're going to need to hold tight, girl. The sun's rising, and we need to catch it to the universe next door."

And that is all the warning I get.

His grip on me fastens a little but nowhere near enough for what is about to happen.

I don't know whether I quite have the words to fully describe how it feels to be flung through the cosmos.

A few years before, I'd gone to SeaWorld in San Diego with my great-uncle and aunt. Their children are abysmal, and they like me much better and say that I class up the whole holiday experience, so they bring me on most of them.

At SeaWorld, they have waterslides, and though this is an imperfect comparison, it is the best way I think I could describe it.

A rushing sensation, almost wet, very dark. At once smooth but also dippy in its turns and corners. A whooshing sound and you go faster at the end and then light! Everywhere, light.

And I don't know how I managed to do it, but I'm still holding on to Peter Pan.

Or with how he's looking at me, my hand still in his, his face now lit up with the light of three rather close suns and I can see his cheeks are the slightest bit pink, perhaps actually it's him who's still holding on to me.

We ride the rising sun like a Ferris wheel, and my hand is still in his and I wonder if he's forgotten it's there, and is that a good thing or a bad thing? I can't tell.

"This is us," he tells me, standing up and pulling me with him.

We fall a few feet and land on a cloud.

"Do you know on Earth they tell us that clouds are just made of water vapor? You can't stand on them."

Peter looks at me, outraged. "Liars."

Then he pulls me down the cloud on what looks like a path that leads somewhere I can't yet see.

It's around now that he lets go of my hand, and I don't want to sound needy, but as soon as he's not touching me anymore, I kind of wish that he were again.

He leads me down the cloud path, bounding ahead like a puppy off its leash until we arrive at a small shack in the middle of a cloudy field that's sitting above a great big mountain.

I look around, confused. "What's this?"

"Bag check," says a man sitting in front of the shack who I hadn't noticed till now. He's reclined on a wooden chair with a fishing pole cast off into a faraway cloud. His skin is leathery, a bit tan like yours would be too if you spent your days on a chair in a cloud. I can't see his hair color because he's wearing a red fisherman's beanie, but I suspect whatever color it once was, it now is graying. His eyes, however, are incredibly blue. He looks in his sixties. Seventies perhaps?

He stands, extending his hand to me. "I'm John."

I shake his hand. "Daphne."

"All right then, Peter?" John nods over at him.

"All right." Peter shrugs back.

"You're a good bit taller." John nods his chin at him. "You'll give that Hook a run for his money."

Peter glares at John a little, as though he resents the insinuation that he didn't already. He shoves his hand through his hair, then looks at me a little gruffly. "Be back in a minute."

I nod once.

John smiles at me and leans in, whispering, "You have your mother's eyes."

I falter. "How do you know who my mother is?"

He smiles a tiny bit, but it might be a sad one. "I never lose baggage."

And before I even have a chance to wonder what he means, Peter strolls on out of the shack looking lighter than he did just a moment ago.

He skims the clouds, not quite walking on them, like nothing in the world is weighing him down anymore.

"Your turn, girl." Peter nods his head in the direction of the shack.

"Don't be scared now," John says, putting a guiding arm around me.

"What am I doing?" I ask, blinking a lot.

"Checking your baggage."

"But I didn't bring anything." I shrug, showing him my empty hands.

He gives me a small smile, then whispers, "Not that kind of baggage. You'll see. Straight to the mirror, if you don't mind." Then he walks away, closing the door behind him.

It's quite dark, dimly lit by silver light, and the room is bigger and deeper and wider than the shack looks from the outside.

In the middle of the room is a mirror. Quite plain, nothing ornate about it.

There's a big X on the floor a foot or so in front of it, so logic has me stand on it.

I stare at myself. Long brown hair. Eyes blue, like my mother's apparently. "Surprisingly swarthy skin," as my dorm mistress would say, with arms and legs a little too long in my personal opinion, but I do hope that Peter likes them.

I look down at myself, wondering how to find the baggage of which they speak, and then I catch in my peripheral vision a glimpse—

There's my reflection, thwarted with and by fifty bags.

Bags of all shapes and all sizes. Different colors, different materials. Tiny ones, giant ones. Each bag has a label on it, but I'm scared to read them. It would be horrifically confronting to find out what exactly has been weighing me down these seventeen long years, but evidently here I stand, dreadfully bogged down and not even remotely as carefree as I thought I was.

Care-filled, you might even say.

I tilt my head left, just to double-check that it's not a trick and the reflection is mine, and it follows me. It does.

I take a step closer. So does it.

There's a plum-round shoulder bag draped right around the neck of my reflection, so slowly, watching myself in the mirror, I reach for it, then peel it off of me. And though I can't see it in my hands, I can feel it in my hands and I can feel the difference in me when I drop it to the floor, and when I do, I become quietly quite sure that that bag in particular has something to do with my mother.

Whatever it was, to no longer be carrying it feels incredible.

So I do it again with another.

And then another.

And then it's like the penny drops and I shed it all. All of it. All my baggage.

They fall off me like scales, and I feel like I could float, and maybe for the smallest second, I do.

I walk back out, but it feels more like gliding now, a bit like ice-skating, and I glide—smack!—right into John, to whom I give an apologetic look.

"I didn't know where to put them. I'm sorry."

He swats his hand. "I'll take care of it."

"Thank you." I reach for his arm, smiling at him.

"I'll be seeing ya." He gives me a look, and I don't know what he means by that, but do you ever sometimes get a feeling that someone knows the future? And you maybe?

"You look lighter." Peter Pan smiles at me as I float over.

"Did I look heavy before?" I frown, glancing down at myself.

"Very." He nods and gives me a look, and I feel annoyed at the rudeness of him.

Peter kicks up some cloud and stands at the edge, looking down, and it's all horrifically unfair because there are so many suns here that he's illuminated from all angles, and it makes him look like he's encased in a halo.

His shoulders are dusted with freckles, and I wonder under what circumstance he might be still enough for me to count them one day. Asleep, probably. If I were to give him a cup of chamomile, perhaps.[*]

"What are you looking at?" Peter frowns, glancing at his shoulder, then up at me.

"What?" I blink, clearing my throat. "Nothing."

Peter gives me a distrusting look and then gasps happily. He pulls out a monocular from his back pocket, flashing it at me.

---

[*] Slip, more like. He won't take that voluntarily.

"Stole this from Captain Hook." He grins as he stretches it open and peers through. "The mermaids are lying out on Skull Rock! I need to show them that I'm big now." He looks over at me, smug. "And a dish."

I falter, and before I can even say anything in response, he winds up for a running start.

"Follow me!" he tells me, and then he bounds forwards.

"Wait!" I call after him, running to the edge. "Where are you—"

And then he nose-dives off the clouds. "Jump, Wendy! Just make sure you don't—"

And that's it.

He's gone.

I can't hear him after that.

Now, listen. I don't know why I do it. It's a crazy thing to do, and in retrospect, I too would find this plan to be as shabby and ill-formed as I'm sure you will, hearing it the first time, but with very little thought towards my chances of survival and with minimal consideration for my own personal well-being, I fling myself from the cloud just as Peter had done.

And so it begins. My rapid descent, my tumbling after him.

Clouds are whipping past my head, I'm gaining speed, and the planet below me that I know for certain* is not Earth is getting closer and closer, and it is then, right then, that I am met with a horrible revelation. I realize that I'm not flying—I'm falling.

Funny, don't you think, how similar those two things can feel at the start?

Now so far from my mind are those fucking happy thoughts, and all that remains at present are my extremely bitter ones. I'm acutely aware that I am, in fact, hurtling towards imminent death, and I could have sworn to you that out of the corner of my eye, I saw Peter Pan use my newfound (but regrettably and inarguably present) affections for him as a parachute to land.

Maybe someday, much later in life, I'll be able to eventually draw the comparison of how this feels right now—plummeting to my death and all—to how it will feel when I fall in love. Alas, I am not yet equipped to make such a comparison. Not really.

---

* Just by the sheer colors of it.

It somehow feels as though I'm falling faster and faster the closer I get to that magnificent blue that I'm plunging towards, and I brace myself as best I can to die.

There is no clarity. No peace. Just a pounding fear and a screaming that I think is coming from me, but it still somehow sounds strangely far away.

I will say this: it is a terrible crash when I hit the water. It feels like glass breaking beneath me, over on top of me, around me, and through me.

The pain of it all takes my breath away in such a manner that I don't immediately realize that as fate would have it, now that I've landed on Neverland, I am—rather regrettably—drowning on Neverland.

The irony of this is and will remain lost on me for quite some time.

The water swallows all of me. I can't tell you which way is up anymore; there seems to be light coming in from all directions.

It's so beautiful, the water. All the bluest blues kissing the aquas, and there's a lot to be said about drowning, I suppose.

Taking in all that water isn't too pleasant at first, but after a short while, it's not so bad.

And I'm thinking, as I float here dying, how tremendously sorry I am for coming to this stupid place, that my mother was right all along, that I should have just gone to Cambridge.

And then something drops into the water next to me. And my heart rejoices a little bit because Peter Pan has come to save me, and I will later recall this moment that's about to happen next as the part where everything—everything—henceforth changes.

I won't realize that for quite some time though.

I'm pulled to the surface, I think, because suddenly there's breath in my lungs again, and I'm coughing and spluttering, and the four suns are so bright that I can't see a damned thing, but I can feel that I'm safe again because I'm scooped up in his arms, and then he lays me flat on a warm deck.

I'm hacking up water like a burst hydrant, and I still can't see anything more than a figure looking down at me, but he tilts his head, and that's when my eyes go clear and I see it isn't Peter with his head tilted. It's someone else entirely.

Is there a word that encapsulates being terrified and enthralled at once?

If there is, I should like to invoke it now.

Awe, maybe? The etymological meaning of the word from the fourteenth century. Fear and great reverence. Strange, this terrible awe I have for the man who's frowning down at me with the most serious pair of eyes I've ever seen. I swallow heavy at the sight of them. Something a bit like home in them. Like all the darkest blues of the water on that planet I'm so very fond of. They belong to a man—definitely a man, not a boy. I can tell he's a man because he has facial hair, and he wears the serious kind of face only men do. That and he's very tall. Not just in stature but in how he stands too, even though he's not standing. He's on his knees beside me. I can tell he's tall and that given a chance, he'd stand a certain way. Shoulders square, eyes straight ahead.

His hair at first glance is mostly brown, but it's lighter than you think it is. Longer than it is short too. Around his chin, all wavy. His skin is darkened by the sun, and he's wet. From head to toe, he's soaked right through.

"Are ye right?"* The stranger shifts some hair from my face, brow furrowing as he stares at me.

He's not blinking; he's just staring at me, waiting. But me? I'm blinking like a maniac because he is deplorably beautiful.

Dug-out cheeks, heavy brow, the best nose I've ever seen on any human being ever in all my life,† and even though there's probably a bit too much facial hair for me to say with absolute certainty, I suspect that one might be able to cut oneself on his presumably immaculate jawline.

I sit up.

"Does nobody wear shirts here?" I ask, sounding cross about it, but I'm using it as a crafty deflection to distract from the fact that I'm overtly staring at his tattooed arms and chest.

He glances down at himself, bare chested and unfortunately chiseled, then back up at me, amused.

"I took it off‡ ye before I saved yer life." He gives me a look, and I immediately resent his tone and can't pick his accent all at once.

---

* He says it like "ya," not Old English "hear ye, hear ye." It's less refined than that.

† And I'm not even sure he is a human?

‡ Though he says it more like "aff"

Scottish? Irish? Somewhere in the middle. From the Isles for certain.

I fold my arms over my chest and sit up a little straighter still.

"Are ye right though?" he asks, a touch gentler.

"Yes." I glare.

"Are ye sure?"

"Yes," I tell him, a bit indignant. I clear my throat. "Who are you anyway?"

"Who am I?" He blinks, throwing a look at the men who've appeared behind him. "A'm no' the one who came hurtling down from abain,§ lass. Who are ye?"

He nods his chin at me as he takes my hand, pulling me up off the ground, and when we touch, it feels as though something gets knocked off of a shelf that I've kept very neat and very tidy for my whole entire life. It's a very organized shelf—color coordinated and alphabetized—but somewhere inside of me, I hear something shatter, and it frightens me, so I snatch my hand away and fold it uncomfortably across myself.

I raise my eyebrows impatiently as I wait for his answer. "I asked you first."

He cocks a smile, and the trigger in my heart cocks also.

"I'm Hook."

I freeze, a little horrified, a lot confused.

"No, you aren't." I shake my head.

He looks over his shoulder again at his friends, face all amused. "Aye, sure I am."

"No." I shake my head. For one, the person in front of me isn't that old. Does no one age here? The way my grandmothers described him, Hook was older—a man of at least thirty-five, if not more—and sure, old Perfect Face here has facial hair that other boys his age might be jealous of, but I know without doubt, he couldn't be close to thirty anything at all.

As well, they told me Hook's eyes were the color of forget-me-nots, an eerie sort of light blue, but this person's eyes are made of the sort of colors you'd see out in the most unexplored parts of the Maldives—

And then, most damning of all, my eyes fall to his hand, the one I'd just been holding, and then I flick my eyes over to his other one…both very much there and very unfed to a crocodile.

---

§ Which means "above."

I look up at him, suspicious. "Where's your hook then?"

"Ah." He nods once, amused. "Yer thinking of my da,*"

I raise my eyebrows as though I'm impatient with him, as though his very presence isn't a complete and total thrill.

"And you are…?"

His eyes fall down my body, and I remember I'm in my little pajamas, and I feel self-conscious.[†]

"Jamison," he tells me when he eventually drags his eyes back up to mine. "Hook."

I stare up at him, and on my shoulders, I feel the weight of those stories my grandmothers told me all my life bearing down on me, even though I know I definitely took that off up in the room in the clouds.

"Jam." A tall, fair Scotsman rounds the corner, walking quickly. He looks early twenties. "There's a—" He stops talking when he spots me, glances back at Jamison.

Jamison flicks him a look that men may give one another in precarious scenarios. "Give me a minute, mate." He cocks his head for him to go away. "And go get me a blanket, forbye.[‡] She's soaked ri' through."

The man nods once and walks away.

I shift uncomfortably on my feet. "Aren't you supposed to be bad?"

"Aye," he sniffs a laugh. "So yer friends with the wee man then?"

"With Peter?" I clarify.

He nods and smirks.

"Yes?" I shrug. "I suppose you could call us friends."

"Sure, so where is he?" he asks, and he does this thing with his mouth, this cocky jaw grind that vexes me, and I don't like his tone, so I frown at him, indignant.

"We were separated in the nosedive down."

He raises his eyebrows. "Were ye?"

"Yes." My nose in the air. "In fact, I bet he's looking for me right now."

---

* Which means "father."

† Neither because of their wetness nor their shortness but because he feels like the sort of person I might like to look my best in front of. I'm not sure why.

‡ "Forbye," I'd eventually find out, means "as well."

"Probably." He nods, understanding. "If only ye were in that gaggle of mermaids thonner on that rock." He points his chin across the water.

I turn and feel my face falter.

Peter Pan is standing in the middle of some boulders, hands on his hips, crowing and beating his chest, and there are easily six or seven of the most beautiful creatures I've ever seen, ever, in my life batting their eyes at him, clapping and cheering, and Peter's tilting his head at them and crouching down and touching their faces, and my stomach falls five feet back into the ocean.

"Here ye go." The Scotsman's returned, and it snaps me back.

I look over at him, and Jamison Hook is watching me with a closeness that feels invasive. He looks at the blanket that's been placed in his arms.

"Is this off my bed, ye eejit?"

The Scotsman scoffs. "Well, I sure wusnae giving her mine, ye ken."

Hook stares at him for a few seconds, eyes dark and furrowed, and I wonder whether there's trouble ahead for the Scotsman, and then Jamison Hook's face cracks into a smile and he smacks his arm.

"This is Orson Calhoun." He gestures at him.

"Pleasure." Orson extends his hand. "And y'are?"

"Daphne." I shake his. "Belle Beaumont-Darling," I tell him for no particular reason.

"Fuck." Jamison Hook's head pulls back. "That's a bit o'a mouthful."

I turn and give him a dark look. "I beg your pardon?"

"Nothin'." He shrugs, but out of my peripheral vision, I can see that Hook's staring at me, and behind his eyes, I think there's something more than nothing.

"What?" I frown at him, all indignant, crossing my arms over myself in some sort of defense.

He stares at me for a split second more, then shakes his head. "Just like that name is all," he tells me, and I do find myself strangely aware of the way the wind blows gently over my face, kissing my cheek as though it's whispering something to me.

He points at the right-hand corner of my lip. "You've got yer kin's kiss."

I blink at him, confused. "My what?"

"Yer family's kiss," he says again.

My hand flies to my face, and my cheeks go pink. "Do I?"

"Aye." He nods, staring at me as he gestures to it. "Perfectly conspicuous."
I am completely delighted.

To be entirely frank with you, I've always quite wanted it; of all the things I could inherit from my family, that was one I hoped for most. I asked my mother once if I had it, and she gave me the most unimpressed look. She asked me why on earth I'd ever want a kiss in the corner of my mouth that no one could reach.

Grandma Mary shushed her at that and told me that the kiss isn't for reaching anyway. It's for giving to whom it truly belongs.

It is a rather intimidating experience, having a beautiful man stare at your mouth, and please be sure of these two things: he is staring, and he is, undeniably, beautiful.

Jamison blinks, and the look between us dissipates. He nods down at Calhoun. "What were ye going to say before?"

Calhoun nods his head behind him. "MacDuff and Brown are at it again."

Jamison rolls his eyes and looks over at me again, but I don't notice because I can't look away from Peter on the rocks with the fawning mermaids.

He's forgotten me completely already.

"I hae t' go break this up," Jamison starts. "Would ye fancy a dander? See the town?"

I give Peter one last look, but I know in the center of me that in this moment, I am less than nothing to him, so I give Jamison a singular nod.

"Did yer fall hurt then?" he asks, staring straight ahead, shoving a hand through his hair.

"Yes." I throw him a look. "Rather."

He bites back a smile. "Yer welcome, by the way."

Jamison cocks an eyebrow as he leads me off the boat, down into the streets, and something about how the village looks gives me a nervous-excited feeling, like maybe I might love it here. It feels like I've fallen into the past and through it into a dream. My grandmothers took me earlier this year to Disneyland. Have you been on the Pirates of the Caribbean ride? It's rather comparable to what their town is like, but incomparable is Jamison Hook who, unlike the filthy robots on that ride, looks more like he might belong in an art gallery, perhaps right next to the Venus de Milo.

"For what?" I ask him, my eyebrows up again.

He gives me a look as he leads me off the boat. "For saving ye, you hallion."

I roll my eyes exaggeratively. "Hardly."

He grabs me by the waist and moves me backwards towards the water. "I can clod you back in if ye'd prefer?" He smirks playfully. "Unsave ye."

"You wouldn't!" I tell him, my nose in the air, liking his hands very much on my waist, but hoping he doesn't know it.

He shrugs. "I make no promises for what I would and wudnae be willing to do to see ye all wet again." He gives me a cheeky smile, and I smack him in the arm.

He's fun to touch. Have you ever had a person who just feels fun to touch?

He laughs again. He thinks he's so suave and so charming* that the only response I consider appropriate is to race ahead of him and make him walk after me—remind him of the sexual revolution that's taking place on my planet (and that I'm currently losing on this one).

"So yer one of the Darling girls." He calls as he walks after me, just as I wanted him to.

"Yes," I tell him, my nose in the air.

"It's been a wee while since one o' ye were here," he tells me, and I keep walking ahead. "What happe—Oh. Morrigan. How 'bout ye?"

I glance back at him, and there's a rather lovely girl[†] standing next to him with two loaves of bread in her arms. Long, wavy auburn hair flowing over her shoulders, pale skin that's freckled like crazy in the sun, and eyes that are watching me coldly, but I imagine they look upon Jamison Hook rather warmly.

She doesn't say hello back to him.[‡] She just looks from him to me and back to him, but he doesn't seem to mind. He throws her a sort of lazy, indifferent smile.

She gives me a long look.

"Who's this?" she asks him and not me.

---

* He is.

† Girl? Woman? Young woman? Older than me, for certain.

‡ If that is, indeed, what he said to her. It's hard to know with that accent of his.

"Morrigan, this is…" He looks over at me. "This is Daphne Tallulah Bowing-Darling."

I glare at him because I know he got that wrong on purpose. The way he's smiling at me, he's being facetious; he's done it to annoy me. And unfortunately, it does annoy me.

"Pleasure." I ignore him and extend my hand to her, but she doesn't shake it, just eyes it instead, which is quite rude, no? And it's definitely awkward, me with my hand extended for a good four seconds before Jamison takes it and gives it a merry shake, all pleased with himself, which I, frankly, am grateful for, but I don't think it endears me any more to his friend.

Her eyes pinch.

"And how do you know each other?"

Jamison opens his mouth, but I cut in.

"I just dropped in." I shrug breezily. "I got in a spot of trouble, and Jay-muh-son"—I pronounce it wrong intentionally and look at him as I do; he rolls his eyes, but he's fighting a smile—"was kind enough to help me."

She eyes me suspiciously. "Pan's latest?" She nods in my direction though the question isn't directed at me.

"Aye." Jamison nods and catches my eye. "Sure, but the fairest one yet, wudnae ye say?"

"If you like skin and bones, I s'pose."

She tosses me another unimpressed look. A bit like how you might look at a spider in your bedroom if you were particularly unfond of spiders.

And then she walks away.

Hook watches after her before he looks down at me, eyebrows up all amused. "Dinnae mind her."

"Girlfriend?" I ask nosily.

"Are we together, ye mean?" he clarifies, and I nod. He scoffs like the absolute arsehole I'm positive he is. "Aye, sometimes, but strictly in the biblical sense."

I give him an unimpressed look, and the way he smiles at me for a second makes me forget that I flew here with a boy who has forgotten me already, who, for all I know, thinks I've drowned and isn't even bothering to search for my body.

And then there's the sound of glass smashing, and two men tumble out into the street.

A rowdy crowd follows them, and it all happens so quickly.

A fight breaks out, and there's shoving. Calhoun's in the middle of it, and Jamison's on the outskirts looking in, hovering close behind me, and I find myself watching him, not the unfolding mess, and I decide I like how his mouth looks when he goes serious.

And I suppose if you were to ask me what was happening and why I was standing in the middle of a town's square I'd never been in before with a man I've never met before with a brawl raging around us but both of us only holding the gaze of the other with a reverent silence, the best answer I could muster for you is that for the second time in my life (and strangely on the very same day), I saw some kind of future unfolding in front of me. And through me, like a flash, ripped pain and sadness and losing and loss and death and blood and fear and trembling and lust and wonder and love and promise and—

Then one of the men fighting is tossed. Drunk and off balance, he barrels over, and while the rest of the crowd sees it and parts so that he can't hit them, I don't see it because I'm back to drowning again, except this time it's on dry land and in the eyes of a pirate.

The drunkard crashes into me, knocking me clean off my feet, and I almost hit the ground, but Jamison Hook catches me and plants me back on the ground, and then he doesn't let go.

He ducks his head to meet my eyes. "Are y'okay?"

I nod, a little shaken but happy to have his hands on me again. Why am I happy to have his hands on me again?

He nods once and spins on his heel, and had I known what was about to happen, I'd have stopped him—I swear it!—but he moves quickly. I'll come to learn that about him—he moves quickly in almost every way but one.

His hand reaches downward, and then a glint of light, a ripple of a gasp through the crowd, and then the man who fell into me falls down dead. Throat cut. Blood spilling everywhere.

My eyes go wide in horror, and I stumble backwards, away from Jamison Hook because I remember with a suddenness that hits me a train—Jamison Hook is a pirate. A real one. A walk-the-other-way-when-you-see-him-coming pirate, and he sees it on my face, that change. The way I was looking at him before is gone now, smothered in the blood of a dead man.

"Do ye still want to see the town?" Orson asks, coming up behind us, as though he didn't have to step over a body to get there.

I shake my head. "I've seen enough." I look at Hook. "Just take me to Peter."

He scoffs. "What am I, yer fucking guide? Find him yerself." He nods his head back towards the water.

He's angry, I think. I don't know why. He's the murderer, not me.

"I'll take her," Orson tells him, and it's only now he glances between us.

I don't say anything, but I nod once and then he leads me away.

Once I'm a couple of meters away, I glance back at Hook right in time for him to snatch an ale from someone else and throw it back with an ease that would make one's mother worry.*

And I wouldn't know it at the time, because unfortunately I don't have eyes in the back of my head, but if I did, I would have seen how Jamison Hook watched me walk away, a scowl on his face, impatient and annoyed and ever so slightly sad to see me go.

Orson and I walk out of the town center and down a white, stony path, and it's beautiful. Somewhere between Milos and Cortona, olive trees and white cliffs and bougainvillea spilling everywhere, and then we get to a clearing.

Calhoun points straight down into a bay. "Yer boy's that way."

I swallow and look over at him. "He's not my boy."

He cocks an eyebrow. "I'll feckin' say." And then he walks away.

I climb down to the shore's edge and watch for a few moments.

Peter's lying out on a rock, face turned up against the sun, squinting into it, and a mermaid's resting her head on his shoulder, tracing her finger over his chest.

And for a second, I wonder if I should leave.

Forget Neverland, forget these two boys that I've just met, and I know what you're thinking: not even a day ago, they were strangers, no one to me, and this place was nothing but a rumor of a dream that my ancestors had, so I could leave. Perhaps I should…

---

* Not my mother, per se, because they're quite fond of rum in Belize, but a mother may worry.

But were I to leave, somehow I just know I'd spend the rest of my days wishing to be back here, wondering with an abominable curiosity about what might have been had I stayed, because Neverland is like quicksand for your soul and like the Mafia is to your heart. Once you're in, you're in.

"Wendy!" Peter cheers from the rock. He jumps up, laughing happily, and flies over to me.

I want to be cross at him for forgetting my name again, but a bit of me is just happy he's happy to see me.

"I thought you died." He laughs carelessly.

I frown. He doesn't notice.

"Where did you go?"

Where did I go? I wasn't even sure. Alone for five minutes in Neverland, and I was momentarily (and grievously) seduced by the eyes of a guileful pirate. Embarrassing, really. And pathetic.

I wonder for a second whether I should mention Jamison but decide there's nothing to mention. Nothing at all, and there isn't.[†]

I glance back over to the town, over by the dock where I landed, looking for—never mind. Looking for trouble, I suppose.

I flash Peter a smile instead.

"Looking for you," I lie.

---

† Right?

CHAPTER
THREE

I WANT TO REITERATE FOR YOU BEFORE I SAY WHAT I'M ABOUT TO SAY NEXT that I am actually quite clever. I have a good grasp on the English language and a substantial lexicon under my belt, but even so, I don't know whether I presently have in my vocabulary the kinds of words that would be necessary to communicate with you what Neverland is actually like. Nevertheless, I will try.

The island itself is divided into four sections, but it's not quartered like pies are.

For lack of a better explanation, it's shaped like a croissant and then quartered rather oddly. The bays and the beach run along the inner curvature of the island. and the curve is technically divided in to two, but not in a way that you can see it from the ground.

The part where Jamison Hook lives and the village is feels like summertime, and I'm led to believe that they call it Zomertierra.

The other half of the crescent looks and smells awfully like spring, and this is where Peter lives, and I'm told the First People of the island also,* and they call this Preterra.

Rimming both Zomertierra and Preterra the whole length of the island is Haustland, which is golden autumn all year round (whether or not they have seasons here, I'm yet to be sure), but behind Haustland, bordering and overshadowing the entire island, is Vinterlun, mountains and snow. I think almost all the mountains on the island exist in Vinterlun with perhaps the

---

* Both human and fae.

exception of Mount Carnealian, which is on the far left of the island, and I think it could be argued it's in the Zomertierra province.

Each province seems to slowly fade into the next, so you aren't always sure where one ends and the other begins. There's also an offensively turquoise bay that sits between where the Never Wood is and where Jamison Hook resides—not that we'll be thinking of him again.

Peter did show me off a bit to the mermaids,[†] and not a single one of them spoke to me. Not one!

"Don't take it personal," he told me. "As a species, they're not so friendly to your kind."

"My kind?" I repeated.

"You know, a"—he nodded his chin at me as he lowered his voice—"girl."

Quite fond of boys though, so it would appear. I might even go as far as to say that they're uncomfortably taken by him, completely enraptured, lying on their bellies, chins in hands, staring up at him while he performed for them tricks, sometimes using me as a part of them. Balancing me on one finger. Tossing me high into the air and catching me right before I'd hit the water. He didn't ask me to partake. I was just partaking, and I don't think I minded because he's Peter Pan, and it's maybe the most brilliant feeling I've ever had, having his eyes on me, even if they aren't entirely on me all the time. The one he calls Marin likes his attention a lot, and Peter seems to like giving it to her.

"You are ever so dreamy now, Peter." She batted her eyes up at him.

He lay down, mirroring her, almost nose to nose. "I know I am."

When the suns became close to setting and the mermaids started to complain about how the rocks were getting too cold to lie on, Peter whispered to me that he was bored and we should go, and that was fine with me, because if I'm being entirely truthful, I wasn't all that mad on how the shadows make the mermaids faces look.

You want creatures like mermaids to live in your mind on a pedestal, stay up there all lofty and gorgeous. I shouldn't care to see how they may go in the darkness, though I suppose that could be said and true about all of us.

---

† Marin, beautiful olive skin, golden hair, purple eyes; Crystal, beautiful white skin, blue hair, blue eyes; Pania, beautiful dark skin, brown hair, golden eyes; Delphine, beautiful brown skin, blonde hair, green eyes.

I asked him if we could please walk to the Never Wood, as I'd have liked to have gotten the lay of the land (you know how walking helps with that), but you should have seen the look Peter gave me when I did—you'd nearly have thought I asked him for a kidney—so we flew, of course. Because it's what he wanted, and also it's faster, which means it was probably the sensible choice.

Besides, flying comes with its benefits. I made so many mental notes of places I've to visit, s. Some I'd heard of from my grandmothers' stories, like Skull Rock, the Old Valley, which is the grounds where Neverland's First People live, Cannibal Cove, which is actually a separate island off the east coast, and then of course the Neverpeak Mountains. There are quite a few islands and atolls littered around the mainland of Neverland, and some look probably just how you'd imagine, but others are quite bizarre. There's one that looks like an island's grown on the back of a giant shell, there's one of dense and heavy jungle, there's one entirely shrouded by clouds, and that's all I can see from here with my normal eyes, but Peter says there's more and that I'll see them in time.

But I did spot what looked to me like a castle I've never heard of. And there's a handful of active volcanoes here, which is incredible, and I need to visit each of them. Obviously the geology of a volcano is fascinating for everyone, not just a hopeful geologist like myself, so I ask Peter a lot of questions about them. What kind of volcano is it? How active is it? How accessible is it? Is someone monitoring it? The volcano is where I channel all my mental energy. I don't think for a second about whether I am culpable for the death of the man Jamison Hook killed, and I certainly don't think about what it felt like with his stupid pirate hands on my waist or how serious his eyes are, and were I to be thinking about his eyes—which I'm not—it would only be because they're rather like water in color, and water is the ocean and the ocean is the thing I nearly drowned in yesterday, therefore, I'm not at all even thinking about his eyes, but the ocean. And/or drowning. I barely even like the ocean[*]. I don't want to be a marine biologist, if you'll recall, I want to be a geologist and thus I should really channel all this attention to the volcanos here—which Peter evidently knows nothing about. When I asked what kind the one near Zomertierra was he said "the hot kind," but I try not to pass judgment because I

---

[*] A lie.

doubt he's had a formal education. It looks neither like a super nor a composite volcano, and I hope it's not a cone, because that would be boring. Probably a shield volcano then, don't you think? That would be lovely.

He did kill him without a thought though, as though it were reflex. And I have a suspicion that the death in question arose because of me and me alone. Were that man to have fallen on anyone else, I feel as though perhaps he'd still be alive, and that's confusing and horrible and confronting, particularly because I must admit (rather reluctantly) that there is some level of (strange) comfort in knowing[†] that Jamison Hook would kill a man for or because of me. Why he did it, I don't know. I suppose I might never know, which would be a little bit rotten, because I do like to know things, but then it snags on my mind what they've always said of his kind—how you can never trust a pirate.

How much truth is in that sentence, I wonder. And a little piece of panic seeds in my chest as I do because yesterday morning, if someone killed another person for me, in front of me, in the name of me, I'd have immediately flagged that person as bad and untrustworthy, and while I do regard Hook as bad because he's evidently a murderer and probably a philanderer, I fear I might not entirely consider him the latter.

Which, all of that's to say, if you were to ask me for directions from the village to the Never Wood to the part of it where Peter lives, I'm quite afraid I'd fall short. I did wonder a few times en route if perhaps Peter might have forgotten the way to his own home, as I know for certain that we went around in circles twice. Now, whether that was us being lost or Peter just enjoying making me feel confused, I can neither confirm nor deny, but I will tell you this much for certain:

From the air, looking down, his home is on the east part of the crescent, on the inner cove by the dock. The landscape is confusing, actually, and I suspect that it was Peter himself who named it the Never Wood merely for lack of a better term. It's not *not* a wood, but it also isn't only that. It's quite a bit more.

It's an all-encompassing wilderness—woods, forests, jungles, shores, bays. Mostly each part keeps to itself, but occasionally there'll be an overlap, and it could be jarring. For example, there was a jaguar with emerald eyes

---

† Or at least it would appear.

lounging in the branch of the Never Tree, which struck me as odd because I've never seen a jaguar in an oak tree before. Although I suppose I haven't seen many jaguars in general. An owl in a palm tree. A toucan in some clover. Lots of life bursting forth and tumbling out over onto one another, that's what Neverland feels like.

The tree the boys live in itself is a wonder, and I realize the moment I step inside it that it must be spelled somehow, because it opens out into a maze of a room that backs onto what looks like an Indonesian jungle.

It's all spiral stairs made of logs and twigs and nets that sprawl the length of the rooms and I suppose act as a kind of balcony. The roofs are thatched with palm fronds, and everything seems to be held together by sticks and rope and other things that should hold this together, but things are never what they seem here. You must remember that.

Scattered about also are these… I don't know what to call them other than nests? All of them look incredibly inviting, but none more so than the nest at the very top, which is piled high with quilts and pillows, and of all the beds I can see, it's overtly and obnoxiously the best one, so I know immediately that one belongs to Peter.

"Have you got her?" asks a young boy, racing out. He has dark brown hair and dark eyes.

"Yes, do you?" demands another with light brown hair and glasses without any glass in them.

They both look about eleven or twelve years old.

Another boy, bigger and broader than the first two—yet still ever so much less than Peter*—strolls out, arms folded. He has almost black hair and a cheeky face.

"She's right there, gents." He nods over at me. "You must look before asking your inane questions."

"Boys!" Peter hollers as he balances on a roof beam. "I got one!"

I stare over at Peter, scowling a bit at being referred to as a "one," before I look over at the other boys, giving them a collective, uncomfortable nod.

"Hello."

---

* I dare say that's on purpose too.

"Hello!" says the first one with the dark hair. "I'm Kinley." He shakes my hand vigorously. "Never met a girl before. This is so exciting." He has a little cockney accent, so cute.

"Never?" I blink.

"No." Kinley shakes his head solemnly.

The one with the glasses frowns over at him. "You know Feather and Calla and Sahara and—"

"Are those girls?" Kinley asks, completely shocked.

"Yes!" the boys and Peter say loudly in unison.

Kinley thumbs over in Peter's direction and whispers, "What's he always banging on about girls for then, like they're special?"

"They are," the one with the glasses says. He sounds a little more like he might have been from West London once upon a lifetime ago. He shoves Kinley away. "My name is Percival, and unlike my foolish friend, I understand the tender seriousness of the feminine ways."

And I have no idea what he means by that, but I swear to you, I keep a straight face as he says it.

"How noble," I tell him, trying not to dishearten him.

"You may call me Perce," he tells me nobly.

I nod and smile politely. "I'm Daphne."

"Brodie." The bigger one holds out his hand. He has the remnants of an accent that's rather hard to pick. A bit Scottish? Maybe American? Either way, I get the feeling that he might be quite stern with the other two.

"Where did you find her, Peter?" Percival asks, flying up to the beam Peter's on.

"I found her in the bedroom window, like I knew I would!" Peter declares. "I told you she'd be waiting for me. They're always waiting for me," he says and then shoves Percival off the beam.

I gasp because I'm new here, and for a moment, I forgot where I was as the boy tumbles through the air and lands in one of the nets below. He laughs merrily and stares up adoringly at Peter like he's a god.

He stands there, Peter Pan, hands on his hips, how they've always described him except for bigger and so much more beautiful (and perhaps mildly more frightening). He stares down at me, eyes locked, and then he gives me a half-baked smile, and I feel it in my stomach. Have you ever had a person give you a look and you feel it in your stomach? Multiple times throughout this day, I have been entirely certain (and it's been empirically proven) that I am not the only person Peter Pan sees, but right now, in this moment, I know I am, and I feel myself grow a centimeter taller because that's what happens when Peter Pan looks at you. And then it's gone. The moment wisps away, and his face changes from the curious sweetness he was gazing at me with to the look he gets in his eye when he's about to jump off a high thing, and then he leaps off the beam, flipping through the air and landing on one of the nets.

The other two boys copy him, soaring up for a few seconds, then nose-diving down.

"Can you all fly then?" I ask loudly, looking down at them.

"Only while we're with Peter," says the one without glass in his glasses.

"Why?" I look between them.

Kinley shrugs. "Those are the rules."

I arch an eyebrow. "According to whom?"

Peter stares up at me, a defiant sparkle in his eye as he cocks a brow.

"So no one can fly here except those with your permission?" I frown at him, the beautiful dictator that he appears to be.

Peter flies back up to me, this sweet grin on his face.

"That's right."

I roll my eyes at him. I think he might fancy himself clever for controlling gravity.*

I peer around the tree house as I listen.

"Where are the others?" I ask no one in particular, but Brodie hears me, and his eyes tighten a little.

"We are the Lost Boys," he says.

"Yes, but there were many before, were there not?" I frown, confused. "Where are they now?"

"Gone, I guess?" He shrugs.

I frown more at that. "Gone where?"

"Just gone," he says, looking around as though he himself just noticed their

---

* And I suppose he might just be.

absence now. "I used to have a brother, I think, maybe?" He looks up at the ceiling, but I can tell he's actually looking back inside his mind, like he's trying to remember a thing he has forgotten.

I blink twice. "And he's gone?"

Brodie holds my eyes for a sliver of a moment and then he shrugs a little. "I must have made him up," he says before he bounds off, diving back into the nets.

The four of them are fighting and wrestling in the nets, and it occurs to me that all three of the Lost Boys are younger than Peter, and that would have struck me as odd and maybe I would have even thought on it more were it not for the ball of light that flies in, bouncing off the beams and then finally hovering right in front of my face. It's not so big, no larger than my fist, but oh my god, once it's still, I see what it is, and she is beautiful.

So now, I know what you're thinking—we all know what they say about fairies, and some of it is true, but a lot of it's slander.

Tinker Bell did not like Wendy, that we know, but Grandmother Mary didn't know Tinker Bell; she had a different fairy, and hers was rather friendly to her. And me, well, I've never till now seen one in my life, but I've had many a pleasant dream about fairies and—in retrospect now—I'm not convinced that all of them were dreams after all as much as they were a prologue to the life awaiting me here.

Yes, it's true that their tininess can inhibit the diversity of what they might feel in a single instant, but it is my personal opinion that Tinker Bell was occasionally (and particularly) ill-tempered and frightfully bold.

That said, I did arrive in Neverland a tinge nervous that perhaps in the same way Pan was fated to always find a girl like me, maybe too was the same girl fated to be hated by the fairies.

But the little fairy hovering in my face, she's like a speck of sunshine. Very pale, almost translucent skin, huge light blue eyes and long, straight,[†] nearly white-blond hair.

"Well, hello." I give her my warmest smile.

She sounds like chimes when she speaks.

---

† But rather messy.

"No, I can understand you." I nod at her, and Peter looks over, frowning and curious.

"You speak Stjär?" he asks me, floating over. He swats the fairy away carelessly as he zones in on me.

"I don't—I didn't know I did." I give him a look. "But maybe?"

The fairy chimes again, landing on top of Peter's head, strutting around, ignoring how he'd just shooed her away a moment ago.

"I think my grandmothers taught me." I look from her to Peter. "I thought we were playing, but—I'm Daphne," I tell her as I extend my finger out for her to shake. She shakes it back. "Rune?" I repeat her name back to her and look over at Peter to check.

He nods, glaring at the fairy, who zips down his arm like it's a water slide before flying back up to my ear and tinkering

"Oh!" I beam at her. "Well, it's my absolute pleasure! Yes, I arrived today, just." I nod. "Yes, from London. Oh, it wasn't so bad. I'd never seen the inside of a black hole before, so that was rather special."

I can see in my peripheral vision Peter and the Lost Boys hovering behind us, watching, curious.

"She likes you," says Brodie.

"Should she not?" I frown, a bit confused.

"Oh." He jumps over to me. "I meant nothing by it. How good that she does." Then he leans in close and whispers quietly, "Just that this one doesn't like Peter much."

That strikes me as interesting because, as far as I knew, all fairies like Peter. Actually, all female creatures like Peter, as though he has a magic kind of pull over us. There is an innate assumption that men are immune to whatever it is about Peter that we* tend to love, and of course that's occasionally true,† but it's not always (nor often) the case.

Girls might be drawn in by his boyish charm and those stupid stars he has stuck in his eyes, but Wendy says the boys often find that Peter has a gravity for them also. Not in the same ways, necessarily, but in how he can climb anything

---

* We being womankind.

† Evidently immunity runs in the Hook family line.

or that he catches lightning bolts and spears them back at the clouds or the way he flies so low just above the water's surface that he skims the sharks' fins the same way you do mindlessly with a stair railing.

My point is, really, that to find anyone immune to him is a rarity, thus I like her already.

I nod. "Well, Rune, I'm entirely delighted to meet you." I give her my warmest smile as Peter floats on over.

"What are you two birds saying?"

Rune jingles angrily.

"I like birds. I didn't mean anything by it." Peter frowns.

More jingles.

"Fine." Peter looks quite sheepish. "I'm sorry then." His cheeks are pink now, and I can't imagine he gets scolded all that often, because he swats his hand. "You can go."

Rune chimes again and it's mocking. She grins at me and flits away, and I feel a bit sad that she's gone.

"Where does she live then?" I look around.

"Just around a corner." Peter shrugs as he looks at his own bicep.

"Which?"

Percival shrugs. "Dunno."

"Well then." I give them all a pointed look, and each of their faces (bar Peter's) falters at it. "Where am I to live?"

Peter glances around. "Here, stupid," he says after a moment.

"Here?" I repeat. "With all of you?"

Peter nods again, exchanging quizzical looks with the other boys.

"What will the neighbors think?"

Kinley looks over his shoulder. "What neighbors?"

"I can't very well stay here," I tell them all with a look.

Peter shrugs. "Of course you can."

I lift an eyebrow. "But where would I sleep?"

Peter snorts a laugh as he shakes his head. "With me."

I blink. A lot. "I beg your pardon?"

All those boys stare over at me, frowns on their faces as though my reaction is the odd one.

"Maybe she's hard of hearing?" Percival whispers to Peter.

"With. Me." Peter overenunciates.

I give him an exasperated look. "I. Heard. You. The. First. Time."

"Oh." Peter floats over, arms folded over his chest. "What is the problem then, girl?"

"Well—" I give him a cautious look, glancing around at the younger boys before I lower my voice. "What would people say?"

Peter shakes his head with a perplexed smile. "Whatever you want them to!"

I sigh. "No. I mean—"

Peter raises his eyebrows, waiting.

I purse my lips. "A boy…and a girl…in a bed… It's very—" I trail my eyes over the boys, hoping one of them might jump in nobly, finish this car wreck of a sentence so I mightn't have to.

"Cozy?" offers Kinley.

I shake my head. "No. I mean—Well—" I stifle a smile. "You know about—" I swallow nervously and clear my throat. "Sex?"

"Yes, of course." says Percival. "How do you spell it again?"

"S-E-X."

"Ah, yes. A German word." Percival nods knowledgeably. "For the number after five and before seven, I believe?"

"It's—" I shake my head. "No, ah—that's. No."

Brodie frowns, folding his arms again. "Well, what is it then?"

"Um—" I scratch behind my ear delicately, and I suppose my cheeks must be looking pink because suddenly Percival takes flight and brings me over a chair.

"Are you feeling flushed, my lady?"

"No, I'm—"

He shoves me backwards into the chair anyway. "Much better." He smiles, pleased with himself.

Kinley and Percival sit on the floor in front of me, Brodie pulls up a chair, and Peter leans coolly against a beam, watching closely.

"Well." Brodie waves his hand impatiently. "Tell us about it then."

"Uh…" I grimace. "No."

"You must!" Percival cries, horrified.

"Yes!" Kinley.

"Wendy used to tell Peter stories," Percival offers. "Perhaps you could tell us a story about sex so we understand it."

And then a little burst of laughter escapes me, and I clap my hands over my mouth to contain it, but the damage is already done. That sweet little Percival sits at my feet looking a little bit rejected, what with being laughed at by an older woman and all, so I give him a sweet smile.

"Sorry." I give him another smile. "I don't mean to laugh. It's just—"

Peter gives me a suspicious look. "What's so funny, girl?"

"Nothing." I shake my head, not wanting to drum on Percival's discomfort.

Peter leaps in the air and glides over, standing awfully close to my face, peering at me.

"She doesn't know," he announces.

I roll my eyes at him. "I do too."

He gives me a spiteful look that's mostly all eyebrows. "Prove it."

I don't like being challenged by anyone; it's a weakness of mine, I'll readily admit. But a particular weakness I have is when I'm challenged by a man. I didn't grow up around too many, just my grandfather, you see? And he was one of those men who believed women were the superior of the sexes, that the sun rose and set purely for the honor to shine on my grandmother's face.

I'm bullheaded, Grandmother Mary says. And I'm used to being the cleverest person in the room, so any time that's contested, I take issue with it.

"Fine," I tell him, nose in the air.

Probably pertinent to point out here that I've never had sex.

Not yet. I've been presented with the opportunity a couple of times. I've just never felt like I wanted to, so I'm not overly qualified to give this lesson, but I take a big breath and give it a crack anyway.

I purse my lips.

How do you explain sex to boys who've never really seen or known romance, in a world without Marilyn Monroe or Sophia Loren.

"Okay," I start, grimacing already. "Well, have you ever spent time with someone, a girl—or a boy!" I add as an urgent afterthought. "I'm not judgm—I don't—You may like who you li—"They're all looking at me blankly, and Peter's frowning. "Never mind." I shake my head. I breathe out. "Um, so sometimes, if you've been spending time with someone, and you like spending time with them, and then sometimes when you see them, you get this feeling in your stomach, that's sort of like…being…erm…kicked?"

"What?" Percival frowns.

"But it's not…all bad?"

Kinley shakes his head. "In my experience, being kicked is never good."

"No, it's not real kicking. It's—" I shake my head. "The feelings. It's just feelings—and it's a weird feeling, but sort of good?"

"I know what you mean." Peter nods, thinking to himself. "I get that feeling with you." He shrugs like he's told me the weather.

I breathe in the fullness of that comment. I'd quite like to roll around in it, relish the moment, but then he keeps talking.

"Is that sex?" Peter asks pleasantly. "Is that what we're doing?"

"Aye." Percival nods wisely.

I clap my hand over my mouth because it's all I can do not to laugh.

"Sounds boring," Kinley says, looking at me suspiciously.

"Look, no." I sigh. "Sex is not boring. Usually. Though, I suppose it could be."

"I hate boring things." Peter shakes his head.

"Me too." Brodie nods.

"It's not boring!" I growl as I shake my head, impatient. "Listen…um… have you ever…" I rack my brain. "Kissed anyone before?"

"Kissed anyone?" Kinley frowns.

"Yes!" I roll my eyes. "Kissed! Like…" I peck the back of my hand.

"Oh!" Brodie nods. "You mean thimbles."

"Yes!" I point at him triumphantly, remembering that faux pas my grand-mother made. "Have you ever 'thimbled' someone?"

"Yes!" Peter nods enthusiastically because he never likes to miss out. "I've thimbled Wendy! And the other two. And a bunch of the ones before. Just like that—" He points over at me and gives me a proud smile. "I love thimbles."

I swallow heavily and gag internally, give Percival a little look.

"Okay, if we're keeping tabs, I'm feeling dramatically unkicked in the stomach." Percival looks confused, and I see him shrug at Kinley.

"Anyway," I continue. "It's sort of like...lots of thimbles, but bigger thimbles than"—I peck my hand again—"that."

"Oh, I know all about sex then!" Peter declares proudly, stretching his arms over his head, which is nearly sexy but isn't on account of what he just said a second ago.

"No, you don't," I tell him sternly.

"Yeah, I do. I've thimbled heaps of girls."

I stare at him; that bothers me in a handful of ways. That he thinks he knows about sex when clearly he doesn't, that he's apparently kissed lots of girls who aren't me, and also that at least three of them are from my maternal bloodline.

"Okay." I give him a look. "I will try to explain to you what sex is in its crudest form."

"Didn't you just?" Peter yawns. "I know all about it."

"Thimbles are a part of it," I tell him a bit waspishly. "Also, they're not called thimbles. They're called kisses, so you obviously don't know that much, so you can be quiet and listen."

Peter's eyes go to slits, and he looks annoyed, but I don't stop because he's such a know-it-all but he knows barely anything, and it's a man's worst trait to pretend he knows about things that he doesn't; but I remind myself how unique a circumstance this is. No mother, no father, no reason to know about anything to do with sex until now.

"And second, kisses are a part of sex and sometimes lead to it—"

"What's 'it'?" Brodie asks, bored again.

"Okay." I take a big breath and clap my hands together.* "The thing in your trousers is different from the thing in my trousers, and you can combine the thing in your trousers with the thing in other people's trousers, and that's sort of sex."

Sort of.

Peter Pan peers down at his linen trousers. He and Brodie trade confused looks, and I hear the littlest one say, "She's very pretty but she can't tell stories like the other ones."

---

* I place my hand over my mouth and swallow. Oh, to die right now.

And with that, I cover my face with both my hands, both sighing and combusting into flames at once.

Then Peter snaps his head in Kinley's direction, and his eyes might have gone a way I don't think I like. "What did you say?"

"Nothing!" Kinley says quickly, shaking his head and looking a bit scared.

Peter eyes him murderously for a few seconds too long, then peers around at the rest of them. "I'm not sharing this Wendy, boys."

And without my permission, I begin to float a tiny bit off the ground. I can't help it. Happy thoughts and all, those traitors.

"Why not?" They all frown.

Peter shrugs. "I like this one's face so much, I don't want anyone else looking at it."

Percival sighs. "This will make for a difficult home environment."

I clear my throat. "Don't I get a say?" I ask, eyebrows high.

Peter rolls his eyes. "Go on then."

"I'd just like to clarify that I'm not going to be all your mothers."

"That's fine," Kinley says.

"I'm not going to be anyone's mother," I clarify.

"That's fine." Percival nods. "We don't need mothers. We're big now. We need a girlfriend."

I give him a look. "Well, I'm not going to be your girlfriend either."

He swipes the air in frustration.

"Where am I supposed to put my eyes then?" Kinley asks, staring wide-eyed and dutifully at Peter and absolutely not at all at me.

I touch his cheek, moving it to face me. "You can look at me, Kinley."

"Fine," barks Peter. "You can look at her, but she's just mine though."

And maybe, perhaps, my heart swells an inch.

After that, we have a dinner that's divine. Sunday roast, except I don't think it's a Sunday.

Brodie told me that there's a type of fairy that lives here called a hob. They're little house fairies who cook and clean, and in return, you make them porridge, which apparently Peter never does, so I make it my personal business to rectify that effective immediately. They don't like being seen, and they like to work alone, but one night when I'm not tired and I've not just traveled through a black hole or watched a man be murdered by a sexy pirate or had to explain sex to a ragtag group of preteens and teenagers, on that day, I'm going to sit up late and try to spot it and thank it for its service because it's the polite thing to do and also because I should like to see all the creatures on this island.

"Come on." Peter takes my hand in his and guides me from the table. "Dinner's over."

And then he floats me upwards.

It takes me a few moments to realize he's taking me to his bedroom.

I've never been taken to a boy's bedroom before—though I did sneak a boy into my dormitory room once,[*][†][‡] and Jasper England did sort of feel me up in his car once, and then that Welsh boy and I spent a lot of the summer swimming and kissing[§]—but I've never been in a boy's room before. Though admittedly, Peter's room is barely Peter's room. It's all just one big room, but his nest is rather a bit higher than everyone else's.

"This is where you will live," he tells me as he lowers me down into it. "It's the best spot, which is why it's mine. It's still mine, but you can be here too."

I give him a small smile and a small nod.

He dives into the air and then tumbles onto his nest, shakes his hair so it falls and frames his face perfectly, and then shifts the covers over himself. He peers up at me.

"Are you coming in?" he asks, and his voice has a curious innocence. And it is odd, admittedly. I don't know how old he is, nineteen, maybe?[¶] "Older than me" is what he said. It's strange that a boy older than me doesn't know a thing about sex, doesn't know why I might worry about what the nonexistent neighbors might say (if they existed) about us sharing a nest, but the fact that he doesn't understand why it might be perceived a certain way makes me feel as though anything one might worry about in such a scenario is incredibly unlikely to transpire.

Peter nods his head towards his nest again, inviting me wordlessly now

---

[*] Sorry, Charlotte!

[†] Evidently immunity runs in the Hook family line.

[‡] Thanks, Charlotte!

[§] Ever so much more than those stupid pecks on the back of one's hand.

[¶] But for how many years was he twelve?

to join him, and against my better judgment, I'm feeling somewhat kicked in the stomach again.

I've never slept with a boy before either.

Not in this way and not in the other way either. I actually don't know how many ways there are to truly sleep with a boy, but be sure of this: I've experienced none of them.

And it's one of those things I've thought of—how nice it would be, especially in the winter when it's cold and you can snuggle up close to them for warmth. But here, the coolest thing is the breeze, and it's barely there. And I'm sure I'm overthinking things now, but I don't even know how to casually lie down next to a boy in a bed, let alone a nest.

I swallow nervously and walk over, too distracted for happy thoughts to make me float.

I lie down slowly, next to him, and stare up at the ceiling. Peter's watching my mouth closely, and then he pokes the top right corner of it.

"These are so hard to catch," he tells me. "And rare!"

"Yes." I give him a demure smile. "So I'm told."

"I'll catch yours," he tells me, sure of it.

I cover my kiss with my hand, make sure he didn't snatch it away while I blinked.

He doesn't stop watching me still, smiling a tiny bit as he does.

"What?" I frown.

"You look nervous," he tells me.

I frown more. "And why does that make you smile?"

"I don't know." He smiles more. "It just does."

I lie back next to him, arms folded across my chest, stiff as a board.

He rolls in towards me and leans on his arm, looking down at me. His eyes flicker over my face.

"Don't worry," he whispers. "I feel nervous too."

And I know my cheeks go pink in an obvious way because Peter touches them, and I love feeling his hands on my face like compresses.

"Peter." I purse my lips and my eyes go wide. "Before, you said that you wouldn't care to share me like you shared the others."

He nods.

"Why?" I press.

"I don't know." He shrugs, settling in on his pillow. "There's just—" He shrugs again. "I just don't want to. And I never do anything I don't want to do."

Pause.

"Even just thinking about anyone else looking at you makes me want punch everything and keep you just up here where no one can see you."

I give him a look. "Well, that's not my favorite plan."

Peter looks at me out of the corner of his eye. "Don't sleep in someone else's hammock, okay?"

I nod once. "Okay."

He stretches his arms up over his head as he yawns. "Mine's the best one anyway."

CHAPTER
FOUR

I SUPPOSE I PROBABLY SHOULD HAVE SEEN THIS COMING OR AT LEAST TOYED with the idea of it, that there are other people here who Peter spends significant sorts of time with, but it wasn't until Peter Pan came right out and said, "I should go visit Calla, because I'm big now, and she will want to see."

And then I said, "Who's Calla?"

And then no one said anything, and they didn't have to, because Peter's thimbled a lot of girls, if you recall, but the small flick of Brodie's eyebrows confirmed it for me.

Peter didn't answer either, by the way. He just took flight straight out the window like he'd forgotten all about me at the mere mention of her.

I've been there a few days by now, I think? It's hard to tell. You know the strange few days between Christmas and New Year's on Earth, where real life feels suspended and you sort of drift through the days without any real notion of time? It's like that here, only always. Time is incredibly slippery here. I think it has only been a few days, and I think that because I can count in my head how many times I've left out porridge for the Hobb, which is three,* not including today, and how many times we've had to take our medicine, which is also three.† I think.

First thing in the morning, no matter what.

Peter said it's my job to make the littlest ones take it, so I take mine first to prove to the boys that it's takable. Which it is. It's mostly sweet, sickly almost. Like agave syrup. But there's a bitterness that cuts through at the end.

---

* Or maybe it's eight?

† Or is it twelve?

"Come on." Brodie nods his head towards the window. "I'll take you."

"Take me where?" I frown.

"To the Stjärna."

It's not a terrible far walk to the Old Valley—as they call it—just maybe thirty or so minutes on foot. It's where the Stjärna people live. It borders Zomertierra. Most of their land is found in the springtime land, and it's all lakes and pine trees and boulders and wildflowers, and I might have been lost to the beauty of it all if I wasn't staring down the barrel of my worst nightmare realized.

Peter Pan diving off a rock and playing in the water with the most beautiful girl I've ever seen in my whole entire terrible life.

Dark brown skin, chocolate eyes, raven hair. Beautiful jagua flowers crawling up her arm.[‡] The biggest, whitest, widest smile I've ever seen—

The wonder of him dims a little as I watch them, and I remind myself that I've known him perhaps not even five days[§] (dimming wonder can help you to remember things here), and then the wonder pipes back up again and reminds me that sometimes abstract things such as affections exist outside the pocket of regular space-time and actually dwell in the special corner of the universe reserved exclusively for the fated hearts.

The girl's very presence around him is—and this is the best I could describe it—akin to watching a stranger deface a family heirloom.

Every time she touches his hair or jumps on his shoulders, I feel a sharpness in my breath as my heels dig in to him a little deeper, and all of me feels on edge the same way it would if I were watching an incredibly expensive crystal vase wobbling on the edge of a shelf.

"Don't worry about them," says a boy.

I glance over at him.

Dark skin, long dark hair, dark eyes, same wide smile as the girl though— obviously her brother. Also shirtless. My god—the shirts! Where are the shirts?

"I wasn't worried," I tell him, my nose in the air.

"Oh." He gives me a look. "Does your face always look that strained then?"

[‡] Which I know about because of my mother's time in Peru.

[§] Or is it nine?

I flick him a look and Brodie laughs.

"Brodie." The shirtless boy smiles over at him, whacking him in the arm playfully. "Filling out."

Brodie smiles but the edges of it are tucked strangely, as though him filling out maybe isn't the great thing it would be to a teenager on Earth. He points back behind us. "I should go find the little ones," he says to me before he looks at the shirtless boy. "If Peter forgets about her again, will you bring her back to the tree?"

The shirtless boy nods, and I hope my face doesn't show (though I am quite sure that it does) how hurt I am not only that Peter's forgotten about me but that it's obvious to other people as well.

"I'm Rye." The shirtless boy extends his hand to me with a warm smile.

I stare at it for a second, sort of mortified that he knows so immediately upon meeting me how forgettable I am, but he doesn't seem put off by me for it—standing there, hand all out, smiling, waiting.

I take his hand and shake it. "Daphne."

He nods once, smiling more, and actually, he really does have a very lovely smile.

"The trees were whispering about a new girl on the island."

"Were they?" I beam.

He nods again, and I decide I like his eyes. "Come on. I'll introduce you." He nods his head towards Peter and his sister.

I pull back, unsure, but he rolls his eyes.

"She's not so bad."

She is, however, more beautiful up close than she is from afar, which is desperately not what I wanted. It's as though her eyes are actually made of garnets, and they do not look pleased when they fall on me.

"Cal," Rye calls to her. "This is Daphne."

Peter turns around in the water, squinting up at me. "Oh yeah! I forgot about you!"

I press my lips together, trying to hide yet another look of crushing disappointment on my face.

"Hello," I say to her as I muster my warmest smile.

"This is Calla." Rye glances from her to me.

Calla says nothing, just stares up at me with pinched eyes.

I offer her another smile. "Pleasure."

She still says nothing.

I glance at her brother.

"Callie." He kicks the water from the shore. "Say hi."

She stares at me for a long few seconds, then rolls her eyes. "Hi."

And then she dives on Peter again, and away they play.

The water sounds quite loud, both the splashing and lapping against the shore, but none of it nearly as loud as the sound of them laughing.

There's too much skin on skin. Peter's scooping her up in his arms and tossing her about like he was doing to me a few hours ago in the nets, and her legs fan delicately through the air before she crashes into the water and he dives down and scoops her up again.

She jumps on his shoulders, wrapping her legs around him, and I have never felt invisible before, but I do. And I hate it. If I had the proper ears for such things, I'd hear it put a crack in the lens, not the one through which I see Peter but the one through which I see myself. Him ignoring me, him all over Calla, doesn't make me like Peter less—though I wish it did. All it does is bubble up within me the most tragic of side effects. A terrible thirst.

I am invisible to him. And now I must be seen.

Rye stares over at his sister and Peter, gives me a long look, and then all too knowingly nods his head in another direction.

"Should we go for a walk?"

I probably nod too eagerly, but I need to get out of here. It's rather demoralizing watching yourself fade from someone's focus.

Fate and all, I remind myself. It's my window he came to. It's me he brought here.

It's also me who he's forgotten.

Rye bounds up ahead of me a few steps before turning back, eyes warm and sunny, and he reminds me a bit of a golden retriever.

"Where to?" He grins.

I shrug. "You tell me."

He thinks for a minute. "Have you been into town yet?"

Yes is obviously the answer, but I find myself shrugging and saying, "Barely, only for a minute, just—"

I shouldn't like to admit it,* but I know I want to go into town because I want to see the pirate again.

You can forget a lot of things in Neverland, quite easily if I'm honest. I don't think of my grandmothers so much. Well, I mean, I do because Peter calls me Wendy all the time, so I remember her that way, but I don't think of her in the way where my heart is sore and I miss her. I don't think of my friends back in London. I don't think of how the flowers smell in our garden. I don't think about warm cups of tea. But I do think about Jamison's hands on my waist and the color of his eyes† and the shape of his mouth.

Mostly I think about the shape of his mouth, I think because I don't feel I have a particularly good grasp on it.

I like to have a grasp on everything, that's all. I just like knowing everything. I consider myself rather well learned, yet I'm insufficiently educated on the shape of that pirate's top lip, and sometimes when Peter's fallen asleep and I haven't quite yet, in between that place of sleeping and waking where you're meant to find Peter Pan, with him right next to me, my mind wanders to wondering how it might feel to trace the outline of Jamison's jawline with my middle finger. I do suspect it might feel like running one's hand along the edge of a marble countertop.

Rye and I walk for a while in silence, but thankfully, it's a nice enough silence that's still filled richly with the wildness of Neverland. Twigs snapping under our feet, rivers racing, birds chirping, and Rye humming away tunelessly.

"Thank you," I call to him. "For offering to take me away."

He looks back and throws me a quick smile. "I want to see that about as much as you do." He laughs. "Trust me."

"So they're close then?" I ask after a minute.

"Used to be." He glances back. "They had that golden age from when Calla was about nine till she was fourteen or something, I don't know. Back then, they were inseparable."

"What happened when she was fourteen?"

"She turned fourteen."

---

* Though I do know that it's true whether I admit it or not.

† Which I'll remind you are a bit like that water planet I grew up on a few galaxies over.

"So?" I frown.

Rye turns around and cups imaginary boobs, smirking at himself. "He couldn't pretend she wasn't growing up anymore." He turns back around, touching trees gently as we pass them as though he's greeting old friends. "But now that he's older, they"—he spins around and cups the imaginary boobs again—"probably act more as an incentive than anything."

I sigh.

"Don't worry." He gives me a quick smile. "He'll forget about her later too."

I sniff an indignant laugh. "Why do we like him again?"

"Beats me." He shrugs as we step through a clearing onto a beach.

He points at a pirate ship I recognize. Gorgeous white sails that fold like duvets, dark wood, lots of navy, lots of gold. The ship's figurehead is a tiger. I thought that was strange initially. Actually, I suppose I still find it rather odd now.

"That's Hook's. Do you know who that is?"

I purse my lips. "We've met."

Rye glances down at me, intrigued. "Really?"

"Briefly!"

He smirks.

"What?" I frown, cheeks pink.

"And?" He says, eyebrows up, hint of a smirk a bit present. "What do you think?"

I frown defensively. "What are you making that face for?"

"Right." He chuckles. "So you thought he was attractive."

"What! I—" I shake my head. "No, I didn—"

"Sorry." He rolls his eyes, grinning. "I meant dreamy."

"No." I scowl. "I—"‡

Rye snorts, rolls his eyes, and keeps walking.

"Liar." He calls back to me, and I chase after him down the beach and into the town, feeling a bit indignant and honestly rather embarrassed because I indeed did find the pirate to be both attractive and dreamy. That is until he murdered someone in front of me, whence I found myself, once again, dramatically unkicked.

---

‡ I definitely do think he's dreamy.

Kind of. A bit. Well fine, I didn't, but I should have.

And yes, sure, it was the tiniest bit attractive to be so defended, but defended so horribly! Ugh, grotesque! So actually, he isn't dreamy, even if he is.

And besides, he isn't. I'm just probably upset that Peter's in a river with his hands all over the most beautiful girl in the world, whom he previously shared a deep-rooted, childhood connection with.*

"Well, well," says a familiar voice.

I spin around and there he is. Jamison Hook. Arms folded over his now shirt-clad chest.†

I'm blushing instantly. I don't know why I am blushing.

I say nothing, just stare up at him, and then he leans down close to me and whispers, "This here now would be the part where ye say hello, Daphne Belle Burmont-Darling."

"It's Beaumont." I flick him a look.

"What is?" Rye asks, poking his head in.

I breathe out my nose. "Nothing—"

"Native." Hook nods, and my mouth falls open in protest.

I go to say, "I don't think you can call him tha—" but Rye cuts me off.

"Pirate." Rye nods back at Hook, and it is then and only then that I realize they're not actually being hostile.

"Girl." Hook nods at me, suppressing a smile.

"Arse." I glare at him, and his suppressed smile turns into a grin. I look over at Rye curiously. "Have your people always been on the island then?"

Hook looks between Rye and I. "Technically, they were colonists."

I straighten myself up. "Be quiet! I don't believe you for a second."

Rye looks between us both and rolls his eyes, unfazed. "Calm yourselves." Then he focuses on me. "We weren't the first ones here."

Jamison gives me a look. "Quite racist o' ye to assume otherwise."

"Well, who were first here then?" I frown.

"Well…" Hook shrugs. "Depending on yer persuasions, the true first people here might be the wee fae."

---

* Existential question: If your entire existence has been a childhood, do you still have one?

† Bollocks.

"And the animals," Rye adds.

Hook nods. "And the merfolk, I s'pose, but they're part fae."

"Are they?" I ask brightly, and both of them give me a strange look.

Rye blinks twice. "What do they even teach you in schools in England?"

I roll my eyes at him. "Oh, just useful things like maths and English and history and geography and biology—"

Jamison pulls a face. "No' very comprehensive if they've missed a whole fecking planet, is it?"

I give him a long-suffering look before I look back at Rye. "If you're not originally from Neverland, where are you from?" I shake my head and ask a further question. "What are you?"

"Human." Rye shrugs.

I roll my eyes, a bit miffed at the evasive answer. "Well, what kind of human?"

"Just human," Hook answers for him with a shrug.

"But where did you come from?" I stare between them.

They both point to the sky.

"Well, when?"

They both stare over at me before Hook leans over towards Rye and quietly says, "She asks so many questions."

Rye pulls a face and sort of gives him a nod.

Hook goes on. "It's all a wee bit annoying, no?"

Rye sniffs a laugh, and don't think for a minute I don't notice that neither of them answer me.

"So what brings y'round this part o' the island?" Jamison asks Rye, but he's looking at me.

"Daphne wants a tour of the village."

"Aye, does she now?" Jamison looks at me, smirking. "Odd considering I gave 'er one just a week back—"

I freeze and Rye glances at me, eyes wide and bright with amusement.

"Well…" I clear my throat. "I…um…I mean it was hardly comprehensive." I look at Jamison. "You were honestly a rather terrible tour guide."

"I was a grand tour guide!"

"No, you weren't."

And then, at the same time, I say, "You killed a man!" and he says, "I killed a man!"

And then our eyes lock, and we squint at each other.

"Midtour," I remind him.

Jamison shrugs. "Aye, some folk would pay extra for that."

I give him a look. "Well, not I." I sniff. "And color me suspicious, but I don't trust you at all, in general nor as a tour guide, so…"

"Sure, yeah." Hook smirks. "Pirate and all."

"Right." I give him a stern nod.

"That sounds like quite the tour," Rye whispers playfully.

"Shut up," I snap.

I don't know when it happened or how even—certainly it was without invitation—but Jamison Hook strolls with us through the village market.

He greets people as we pass them, and sometimes I think there's an audible swoon from girls around us.

An older woman at a fruit stall tosses him an apple, and he catches it with a wink, then offers it to me.

I shake my head, and he takes a bite. The crunch is loud, and the juice of it runs over his bottom lip. He wipes it away with the back of his hand, and I swallow heavy.

Jamison Hook spins around on his heel, and his eyes catch the light and they look a bit like the surface of Neptune, which I know about now because I believe I passed it to get here. Dark and light, like the shifting and moving all swirly blue and ultramarine.

"So." Jamison clears his throat. "Where's the Never Boy today?"

I flash him a little look. "With the Never Girl."

He squints. "Is that no' ye?"

I give him a tired, amused look. "Not today."

"He's with my sister." Rye doesn't look up from the gold lamp he's inspecting.

"Ah!" Hook gives me a pointed look. "How wile* unlike him."

I roll my eyes and keep walking ahead.

---

* Which means "very."

"How's it going thonner with the wee man anyway?" Jamison calls after me, and it sounds like a sincere question though I won't trust his sincerity, even if I feel like it.

I like it when he refers to Peter as the "wee man." It's so mildly derogatory, so technically inoffensive, yet it would offend Peter so terribly; I do my best not to smile at him for it, squashing it away every time it comes. "I can't imagine he much likes you calling him that."

"Sure but that's my primary reason fer doing it." He gives me a playful look, and I roll my eyes like it annoys me and I don't love it a little bit. Peter's just so big for his boots sometimes, you know?

"It's going fine."

"What's it like living with the Lost Boys?" Rye asks.

"It's fine," I say, but it comes out all high-pitched.

"Fine?" Hook repeats skeptically, and Rye turns around, intrigued.

"Fine." I grimace. "Well, weird."

"Weird how?" Rye frowns.

"I don't know. Weird like—they're very removed from regular life and... societal norms."

"Right, sure." Jamison gives me a look. "They're a bunch o' half teens who live all together in a tree house that's captained by a maniacal...I want to say fifteen-year-old?"

Rye tilts his head, considering this. "I think he's a good bit older than that now."

"Literally?" Hook blinks. "Aye, he's about four hundred years older than that."

"They're not regular teenagers is what I mean." I flick him a look that I hope communicates my point, which he still misses. "I mean...it would appear that they don't know about a lot of"—how do I put this delicately?—"stuff."

Rye frowns more, and I'm wondering if I'll have to have the ruddy conversation all over again.

"They didn't know about sex."

"What?" blinks Rye, eyes wide and surprised.

I nod at him, exasperated.

"And you told them?" He balks.

Hook snorts a laugh, and I toss him an unimpressed look because I give Rye a hopeless shrug. "Well, they didn't know!"

Rye's jaw has dropped, and his eyes are bright. "How did you—why did that—what?"

I whack my hands on my cheeks, feeling hot again. "Oh, and I suppose, how would they know! No one's told them." I sigh. "The importance of mothers, honestly—or fathers! Or just, you know, community knowledge that's sort of… passed down." I eye Rye. "Someone should have told them!"

Rye shakes his head, grinning big. "So happy to have let that baton pass me right by."

"Well, so anyway." I give Rye a little glare. "I told them and, my god"—I rub my temples—"I might have really put them on a bad path. I wouldn't be entirely surprised if one of them goes up and kicks someone they're attracted to right in the stomach."

Hook eyes me cautiously. "For why?"

"Because that's what it feels like when you're attracted to someone, you know? A punch in the gut."

Rye considers this, then shrugs. "For me, I just can't get them out of my head." Then his gaze trails behind me. "Hey, I'll just be back in a minute."

Hook and I watch him duck into a shop. Hook watches the shop for a minute, then turns back to me, something processing behind his eyes, but it dissipates when he looks at me.

He walks a few paces faster than I do, and I wonder if he does this so I'll stare after him.

He's wearing dark trousers that don't fit very well, but somehow I mean that in a positive way, a white shirt with a navy jacket with big buttons, and high-top leather boots that are undone.

He looks back at me, smile cocked. "Ye get the punch in the gut around me, don't ye?"

I scoff, indignant. "I do not."

"Aye, you do." He smirks, eyes all lit up. "I ken ye do. You buckle a wee bit whenever ye see me."

I stare at him, wide-eyed, shaking my head. "You're crazy."

"Am I?" He tilts his head playfully, and maybe, just maybe, I'm not kicked in the gut, just perhaps a little bit flicked or something, but that doesn't really count.

"Well." I take a huffy breath and put my hands on my hips as I stare up at him. "You feel a punch in the gut when you see me too."

"No." He shrugs indifferently as he shakes his head, and I feel my cheeks flush again but differently. My face falls a little.

He lets it hang there—the awkwardness, the disappointment that shouldn't be there but nevertheless is disastrously evident on my face—and then he leans in towards me. His face is close enough to mine that I can feel his breath. His eyes flicker to my mouth, and he runs his tongue over his bottom lip.

"That's no'where I feel it," he whispers. He takes out a flask and has a swig before he offers it to me.

"Well, so—" I shake my head at him as I glare over. Swallow. "Where do you feel it then?"

He lifts his eyebrows playfully.

"Ah!" I stomp my foot, annoyed to have fallen into that trap. "You're disgusting." I walk quickly down the street, shaking my head at him. "Filthy! You're deplorable even! I can't believe   "

He grabs my wrist and spins me around so we're toe-to-toe. "That yer attracted to me?"

"No!" I yank my hand away from him, smacking him with it. "That I'm even…spending time with you!"

"Aye." He nods, conceding as he swallows. "But y'are attracted to me."

"I…" I scoff, shaking my head.

"Look at ye!" Jamison beams, all smug. "Yer lost for words."

I scoff again, reach into his internal coat pocket, and grab his flask. I yank off the lid and take a big sip, and he stares down at me, eyebrows up, but I think perhaps a little impressed. I rather like the feeling of impressing him, and maybe my brain runs through a few hypothetical scenarios where I might be able to impress him again.* I screw the lid back on extra tight and hand it back to him.

Our hands brush as I do, and for a sliver of a second, the smug look on his

---

* Or maybe it doesn't. Who's to say?

face is knocked off, and he's looking over at me with a face that looks like my heart feels—caught off guard and a tiny bit afraid. It's just for a moment, but I see it before he blinks it away and he's back to smug all over again.

"Did that help?" He gestures to his flask. "Do ye feel more in control of yerself around me now?"

I give him my biggest eye roll and walk past him.

I hear him laugh and then he's next to me again. "Dinnae worry. I have that effect on many a girl."

My chin drops to my chest a bit. "How many girls?"

His eyebrows go tall. "Many," he overenunciates.

I make a sound at the back of my throat. Jamison Hook is probably the most annoying man I've ever met, but let's be sure about this: he is terribly manly.

He flicks his eyes over at me, amused. "Sure, but how'd sex come up anyway?" He takes another swig from his flask.

"Well," I sigh. "Peter said for me to sleep with him—"

Jamison chokes on his rum.

"Not like that!" I clarify quickly, shaking my head, though I did enjoy how his hearing that made him react. That makes me feel a good bit better. I peer up at him, and our eyes catch, and my heart trips a little.

"What way then?" he asks, shaking his head as he squashes away a smile. Always squashing smiles… I wonder if it's a pirate thing? Are they not supposed to be happy?

"In his hammock. With him."

"A hammock." He eyes me. "Yer sleeping in a hammock?"

"Mmm—" I purse my lips, considering this. "it's a cross between a hammock and a nest."

I can see him trying to imagine it, but to his credit, it's hard to picture.

"Do ye enjoy that?" he asks.

I shrug.

"Well." He gives me a look. "I hae a bed, should ye ever care to use it."

I roll my eyes and walk ahead of him.

"I'm just being a gentleman," he calls after me.

"Is that what they're calling it these days?" I say without looking back at him.

And he goes "hah," and I feel quite pleased with myself.

Jamison leans back against a wall, head tilted as he watches me, brows a little furrowed. "Are ye at all equipped to be giving them thon lesson?"

I turn around, frowning. "What do you mean?"

He nods his chin at me. "Have ye even had sex?"

My cheeks creep pink again, and I feel like I should feel embarrassed, but I don't want to be, so I fold my arms over my chest, square them, and go stand toe-to-toe with that pirate. I back him up into the wall as far as he'll go, and nose in the air, I tell him, proud as I can, "No."

"All right then," His eyes fall down my body, and he nods once and then he swallows heavy. "Good to know."

I put my hands on my hips and try to look superior. "Why is that good to know?"

He shakes his head. "Just good t' ken." He squashes another smile and presses his tongue into his bottom lip but says nothing else, and I don't know why, but I feel myself smiling back at him too.

I walk a few steps away from him, as I suspect keeping my distance from Jamison will be a key component in maintaining a healthy relationship with him, and then spin back to face him. "How old are you?"

He breathes out a laugh. "Twenty-two," he tells me.

Quite grown-up, really, don't you think? Quite a man—especially compared to Peter. Except I'm not comparing him to Peter, because why on earth would I?* Peter's a boy, and Jamison's a man, and I'm a—

"And you?" Jamison asks breezily, and across my face, I feel a flicker of a frown. "How old are ye?" he asks again.

I'm a woman. That's what I consider myself to be, I think. Except when I'm around Peter, and then maybe I'm a girl, because I don't imagine he much cares for women. But if I were on my own, and a voice inside me were to ask whether I'm a woman or a girl, probably—truthfully—the answer is that I'm right on the cusp of both. I feel a pull backwards and one forward—to grow up and to grow down. A leaning towards responsibility and a nervous panic within me to run from it. Which is new. I've never had that before. As though Peter

---

* Perhaps because we're not on Earth?

himself planted a seed in my mind where, for the first time ever, the future is a thing I'm a little bit afraid of.

Fear is contagious, in case you didn't know.

And my brain is moving very fast right now, in this moment. Only a second or so has passed since Hook asked me my age, which is a regular, non-weighty question (that I, myself, asked him first!), but something about it now that it's pointed back at me feels weighted, and the answer bears heavy on my mind. As though my allegiance to girlhood or womanhood might infer something more.

I'm ever so slightly reluctant to tell him because I don't want him to stop looking at me how he is right now, eyes flickering up and down my body like a tiger sizing up an antelope, and I know I shouldn't like it and maybe I should be scared, but I do ever so like the feeling. I like it much more than I wish I did in general and absolutely more than how I felt before when I saw Peter's hands on that Calla girl's waist, so maybe what I'm really feeling is a kind of desperate recklessness to be seen and nothing else more complicated or subversive to the real reason I'm here.

I clear my throat, stand all tall again, relax my face, and calmly answer him.

"Eighteen," I lie before saying quietly under my breath, "Almost."

Jamison's mouth pulls as he breathes out, and he squints again, a bit dubious as he shakes his head. "How 'almost'?"

"November 1," I tell him, and I sound hopeful as I say it, like I want my birthday to be acceptable to him.

He thinks to himself for a minute. His eyes flick up and left, his mouth forming a thinking kind of pout, and then after a moment, he nods once. "All right."

I swallow, standing very still but rather relieved that he doesn't seem entirely put off by me.

"All right?" I repeat back at him, eyebrows up a little.

Jamison clears his throat as he takes a step closer towards me, his mouth as close to my ear as it can be before it touches. "Between my shoulders. Like a weight." He shifts his head so we catch again, his gaze going from my eyes to my mouth to my eyes again. "And I feel it in my bones." He pauses. "Not that bone!" He nudges me playfully, and where his elbow touches my ribs, the feeling of him being there lasts so much longer than it should. "Get yer mind out o' the gutter." He smirks at me.

I breathe out loudly. "I wasn't even—"

"In my normal bones." He keeps going, ignoring me. "I feel it all over. Like a flu."

Then he holds my eyes for a few seconds, and he's looking at me now in a way that feels different from before. It's heavier. Before, his eyes on me felt like a cardigan, and now it feels like a winter coat.

"Afternoon, Jam." An older man nods at him cordially, and Jamison nods back, giving him a warm smile.

I frown up at him, thinking. "Are they calling you Jem?"

He shakes his head. "Jam."

I smirk a little. "Like the preserve?"

He rolls his eyes. "Sure, or like the first three letters o' my name."

I smile, pleased to have annoyed him a little. I put my hands behind my back as we walk through the town.

The eyes of the townsfolk are on us, and I quite like the feeling.

He's much taller than me. At least a full head and probably some extra.

"Is that what people call you?"

"It's what my friends call me." He shrugs and then thinks to himself for a minute. "My mum calls me Jammie."

I look over at him and make no efforts whatsoever to conceal my smile. "Well, that's entirely adorable."

"Quiet now." He stares straight ahead, but he's not actually annoyed, he's just trying to look like it. He looks at me out of the corner of my eye. "I dïnnae mind Jem though."

"Do you not?" I give him a pleased look.

He nods. "Ye may call me that."

That makes me happy. "Okay."

"Okay." He nods again, but just once this time, and then he pauses. "And what will I call ye?"

I roll my eyes. "Daphne."

He shakes his head. "You dïnnae have any nicknames?"

"Daphne's rather horrible to shorten." I shrug helplessly.

"Nothing yer mother calls ye?"

My mother barely calls me at all, not even by name. I don't tell him that though. How can I? The confession of such a thing would imply to him that I am perhaps, inherently, unwantable. I don't want that thought so much as whispered into the ear of his mind.

I just shake my head.

He looks at me, equal parts annoyed and confused. "Nothing affectionate at all?"

"Well, my mother thinks nicknames are superfluous and a waste of time," I tell him with a quick smile. Also I suspect there's some element of a lack of care at play, but I can neither conclusively confirm nor deny that. I clear my throat. "So she named me something that you can't really shorten."

His face pulls in a curious sort of discomfort, then he lifts an eyebrow. "Daphne Belle Beemont-Darling. Wee bit long, dinnae you thi—"

"It's Beau! Pronounced 'bow,' as in tie a bow, Beaumont," I interrupt him with a growl. "Bow!"

"Bow, is it?" He tilts his head, smirking. "Sure, but that'll do."

Our eyes catch, and he swallows, and the sun feels like it's kissing my cheek, and I feel a strange, new kind of warmth fall upon me as his eyes flicker over me.

"Jam!" says that pirate from the other day, Orson Calhoun. He grabs his shoulder. "We've go' trouble."

Jamison rolls his eyes. "What now?"

Rye appears behind Calhoun, a little frown on his brow.

"One of the wee bairns stole a loaf o' bread from the bleeding prick baker, and he's demanding his hand fer it."

"Oh, fuck." Jem rolls his eyes and moves past me quickly.

"You okay?" Rye asks, shoving his hands through his hair as we walk quickly after Hook.

"Fine, yes." I nod. "Where did you go?"

He shrugs. "Just lost you for a minute."

Actually, he lost me for a little more than twenty, but I didn't mind it (all things considered*), so I don't say anything.

Jamison's pace picks up as though he feels the urgency of the moment,

---

* All things being Jamison.

72

and the way people move out of his way, it's almost as if he's the mayor of this odd town.

There's a crowd gathering at the other end, a bunch of kids yelling and screaming, and Hook pushes his way through them all, and then I see it—this horrible-looking man with greasy hair and about nineteen chins, one hand raised in the air, clutching a butcher's knife, the other holding down the arm of a sweet, little blond angel boy.

He's squirming and crying, and I gasp at the sight of it. Jem looks over his shoulder at me as though he's just remembered I'm there. It's just for a second before he looks back at the unfolding situation.

"Redvers," Jamison says in a calm voice. "Put that cleaver down. Yer bread's not thon good."

The man glares over at Jamison. "Wee bastard stole a loaf from me."

"I wasn't stealing it!" the boy cries. "I knocked it over. I was picking it up!"

"Fibbing scunner!" the baker yells and grips his cleaver tighter. I see him pull back a bit, so I cover my eyes for a moment, then peek out my fingers.

"Aye." Jem nods and gives him a tight smile. "But I wudnae think it's worth dying over."

The baker glances over at Jem, then gives him a sinister smile. "I'm not going to kill him. Just a hand."

Jamison shrugs. "Aye, but see, then I'd have to kill ye, so..."

The baker peers over at Hook right as he takes out his pistol and points it straight at the baker's horrible head.

But then something happens that I don't think Jamison was prepared for.

Another boy—older than the sweet, little blond one, maybe thirteen or fourteen—appears with a gun of his own, pointing it at Jamison.

"Put your gun down," he tells Hook, voice shaking as he does. He's got the same pinkish skin, the same greasy sheen as the baker. It's his son, for certain.

I inhale sharply, nervous. A teensy bit because I don't want Jamison to kill yet another person but a lot because I definitely don't want another person killing Jamison.

"Milton!" the baker growls, looking scared himself now. "No, put it away."

The boy shakes his head. "Fair is fair," the boy says, trying to sound braver. "We just want his hand."

The baker shakes his head quickly, staring at Hook. "I'm just down a shilling. I'm not after trouble."

I hear Hook breathe out his nose loudly. He's annoyed, but he's calm.

"Daphne?" he calls, not moving a muscle, eyes still on the cleaver, hands still on the pistol. "Come here, would ye, please?"

Rye shoves me wordlessly forwards, and I take a few nervous steps towards him. The baker and the son are staring at me, frowning as I approach them cautiously.

"Here," Jem says, catching my eyes and nodding me closer to him. "Reach into my pocket now."

I stare at Hook and he gives me a somewhat pleasant and indifferent look.

"Get this man a couple o' shillings fer his bother."

I stare from Jamison to the baker to the little boy, and then Jem rolls his eyes. "Come on, Bow. We dinnae have all day."

I give him an unimpressed look and move directly in front of him. I glance over at the baker's son nervously, but Hook ducks his head to catch my eye, and he does this clever thing where he tells me we're fine without saying a word.

I reach my hands into his coat and pat down Jem's body. His eyes catch mine, amused, and I don't ask for a few seconds where I'm meant to be feeling.

He presses his tongue into his bottom lip. "Front left pocket," he tells me without looking away.

I swallow heavy.

"Ye watch those hands," he says so quietly no one but us could hear it.

I pull out a handful of coins—gold, silver, and bronze, just as you'd expect—but none of them look like our shillings from back home.

I hold them out in my hands and stare up at Jamison, waiting.

He glances down at my hand and then past me back to the baker, monitoring it all.

"Two of the silver ones with the lass who has flowers in her hair," he tells me without looking at me.

I pick out two of those and then put the rest back in his pocket. And though you might have missed it if you blinked, Jamison winks at me as I do it, and my heart skips a little beat.

"Thonder to Redvers, Daphne, if ye dïnnae mind." Hook nods his head, still not lowering his gun. "On the table in front of him."

I nod and do it, staring at the little boy with his arm pinned, wondering when the baker will let him go.

The baker looks at the coins on the table, then over to his son. He nods his head, telling him to lower the gun. And then, finally, he lowers the cleaver.

Hook sighs pleasantly and lowers his pistol, tucking it away. He walks over to the little boy and picks him up with a great and wonderful ease and then walks over to the butcher.

I'm still standing there, a little paralyzed by all of it, of what I nearly just saw—

Jamison leans in close to the baker and whispers to him, "Ye even look as though y'are about to hurt a bairn again, I'm gonna take a cleaver to yer fucking face."

I don't even have a chance to gasp at that (though it did deserve one) before Jem reaches over and grabs my hand, pulling me away and through the crowd.

Once we're through the crowd, he lowers the little boy to the ground.

"Farley." Jem gives him a look. "I've told ye before, if ye need something, just tell me."

"I didn't steal it, Jam!" The boy stomps his foot. "I swear it, I was running and I knocked it and it fell."

Jamison groans and swats his hand through the air. "Then just fecking stay away from the square, ye ken?"

"Okay." The little boy nods, smiling up at him. "Thanks, Jam."

And then he races off.

I look up at him,* and I guess if I could feel the galaxies or even just see them, maybe I could have seen a new moon peeling open behind Jamison Hook, but my eyes aren't quite yet that way inclined.

I nearly shake my head at him, in a tiny bit of awe.

"You're not half as bad as he says you are," I tell him.

Jamison's head tilts, and his brow furrows. "And yer twice as brave and beautiful than he lets ye think y'are."

---

* Extra tall now. I think he grew about a foot through all that. At least in my mind's eye.

The tension in my face melts away like rain does in a puddle, and I feel like I'm staring up at a big tree I'd really like to climb or breathe in or lie under. He's strangely grounding to be near. The feeling you get when you're near a giant calm lake or when you're sitting by a fire outside on a cold night or when you're watching a big storm roll in from the safety of under a blanket and behind a window. That's what it's like to be next to him, and that's what I'm thinking about as I'm looking up at him and he's staring back at me, jaw tight, kind of frowning.* Then he glances down at our hands, his holding mine, me now terribly conscious of the fact that I'm gripping his impossibly tight. He stares at them for a couple of seconds and then back up at me, neither saying anything nor moving his hand away, so I move mine. I don't know why.

Not because I want to but because I suppose I should, right? I'm not here for him. And yes, Peter's hands were up and down the body of a girl who's not me, and that made me feel sick and invisible all at once, but there's a part of my brain that tells me that it doesn't matter because they're not fated, so then neither are Jamison and I.

He clears his throat and puts his hand in his pocket as Orson and Rye walk over to us gingerly.

"Nicely done." Orson nods at Hook and then at me. "And you—braver than I pegged for a wee English lass."

I give him a little glare, and Jamison juts his chin in my defense.

"Fuck off and houl yer wheest."†

I look between them all. "Was that in English?"

"Aye," Orson says as Jem nods.

"Barely." Rye looks between then and then he gives me a look. "We should probably head back to the valley."

"For yer help today, thank you." Hook holds my eyes for a second. I flash him a quick smile because my cheeks feel hot, and I don't know why they would, but either way, I don't want anyone to notice.

Jamison nods once as he backs away. "Bow."

I give him a smile I don't mean to give him as I nod back. "Jem."

---

* Always kind of frowning.

† Believe it or not, that means "be quiet."

And then he turns and leaves.

"Nicknames?" Rye asks, blinking.

I roll my eyes and walk ahead of him.

He jogs after me and lets out a laugh. "Do you know what 'briefly' means?"

I asked Peter about his day once I was home. His brow looked heavy, and his face looked complicated. Neither are things that suit him, and he said he couldn't remember and that he'd be back in a minute, and then he flew away.

Once he was gone, immediately Rune zipped in, all light and sparkles, and she jingled into my ear so much more information than I wanted.

"Did they kiss?" I asked.

She tinkers no.

That was the only real relief her story offered me. He took Calla on an adventure: climbing trees, saving a baby tiger, make-believing she was drowning in a cave and the rest of the Lost Boys were the pirates trying to kill her. Rune said when Peter saved her in the end, Calla tried to kiss him, but his cheeks went red and he started laughing.

I couldn't tell—truly—before he zipped off whether he actually couldn't remember his day or whether his not remembering was a convenient way to avoid telling the truth.

And that much is true: it's hard to remember some things here but not all things.

For instance, I can't entirely remember what I had for dinner last night or the way Wendy smells, but I seem to be able to remember the feeling of my hand in Hook's, and I can't quite shake the glistening of the cleaver and the scared look in that boy's eye.

When Peter comes back, his face is different, all light now with his dreamy sort of forgetfulness, and he floats me up to his room.

"What did you do today?" he asks me as he settles into his bed.

I pause for a fraction longer than natural. "Rye took me into the village."

"Oh." Peter nods. "What did you do?"

"Nothing really," I say, too fast. I'd already felt like I was lying to him a bit, not telling him about Hook when I met him on that first day, and now I'm lying again.

Nothing really?

I suppose that's technically true. We didn't do anything specifically.

"We just wandered the town a little bit." I force a smile.

"Did you see Hook?" Peter asks, staring up at the thatched roof.

I purse my lips. "Met him, actually."*

Peter sharply turns to face me. "You met him?"

I nod, swallowing nervously.

He glares at me for a second, then rolls on his back again. "Dog," Peter spits, and I frown up in the darkness.

"I didn't think he was so bad."

Peter head snaps in my direction with a sharpness that makes me nervous. "What did you say?"

"I mean—" I swallow. "I barely know him. I just…he seemed nice. He saved a boy."

"I save boys," he tells me gruffly.

"I'm sure you do." I nod quickly. "I didn't mean to imply that you don't by saying that he does." I swallow. "He just…did. In front of me."

"Show-off," Peter says under his breath before he gives me a look. "Don't see him again."

I prop myself up on my elbows and frown. "Are you going to see Calla again?"

"Who?" Peter frowns, confused. "Tiger Lily, do you mean?"

"That's not her name, Peter," I remind him.

"I know her name!" he snaps. "And it's not the same thing."

"How is it not the same thing?"

"Because." Peter eyes me. "Calla is my friend."

I square my shoulders a bit. "Well, maybe Hook is mine."

Peter stares over at me through the darkness, and even through it, I can see his light eyes clouding over. "I'm your friend."

---

* About a week ago, I don't say aloud.

"Am I not allowed others?" I ask, and my voice goes up strangely at the end.

Peter lies back down as he shakes his head. He sighs impatiently. "I'm trying to protect you."

"From what?" I lie back down next to him. I must admit, I do like being next to him. There's no feeling exactly quite like it, but were I able to liken it to anything, I suppose it would be similar to the feeling of lying next to a lion. Scary and wonderful and dangerous and safe all at once.[†]

Peter says nothing for what feels like a long time before he looks over at me, brows as serious as I've ever seen them.

"Everything."

---

† Only if he likes you.

CHAPTER
FIVE

"Wake up, girl!" Peter Pan tells me, nose pressed up against mine.

I blink my eyes open and give him a tired smile as I breathe in deeply. Do I smell sweets? There's a lovely, familiar smell. Something like home?

I rub my eye.

"Do you have sweets in your pocket?" I ask him.

"No." Peter frowns a bit, and my heart pangs at the frown, as though I'm sad he's sad. "Why?" Peter asks.

"Oh, nothing." I smile up at him. "I just can smell pink bonbons, I think?"

Peter rolls his eyes. "Don't be silly," he says as he pulls me up from lying down, waving his hands through the air to get rid of the smell.

I have a big stretch as I yawn.

They don't believe in blinds here. I haven't had a lie in since I arrived. Quite frankly, I'm exhausted.

Peter thinks sleep is a waste of time. No surprises there.

I partly think much of his attitude comes from years of being grossly under slept.

"The day is waiting!" he tells me, flying up into the rafters and landing on a beam. He perches there, legs kicking and swinging as he beams down on me like my own personal sun, and it feels like lying out on a hot day when Peter's focus is on you. A sort of saturating warmth.*

"I want to take you somewhere today," he tells me with a smile.

---

* Do you know what I mean? The kind that can feel almost too warm at times, yet it is the most beautiful, intoxicating summer's day so you'll never leave it.

I sit up, rubbing my eyes tiredly. "Where?" I give him a sleepy smile.

"Just one of my best places." He shrugs before he triple backflips off the beam and lands right in front of me. "But first"—stern look—"medicine."

Peter bounds away, and I go and wake Kinley and Percival. I walk to them; I don't fly. I find flying a bit arduous in the morning.

"Good morning, boys," I say, brushing a hand through each of their hair. They blink awake.

"Breakfast." I give them a smile, and they nod, tired, flopping their heads back down on their respective pillows.

I've not caught sight of the hob yet, but I have started leaving out complimentary notes, because their cooking is sublime. I can't remember what I ate for breakfast yesterday, but I remember I could have died over it, and today, it's the most incredible pile of thick, fluffy ricotta pancakes, honeys and combs and syrups and compotes, butters and fruits. Once Brodie, Kinley, and Percival join us at the table, we each take our medicine.

"It's not so bad!" I tell Kinley, like I do every morning. "Think of how strong it'll make you."

"But I'm strong now." He frowns, offended.

I give him an encouraging nudge. "Imagine then, all the more! So where are we going, Peter?" I ask him as I bite down on a strawberry.

"Swimming," he tells me with a smile.

"Swimming?" I repeat back with a frown. "But I have no swimming costume?"

"Why not?" He scrunches his face up. "And what are those?"

I roll my eyes. "The clothes that you swim in."

Peter rolls his back. "Well, why didn't you bring them?"

"You told me not to!" I stand up, feeling cross.

So he stands up, frowning defensively. "No, I didn't!"

"You did too!" I stare at him indignant. "You said you were all I needed!"

"I am!"

Percival leans in towards Kinley and whispers ever so quietly, "Evidently not so."

And then Rune zooms in, hovering, all sparkles in front of my face.

I put out my hand for her to land.

"I know!" I shake my head at her. "He's so conceited."

"Hey!" Peter growls and throws a blueberry at the fairy.

She flies over to him at the speed of light and pulls his hair before she flies back over to me.

"He said he was all I'd need. Can you believe it?" I roll my eyes. "That's my fault though, isn't it, for believing him. Men are such terrible packers."

She jingles.

"Oh, no. I shouldn't like to trouble you." I shake my head at her offer. "Well, if you're sure it's no bother?"

She chimes again and zooms away.

"There." Peter shrugs. "Problem solved. The fairies will make you a bathers."

I give him a look. "If you'd told me, I could have just brought my own and saved them the time."

He swipes his hand through the air and yawns.

Right as breakfast is finishing up, Rune zooms back in and drops a bikini made of tightly woven together daisy chains.

"Oh my goodness!" I stare down at it. "It's so beautiful."

She chimes.

"Will it fall apart?" I hold it delicately in my hands.

She shakes her tiny, gorgeous head, because I've misunderstood.

"Oh!" I blink, delighted. "It's spelled!"

And she tinkles again.

"Yeah!" Brodie nods, agreeing with her. "Put it on."

Peter gives Brodie a cross look, but it only lasts for a second, because down a slide I didn't even know was there slides Calla, and I frown immediately.

Rye tumbles down a second after her and gives me a little wave.

Calla straightens herself up, standing tall, brushing the dirt from her hands, and when I tell you that she's beautiful, I want you to imagine with me a dark-skinned Raquel Welch. There's a film that came out last December, maybe you've heard of it? *One Million Years B.C.* She's on the poster in a fur bikini? Well, that's essentially what Calla is wearing, and she looks every bit as gorgeous as Raquel Welch.

Rune lets out a sigh.

NEVER

I glance down at myself—at the same little frilly, baby-doll shortie pajamas I arrived in. White.* My favorite pair, and I used to think I looked quite pretty in them until bloody Raquel bloody Welch appeared.

Peter's staring over at her, almost like he's unsure of what to do, like it's too much—too much hotness—and she knows it. She knows she's beautiful; you can't be that beautiful and not know it, and I know she knows she's beautiful because she's wielding it around in front of me like a terrible weapon that she knows might be the end of me.

Kinley nudges me with his arm and tugs me down by the hair so as to whisper to me. "Perhaps you should change now."

I leave the room—not that anyone notices except for Rune, who comes with me.

I'm happy to take off my clothes though. I haven't really since I got here.

I think I've showered?† Showering seems like the sort of thing one might forget about doing here.

Daily to-dos are done here, but they're not oft remembered.

The things I've noticed I'm able to recall are the way things make me feel if I feel them with enough gravitas.

I try to remember when I last showered and if I just put back on my old pajamas afterwards—I suppose I must have? I brought nothing else with me, and Peter's honestly done a rather terrible job of living up to what he said about being all I need.‡

Nevertheless, I put on the fairy bikini, and Rune ties the daisies off at the neck and flits around excited, clapping her hands.

There's no mirror here, so I can't see how I look, but I try to peer down at myself.

"It fits like a glove," I tell her.

She shrugs. It's magic, she tells me, and then she kicks me back out towards them.

"Whoa!" Percival yells dramatically when I walk back in.

---

* Though admittedly increasingly less so as the days trickle on.

† Haven't I?

‡ I clean my teeth with sand and chew on mint leaves afterwards.

Rye pulls back, blinking, surprised. Calla rolls her eyes and looks away, but Peter—his mouth falls open ever so slightly, and then he swallows heavy. He says nothing, but his face has gone serious, and I can't decide whether it's a wonderful feeling or a horrible one, being stared at like this. Somewhere in between maybe.

"Should we go?" Rye asks a bit uncomfortably.

I nod eagerly before I turn to Rune.

"Thank you," I tell her, and in turn, she claps her tiny hands, and a rose petal appears. She swipes it across my cheeks, my nose, and then over my lips.

She jingles and gives me a wink.

I walk out into the woods, and Rye walks after me. "Are you trying to kill him?"

"Just trying to get a look in with your sister about." I roll my eyes.

He rolls his eyes back. "You got a look in, all right."

Peter and Calla walk out after us, and Peter's still staring. We catch eyes, and he stares at his hands immediately.

I walk over to him, catching his eye again. "Are you okay?" I whisper.

"Fine." He nods. "Yeah, of course I am. Why wouldn't I be?"

I shake my head a lot. "I don't know. You just seem—"

"I'm kicked," he tells me with a nod. He says it so unemotionally, just like it's fact.

"Oh." I nod once, trying not to float away with that. He sees it anyway, the delight in my eyes, and he squints at me playfully.

"Are you kicked?"

"Not yet." I hold my chin in the air, and he frowns immediately. "Maybe when you take your shirt off."

He grins at me and laughs before he takes a running leap and soars for a bit.

I turn to look at Calla, who's just staring at me. Staring is the wrong word. It's more of a scowl—a murderous, hateful scowl.

"I don't feel like we've had a proper chance to meet. You're the only other girl I've really seen here, besides Rune—that's the fairy," I clarify for her because she's still just frowning at me. "And she's a girl, of course, but she's not a human girl, and you're the first human girl I've seen, besides one in the village who's actually—well, she's sort of rude, so I'm glad to—"

I shake my head nervously and give her a big, apologetic smile. "I'm sorry. I'm wafting—"

"Hi, Wafting," she says, deadpan.

"No." I shake my head and laugh. "Sorry, I meant I was blathering."

She gives me an up-and-down look. "I'll say."

I stand in front of her, blocking her path. "I'm Daphne." I extend my hand to her, and you best be sure, she does not shake it. She does stare at it though, as though I'm holding out a slug for her to pet.

"I know." She steps around me.

"Calla—" Rye growls.

"What?" She sighs, bored.

"Be nice."

"Why?" She shrugs, looking at her brother and not me. "She's just going to grow up and get old, and he'll get bored of her how he gets bored of all of them, and then he'll take her back and she'll spend her whole sad life wishing she was still with a boy who has forgotten all about her." And then she looks at me, stares me down with these dark eyes, hemmed with a kind of hurt that tells me that's her story as much as it could be mine. "That's the real Darling family legacy."

And then she sprints off, prancing up a log like a gazelle, and right as she dives off it, she yells for Peter, and he swoops down and catches her, and it's all done with a spectacular and rehearsed ease. One must wonder after seeing a thing like that how many times he's caught and touched that body to catch it now so mindlessly and well—

Rye glances over at me. "She's territorial."

I give him a look. "No kidding."

He gives me a little shrug as he eyes me up and down. "Not like you didn't come out swinging in that—" He nods his chin at what I'm wearing.

"Do you like it?" I ask him proudly.

He gives me one very exaggerated nod.

"Do you think she'll like me?" I ask, staring at his sister in Peter's arms, winding above us through the air.

"Probably not." He shrugs. "But can you blame her?"

I sigh.

"How old is she?" I ask, watching her.

"Same as me." Rye shrugs. "Sixteen. Seventeen next week."

"You're twins?"

He nods. I knew some twins at primary school, actually. They were strange. Their connection to one another always seemed beyond the realm of regular understanding.

"I'm seventeen," I tell him with a smile. "But I'm eighteen rather soon." I frown a bit, thinking about what that means. I've never frowned at the thought of getting older before—at being an adult—but the longer I'm here, the more it begins to feel as though aging might be more of an imposition than I'd hitherto realized, except in the context of Jamison. I have a quiet suspicion that growing up might be the opposite of an imposition when it comes to him.

"Peter was thirteen the last time you saw him?" I look over at Rye.

He nods.

"And was he thirteen for a long time?" I ask.

Rye nods again, thinking it through. "A few hundred years at least." Rye shrugs as he adds, "Or so I'm told."

"And now?" I look up at Peter, still soaring above us—all the angles of a Greek god, with the sun behind his hair making him all golden and bronze and light.

Rye watches him, squinting. "Eighteen? Nineteen, maybe?"

I purse my mouth. Not too long till I'll be too old for him too then.

"Say—" Rye eyes me with a smirk. "How old's Hook these days?"

I say nothing for a moment as I stare straight ahead before I give him a demure shrug.

"I'm not sure." And then I glance at him from the corner of my eye. "And I'm quite sure I've no idea why you even mentioned him."

He gives me an amused look. "Yeah, okay."

Now, Skull Rock is not at all the way that you might imagine it to be. The mere name of it conjures up images of dark skies, clapping thunder, and crashing waves, but those images are wrong.

Is the standalone rock strikingly similar to a skull? Yes.

Are there legends about whether the rock is actually the skull of an ancient giant? Also yes.

But there's nothing macabre about it.

The submerged part of it is alive with coral and inhabited by the most glorious fish you could ever even imagine. Rainbow fish, shimmering fish, fish whose scales change color as they swim. The way they move under the water, they sparkle like jewels, and I can't help but frown as Peter casts out his fishing line.

"But they're so pretty," I pout.

He shrugs, indifferent. "You can kill pretty things."

My face falters. "You mean eat pretty things."

"Right." He nods, sitting down on the rock, yawning.

Calla's and my eyes catch. Funny isn't it, the camaraderie women can find in the darker places we sometimes find ourselves in, which isn't now! I'm nowhere dark. In fact, it's impossibly light! And wonderful. I just—I suppose both of us each were the slightest bit silently uncomfortable with what Peter may have just inadvertently and probably accidentally implied and our minds will bury soon anyway.

Rye drops a crabbing net into the water and then goes and sits next to Peter, glancing over at him, equal parts confused and curious.

"I've got to ask, Pan." He grimaces for a second. "How did you do it?"

Peter frowns. "Do what?"

Rye gestures to his form vaguely. "Grow…up?"

I shake my head at him. "Isn't that the wrong question?"

They all look over at me.

"I mean—" I shrug. "The question really is how on earth did he stay young?"

"We're not on Earth," Calla tells me unceremoniously.

I roll my eyes at her, but then I hone in on Peter. "How did you do it?"

Peter's eyes flicker with a sort of excitement that he gets when he knows something you don't. He likes to have things other people don't have. He likes to know things other people don't know. To call it a superiority complex would be oversimplifying it. To say he loves control sounds incredibly harsh, but perhaps still it is more apt.

Calla doesn't like how Peter's looking at me, with his half-baked smile, like it's a secret he'll make me work for, and I would. There's not much I wouldn't do to keep him looking at me like that, because I'm sure his gaze is at least fifty percent comprised of the breadseed poppy.

A sound from the back of Calla's testy throat and the mood breaks. "Everyone knows how he stays young."

I lay my hands in my lap and sit up a bit straighter. "I don't," I tell her pointedly.

Peter stares at me a few seconds before he pats the ground next to him.

A little bit to annoy Calla and a lot because I just want to, I go and sit by him. He wriggles in closer to me, and we're shoulder to shoulder.

You'd think maybe I'd be used to it by now—because we share a nest—that we'd brush up against each other at night, but he rolls as far from me as possible. Sometimes he builds almost a pillow wall that goes between us. The first night I asked him what he was doing, he said he didn't want me to kick him in the middle of the night. I couldn't tell whether he meant it in our metaphorical way or in a literal way, but ultimately the takeaway should be that he touches me less than you might have thought.

That sort of thing can do a number on your thinking when you watch him so easily touch someone else.

So sitting next to him on this magical, mysterious rock, our shoulders brushing when he moves his hand so it's a bit behind my back, almost like his arm is around me—but not quite, because he wouldn't, because he's Peter Pan and that's too grown-up—; but in this particular moment, I feel how I thought I'd feel this whole time I've been in Neverland, I suppose.

Peter leans in close to me and whispers, "I found it."

I glance at him with waiting eyes. "You found what?"

He gives me a look. "The fountain."

I frown a little. "Of…"

Calla groans again. "Youth, stupid."

That makes Peter laugh more than I'd have liked it to, like he thinks I really might be, so I glare over at her. My feelings are wearing thin now. I've never felt stupid before. Never been called it so often either actually.

Also because Calla's just mean for no reason.

"Did you really?" I ask, looking back at Peter—just Peter. I widen my eyes, make myself look more enraptured by his story than I am hurt by his disregard.

I will, in time, learn the art of this incredibly well.

Peter nods proudly.

I lean into his arm a bit, stare over at Calla as I do, and Peter swallows.

"Did you know on Earth that they think it's in Florida!"

"What's Florida?" Rye asks, and I give him a dismissive shrug.

"It's just like a giant swamp and the bottom of America."

Calla lifts an impatient eyebrow. "What's America?"

I purse my lips. "The place where the queen doesn't live."

"A queen doesn't live here either," Peter tells me.

"We did used to have a king though," Rye tells me. "A fairy king."

"Oh." I blink, interested. "What happened to him?"

Calla shrugs and so does Rye but differently—she shrugs as though she's bored, and he shrugs as though he's sad not to have the answer—but Peter drags his hand over his throat, holding my eye.

"Dead?" I balk.

Peter nods firmly.

"How do you know?" I look from him to Rye.

Rye sighs placatingly. "He doesn't. It's a long story." He pauses. "It's a bad story."

"And I," Peter straightens up, "have a good one."

"Sorry," I shake my head. "The fountain of youth.—Well, so where is it?"

Peter stares at me a few seconds before he tosses his head back and laughs. "Nice try."

I blink at him, a bit in disbelief. "You're not going to tell me?"

Rye looks past Peter to catch my eye. "He won't tell anyone."

"No one knows." Peter shrugs. "Just me and, like, three grown-ups."

"Well, who?" I ask, feeling annoyed about it in case I should like to be young forever.

Peter yawns. "Dunno."

"So you just found it?" I ask with a frown.

He nods. "There was a nice shimmer to it, so I tried it, and then I just didn't get old after that." He lies back on the rock behind, but not before taking his shirt off and tossing it away.

He is regrettably handsome like this. Actually, he's regrettably handsome whichever way you slice him.

I swallow and he notices, grinning up at me. "Kicked now?"

I lie down, facing him on my side. "Yes," I whisper quietly.

He moves in closer towards me. "Good," he whispers back.

Then there's a big splash as Calla dives in. "Peter!" she calls. "Peter, come in. The water's perfect! Your favorite kind of temperature."

"Just a bit cooler than a cool bath?" Peter asks, sitting up immediately.

Calla is barely through her nod when he dives in after her. His head pops back up after a moment, and he sighs with a deep contentment.

Rye and I catch eyes, and he gives me a look.

"But still then," I call to Peter. "How are you big now?"

He shrugs, shoving his hands through his hair. "I just didn't take any for a while."

Rye frowns, interested. "How long a while?"

Peter shrugs again and duck-dives under the water, and it feels incredibly deliberate and well timed. He stays down long enough that the fact that we asked him a question and he didn't answer drifts gently from our minds, like a cloud floating through a portion of sky.

His head breaks the surface of the water, and he swims towards me, something in his hand. He offers it to me, and I hold my hand out.

He drops into my hand the biggest pearl I've ever seen—the size of an apple. I stare down at it, eyes wide.

"For you." He smiles at me angelically before he backstrokes away.

I see Rye peer over at it out of the corner of his eye, and his mouth twitches in a way I don't understand, and it doesn't really matter anyway, because there's a sunbeam that casts Peter in an terribly wonderful light, and all my other thoughts dissipate like the white on a wave.

"Gosh," I sigh, putting my chin in my hands and staring after him. "You must have the most brilliant stories."

"I do." Peter nods coolly.

"I have a good one, Peter," Calla says.

Peter lets out a little sigh, like he can't quite be bothered to hear it. "It won't be as good as mine, but all right. Go on then."

"Well, I was on the riverbank between Preterra and Zomertierra with—"

"With who?" Peter cuts her off sharply with a frown.

This pleases Calla the same way it makes my mind feel like it's tripping on a stone.

Disappointment's such a nuisance. It creeps up on you, shines an annoying light on the things that you care about that you didn't know you did.

"With Heron," she tells him with a glint in her eye. She pushes her dark hair over her shoulder and looks over at me. "He's the son of the chief. Next in line."

She's looking at me as she says it, but I feel quite sure the information isn't being shared for my benefit. She's saying it to me, but she's dangling it over Peter's head.

"Why were you on a riverbank with him?" He frowns.

"Because." She shrugs as though she's entirely indifferent about it. "You weren't speaking to me. I was too big, remember?" She gives him a look.

Peter shakes his head. "I was stupid back then."

She nods. "I agree."

Rye breathes out his nose and scoots over closer to me.

"Anyway, we were walking along the riverbank, and this thing came and attacked us—"

"What thing?" Peter's eyes brighten at the very mention of danger.

"I don't know. It was strange—" She shakes her head. "I didn't get a good look at it, but I saw it for a second through the reflection in the water, and I think it looked like a person?" She pauses, thinking back to it. "But then, kind of not really?"

Peter swims to her, eyes wide and spellbound.

My grandmothers always said he's a sucker for a story.

"And then what?"

"Well, then"—Calla eyes him dramatically—"it grabbed Heron by the ankle and started to drown him—"

"It's a curse," Rye whispers to me. "All the firstborns of the chief die."

"He died?" I look from Rye to Calla, horrified.

She shakes her head, looking smug. "I saved him."

"How?" Peter demands. "Tell me, how did you beat it?"

"I hit it over the head with a branch." She shrugs. "And then, by the time I pulled Heron back up onto the bank, it was gone."

"Whoa." I sit back, feeling a tiny bit nervous. "Are there really monsters here?"

"Not really,"* "Sometimes,"† and "Yes"‡ are the collective answers.

Rye clears his throat. "I saved a baby from town from that rogue panther the other week."

"Did you?" I stare over at him.

"He did." Calla nods, proud of him, and that's the first thing she's done that makes her seem a bit likable to me.

"How!" I ask.

"Yeah." Peter frowns. "How?"

Rye shrugs. "I saw the panther climb through the window from the street, and then I heard the baby crying—"

"What were you doing in town?" Peter asks.

Calla shrugs. "Rye goes to town a lot."

Peter looks at him suspiciously. "What for?"

Neither Rye nor Calla says anything.

"I like the town," I offer, and Peter glares at me.

Rye gives me a little grateful smile.

"The panther had the baby, and it jumped out the window, scaling the walls. I shot it with an arrow."

"Oh my god." I blink. "Was the baby okay?"

Rye nods at the same time as Peter groans, "Who cares?"

I stare over at him, shocked if I'm honest.

Rye shifts, looking away.

"Well, for one"—I give Peter a pointed look—"the baby's mother, I'm quite sure,"

---

* Rye.

† Calla.

‡ Peter.

Rye flicks me another grateful look.

Peter floats up out of the water. "My best story is the one where I kill Hook," he announces, and I swear to god, I gasp a little, and I will very quietly admit to you (and no other) that my heart goes rather tense for a full four seconds before I realize he's talking about the elder Hook and not the one with the perfect face and the ocean eyes.

I push my hair behind my ears and breathe out a measured breath.

If I were to be entirely honest, that gave me such a horrible fright that I don't completely understand, nor do I care to think any more than that.

"Tell us, Peter," Calla says. "It's one of my favorite stories."

Rye leans back on the rocks, eyes closed but squinting still with the sun.

"It was my cleverest death yet," he tells me, eyes wide and excited. "I lured the crocodile from his cave."

"How?" I ask, because he's not big on the details, but I am.

"With blood," Peter says.

Rye opens an eye, looking up.

"What blood?" I frown.

Peter shrugs. "Just blood."

"From where?" I press.

"I don't know." Peter flies higher into the air before he dives into the sea like a cormorant and back up again, holding a fish he's caught with his bare hands. "Just from somewhere." He flies back up, holding the fish still. "So then I get the crocodile to this island that's really far away. It's far. It would take you nearly a full day in the *Jolly Roger* to get there…and then I kept the crocodile there by feeding it things it likes."

"What does it like?"

"I don't know." Peter shrugs again. "Hands and stuff."

My head pulls back. "Did you say 'hands'?"

"Ham," Calla says, over-enunciating. "Right, Peter?"

"Right." Peter nods.

I swallow, watching that fish in his hand squirm, and all he does is hold it tighter.

"Then I started a rumor in the village about that island being the place where the fountain of youth is." Peter looks over at me. "He was always obsessed

93

with finding the fountain of youth, so he went. By himself! Like I knew he would, because he's greedy and selfish, and he wouldn't want anyone but him knowing where to find it."

I stare at him, wondering if he knows what he's saying, whether he's aware of the hypocrisy, but I don't think he cares either way.

"Then I tricked the fairies into making me a fountain that looked like it was from the olden days, like the real one but not exactly like the real one, and then I put it in the middle of some quicksand."

I frown. "Why didn't the fountain sink?"

He growls, impatient. "Why do you ask so many questions?"

Rye props himself up on his elbows, listening, waiting for an answer.

Calla looks up at Pan like he's her hero—he is, I suppose. Her eyes are practically glazed over with awe, but mine aren't. I lift an eyebrow, waiting.

Peter rolls his eyes again.

"I made a fairy spell it," he tells me, annoyed.

Rye sits all the way up now, frowning himself. "How do you make a fairy do something?"

Peter gives him a long, blank look. "There are ways."

I get that feeling again. It's small and I bury it immediately, throw some sand over it, focus on the wonder of it all. No one does the right thing one hundred percent of the time, right? Least of all me. I'm not perfect—I lied to him the other night, and I can be quite a know-it-all sometimes. Oftentimes I think I'm learning more and more, and actually I'm not learning at all. If anything, I'm unlearning everything I thought I knew, but maybe that's okay. And anyway, Peter is the literal embodiment of youth and freedom and joy, and sometimes those things have prices.

"And then it was easy, really," Peter says, glancing down at the fish in his hands. It's stopped flip-flopping now. Just its tail's moving every now and then.

"Once Hook was on the island, he searched till he found the fountain the fairies made, and he went straight to it, grinning like the big idiot he was. It took him just a second or two to realize he was sinking and th—"

"Can you let the fish go?" I interrupt him.

Peter scowls down at me, cross now. "What?"

"The fish." I nod at his hands. "Please?"

He looks at his hands again, like he's just remembered it's there and it's real and it's alive and he's maybe killing it. He gives it a kiss and tosses it over his shoulder.

I watch it tumble through the air and splash back into the ocean, but I hadn't the heart to check whether it floated back up to the surface.

"Once he was stuck, I let the crocodile out of the cage I made it, and he went straight to Hook because Hook is his best flavor of blood, and I cut his cheek so that he could smell it. Crocodiles are like sharks, did you know?" He smiles at me pleasantly. "They can smell blood."

I cross my arms over my chest, feeling uncomfortable now.

"Didn't the crocodile start sinking too?"

"Yeah." Peter nods and shrugs at once. "They both died. It was pretty amazing."

I stare up at him, my mouth agape, but he's just smiling away, and I feel broken for a second, confused in my mind about all the things I'm hearing, because he's saying it like it doesn't matter. Calla doesn't seem fazed, and Rye looks maybe a little bothered, but all I can think is that was Jamison's father, and Peter fed him to a crocodile, and he's proud of that. My heart pricks in a strange way, imagining how Jamison felt when he learned that his father had died. When did it happen? Was he sad? Was he relieved? Sometimes death can bring relief, I know that. That's true enough on Earth, so maybe that's true here too.

Or maybe death works entirely differently here?

Maybe it's not the terrible affair we make it back home? Maybe on Neverland, they're more evolved, and they've found a way to visit people from the past? Maybe death is the next step up, and that's why they're so cavalier about it. Maybe death really would be an awfully big adventure.

"What's your best story, Daphne?" Rye says, catching my eye, nodding his head. It feels like he's telling me to speak.

"Um." I shake my head, try to shake away the strange feelings I have but am actively trying to ignore. I look from Rye to Peter and offer them a shrug. "Last summer, I saved the queen's nephew from drowning." I look between them all; Rye's listening, Peter's frowning, and Calla's staring at her nails. "I was at a pool party with my b—" I stop myself. "My friend, he's friends with them all, and this little boy fell in the pool, and no one noticed, but I saw him there, sunk at the bottom, so I dove down to him, and he was okay in the end, actually, so that was nice."

Peter frowns, unimpressed.

"She gave me an RVO," I tell them.

"What's that?" Calla asks with a frown.

"Oh." I shrug. "It's an award you get from the queen when—"

"Who cares about queens?" Peter crows. "Kings, maybe. But queens?" He makes a *pfft* sound.

And with that, I've had enough. I push myself up off the rocks and start to head back.

Back where? I'm not sure. Just away. From him.

I stomp down Skull Rock. The tide is low enough that there's a sandbar connecting it to the mainland, and thank goodness for that. I don't have the happy thoughts to fly.

He's terrible. Honestly, he's horrible, don't you think?

He's completely, entirely, completely awful.

Self-involved, petulant, vain—

"Wait," he calls, flying after me. "What's wrong? Where are you going?"

He lands in front of me, and I stare up at him.

The sun's behind him now; his face is in the shade.

I know you'd like me to say he's less beautiful, but that would be a lie.

Peter Pan is spectacular in all manners of lighting, at every time of day, regardless of where the sun may fall on him. Shadows on his face don't dull his beauty; they sharpen it. The sweet angle of his nose is accentuated now with the new freckles the day awarded it, and his eyes are, in fact, noticeably brighter now that the sun is setting, as though all day long, the two have been competing to be the shiniest thing around us. There's just a flicker of light that rests atop his cupid's bow, as if almost there by some kind of magic, and I swallow heavily, because three seconds ago, I hated him, but now he's in front of me again and it's waning. What is that?

I shake my head at him. "You're the worst."

"No, I'm not." Peter's face pulls. "I'm the best."

I give him an exasperated look. "No, you aren't. You're infuriating and rude and—"

"How am I rude?" he interrupts me.

"You interrupt me."

He rolls his eyes. "Just now."

"Still rude."

He sticks his chin out a bit, crossing his arms over his chest. "Before that then?"

I stare up at him, my nose in the air. "To normal people, my story is impressive."

He rolls his eyes. "Well, who cares about normal people?"

I point at him. "Rude!"

"Fine!" Peter rolls his head back, tired. "I'm impressed."

I smack my hands on my face, annoyed as I push past him. "Don't just say it!"

He growls at the back of his throat. "You don't know what you want!"

I spin around to face him again. "What I want?"

"Yes!" he yells, getting right up in my face. "You don't know! You're just yelling because you're a girl, and girls go stupid like this!"

"No!" I stare him in the eyes. "I'm yelling because I'm angry at you!"

He stares at me for a few seconds, blinking. Five times, to be precise. I counted them. They demanded me to.

Blink. Blink-blink. Blink. Blink.

"Girl…" Peter ducks to hold my gaze. "Why are you angry at me?"

I do try my best to glare up at him, to remain angry, but it's difficult. Counterintuitive almost? It's not what you want to do.

I remind myself that being cross at a man is one of a woman's main advantages in life and love, so I cross my arms over my chest and try my best to look like I'm not thinking about his shoulders and how big they are.

"'Girl' is not my name."

"Daphne." He tilts his head the other way. "Beautiful Daphne."

I turn my back to him for the sole purpose of making him fight for me more.

"Clever Daphne," he says, moving around me so we're face-to-face again, one hand on my waist, the other on my arm. "Infinitely-more-beautiful-and-clever-than-everyone-else-in-the-entire-universe-except-for-me Daphne."

I roll my eyes at that, yet still, I'm swooning a tiny bit on the inside.

"Girl, why are you angry?"

I breathe out a breath I didn't realize I was holding.

"You spent the day with Calla," I tell him, trying my best not to sound pouty about it, even if I am a bit.

"Today, you mean?"

"A bit." I shrug.

Peter gives me a grumpy look. "Well, don't be angry for just a bit."

I put my hands on my hips. "And about a hundred other days since I've been here."

"Have I?" he asks, curious.

"Yes."

He thinks about it, like it's news to him. "What do we do?"

"I don't know." I shrug, not wanting to sound stupid but absolutely feeling it either way. "You touch her, and you pay all your attention to her and—"

He's smiling now, pleased. Like he knew all along what he does with her, and he just wanted to make me say it out loud.

"You don't like it," he says, frowning a little, thinking about it. And it may be worth noting that I think he's really, actually thinking about it.

I put my nose in the air, indignant. "No."

He lifts his eyebrows a tiny bit. "Were you jealous?"

I purse my lips, feeling stupid again and hating it. "Yes."

Peter nods once, frowning, as he licks his bottom lip. "What's that word you say that's for thimbles? But it's the fake word, not the real word?"

I give him a look and a curt smile. "Thimbles is the fake word. Kissing is the real word."

He blows air out of his mouth. "Kissing's not a real word."

"It definitely is." I nod emphatically.

He gives me a look like I'm an idiot. "A kiss goes on your finger."

"A kiss can go anywhere!"

"Well, I'd like to put one on your mouth," he tells me unflinchingly.

"Oh," I say rather quietly. I swallow, my heart suddenly bouncing around like a bird trying to get out of a cage. "Now?"

He takes a step closer towards me, swallows once himself. "Yes."

"Okay." I nod.

He tilts his head. "Ready?"

I just nod. I don't have words left in my body now, just jitters.

And then he just stands there.

He doesn't do…anything. He stands there, toe-to-toe with me, eyes open and staring at me.

I stare up at him. "You said you've kissed lots of girls."

"I have." He breathes out, looking confused and frustrated. "This is different."

"Why?" I ask, and my voice sounds quiet. Nervous, maybe.

Peter shrugs. "Just is."

"Okay." I nod. "Do you know what to do?"

He scowls at me. "Course I do."

I stare up at him, his eyes rounder than they were a moment ago.

"Okay." I flash him a quick smile and take his left hand. "Well, as you'd know then, your hand goes on my waist, here, like this—" I place it on me.

Peter nods once. Swallows. "And this hand?"

"Here, if you like." I wrap it around my lower back.

He nods again.

"My hand"—I lift it up to his cheek, laying it on it gently—"will go here."

"Just like I knew it," he says, voice low and throaty.

He swallows, and I get on my tiptoes.

"And then, of course, you close your eyes," I whisper, and his eyes squeeze shut.

I stare at him for a few seconds, lock it away in the keepsake box in my mind, make sure I remember forever the splendor of the moment, how he looks right now, this tender clash of innocence and growing up.

And then, slowly, I press my lips against his.

I feel the sea kicking up around our ankles, and the sand under out feet pulls away and it feels like I'm sinking—maybe I am?—the smell of flowers blooming, and I swear to you, I felt butterflies flapping against our cheeks, kissing us as we kiss each other.

It's slow and gentle and sweet. There aren't fireworks, no big bang—just my kite-shaped heart floating up, up and away into a Botticelli sky.

"Whoa!" He pulls back a bit. "You're good at that."

I sniff a laugh. "Thank you."

He frowns a little. "Now you say I'm good too."

I roll my eyes, amused. "You're good too."

He cracks a smile, and I think the sun climbs back a bit higher into the sky again.

And this was the night he stopped building the pillow wall between us.

CHAPTER
SIX

It doesn't take long for Peter's kisses to get more and better and longer and braver. Their occurrences become more frequent, and the placement of his hands gets bolder as the days breeze by us. It is funny though, no matter what he does or how he kisses me, he still can't quite seem to catch my kiss.

It maddens him. It could actually be why we do it so often?

Sometimes it feels as though it's a game that he can't stop playing; the prize is the kiss, and I'm merely the field on which the game is played.

That sounds worse than I mean it to. It's not bad at all… His kisses are as you'd imagine they'd be: they run through your whole body like the warmth of a rising sun, taste like waterfalls and springtime and rainbows and Milky Ways and all the good stars. I do like kissing him very much. Though there's nothing particularly affirming in his eyes that makes me sure of what I am to him.

If I sit next to him, his arm goes around my shoulders, especially if there's another person in the room—he's not a good sharer. He's innately more suspicious of all the boys now, particularly Brodie because he's the biggest and thus to Peter, I am learning, the most threatening.

Now, I don't want you to think I'm complaining about it. I'm not horribly difficult to please, and I am happy here. The kisses are good, verging on great even. I just don't know so much that it's indicative of something we are as much as it's just something we do because why wouldn't we?

It's proving somewhat difficult to know him more though, particularly in the ways that I'd like to know him—do you know what I mean?—to know him in a way that feels similar to how I now know his body and he mine.

But getting to know Peter is like trying to study water as it runs over a fall. Always moving, always rushing, somehow constant, and never the same all at once.

To make matters worse and harder, there are the obvious complications in that he nearly forgets absolutely everything.

He'll disappear for chunks of time in the day, and he could be with Calla, or he might be out fishing or playing with the mermaids, or he could be soaring treetops with the boys, or actually, he might be doing none of that.

And I don't think he's being evasive, though it's impossible to ever be entirely sure. It's easier to presume he's actually just as forgetful as he says he is.

He's not home at dinnertime. It's just me and the boys, and that's fine. I don't need to be around Peter all the time, though I see why it might sound like I think I do. I don't. It's just a strange feeling to be in a foreign place, almost entirely dependent on an undependable person. It feels like you're playing a game of chess for the first time in your life against a master, in the dark, and only his pieces glow. That's what it feels like to be with him.

"So how long have you been a Lost Boy, Brodie?" I ask as I have a big sip of water from a coconut shell. The water here, how it tastes, you wouldn't believe it. Somehow sweet like nectar but not remotely overbearing, just perfectly balanced to nothing.

"I don't know." Brodie squints to remember. "A bit of time now."

"Were you always bigger than the others?"

He shakes his head. "I think I was small once."

"Does everyone get old here?"

He nods. "Except for Peter."

"Were you very young then, when he found you?"

Brodie puts his chin in his hand, thinking back. "We were on a boat, I think?" He blinks a few times. "I can remember it only a bit. I can hear seagulls in my mind when I think of it."

"We?" I tilt my head at him. "Your brother, you mean?"

He nods, straining at the thought. "I think so."

"Did he not come with you?"

"No, Peter took us both." He nods.

"Took?" I blink, confused, and Brodie shakes his head.

"No. Saved." He shakes his head, looking past me to the memory. "He saved us. Our parents, my mum, she wasn't"—he pauses, breathes out—"paying attention, and I went overboard. Maybe we both did?"

"And Peter saved you?" I smile at Brodie, feeling a rush of pride for Peter. How good of him.

Brodie nods, but he's frowning still, a thought cracking over his face like an egg. "Yes," he still says anyway.

I tilt my head and ask him gently, "And where's your brother now?"

Brodie looks over at me like he's just remembered I'm here. He blinks and breathes out. "I don't know."

And then there's a smash.

I gasp in fright and grab Brodie's arm instinctively before I look over and see Peter standing there in the sort of frame of the sort of door that leads to the dining room.

He's just staring at us, broken glass around his foot.

"Oops," he says, stepping over it and walking towards us.

"Hi." I smile quickly, and I don't realize that I don't breathe out upon realizing it's Peter. I bring my knees up to my chest, because I'm relaxed, I think? That seems like something a relaxed person might do, don't you think? Brodie's shoulders stay rather tense though.

Then Peter walks over and sits down next to me, throws an arm around my shoulders, and stares at Brodie, saying nothing.

Brodie swallows, clears his throat, and then stands.

"Thanks for having dinner with me," I call to him.

He doesn't say anything as he looks over his shoulder, just nods.

"What were you talking about?" Peter asks once he leaves the room.

"Oh, nothing." I shrug. "Just how he came to Neverland."

"Did he tell you I saved him?"

I nod. "He did."

Peter gives me a triumphant look. "Were you very proud of me?"

I brush my lips against his cheek. "I was."

He leans back in his chair and smiles, breathing out, content.

"Where did you go tonight?" I ask, even though I already know the answer.

"Dunno." He shrugs.

"Did you see anyone?"

He inspects his thumb. "Could have."

"Calla?" I ask, feeling a hint of insecurity.

He stares at me for a long second, then flies off and tosses himself into one of the giant nets. I sigh and fly after him, less exuberant, and I supposed I collapse into the net more than throw myself into it.

He rolls from where he's lying over to me, as though he's tumbling down a hill, stopping when the whole side of his body is pressed up against mine.

"Do you know how I got here?" he asks me brightly.

I glance around, a bit confused. "Here…where?"

"Here, here." Peter shrugs. "Neverland here."

I should say—in case I wasn't clear before—there's something almost addicting about kissing him. Whenever he kisses me, there's always the inevitable end of that particular kiss, and from that moment until I reach the next, I wonder about kissing him…when it'll happen again, how it'll happen again, why it feels like when you have a little bit too much champagne and your arms go heavy and your whole body falls to a funny, heavy kind of relaxed.

"Mmm." I frown a little. "I should think that I've heard the story from Mary or Wendy before, but you'll tell it better, I'm sure."

He kisses me for saying that. I knew he would; that's why I said it. So he'd duck his face lower than mine a bit, knock my mouth where he wants it, and press his lips that get bolder and bolder by the second up against mine.

He shifts a bit, pulls me on top of him, rolls himself underneath me.

He puts his right hand on my lower back and frowns at me for a second.

"It's okay if I put just one hand on you here and the other behind my head, right?"

I nearly laugh, but I don't because his eyes get a look in them if he feels you're laughing at him.[*]

"You don't have to hold me the same way every time, Peter."

"Oh, I know." He shrugs. "I was just making sure you knew that because I want my hand behind here, but I didn't want you to be a girl about it."

I breathe out, flicking him a look. "How did you get to Neverland, Peter?" I ask so as to avoid starting an argument.

---

[*] It's not a terrible look, and it's really only actually sort of scary if it's getting dark out.

"Well, it was a springtime morning, and I was in Kensington Gardens with my mother," he starts. "I was the cutest baby you've ever seen."

"I'm sure you were." I nod.

"I was in a stroller, and she was talking away to some lady—you know how girls love to talk—"

I roll my eyes again.

"She wasn't paying so much attention to me. Why do you think mothers do that?"

"What?" I frown at him. "Ignore their children, do you mean?"

He nods, waiting for an answer—very unlike him.

I swallow, thinking back to my own. I think she used to ignore me too. It was a nice thing to have forgotten. Actually, I don't think I should like to remember with pinpoint accuracy the depth of how much she ignored me.

"Busyness, I suppose."

"Busyness," he growls under his breath like he's trying to scare it away. "I hate busyness."

How his face goes—so angry about it, so hurt—as though he's losing the wonder from his own story and the memory is being waterlogged by the emotions surrounding what it might be like to be abandoned in a park by your mother when the reality isn't numbed fully by one's being saved by fairies and magic.

"And then what?" I ask him, catching his eyes and not letting them go. "Your mother was talking to a woman…"

"And then there was a gust of wind!" Peter declares dramatically. "The biggest gust of wind that there's ever been in the history of time!"[†]

"And then what?" I smile over at him.

"And then I just rolled away." He shrugs like it was nothing. "Away and away, down a hill and another hill until I was lost and alone."

Funny, but there aren't that many hills in Kensington Gardens. I don't say that though.

"Were you terribly afraid?" I ask instead.

"A bit." He shrugs again. "But less afraid than a normal baby would be."

---

† That does feel debatable, but it's not a hill I'm willing to die on.

"So you were alone?"

He nods, his face different now. He blinks twice. "I was alone."

I put my hand on his cheek, and he kisses me mindlessly, because I think he thinks a hand on his cheek means he must.

"And then Tink found me."

I smile up at him. "What was she like?"

"Tinker Bell?" he asks, eyebrows up for a second before they go low again. "She was…" He trails to a frown. He swallows and wipes his nose, looking away a bit. I can't tell whether he's forgotten or he's upset.

I watch him for a few seconds before I gently ask, "Where is she?"

"Hmm?" He looks over at me, frowning.

"Where is she?"

"Who?" he asks, and my face tugs.

I clear my throat. "Tink."

He shakes his head. "You wouldn't be allowed to call her that. Just I was."

"Okay." I nod. "But where is she?"

Peter yawns, stretching his arms up over his head. "What do you mean?"

"I mean, where did she go?"

"I don't know!" he says loudly, sitting up.

"Well." I look around, confused. "Do fairies die?"

"They can."

"And did she?"

"Why would you ask me that?" He stands, arms crossed over his chest, and outside, the wind picks up. It's quiet enough I don't notice it in a conscious way, but that doesn't mean it doesn't happen.

I stand up too because I don't like the feeling of him towering over me.

"Why do you remember some things, but others you don't?" I ask him carefully.

Peter shakes his head. "What are you talking about?"

"I mean—" I shrug. "You don't remember what you did tonight or what you had for lunch today—and they're small, sure, that's fine, forget them, who cares if you forget them—but how can you remember how you came here when you were a baby? Because no one can remember anything from when they're a baby." I shake my head at him, eyes wide. "No one at all, but you can?"

"I'm just clever, that's all." He starts to walk away.

Walk, not fly.

"But you can't remember what happened to your best friend?" I call after him.

"Tinker Bell wasn't my best friend," he says without turning around, but he does stop moving.

"Of course she was." I move off the nets onto solid ground.

He shakes his head. "She wasn't."

"Who is then?"

"No one." Peter shrugs. "I don't need one."

I frown at him, a bit put off.

"Well, she was important to you, was she not?"

He shrugs again. "I s'pose."

"Yet you've forgotten entirely where she's gone?" I ask loudly and slowly.

"Yes," he says back in the same tone, and his face pulls tight and ugly.

I've never seen him ugly before.

And it's not the normal kind of ugly, where something is physically repulsive, which he could never be. It's the other kind.

The waves are loud now. And they must be big because we aren't on the water.

We're not far from it, less than a half a kilometer back. The tree house isn't built right on the shore, but I can hear the waves splashing up against the trees now.

"And what even happened to her?" I ask, shaking my head at him.

Peter scowls at me. "Why do you think something happened?"

I lift my eyebrows. "Well, did it?"

"I—" He scoffs, shaking his head. "No."

"No?" I repeat. "Or you don't know?"

"I don't remember!"

"But you remember how you got here!" I yell.

And then he launches at me, flies from where he was standing ten meters away, and in a single second, he's right in my face.

"I lied!"

My heart's pounding. "What?"

"That's not how I got here," he tells me, still sort of yelling. "I tell everyone it is, but it's not. I stole that story from a Lost Boy," he tells me, but he's not floating anymore; his feet are very much so grounded. "He was in Kensington Gardens, and his mother was ignoring him, so I took him."

"Peter!"

"It's better like this." He shakes his head. "He was happy with me."

"And now?"

He shrugs, rolls his eyes, says what he says next like it's a betrayal lobbed against him specifically.

"He grew up."

He starts to walk away from me, but I chase after him.

"So where is he?" I ask him, reaching for his wrist.

He shakes me off. "I don't know!"

"What do you mean 'you don't know'?"

He looks at me, angry and frustrated. "I forgot where I put him, that's all."

"Put him?" I blink over at him. "Why would you put him anywhere?"

Peter throws me a look. "That's an expression."

"For what?" I ask loudly, and he doesn't say anything back, so I take another run at it. "So you stole a boy from his mother in Kensington Gardens, and you've since misplaced him somewhere in Neverland?"

"Yep." He overenunciates, and he sounds unaffected.

"Well, did someone steal you?" I stare over at him. "How did you get here?" I try to pull on his arm, and he spins on his heel as I do.

"I don't know!" he bellows. "I don't know! Stop asking me. I don't know." His eyes are dark now, no green or gold in sight. More like molasses. Wild now too, like those Atlantic storms get. "I don't like your questions." Peter growls, standing above me, nose pressed against mine but not in a way that feels sweet or good. "I don't like how they make me feel. I feel sick with your talking. Always talking! I need you to stop. I remember what I remember and I forget what I forget, and if you ask me any more things, then I will forget you." He roars, and thunder claps so loudly and directly above us that I jump in fright, right off the ground, and once my feet aren't touching it anymore, I swim through the air to my bed.

Only my bed is his bed, and he chases right after me.

"Wendy!"

"Daphne!" I yell at him, staring up ragged from the nest.

"Daphne." He sighs almost like he's sad at himself. "I'm sorry. I know you're just a nosy girl."

I scoff, looking away.

"Sorry." He frowns as he sits down next to me. He touches my cheek with his finger—pokes it almost. "Was that bad to say?"

I glance over at him, my anger from a second ago a bit destabilized by his touch. "Yes."

He gives me a pointed look. "You are nosy though."

"I'm not nosy." I cross my arms, indignant. "I'm just trying to know you."

Peter shrugs, a lightness to him again. "You know me."

"No." I shake my head, and I tell myself that I'm not even remotely unnerved by how quickly the tides of him can change. Because the ocean changes quickly too, and it's fine and safe and people hardly ever die in it.

"I don't," I tell him. "Not really."

"Yes, you do!" He sighs. "I love the sun and flying and treasure and adventure and—"

"That's not who you are. That's what you love."

Peter gives me a look like I'm stupid. "We are what we love, girl."

"I love rocks and the earth and learning, but I'm not those things!"

"Well, I love danger and I love freedom, but try to tell me for a second that I'm not those." He lifts an eyebrow, daring me.

I nod and my shoulders slump, because I'm tired and he's right. He is.

"You are those things," I concede.

He nudges me with his elbow. "The good kind of dangerous…"

"Yes." I nod. Even though I'm not entirely sure.

He sighs, looking at his hands. "I shouldn't have stormed at you."

I stare over at him, taken aback. "Was that you?"

I had wondered.

"Yes," he says, staring at his hands.

My face lightens up a bit. Maybe it shouldn't, but awe happens without your permission most of the time. "How do you do it?"

"I don't know. Just happens." He shrugs. "Sometimes when I think about you, the sky turns pink."

My eyes go round.* "Really?"

He shrugs again. "The first time we kissed, there was a meteor shower that night after."

"Why didn't you tell me?"

He shrugs.

"Felt dumb." He flashes me a smile as he looks away.

I duck so our eyes catch. "Peter, how could that possibly feel dumb?"

"I don't know how I got here." he says rather suddenly, and his brows bend in the middle in a way that makes my heart's knees bend. "Or where I came from or who my parents are. They just didn't want me or to know me, because I'm here, and that's all I know."

"Oh," I say, wishing we didn't have that in common. It's an awful club to belong to.

"The fairies raised me though," he says, catching my eye. "Together with the land. I think that's why it happens. The land's my friend."

I reach for his hand, and he lets me take it now. "It listens to you?"

Peter nods. "And feels with me."

"Do the animals?"

"Most of them."

And I'm back in awe now, staring up at him all wide-eyed and stupid.

"Are you impressed?" He smirks.

I nod a bit solemnly. "Yes."

Peter puts one arm on my waist and the other around my back, brushing his lips over mine.

"Good."

---

* And all the things I was worried about just a minute ago topple straight out of my head.

CHAPTER SEVEN

SLEEPING IS BETTER WHEN THERE'S NOT A PILLOW WALL BETWEEN YOU.

Not that he's holding me or touching me. Sometimes I'll wake, and his leg will be kicked over me, but that's about it as far as nightly affections go.

But the wall being down does afford me one thing.

A spectacular morning view.

It might be a contentious thing to say, and he himself would most definitely disagree with it, but I think Peter is his most beautiful while he is sleeping. When he's awake, he's never still long enough to be able to take him in properly, and truthfully, there's much to take in.

There's almost a luster to his skin—fairy dust, maybe? I don't know—something golden that's over him; he's gorgeously olive. Freckles that kiss his cheeks and his shoulders like I wish I was allowed to, but he doesn't like affection on anyone's terms but his own. His hair is styled every morning by the sea and the wind, and they push it the perfect, wavy way.

His eyes flutter open, and I close mine quickly.

He'd be altogether too smug if he knew I watch him while he sleeps sometimes.

He sits up and shakes me because I'm good at pretending.

"Get up, sleepyhead girl. It's morning." He jumps to his feet and flies straight to the beam, flipping off it and soaring over the boys' beds below us. "Morning, everyone!" Peter yells.

The littlest boys rub their tired eyes awake.

"Medicine!" Peter hollers, and we all groan, but I follow him down and hand it out.

Brodie gives me a tight smile when I hand him his, and I give him an extra warm smile because I feel as though he needs it.

"You're looking rather tall today, Brodie."

Something flickers over his face, and he says nothing, but he sits down quickly before Peter has a chance to look over at him.

I slide into the seat next to Peter and reach across him to a bowl of berries, pulling them closer to me.

"Gorgeous spread, Hobb! Thank you!" I call out in the hopes that they'll hear me.

"You don't have to thank him," Peter says as he shovels some bacon into his mouth.

I shrug breezily. "But isn't it nice to?"

Peter pulls a face. "He has to. He's a slave."

I peer over at Peter. "Not an actual slave?"

He frowns at an apple he's holding, bites down—big crunch. He glares at the bite mark he made in it, then he looks over at me, straightening up.

"Why do you always wear the same thing?" Peter asks, staring at me with his head tilted.

My head pulls back. "I beg your pardon?"

"The same clothes." Peter squints at me. "You're always in them."

I wave my hand at him. "So are you."

"Tiger Lily never wears the same thing," he says loudly over me and looks back at his apple before he takes another bite from it.

"There is no Tiger Lily, Peter," I tell him, straightening up. "Her name is Calla."

He turns and faces me again. "Calla never wears the same thing."

"Well." I give him a curt smile. "I suppose someone told her to pack appropriately then."

Peter rolls his eyes and pushes back from the table. "This again!"

I shake my head at him, incredulous. "You told me I didn't need anything! Do you know what that implies?"

He glares at me. "Of course I know what it implies."

"And yet—" I lift one eyebrow, pointedly.

"I don't want to talk about this anymore," he says, walking away from the table. "It's boring."

I frown after him. "Where are you going?"

"Just somewhere not with you," he says before he takes off out the window.

I stare after him, my cheeks a bit pink, mildly mortified, and the silence from the Lost Boys makes it worse.

They all stare at their plates, not daring to say anything in case Peter's spying. He would spy too, to listen to see if someone said anything that went against what he thinks.

It's the closest I've come to crying this whole time I've been here, so suddenly and strangely stripped of confidence, I might as well be sitting here naked in front of them.

They don't know what to do. I don't know what to do. They just sit there in this horrible silence, sad for me, looking at their hands, their plates, their toes, the wall, anything but me, and it's awful.

"Well, that was a lovely meal," Percival says. "I'll just be right—" And then he scurries away.

Kinley goes after him.

Brodie stands up, chin low, and his eyes flick up at me. They're weighted and they're saying something, but I don't know what, and then he leaves.

It's my turn to go then. As I get up, I hear the scurrying sound of little feet. I turn and I think I see the wisp of tattered clothing, and I'm about to say something when I see a little choux pastry bun by my feet. Just one. On a little pink plate.

I stare at it for a few seconds, then smile a tiny bit.

"Hobb?" I call, then wait for a second—nothing. "Thank you, whoever you are."

I fold it up in a napkin and tuck it away.

I can't fly on my own (I've tried before, but it appears gravity won't allow it), and I haven't walked to town by myself yet, but the latter seems more my speed anyway.

From where the tree house is to the town is just one big crescent shape, so it's hard to get wrong.

I walk along the water's edge. It's not a terribly long walk. Maybe an hour? A bit less.

You know how sand on Earth is made of crushed-up sandstone and quartz and bits of shells and skeletons from marine life? The sand here kind of looks a bit like ours—grainier, bigger, the shells are more obvious—but the most jarring thing is that I think a great deal of the sand is made up of crushed-up gemstones.

I can't be sure because I don't have a microscope with me, but when the suns hit the sand, it could nearly take your eyes out with the shine. And when I pick it up and run it through my fingers, I see specks of what looks like rubies and topazes and tourmalines and tsavorites. They're tiny, just specks of glitter, really. Except they're not specks of glitter; they're jewels, and the sight is dazzling.

I concentrate on the sand for a great deal of the walk and try my hardest for what Peter said to me not to knock around inside my brain like a bird trapped in a cage, flapping everywhere, hurting its own wings in the process.

Truthfully, I hadn't thought about how I looked for weeks, but after what Peter said this morning, it's become one of my more consuming thoughts. It's horrible to be made to feel small, and while he is good at nearly most things, he is ever so good at that in particular.

There's this running thought in my mind that's like, *I'll buy some new dresses and I'll show him!* But what will I show him? That he can say unkind things to me and I'll bend like a reed in the wind to gain his approval? Or the alternative: I ignore what he said and then just feel uneasy and quietly embarrassed until it passes?

Both sound rather horrible actually, but at least the former results in me getting some new clothes.

The one primary predicament left is I don't have any money.

But I do have emerald earrings my mother gave me once.

Now, I do personally consider myself to be a sentimental, but she isn't, so I'd like to think that in this particular instance, my mother would be more proud of me than less for being pragmatic enough to sell my earrings for clothes.*

When I walk into town, I'm half expecting everyone to stare at me because of my unsightly appearance, but I realize quickly and sort of all at once that

---

* Ignoring the part where I'm doing it because a boy was mean to me. I can't say for certain (as we've never spoken of such things), but I have the distinct suspicion that she would not approve of that specific detail.

(1) no one cares, (2) I look fine, and perhaps most importantly, (3) Peter Pan is a bollocking arsehole.

I have half a mind to turn around and away, but now that I'm actually here, I also have half a mind to see if I can hitch a ride back with someone to London.[†]

The terribleness of him! It feels more tangible away from him, almost as though a fog has lifted.

I blow some air out of my mouth and spin on my heel, maybe to leave,[‡] but I find myself face-to-face with a pirate.

"Aye," Jamison Hook sighs, but he's smiling. "So ye cudnae keep away."

I frown up at him. "I beg your pardon?"

"Ye came to see me." He lifts his eyebrows playfully.

My hands fly to my hips. "I most certainly did not!"

He gives me half a smile. "Sure, I see the way ye look at me."

I scoff, shaking my head, but I swallow nervously in case that's true. "You're awfully cocky."

"Aye." He nods coolly. "And you're holed up in a tree with Peter Pan, so I ken that your fond o' cocky."

I flick him a look. "Well, ever less so by the second."

And do you know what? He could have so easily pried there—it was practically an invitation to—but he doesn't. He doesn't ask for more information, and he doesn't poke. Just a single eyebrow of his goes up, and he tilts his head as he processes what I just said wordlessly.

He crosses his arms over his chest and looks at me in this way I can't quite unpack.

"I am surprised that ye even remember me." He flicks an eyebrow up, and I give him a look as though I think he's being annoying, but truthfully, I'm pleased he's still here. Jamison mashes his lips together. "Are ye finding things a wee bit hazy yet?"

I stare over at him before I blink a few times. It's been years since I felt like someone understood me here, except have I been here years? Or is it just days?

---

† I'd never make it back through the galaxy alone.

‡ Maybe? I don't know. I can't be totally sure.

"Actually, yes." I let out a bewildered laugh. "That's funny, isn't it?"

He presses his lips together, and I don't know why, but something akin to nervousness creeps up my spine a little, so I let out a single laugh to show him that I'm fine even though I'm not sure that I am, except why wouldn't I be?

I give him a bright smile. "Does that happen to you here too?"

"It's no' a here thing." His mouth pulls a little as he shakes his head. "It's a there thing."

My face falters. "What do you mean a 'there thing'? Where?"

He scratches his neck and gives me a long look before he breathes out his nose. "You never wonder why none of ye remember anything thonner?"

"It's Neverland, that's all." I shrug dismissively. "Things…slip."

Jamison shakes his head. "No' for everyone."

I stare up at him, my mouth ajar. "Really?"

"I remember everything." He shrugs like it's nothing.

I frown, confused. "Even from a week ago?" I ask him as though that's some great feat.

"Aye." He sort of breathes out a laugh. "A week ago to the day, I had a salmon skin roll fer lunch. I won a particularly hefty hand o' cards thon same night. The day afore that for breakfast, I had…" He squints, thinking back. "Eggs. Boiled. Runny yolk. Toast."

He nods at his memory,* and I do find myself thinking that he's very, very lovely to look at—

He keeps going.

"I went to the bank that day. Deposited something in my safe. I had sex that night—"

I frown immediately, and I do wish that I didn't because it's an obvious frown, and he catches it, lets it hang there, the invisible implication of my frown, what it's saying without saying, and he—that terrible, beautiful twat of man—says nothing for a full, hideous, awful six seconds. And then he takes a step towards me, eyes locked. He gives me a steadying nod.

"And you, Daphne Belle Beaumont-Darling, fell from the sky forty-one days ago at twenty-seven minutes past the hour."

---

* Even though I think it's a bit like a funny kind of showing off.

"What was the hour?" I ask him, just to be petulant.

"Two," he says, holding my gaze. "In the afternoon."

My cheeks go a bit pink. "Why do you remember that?"

He breathes out, quiet for a second before he nods his chin at me. "Do ye not remember it?"

I twist my mouth up as I think hard as I can back to it. "I remember you didn't have a shirt on," I say without really thinking.

His eyebrows shoot up, pleased. "Aye, ye would remember that."

I roll my eyes. "Stop—"

"It's very memorable." He grins.

I cross my arms over my chest.

He laughs and I like the sound so much. Like you're sitting by a fire with a drink in your hand that you love, that's how his laugh feels when it hits you—it warms you up from the inside out. And even though I'm trying my best to appear as apathetic towards him as I can muster, his laugh unfurls me a tiny bit, and another peculiar confession escapes me.

"I remember your eyes too."

His head tilts a bit, and he takes another half a step closer to me. "What about my eyes?"

I swallow, lick my bottom lip, drop my eyes from his gaze. My heart's beating away now, like an impossible, treacherous little drum.

He pinches his bottom lip mindlessly, then takes a conscious step away from me, nodding as he does it.

He takes a big breath. "Sure, but I'm impressed that ye remember them at all."

"Why?" I shrug airily, as though I don't think about his eyes sometimes how I think about his hand on my waist that day too.

His face goes a bit serious. "Because over on thon part of the island, there's something in the water."

"Jamison." I roll my eyes.

He gives me a look. "A'm no' lying to ye."

"Stop," I tell him, feeling a bit hot around my neck.

"A'm telling ye—" He gives me a tight smile. "The wee man puts something in the water."

"Jem!" I growl.

"Daph." He shakes his head. "He does."

I glare at him. "No, he doesn't."

"How do ye ken?"

"He just doesn't." I shrug.

"But how do ye ken?"

"Because he wouldn't!" I stomp my foot.

"Aye." He nods, a bit vindicated. "So ye dinnae really know."

I shake my head at him. "I don't want to talk about this anymore."

"Because ye know I'm right." He gives me a look.

"No." I give him one back. It's deliberate and controlled. "Because I'm quite sure you're very wrong."

Jamison shakes his head, watching me closely. "I can see it, ye ken. Right there." He reaches over and taps me between the eyebrows. "Yer worried it's true."

"Stop." I whack his hand away. A bit because I want to, a bit just because I felt like touching him. "I didn't come here for this."

"What did ye come for?" he asks, eyebrows up and looking impatient.

I cross my arms over my chest and square my shoulders.

"I need some new clothes." I gesture down to myself. "This is the only outfit I've got here, and it's filthy."

"Aye." He nods solemnly. "True, the first time I saw ye I thought 'that is a filthy lass.'"

I balk and he chuckles, grinning because he wanted a rise and I rose. I think I quite like giving him what he wants.

Then Jem shakes his head. "What's wrong with yer clothes?"

"Nothing." I shrug, staring down at myself, feeling stupid and embarrassed again.

Jamison ducks to catch my eye. "What?"

I shake my head and look back up at him, brave as I can. "It's nothing."

Then I look around the town square for the seamstress. I know I saw a shop here the other day; there was an oversize bobbin sitting on the roof—a bit misleading if it's not a tailor. I look past Hook's shoulder, then over mine. This stupid place is so confusing.

I think my eyes might look glassy, and I wonder if they do because Jamison doesn't seem to drop them.

"Did someone say something to ye?" He takes my wrist in his hand, keeping me still.

I roll my eyes like the whole thing is stupid—which it is. It is stupid. I can be stupid, I know that. But stupid things can still be hurtful.

I spot the shop and walk towards it.

"Was it him?" he calls after me.

I stop walking. I don't say anything, just turn back around to face him.

Jamison's head pulls back. "He teased ye? About what yer wearing?"

I say nothing, but our eyes hold.

"How?" He shakes his head. "There's no' much there of it to tease," he says, barely with a straight face before he puts his hand on my waist, grabbing my eye again. "Thon was a joke." He ducks more to make sure I know it, flicking his eyebrows up in this playful way. "Sure, but I like it." He shrugs, looking me up and down. "Probably prefer there to be less, if I'm being honest."

My jaw falls open, and my eyebrows go up.*

"Joking!" he says again, shoving me playfully. That's flirting, I think. "No." He shakes his head. "I am joking." He pauses, licking his bottom lip. "Till November first, and then a'm probably no' joking anymore."

My eyes go wide again, and instead of laughing how I'd like to, I take a quick breath. Jamison's face falters, and I feel an exciting kind of important.

He swallows a bit nervously. "Ye have no' said anything in about a minute."

I shrug breezily. "Well, you're just saying so much for the both of us."

He squashes away a smile, nodding a couple of times. "There's no' a single thing wrong with what ye've got on." He gives me a look and pauses briefly. "Or not got on."

I fold my arms over my chest and give him an unimpressed look,† and he laughs again.

I sigh and swing open the door to the shop. The door closes behind me, and I check over my shoulder only to see that he's not followed me in.

---

* Completely delighted, I'm very sorry to admit.

† Though just hovering below the surface of me, I am very impressed.

That won't do.

I crack open the door and poke my head back out.

"Are you not coming?" I say to him.

Half a smile crawls up the left side of his face, then he walks in after me.

"Morning, Bets." Jamison beams, walking right over to the older woman at the shop front.

She's got sort of golden, wispy hair, sparkly blue eyes—ones that have wrinkles around them that you trust—and a lovely mouth.

"Jam." She gives him a warm nod, and her eyes fall to me. Her eyes flicker down me how I worried everyone's would, but she is a seamstress, so I suppose it's situationally okay.

"This here is my dear friend Daphne." He gestures to me. "She's looking to procure some new clothes, 'acause she's under the thumb of a maniacal misogynist."

He flashes me a curt smile, and I roll my eyes at him.

"Right." She nods, and I pick up a cockney accent. "He not a fan of your pajamas then?"

"No," I tell her, keeping my nose in the air.

She breathes out her nose and shrugs. "Quite like 'em myself. But what we after?"

"Well." I flash her a smile and clear my throat. "I should like to say at the start, I don't actually have any money."

Bets rolls her eyes, and Jamison looks over at me like I'm crazy, but I quickly push my hair behind my ears, flashing her my earrings.

"But I do have these."

Both she and Jamison stare at my ears, and he pulls back once again, surprised.

"Colombian Muzo emerald earrings. Maybe just a tiny bit smaller than three carats each."

She nods once. "That'll work."

Hook gives her a look, a bit annoyed almost.

"All right, lass." Bets steps out from around the counter. "What are we making for you then?"

"Um." I frown. "Just some clothes?"

"What kind?" she asks. "Do you want to look like us, or you want to look like you?"

"Me, thank you," I tell her politely, and even though Jamison is turning a book over in his hand, not really paying attention to me, I think I see him smile a tiny bit as I say that.

"Right." She nods. "I'll make a few pieces then. Dresses?"

"Sure."

"Shorts? Those little tops you humans like." She pauses, eyes pinching at me. "You are a human, yes?"

I flick my eyes over to Jamison, amused, before I look back at her. "Uh, yes."

She nods again. "All right. Come back in an hour."

"Oh." I frown, looking from her to him. "Should you not like to know what colors I like?"

She writes something down without looking up at me. "I know what colors you like."

I squint, confused. "Or what size I am?"

She sighs, bored, and picks up her cup of tea, staring at Jamison. He puts his arm around me and smiles apologetically as he guides me out of the shop.

"Be back in a wee bit," he calls to her, and she swats us away, looking annoyed.

"What are you doing?" I growl up at him once we're back outside. "She doesn't know what I want!"

"She's magic," he tells me like I should have known.

I look back over my shoulder, excited. "Is she?"

"Yer in Neverland, remember?" He gives me a look, his eyebrows up. "Or hae ye forgotten that too?"

"An hour." I purse my lips. "What shall we do?"

"We?" He blinks and I frown at him. Then he laughs, pushing his hands though his hair. It's in a low ponytail today. "I could finish thon tour."

"Oh." I nod sarcastically. "Because you're so good at those."

"Daen ye come back for seconds?" He smirks down at me, and then I notice something about him.

"Oh, actually." I stare at him. "You're rather incredibly clean."

"What?" His face scrunches up.

"You're very clean."

"Thank…you?" He frowns.

"Can I ask you a strange favor?"

He rolls his eyes as he shakes his head. "It's always take and take with ye." But he bites his bottom lip at the end of that and gives me a half smile as he waves his hand impatiently.

"Do you have a shower?" I ask him, hopeful. "Or a bath?"

He sniffs a laugh. "Aye, a bath." Then he nods his head towards his boat.

We walk to it in silence, and it does a number on me for some reason, walking voluntarily onto the ship of a pirate. It goes against everything my grandmothers told me, I think. Right? Did they say that? I can't quite remember.

"So this is the Jolly Roger?" I ask when I step onto the deck.

It's actually very gorgeous. Very ornate, very clean, I rather like it.

"No." He shakes his head. "This is just my home."

"Oh." I nod once. "Does it have a name?"

"My ship?" He glances around it proudly before he nods. "Aye."

I lift up my eyebrows, waiting for him.

"The Golden Folly."

"And what is yours?" I ask him, eyebrows up.

"My golden folly?" he asks, mostly with his chin. "I'll tell ye November second."

I let out a small laugh as I shake my head at him, and that tongue of his presses into his bottom lip for a second, and then he looks away quickly.

"This way." He leads me towards the back of the ship to a door that he swings open.

I don't know what I was expecting, really. Less, I suppose. Less of a home, but it's just gorgeous.

High wooden beams, dark wooden everything, mismatched Persian carpets, but lots of red and navy. It's very warm. A big dining room table. A very serious-looking desk. A four-poster bed that makes me swallow heavy and my cheeks go pink just at the sight of it. Circle-top bow windows that run the lengths of the back of the ship and look over and across the bay.

And then, behind a six-panel room divider, a bath.

"Briggs?" Jamison calls out. "Briggs, are you in?"

A scuttle and then from (I'm quite sure) somewhere through the wall, a little elf appears.

Only about knee high, big, pointy ears, eyes farther apart than humans, a sweet button nose, messy hair, and big, wide feet. He looks a bit on the older side.

"Sir?" He smiles up pleasantly at Jamison, and I straighten up, delighted.

"This is Ms. Beaumont-Darling."

The elf bows.

"Please." I touch my chest, shaking my head. "Call me Daphne."

The elf shakes his head. "Inappropriate," he grumbles.

"Oh." I look at Jamison, alarmed. "I didn't—I didn't mean to—"

Hook catches my eye, amused, before he looks back at the elf. "Briggs, Daphne would like a bath. Would ye mind running her one, please?"

Briggs nods, then bows to me and moves behind the panel.

"Is that a hob?" I ask, craning my head to see him.

"Shh!" Hook rushes to me, clamping his hand over my mouth. "Ye cannae say that!"

"What?" I say, muffled, under his hand.

He gives me a look. "It's derogatory."

"Oh." I frown. "I didn't know! That's just what Peter calls ours, and I—"

Hook rolls his eyes.

"O' course it is." He sighs once. "They prefer broonics."

I shake my head apologetically. "I didn't know. Broonies?" I repeat.

He adjusts his accent so it's more like the Queen's English. "Brownies." He gives me a long-suffering look. "But aye. That is what he is."

"We have one at the tree, but I've never seen him."

Jamison shrugs. "Aye, that's normal."

"This morning, he did leave me this though." I pull out the pastry, flashing it to him. "Would you like some?"

Jamison looks at it in my hand, then up to my face, a bit like he's actually deciding whether he wants to eat a pastry I've carried with me the whole day. "Aye." He nods after a moment.

I follow him over to the dining room table, and he sits at the head of it as I sit to his right. I set the choux pastry bun in front of him, and he pulls out a beautiful dagger from his boot—silver blade, gold handle, dotted in red jewels—and he cuts it in half.

"That's pretty." I nod at it.

He licks the blade free of cream and flashes it to me.

"It's old. My da gave it to me."

He takes a bite from his half, and his eyebrows lift in pleasant surprise.

"Were you born here?" I ask as I watch him.

He nods.

"And you've been here forever?"

He shakes his head. "My da went to Eton, so I went no' to Eton." He laughs to himself. "I went and boarded in Armagh. The Royal School."

I stare over at him, shocked. "You lived in Ireland?"

He smiles a little. "Aye. Well, back and forth atween here and there."

"Is that where your mother's from?"

He shakes his head, smiling cryptically.

"Is that why your accent's so strange?"

Jamison chuckles.

"My accent…is a mess o' accents that I picked up atween my parents and my nannies and my school. English, Irish, Scottish—I'm a fecking mess."

"Why, exactly?"

"Well, my da, he's from England. London, originally. And me marm— she's an out-of-towner, I suppose ye'd say? I had an Irish nurse, a Scottish nurse, Irish teachers and friends. I s'pose I sound like them all." He gives me a little look. "We are great products of the folk who raise us."

I frown a little. "Do you think that's really true?"

He nods a bit solemnly. "Unfortunately."

And my mind wanders to Peter… Who raised him? The land.

I purse my lips, then look back up at Jamison.

"Is it unfortunate because of your dad?"

His face goes rather serious all of a sudden. "A'm no' like him."

I give him a gentle smile. "Are you like her then?"

His mouth pulls as he thinks about it. "I hope so."

"Where is she now?"

"Mum?" Jamison shrugs, wide-eyed. "God knows."

And I wonder what he means by that, but it feels rude to inquire. Mothers and fathers can be such touchy subjects, and knowing where one is isn't necessarily a measuring stick for anything. Parents come with invisible strings and ties that pull them and fasten them to things besides their children. Sometimes they let you see them. Sometimes they don't.

"May I ask you something?" I purse my lips, and he nods. "And I'm terribly sorry if this is rude and I'm overstepping, but were you close with your father?"

He stares over at me for a few seconds, then shakes his head. "Not really. Sometimes?" He shrugs, then flashes me a quick smile. "He wusnae all bad."

I try to imagine it—the fearsome, loathsome, infamous Captain Hook... not all bad?

"Ye have siblings?"

I shake my head.

"Just ye at home then?" he asks, nodding his chin at me.

I take a bite of the bun, and—oh my god—it's divine.

I give Jamison a nod. "And my grandmothers."

"Where's yer mother?"

"Oh." I take another bite. "Somewhere in Central America on a dig."

He tilts his head, confused.

"She's an archaeologist."

He nods, impressed, and a smile dances over his face. He reaches over and wipes his thumb over my bottom lip, and my heart stops in its tracks. He looks at the cream he just wiped from my mouth, then sucks it from his thumb mindlessly.

I swallow heavily.

"And what do ye want to be when ye grow up?" he asks.* "Or are ye not planning on growing up anymore?"

I give him an unimpressed look. "I'm going to be a geologist."

"Oh." He laughs, almost as though he's confused. "That's...specific."

"Actually." I sit up straighter. "It's not. Geology's terribly broad."

He nods, swallowing, amused. "My mistake."

---

* Yours, perhaps. I don't know.

"Mineralogy," I tell him, even though he didn't ask for the specifics. "I like rocks. And stones and earth. I love the earth."

"Is that why ye left it?" he asks, eyebrow up.

I frown a little, thinking on what he's implying. "I don't know why I left it—a pull away, I guess?" I shrug. "Like fate? But that doesn't mean I don't love it."

He nods a couple of times. "So why do ye like Earth so much?"

"I don't know." I breathe out in the comfort of the question. "I think I find it grounding? I like my bare feet on the earth—the feel of it."

He nods, watching me and letting me prattle on.

"I suppose I've always just liked it. Rocks and nature and volcanos, the history of things, how they form. It's all just fascinating to me. I like how stones feel in your hand, how they feel on your skin. I like how a specific chemical formula and time underground, in the dark, where no one is looking, makes these." I flash him my earrings again, and he smiles a little bit. I shrug, feeling now like I've talked for too long. "I like how rocks tell stories. I suppose I like Earth because it's really just one big rock."

Jamison's watching me, eyebrows bending in the middle like he's almost frowning, but it's not a bad frown. Neither is it entirely confused. More like he's just fascinated.

I squirm a little, embarrassed to have his gaze so intensely on me but also a little bit pleased.

I clear my throat to keep things moving. "Is this a planet?"

"Neverland?" He blinks. "Aye, o' course it's a planet. What dae you think yer wee feet are standing on here?"

I roll my eyes.

"Neverland's no' the planet. It's an isle that's a part o' a realm. The planet itself is called Little Störj." He stands up and walks to a bookshelf that's organized with no rhyme or reason, other than each book is bound in leather. He grabs one with a navy spine and gold foiling and places it in front of me. "'Twas founded around 1300 BC your time."

"By whom?" I ask him, chin in my hand.

He flips open the book and rifles through a few pages to a black-and-white photo of five people. Three women, two men.

I marvel at them for a few seconds. "What were they?" I ask as I stare at them.

"I think the politically correct term is star travelers." He smiles as he glances at the photo.

"They're aliens?" I blink up at him, surprised.

He points at me. "Politically incorrect."

"Sorry!" I flash him a smile. "So it's true then, we're not all alone in the universe?"

Jamison shrugs and looks over his shoulder at the harbor behind us, filled idyllically with fisherman and boats. "Evidently not." His eyes soften a tiny bit around the edges. "Did ye feel ye were?"

Less so by the second, actually, I think as I stare over at him and swallow heavy, ignoring the feeling of all the threads pulling inside me and stepping around one of about a million potholes that exist in my mind about pirates.

"Her bath is ready," Briggs calls and pokes his head from around the divider.

"Thank you, Briggs." Jamison nods at him, and I offer him back the book.

He shakes his head. "Keep it." He wraps his hands around mine and gives the book back to me. Our eyes catch. "Ye need it more than me, thonner with the wee man. I cannae imagine he's that grand a conversationalist."

I stifle a laugh and drop his gaze because his eyes feel too good to hold. He gestures towards the bath.

I give him a quick but grateful smile and slip behind the screen.

I pull my clothes off me and leave them by the foot of the clawed bath.

"I'll leave ye be," Jamison calls from the other side.

"You don't have to!" I say maybe too quickly, and there's a clunky pause from him.

"What?" he says after a few seconds.

I pause. Scratch my cheek. Try to figure out why I said that.

"I like talking to you" is what I say, and ultimately, it is the truth.

Three seconds go by before he says anything.

"Aye," he says, and I hear the sound of him dragging a chair over to the other side of the divide. "I like talking to ye too."

"Just don't peek," I tell him.

Pause. "No promises there."

I smile—a lot—so much that I'm glad he can't see it, and I lower myself into the bath. I don't know whether it's because I haven't bathed properly in apparently forty-one days,* but it's perfect. The perfect temperature, the perfect amount of water—it smells like it has oils in it to the perfect combination. The shape of it holds me to the perfect cradled recline.

I breathe out.

"'Tis a grand bath," he tells me.

"It is." I nod. "Thank you for letting me use it."

"Thank ye for taking yer clothes off in my home," he says nobly, and I try my best not to laugh, but I do and then so does he.

"Grubby, dirty, messy," I hear Briggs say under his breath, and I snap my head in his direction, peering over the side of the bath.

He's so little he can't see in, and when I spot him, he's staring at my pajamas, carrying them away.

"Briggs!" Jamison sputters.

"Filthy girl," Briggs keeps growling as he wanders off.

There's an uncomfortable silence.

"I think he meant my clothes."

Jamison starts laughing. "Well, fingers crossed."

I hear the sound of his chair push back, and he stands. "I'll be back in a second."

"Okay." I nod and he leaves.

I sink down into the bath and try not to look the feeling I've got that I'm doing something wrong directly in the eye.

Why do I feel like this?

As though I owe Peter everything when I'm quite sure he'd be sure he owes me nothing.

He's such a strange boy. All instinct and wild animal, and that is, for the most part, very exciting and almost dreamlike to live alongside.

There is, however, a fine line between dreams and nightmares.

Peter can be callous and impetuous; he's incredibly temperamental. He's hotheaded, he's arrogant, he's proud—but then there's that boyish charm. And

---

* Because the ocean doesn't count.

you can excuse so much because he's never known a parent. Every time I'm with him and he's good to me, it's akin to successfully petting a lion. I'm immensely proud and relieved and delighted that the lion's decided not to bite me, but he can bite me, and when he does, it can be quite severe.

The bites, I think they might be worth it for getting to lie down with a lion—it's a special kind of thing that only happens once in a lifetime, I suppose. I do wonder, though, might the span of my lifetime be significantly less because of it? And if so, is that worth it?

I hear the door open again.

"Jem?" I call.

"Bow," he calls back. "Decent?"

"Not remotely."

He sniffs a laugh from the other side of the divide.

"You didn't leave me a towel," I tell him.

"Did I not?" He pauses, and it hangs there. "How awful o' me. Sure, I'll hand deliver it then, will I?"

"Jamison." I glare at him though he can't see me, and he laughs at his own joke. Then he slings one over the top of one of the panels, and I stand up, wrapping it around myself.

I step out from around the divide, and Jamison's eyes fall down my body and his mouth falls open a little. He blinks twice at my ankles before his eyes pull back up over the rest of me.

I swallow as I fasten the towel to my body, extra tight.

"Your brownie took my clothes." I purse my lips.

He nods once, smirking. "Filthy girl."

I say nothing, just shift my weight between my feet, staring at him, sort of stuck.

It's not the worst feeling though, here with him, like this—him trying not to look at me, me trying not to like it as much as I do.

He holds up a finger and turns to his bed, fetching something.

He carries back a pile of clothes.

"From Bets."

I stare at the clothes in his arms and shake my head.

"I haven't paid for them yet."

"I paid for 'em." He shrugs.

I stare up at him wide-eyed as he puts the clothes in my arms.

"You didn't have to do that," I say quietly.

His mouth pulls a little. "Daen want ye to have to sell your earrings."

"Jem—"

And then he shrugs dismissively. "Sure, I only did it so I could take 'em off ye at a later date."

I drop my chin and squint over at him as though the idea incenses—not excites—me.

"You're awfully presumptuous."

He flicks his eyebrows up. "And you, Bow, dïnnae hide the intrigue behind your eyes all thon well."

CHAPTER
EIGHT

PETER DIDN'T SAY A THING, NOT A SINGLE THING, WHEN I WALKED IN WITH my new clothes…as though he didn't even notice at all.

All the pieces Bets made for me were completely divine, by the way, and he hasn't said a thing about them once—absolutely zero inquiries. No wondering where I got them, no questions about how I paid for them or when I got them, not even a peep about whether a devilishly handsome pirate won me over a tiny bit by sparing my mother's emerald earrings—not a single word.

Which then begs the question: Did he even mean what he said in the first place, or was it merely a throwaway thought he said without thinking (how very much like Peter) that I took to heart when I wasn't meant to take it anywhere?

It is hard not to take the things he says to heart though. I see it happening all around us all the time. I watched him tell Calla that her hair was too long and it was getting in the way; the next day, she arrived with it noticeably shorter.* I heard him tell Kinley that he throws like a girl,† and then I saw him practicing by himself later on. He told Brodie he was taking up too much space on a seat a few days ago, and then Brodie didn't come to dinner that night.

These parts of Peter are a bitter pill to swallow, and every now and then, I get to a point where I wonder why we're all here, why any of us stay loyal to him. And trust me, we are loyal to him. But then there's the other part of Peter where I catch him teaching Percival how to shoot the perfect bow and arrow and showing Kinley how to free dive for huge chunks of time.

---

* Though I'm not so sure that he noticed.

† And knowing him, I doubt he meant it in the way where a girl might throw with focus and precision and a quiet strength that would go over Peter's head.

I saw Calla's face soften when Peter carried in a bucket of clams and lay them in front of an elderly Stjärna woman and kiss her on the cheek before wandering away.

I do have to remind myself that he was raised by fairies and, in part, the land, and thus he behaves like the weather.

It's not often that the weather doesn't dwell in extremes. It's usually hot or cold, sunny or rainy, stormy or brilliant, and he is the same.

Whatever Peter is in that specific moment, he is wholly that thing. When he is petulant, my god, he is hateful, but when he is sweet, he is the human embodiment of birds landing on your fingers and deer feeding freely from your bare hands.

So then, I reason, that one doesn't just simply hate the weather entirely because sometimes it, occasionally, behaves a tiny bit cruelly.

Not that I could ever hate Peter, because it's Peter. I should quite like to if I could; I've lain awake at night after he's spent the day with mermaids, without me. I've tried my best to hate him for it, but I can't, and I know that's peculiar. I know it is. Maybe I've known him days, maybe it's been years by now, but being around him, he just…soaks into you, and I do suspect that were we ever to fully part ways the way my grandmothers did, that I too would grow into one of those old women, cracking open windows, trying to find my way back to him, trying to catch a whiff of freedom and summertime and the way his skin smells like coconuts and salt. But then, maybe it's more than that? Because even when I'm with him, even when he's lying right there next to me, I have this feeling that perhaps if I were to leave him, in any which way, maybe I would die or something? That sounds so odd, I know. It's just a feeling I have sometimes. I'm not sure why.

At this point, I have accepted (for the most part) that Peter and I do have a peculiar connection, which I'm quite sure has traveled both time and space to be present in front of us.

My grandmothers always said that Peter Pan is a part of our family's destiny. I suppose that makes sense. Were he to be some kind of generational destiny, that's fine, but I suspect he's more than that to me.

Destiny and fate, you think you can interchange them, but you can't. Destiny is—I believe—impacted by you and your choices and what you choose, but fate is not. It's concrete. It's the occurrence of events beyond a person's control, as though determined almost by a supernatural power.

There is a part to Peter that feels like fate, and I think that's an important component for me, because I'm self-aware enough to know that I don't like him all the time, yet there is a perceptible pull I have towards him, and it doesn't always feel within my control.

This peculiar drift back towards him even if I were to try to swim in another direction—as though the universe is pulling me to where it wants me, and I do believe in the kind of universe that would do that…

On this planet, if the universe can raise a boy, it can surely fate some hearts, so this, I presume, is my lot.

"You're not going to go, are you?" Peter asked out of the blue the other night.

I was playing a game of go fish with Rune, and I looked up at him.

"Go where?"

He shrugged. "Anywhere."

Rune jingled, and I gave her a look to quiet her.

I give him a delicate look, still not quite entirely sure what he was trying to communicate.

"Um—" I gave him a gentle smile. "I'm sure sometimes I'll go places."

"But not away," he clarified. "The others all left, but you're gonna stay, right?"

I watched him for a few seconds before I suddenly felt myself nodding even though I hadn't agreed to the thought in my mind.

He smiled, pleased with himself, and then flew out the window.

Sometimes it does feel like loving him is something that's happening to me, not through me or in me. An external thing that's disconnected from my day-to-day life and how sometimes I think I might feel, I always feel a different way eventually anyway when I see him call a cloud over to give a wilted flower some shade.

It's fate. It has to be. That's why it doesn't bother me* when he's off gallivanting with Calla or when he spends the day showing off to the mermaids, because

---

* Much.

it's not the same. They don't mean the same things to him that I think I do. He doesn't share his bed with them, he's not kissing them,* and they're not who he comes home to. I think that counts for something, doesn't it?

Rye is coming over today, and we're going out and around in Preterra.

He said he wants to teach me how to forage so I can look after myself. I told him Peter said he'd look after me, but he just smiled and said he thought it would be a good idea just in case.

That made me frown a bit, because in case of what? But he tacked on a shrug at the end and said, "You know, in case you get lost or something?" I don't know if he actually meant that or he was just saying it to soften the blow, but anyway, what blow?

I hide the book that Jem gave me like I have every time I've left the house. I'm enjoying reading about it all so much, learning about this land and how it all came to be, but I suspect for some reason that Peter won't much care for it as, thus far, he doesn't feature in it once. Which, actually, if we're honest, it seems like someone was trying to make a point. I don't know how old Peter Pan is. I don't know how long he's been the boy wonder of this little island, but for there to be a history book written about Neverland and Peter not to be included in it? Well, that feels rather intentional.

I'm wearing one of the outfits Bets made for me. It's a little white boatneck blouse with tailored shorts, and just quietly, between us, I've liked the feeling of wearing the clothes that Jem bought me because I feel like I'm wearing a secret.

It all appeared to be wasted on Peter who, at breakfast, barely looked up at me. Yesterday, he flew to one of the towns on one of the other islands and fought a pirate to the death.

"For what?" I asked.

"For honor!" he cried, and the Lost Boys har-har-ed.

His real prize though, it seems, was the knife he took from the pirate.

The handle is silver and twisted. Some of it's dark, some of it's light, but how sharp it is feels of a particular concern, especially in the hands of a boy like Peter.

---

* I hope.

"Look how sharp it is," he said to no one in particular at breakfast before he gently tapped his finger on the tip of the blade and immediately a drop of blood formed. "It's magically forged," he told us, and the boys "ooh-ed."

Peter held out his hand towards me. "Can I have a hair?" he asked without looking at me.

"What?" I stared over at him, and then he looked up at me and plucked a hair right off my head.

He held the piece of hair between his thumb and his finger like he was trying to thread a needle, except he was literally trying to split a hair just to prove to no one that the knife could do it.

So I kissed his cheek, and he said nothing when I said goodbye.

On my way out, he runs after me and kisses me up against the giant mushroom by the door.

"You look really pretty today, girl," he tells me.

My cheeks go pink. "Do you want to come with me and Rye? We're going for a—"

"Boring," crows Peter, and I roll my eyes, and then he claps both his hands on my face and kisses me again and takes off in the other direction.

"You two seem to be doing better," Rye says, pushing himself up from the tree he's leaning against. I hadn't noticed him there, and I flash him an embarrassed smile.

"Sorry."

"What for?" He shrugs, indifferent. "You ready to go?"

I nod once.

"Got your basket?"

I flash it to him.

"Got your shears?"

I shake my head.

"A knife?" he asks.

I pull a face.

He shrugs. "I've got two. Come on."

"Where are we going?" I ask him after a few minutes.

"The best place to forage."

I lift my eyebrows, waiting for more.

He looks over his shoulder and gives me an excited smile. "The Fallen Kingdom."

I blink at him. "The what?" I guess I've not reached this particular part of history in the book yet.

"The fairies, right? They live in tiny pockets, a few here and there. A lot of the time they're alone."

"Right." I nod. They live in the trees mostly, and you can spot them because there's always this bright light that feels almost too beautiful to be real but feels too warm to be your imagination. The little hollows are usually mossy, baby mushrooms growing around them, the tiniest flowers you've ever seen and so much sparkle. I haven't dared peek in, but it sounds like wind chimes and chirping birds.

"But they used to live in a kingdom."

"Really?" I stare after him.

"They used to be big too."

I stop in my tracks, because now this just sounds fake. "What?"

"They still can be." Rye shrugs.

I shake my head. "Then why?"

"When they're small, they're harder to catch."

I frown over at him. "Who's trying to catch them?"

Rye gives me a sobering look. "Lots of people." He reconsiders this answer. "Lots of things." He doesn't say anything for a couple of minutes again before he stops and crouches down. "This is a type of mycorrhizal mushroom."

"Oh." I nod. "We have those on Earth."

"Yeah." He nods. "I think they're from there originally, but my people brought them with us. Anyway, it's safe and edible." He picks three of them and puts them in his basket. "This one"—he points to a smaller one that's stringier looking— "also edible." He pulls a face, and I squint at him, confused. "But the pirates, they'll come out here looking for these. They'll grind them up and—" He sniffs.

"Oh!" I gasp. "Like drugs?"

"I mean—" He shrugs. "I don't know what that is. That's not what we'd call it here."

I squint over at him. "What would you call it?"

He chuckles and thinks for a half a second. "Herbal recreation."

"Drugs." I nod with a laugh.

We keep walking.

"There's a few plants around that do that. Flowers and leaves and mushrooms—"

"Do you use them?" I ask as Rye stands and keeps walking.

"Sometimes," he says.

"For what?" I ask nosily.

He looks back at me. "When I need to." He stops at a tree and reaches up for a branch, pulling it down. "Come smell this."

He's tall and broad and has such a warm face that it's impossible not to grin up at him as I do. His eyes are dark like leather, short dark brown hair, brown skin, and the loveliest smile. He's handsome too, and I suspect that he knows it, though he doesn't appear to use it to his advantage.[*]

"Lune blå." He breathes them in, and I don't know how I'd explain the wonder of the smell. Maybe muddled blackberries with cream?

"It's the leaves," he tells me. "Not the berries. You make tea from it."

He picks me a bunch and puts it in my basket, flashing me a quick smile as our faces are close enough to feel each other's breath. It's not deliberate; it's just by circumstance.

"Peter likes that." He nods at the leaves in my basket and then he clears his throat.

"So…" I glance around. "Are you seeing anyone?"

Rye's eyebrows flicker, confused. "I can see you…"

"Oh!" I let out a little laugh, shaking my head. "No, on Earth, you'd say—" I purse my mouth as I think. "Are you, um, romantic with anyone? Are you… in a…couple? With someone?"

"Ah." He gets it. "I'm…interested in someone, yeah."

"Oh!" I look over at him, delighted. "That's exciting."

He rolls his eyes and keeps walking. "Is it?"

I nod even though he doesn't see me. "Do they know?"

"I don't know," he calls, not looking back. "Hard to say. They're always preoccupied."

---

[*] How good of him. How very superior to all the other men I know on this island.

I frown. "What with?"

He flicks me a look. "Other people."

"Ah." I nod once and wonder if he's talking about me. He might be.

I wonder. He's been a very good friend to me since I got here, but I thought he was just being my very good friend.

I press my lips together and glance over at him. "Thanks for doing this."

"Yeah." He nods, flashing me a quick smile. "Happy to." Rye blows some air from his mouth and picks a few berries off a bush, tossing them to me.

I look down at them. Beautiful, hot pink, soft, almost velvety. "What are these?"

"Raspberries." He smirks.

"Oh." I laugh once, feeling a bit embarrassed.

He chuckles and walks on ahead of me, and for a minute or so, we say nothing, but I think the silence between us is the okay kind, not the bad kind.

"Can I ask you something?" I call to him.

"Yes," he says without stopping.

"Do you forget things?"

He stops walking, pauses. "What?"

I breathe out my nose and catch up to him. "Why do I forget things here but you don't and Jem doesn't and—"

"Jem?" His head pulls back.

"Sorry." I shake mine. "Jamison."

He blinks, surprised. "Jamison?"

I swallow and sort of roll my eyes a bit.

Rye gives me a look. "When did Jamison become Jem?"

"Why does that matter?" I shrug, turning away from him to pick some flowers like I know what I'm doing.

"Do you see him?"

I pause, press my lips together, and I'm conscious of how my voice sounds before I let myself speak. "Sometimes."

Rye stands a few meters away, just watching me. "Wow."

"Wow what?" I frown.

He cocks an eyebrow and gives me a look, then walks past me, sweeping a branch of weeping willow aside and holding it open for me.

"He's my friend," I give him a look.

"If you say so." He juts his jaw.

"I say so," I tell him, nose in the air.

He nods, but it's weird. He looks bothered with me.

I frown up at him. "Why are you being strange?"

"I'm not." Rye sighs. "I just—nothing." He shakes his head. "I don't know why you forget things." He gives me a shrug.

"Just some things," I clarify even though he didn't ask for clarity, and then I realize he's stopped walking.

He's standing before a giant, overgrown marble arch.

There are wrought-iron gates all grown over with ivy. Rye pushes them, and they creak loudly, and for some reason, the moment turns solemn.

"This is the kingdom?" I ask, staring up at it all in wonder.

It feels almost like we're in a greenhouse with a roof so high you can't see it. The trees stretch ridiculously tall, so there probably isn't a roof, but as soon as I step in, I have the distinct feeling that I'm under some kind of covering.

"Yep." He nods.

"Whoa." I peer around me.

It feels sacred. It really does. We stand under a tree, and the wind blows in, moving around us that way the wind does here, gentle and present all at once, rustling around your ears like a whisper, as though it has something to say. I've never seen anything like it here. It's all marble and stone and overgrown, and life is just teeming from it, crawling from every crack and crevice.

It's gorgeous and decrepit and mesmerizing and agonizing all at once. You know how it hurts sometimes to see something that should be magnificent in complete ruin?

"Oh my god." I bend down to the prettiest pink flowers I've ever seen in my life and go to pick one. "Look at these. They're—"

"Don't touch those!" Rye says quickly, and I freeze. "That's glömmfloare. It…" He pauses, squints, and thinks. "It's bad for you."

"Oh." I brush my hands on my dress, smiling uncomfortably. "What happens?"

He stares over at me for a few seconds, then his eye falls to the ground, and his face lights up. "Oh, come here." He crouches down and nods at a flower that looks like nothing I've ever seen before. It's sort of pink, sort of purple, sort of like a sunset—layers and layers of petals, more dramatic than a peony, but just as elegant, and taller too. "This is the blooming nurse." He gives me a proud smile. "It fixes pretty much everything." He shrugs. "Broken bones, broken hearts, fractured minds, stab wounds, siren kisses, werewolf bites—pretty much everything but some spells and death itself."

I bend down to look at it, oohing.

"They're also really rare and poisonous if not prepared correctly," he adds as an afterthought.

I give him a look. "Oh good."

He smirks.

"Why can't it break certain spells?" I ask, and then my face falters at my own question. "And also, what do you mean, 'spells'?"

"You know." Rye gives me a look. "Magic?"

"From the fairies?"

"No." Rye's face goes a bit serious. "Another kind of magic."

And he doesn't say anything else about it, so I bend down to pick it.

"Wait," he says. "Leave it. We don't need it."

I look over at him, thinking about it. Then I nod. "You're right."

We're back to quiet again, and I'm wondering about that flower he said was bad and as well as why that magic flower can't break spells and also—spells?!

"Can anything break a spell?" I ask him, sitting down next to him under a tree.

He shrugs. "There's a natural counterbalance for the supernatural, most of the time anyway. It depends though."

"On what?" I start braiding the grass.

"On the spell," he says, but he's not looking at me. "I don't know of a plant that can bring you back from a magic death. But I know about a plant that can lift a sleeping spell or a mind fog spell or—"

I frown at him. "Who's casting all these?"

He gives me a longish look and then sort of breathes out a laugh. "No one. Don't worry about it."

And with that, he stands and goes behind the tree, collecting some mushrooms that are growing beneath it, pointing out which ones are safe and which ones aren't.

"So how long have you and Jamison been…" He leaves that open-ended, and I make sure he sees my face as I shake my head.

"No, we aren't…anything." I shake it more. "We're just friends."

He lifts his eyebrows. "Who do…"

I pull a face. "Things together sometimes."

"Like?"

I cross my arms over my chest. "I thought we just established I don't remember things."

Rye rolls his eyes, and I groan, feeling trapped.

"He took me to the library the other day, I think. To a tea shop on another day. One time, he bought me some clothes—" Rye shoots me a look for that one, but I ignore it. "He took me to where the founders landed."

"The founders." He gives me a tight smile and a somber nod.

"Sorry." I shake my head. "Is that bad to say?"

"Colonization is not great no matter how good it goes." He shrugs. "But I guess my people landed once too. Before us, it was just the fae."

"But your people got along?"

"Our people built Neverland." He nods. "Just not according to history."

"Oh." I frown a bit.

"They were okay for the most part, the elders say, nothing like the colonizers on Earth. We're just…not in the books. Not those ones anyway."

"Which ones are you in?" I ask, looking for his eyes. "I'd like to look at them."

He flashes me a quick smile. "There are caves my elders talk about, somewhere on the island that tells the full story—you know, the prophecy and the rest."

"What prophecy?"

He shrugs. "I don't know, something about the kingdom restored." He waves vaguely around us.

I put my hand on the fallen marble head of a giant statue. "What happened here?" I peer up and around.

"Fairies are insanely loyal, like nuts about it. They're pack creatures. They love family, they love each other, and you have a thing—it's a word you use on your planet for wish slaves." He squints at me, trying to remember.

"Genies?" I offer, and Rye snaps his fingers.

"Genies! Yeah." He shrugs again. "That's a caricature of a fairy. Except if you catch one, you don't get three wishes. You get infinite wishes, and they live for so long, unless you kill them on purpose."

"Who would kill one on purpose?" I ask, horrified.

"Themselves if they've got nothing to live for, or someone else if they're trying to control another fairy."

I frown at him. "How can you control a fairy?"

"You can't, really. That's why you have to catch them in pairs. It's the only way you'll get it to do what you want."

My brows get low, but I keep listening.

"If you have two, and you threaten to hurt one, the other will do what you want. It's why fairies tend to spilt up and stay apart. They're so loyal, they're too easy to exploit."

"So what happened here?"

Rye scratches his neck. "People kept pillaging the village to control their magic, for money, for riches, you know—the usual shit people destroy a place that isn't theirs for."

I shake my head at it all. "So the fairies just left?"

"They scattered." He shrugs. "They had to. Once the people worked out if you took two fairies at once they were a lot more compliant, two or more fairies gathering became too dangerous. We tried to shelter them. It worked for a while, my grandfather said, but fairies are so obviously nonhuman, you know? They're too beautiful. You just knew as soon as you saw one what it was, so they took them anyway."

"So that's why they went small?"

"Yeah. Well, that and then the humans started to rape the women fairies to try to make halflings."

My mouth falls open in horror.

"But humans don't get it. A fairy's magic is so powerful and so their own. You do that to a fairy, she's not giving you what you want. They control their magic. So they use it to control their size, stay small, stay alone, survive."

I feel ill as I stare over at him. "People would still try to hurt them?"

"Daphne." He gives me a look like I'm stupid. "Never mind the decade or the planet, but what won't man do for power?"

You have a vision in your mind of other planets, that they'll be better than ours, more advanced, more peaceful, more evolved—

And maybe they would be without humans. Humans seem to be the common denominator when it comes to the downfall of others.

"We should go." Rye nods his head. "I'll take you back down past Cannibal Cove."

I toss him a look. "No, thank you."

He laughs. "It's just a name. It's mostly just mermaids."

And do you know, I really do love it here. For the strangeness and the chaos and the mysteries that seem so above my head, the land is nothing short of spectacular.

Every color that blooms here is insanely intense. You've never seen greens more saturated than this, and there are about a million different shades all layered on top of one another as the fallen fairy kingdom with its forest all overgrown morphs into a proper jungle that spills out onto the most unimaginably beautiful beach. Like no one's ever stepped foot on it before.

The wind blows against me, and there's a sweetness in the air even though there are some grains of sand blowing on my face. I turn my head to shield my eyes and spot a mermaid on the rock.

That still feels like such a ludicrous thing to say.

I recognize her. It's the one with the auburn hair. Marin, I think her name is. Rye told me that she's actually part siren; I don't know what that means though.

Her tail stands out against the backdrop of it all because it's bright and glistening shades of amber and yellow.

And then I notice underneath her a pair of legs. I stop and squint. It's getting hard to see. The suns are all starting to set.

"Hey." Rye grabs my arm. "We should go."

"What?" I blink, confused.

He moves in front of me, shaking his head. "This was a stupid way to come. I don't know what I was thinking, but we should just go back through—"

I peer around him, and that's when my eyes come into proper focus. The mermaid is with someone. Actually, she's kissing someone.

A lot.

"Peter?" I say his name, but it sounds foreign as I do. It's a funny feeling, floating but in the bad way. Like I'm at sea and I'm adrift. I think I call his name again as I walk towards him, but he doesn't stop.

Rye grabs my arm again. "Let's just go." He shakes his head. "We don't want to see this. Marin's a piece of work. We should—"

"Peter Pan!" I yell loud enough for him to finally notice me.

He pulls back from the mermaid and looks around confused till his eyes finally land on me about ten meters away from him.

"Wendy!" He beams.

"Daphne," I say, and Rye's head falls as the mermaid giggles.

"Daphne." Peter nods, smiling indifferently as he props himself up a bit. "Rye! What are you doing out on this side of the island?"

Rye just shakes his head, gives him a little shrug. "Foraging."

I look past Peter to the mermaid leaning on his shoulder, staring up at him dreamily, before I look back at him.

"What are you doing?" I ask, sounding braver than my insides feel.

"Kissing."

And obviously so. I just saw them doing that. I don't know why him saying it out loud feels like somebody's dropped a piano on me. Now that I'm closer, I can see he's sort of shimmery—specks of scales from rubbing up against a mermaid.

"Oh." I nod a couple of times as I stare over at him. "Why?"

"Because it's good." Peter shrugs, and Rye sighs next to me.

"Oh." I nod again. Another piano.

"Daphne," Peter says in a voice that makes me feel stupid. "You're not the only girl I play with."

Piano.

"Did you think you were?" he asks me, smiling like he's confused.

I stare over at him, do my best not to let it show on my face that it feels like a little bit of me is folding up inside myself, tucking itself away into a far back corner where I won't be able to reach it again.

Peter smiles over at me mindlessly, nodding his chin towards Rye. "Come join us."

Rye shifts uncomfortably beside me, and I glare over at Peter, unable to look away.

"No." I shake my head.

Peter looks over at me, head tilted, like he's trying to read a sign in another language.

"Why do you look…stupid and sad?" he calls to me.

Because I am those things, I think.

I say nothing, and Peter gives the mermaid a look as though to imply that I'm the one making things awkward. He sniffs, amused, and the mermaid covers her mouth with her hand, doing a terrible job of suppressing her laugh.

Something about his indifference and how strangely beautiful and cruel she is at once makes my eyes go glassy.

Peter squints over at me in disbelief. "Are you crying?"

And with that, the mermaid lets out a delighted little squeal, and Peter lets out one single laugh, watching me like I'm not the person he shares his bed with every night.

I turn quickly on my heel and walk back into the jungle.

"Where are you going?" Rye calls, walking after me. "I'll bring you back to the grounds. You can stay with us."

I turn to face him, crossing my arms over my chest. "Is he like that with Calla?"

Rye sighs, tilting his head. "Daphne, I—"

"Does he do that with Calla?" I ask tonelessly.

He says nothing.

"Yes or no, Rye?"

Rye sighs. "Yes."

I shake my head at him. "I'm not going back to the Old Valley."

He looks stressed. "Then where are you going?"

Where am I going? I don't know. Except yes, I do. There's only one place left that I can go, really.

I start walking again.

"At least fly there," he calls to me.

I shake my head. "I can't fly without him."

Rye grimaces.

I look back at the rock, and Peter's there, reclined on the rock, hands behind his head, the mermaid gazing at him all adoringly, finger running down over his nose.

And that's enough for me. I take off through the jungle.

Flying would be faster, that's definitely true, and though I've never tried, I really am sure that I couldn't do it without him—that's what Peter says anyway—and I don't know if you can do it when you're sad, because happy thoughts, that's what Peter always says, and I have none. I'm not willing to feel like a failure at the same time as I'm busy feeling like an idiot.

I do eventually get nervous by myself out here, because I don't feel I know it particularly well yet. Whenever we're out here, it never feels like we take the same path. Whenever Rye takes me somewhere, we walk a traveled path, or if one of the Lost Boys takes me, we go down paths that I think look familiar to me, but when Peter's there, we're always going strange ways and taking corners and turns I don't know we need to be taking. A small part of me wonders whether that's on purpose. So I have to depend on him, but who could I say that thought to, and how would I prove it anyway? And to what end?

So I run through the jungle till I reach the shore of the crescent, and then I run along the edge of the bay.

I will say, it is rather difficult to navigate your way around an island you already don't know very well when you're crying; no one tells you that. It's rather hazardous, and I nearly might have fallen a few times were it not for a couple of little birds that flew along beside me, guiding me and keeping me right with little pecks and flapping their wings against my face whenever I began heading the wrong way.

They come with me the whole way to the start of the town, those sweethearts. I check my pockets to see if I have anything I could give them, but I don't. I just give them a sorry wave goodbye, and off they fly.

It's getting dark now. I don't know what time it is—as though time matters here. I haven't yet figured out which sun they attach their time to. It couldn't be too late in the evening, and now that I'm here, I don't know why I've come.

Even though a bit of me does.

I'm sad, obviously. But why have I come here? That's a question whose eyes I've been avoiding because it doesn't make sense. I can't really believe it. Peter's been doing that with Calla and the mermaids? All those times he's not with me, is that what he's been doing?

He doesn't even do that with me, that kind of kissing. It was a lot of kissing… He's progressed without me, without even telling me.

I walk, brave as I can, towards the *Golden Folly*, climbing on board and walking straight to where Jamison took me the other day.

Orson Calhoun stands from the chair he's reclined in on the bridge.

"'Ello." He nods.

"Hi." I wipe my face with my hands and sniff. I know it looks like I've been crying. No way to hide that.

"Are y'okay?" He nods at me.

"Is Jamison here?" I look past him to the door to his room.

"Aye." He nods.

"In there?" I walk towards it.

"Aye, but—" Orson starts but it's too late.

I swing the door open, and there he is with a girl who I think looks familiar, but I can never remember anything these days. It's someone. He's with someone. Bent over a table. She's fully naked, he's partially naked, pumping away.

"Oh my god." I clamp my hand over my mouth, spin around immediately, and cover my eyes too late.

"Bow!" he says, startled.

"Shit. I'm sorry!" I keep walking, quickly as I can, scurrying off the bridge. "I'm—Fuck. Sorry."

I hear movement after me.

"Thank ye for that," Hook says to Calhoun as he passes him and jogs after me. "Whoa, whoa!" He grabs my arm and spins me around to face him. "What's going on? What're ye doing here?"

I snatch my arm away from him, and his face falters.

"Are ye okay?"

"Fine." I nod a lot. "I'm fine." I tell him, except now I'm shaking my head. I'm not sure I am fine. I'm about to not be fine. I need those birds to come back. I'm starting to not be able to see again. I wave my hand vaguely in the direction of his quarters. "Don't let me keep you from—" I swallow heavy. "Finishing."

Hook breathes out once, and it's heavy and he looks down at me with this frown that's confused and maybe even a bit sad.

"What's happening?" He looks over his shoulder, bewildered.

"Nothing." I shrug expressively. "Literally nothing. On all fronts." I nod to myself. "Clearly."

He keeps frowning at me. "What?"

I wave back towards the girl who's now filling the doorway, watching us with a frown. "Enjoy."

"Aye, sure." Jamison scoffs, annoyed. "I will."

I walk backwards away from him and flash him my middle finger before I spin around and walk away.

"I dïnnae ken what that means," he calls after me.

I spin back around to flash him two.

He throws me an unimpressed look and then walks back to the girl, putting his arm around her, closing the door behind him.

Piano.

I don't know where to go or what to do. I can't go back to the tree house. I don't want to go to the Old Valley. I don't know how to get home.

I spot a little lizard that's staring at me from a few meters away. He's glowing this warm sort of yellowy green, perched at the edge of the dock.

I watch him for a few seconds, and briefly I feel better, distracted by something that's so strange it demands my full attention, and then the lizard drops off the edge of the dock.

I dart towards it and peer over the edge, but the lizard's landed in a beached canoe.

He stares up at me, blinks twice. And for some reason, I feel like he's telling me something.

I look over my shoulder to see if anyone else is seeing this, but there aren't many people around, and besides, who's watching a sad, crying girl chase a lizard anyway?

I slip down over the side of the dock and land on the sand.

I stare at the lizard, which stares back at me. "Am I to understand we're to share this?" I gesture to the canoe.

Quite typically of lizards (and as I suspected), he says nothing in return.

I hold out my hand. "Are you a nice lizard?"

He runs onto my hand and immediately curls up in the palm of my hand.

"Well, at least one of us is set for the night."

I climb into the canoe, curling into a ball, being careful not to squash my new lizard friend as I do.

Maybe I was wrong. Maybe there is no such thing as fate, and maybe I hate it here.

CHAPTER NINE

"ARE YE HAVIN' A SLEEP WITH A LIZARD?" SAYS A DEEP* VOICE I DON'T PARTIC-
ularly want to hear first thing in the morning, all things considered, though
were I being honest, I suppose I'm glad to hear it also.

"No." I keep my eyes closed for a few more seconds. "I believe that was you."

Jamison snorts a laugh, and I blink my eyes open, staring at my little lizard
friend and my little lizard friend only. He's still all curled up in my palm, I give
him a smile, then lift my hand up to the top of the canoe and let him climb
off me.

"Look at ye." Jamison nods his chin at me. "So at one with nature."

"Look at you." I glare at him. "So clothed now."

He tilts his head. "Are ye a bit sad about that?"

I give him a stubborn look. "Not even remotely."

Though actually, if I were to be entirely truthful, perhaps I am a bit (but
very remotely).

He crouches down so we're closer to eye level. "What're ye doing in a
canoe?"

"Oh." I sigh. "I just grew tired of all the comforts you get from living in a
tree house and decided I wanted to create some new lower back problems for
myself." I give him a sarcastic look.

Jamison squashes away a smile, nodding. "Ye fighting with the wee man?"

I look away. "I don't want to talk about it."

He moves his head, looking for my eyes. "Ye came to me last night."

---

* And regrettably sexy.

I give him a look. "And you came with someone else entirely, so that's completely brilliant for you."

Jamison frowns. "Is thon what ye were there for?"

I quickly tuck some hair behind my ears. "Of course not!"

He stands, arms folded over himself, staring down at me, brows furrowed. "Yer angry."

"No, I'm not," I tell him hotly, and I don't know when I decided I felt like fighting with him, but I do.

He offers me his hand to help me up, but I brush it away, heaving myself up instead—and rather indelicately so, I might add. He rolls his eyes at me.

I've never fought with a man before, so I can't tell for certain whether that's what we're doing right now, but whatever this is, I must admit that there is a thrill to it.

Jamison nods his chin at me. "I like yer dress. It makes ye look quite swarthy."

I shrug dismissively. "I just get darker in the sun is all."

"I'm complimenting ye." He gives me an unimpressed look. "Actually, I'm complimenting the dress that I bought ye…thon yer wearing."

"I didn't ask you to!"

He shrugs. "Ye could just be grateful."

"I was!" I shoot back.

"Until?" He lifts his eyebrows, waiting, and I say nothing.

I keep saying nothing, quite enjoying all the attention he's giving me, and then he breathes out, annoyed, rolls his eyes, and turns and walks away.

"Where are you going?" I call to him, but he doesn't stop, just keeps walking. So I climb out of the boat and scramble after him. "Hey!" I call again. "Where are you going, I said!"

He spins around, though he doesn't stop walking. "Fer a dander up the mountains." He flicks his eyes. "Would ye care to join me?"

"No," I say quickly. He rolls his eyes, and I regret it immediately. "Maybe?"

He stops walking. "Maybe?" he says, eyes pinched, and I think I see a smile whisper over his face but ever so lightly and only for a second before he puts it away. He might enjoy being angry at me too. Jamison's eyes fall to my bare feet. "Yer gonna need something for those."

I straighten up, offended. "I walked the Fallen Kingdom and the jungle yesterday without shoes."

"Well, thon was stupid of ye." He gives me a look. "And this is a mountain. There'll be jagged rocks and snow and—"

"Oh, never mind then," I growl, crossing my arms, looking away.

He stares over at me. "Yer an absolute punish today."

My mouth falls open, a little bit from hurt, but mostly from the reprimand.

Jem moves in towards me and waves towards the town square. "We can buy ye some shoes, Bow."

"I don't want you to buy me shoes!" I say quickly.

"For why?" He rolls his eyes.

"Why do you want to?" I ask. "So you can hold it over my head again?"

"I never—Fuck!" He shakes his head at me, his face getting closer to mine. "Is yer head cut?"

And then a ball of light zooms in between us, hovering at my eye level.

Jamison pulls back, surprised, as I put my hand out for Rune to land on. She chimes.

"Oh no. I'm fine." I shake my head.

She zips over and jingles aggressively in Jamison's face—he stands there wide-eyed and stunned—before she darts back over and lands on my hand. She jingles.

I give her a look. "Heard about that, did you?"

She trills wildly.

"She's very pretty. Oh, you don't have to say that. Well, thank you. That's kind." More chimes.

"No, I've not spoken to him since." I shake my head, and then I feel Jamison's eyes on me. I turn to him and frown. "What?"

He lifts an eyebrow, surprised. "Ye speak Stjär?"

"Yes." I roll my eyes as though I've been fluent in it all my life. "Don't you?"

He pulls back a little, surprised again. "No' fluently."

I scoff and Rune and I trade unimpressed looks.

"I know." I roll my eyes again as I stare over at him for a moment before looking back at her. She trills something about how handsome he is. "Yes, I suppose, if you're interested in that sort of thing."*

---

* I say as though I'm not.

She jingles.

"Without it on, do you mean?" I lower my voice as I turn my body a little so Jamison can't see so much of us, in case I'm blushing because I could maybe, possibly be. "Well, yes, I have. No! No, no! Not like that! But it is quite nice, actually, if you must know."[†]

I straighten up again, look back at him over my shoulder, and our eyes catch. He swallows a smile before he glances away, and I ignore the feeling I have that he may have just caught all that after all.

Rune jingles.

"Well, we were going to go on a walk, but I have no shoes."

Jamison ducks his head in towards us, raising a finger in protest. "It's no' as though I dïdnae offer to buy ye some."

Rune jingles, pleased.

"Well, she said no." Hook tells her. "Aye, cause she's stubborn."

Rune chimes at me hotly, stomping her foot against the air.

"I don't care to ask people for things," I tell her proudly.

Rune jingles angrily again. Fairies and their emotions, honestly.

"Well, I classify you as people, Rune." She pulls a face, as though being called a human is offensive, and I guess considering us as a species at large, I do understand why she may not have received it exceptionally well. "I meant it in a positive way," I clarify. "As in I wouldn't much like to ask you for anything or expect you to help me either."

The fairy gives me an exasperated look before diving off my palm and whirring around my ankles.

Hook stares on and so do I as she fabricates a beautiful pair of knee-high moccasins from nothing. She zips back up to my hand.

"Oh, Rune, they're gorgeous!" I look from her to my feet. "I love them! Thank you!"

Jamison's just staring, mouth open, eyes wide, like he's never seen a fairy before or magic.

Rune trills, glancing between Jamison and I.

"Just up the mountain, I believe. Would ye care t' join us?"

---

† And Rune tinkles that she indeed must know, and frankly, I do not blame her.

She makes very tiny kissing sounds, and I pull her away from Jamison's line of sight again.

"Oh! Stop that, immediately," I whisper to her, and she jingles, laughing.

Jem cranes his neck, trying to see what's happening, and Rune jumps from my hand and flits over to him, hovering at his eye level for a few seconds and then over to his ear, chiming so quietly I can't hear her.

"I ken." He nods and pulls back, looking at her, confused. "No, say that again, slower now. Oh. Oh, I will, aye." He nods. "I swear. No, I dïnnae like him either."

I frown over at them, and Jem flicks me a smug look as Rune moves away from him.

"Perhaps ye could fashion her up a wee coat fer the mountains too?" he asks her pleasantly, but that absolutely sends her bouncing between us like an enraged pinball.

"He didn't mean it!" I shake my head.

"It's fine!" Hook shakes his head quickly, panicked almost. "She can hae mine. If she's cold, she can hae mine."

That placates her a bit, and the fairy flies right in his face, tinkering and waving a scolding finger at him before flying away at the speed of light.

Jamison looks over at me, eyebrows up.

"All right, dïnnae ask a fairy for a coat. Now we know."

I breathe out a laugh, and we start walking into the rain forest the town blends into.

He stares over at me for a little while before I say anything.

"What?" I ask defensively.

"The fae"—he squints—"dïnnae often take to people."

I purse my lips, not really knowing what to say, but he keeps staring in a strange kind of awe.

Jamison shakes his head a bit. "And never do they do them magic."

"Well." I shrug, giving a tall look for no reason in particular. "I'm very charming."

He catches my eyes and nods to himself. "Aye, I s'pose y'are."

That disarms me a bit, enough for all the fuel I had to be argumentative and cross at him for no reason to be immediately drained from my tank.

Jem shakes his head, still thinking on it. "Ye dïnnae see a lot o' fairies about these days. Good at hiding."

I nod once. "And for good reason."

"Ah." He gives me an impressed look. "So ye've been doing some reading…"

I look over at him, pleased. "I have."

"Come and take my books anytime ye want them," he tells me, which although I don't think he meant to be a sexy thing to say, it was absolutely a sexy thing to say.

Rye told me that it would really only take you a couple of days to walk around the entire island and that from the tree house to Neverpeak Mountain, it would take half a day. Less so from Zomertierra.

We're in the part of the rainforest where it starts bleeding into a regular forest, which I can see up ahead begins to turn to autumn.

Jem and I walk for a bit in silence, and it is the best kind of silence. Peter doesn't offer much of it; to him, silence is boring, silence is to be filled, and he fills it, constantly. Stories of himself, crowing, laughing, kisses sometimes—not exclusively with me alone, it would appear.

But here with Jem, it's just a stillness I've not really been afforded much yet in life.

I can hear birds and the sound of the air moving through the trees around us and not much else.

But silence has a downfall. Silence is when the thoughts come.

Accidental thoughts, ones you're not even trying to think of but there they are, growling away all the same from deep inside your monster of a conscience, ones you've been ignoring all day because if you don't ignore them—if you were, perhaps, to ponder such things—the very fabric of everything as we know it might pull and fray, and then what?

But that is the question, isn't it?

And then what? And actually, really, and then even what?

For all I know, the pirate is dating that girl, and he's just a wonderful (terrible) flirt.*

Then he breathes out this big almost sigh.

---

* This is true regardless of anything else.

"Just say it," Jamison says, watching my face.

I look over at him. "What?"

"Whatever it is yer thinkin' about. Just say it or ask it or—"

"Why didn't you tell me?" I ask, and it's out of my mouth like a horse at the gate.

It sounds more like a demand than a question.

He stops walking.

I stare over at him and conclude quite quickly that we're going to have another fight. It feels like a nice place for it—scenic… Every red and orange and yellow on the color wheel is smeared across where we stand.

It's raining leaves and smells like smoldering logs and cinnamon, and Jamison Hook blends right in because something about him feels like when you've walked inside after being caught in the rain and a fire's already lit.

"Ye never asked—"

"So?" I shrug, impatient.

He gives me a look. "So for why would I tell ye?"

"Because—"

"'Acause why?" he asks, eyebrows up, and I just glare at him, angry and rearmed, ready to fight him for no reason.

"Do you often buy clothes for wayward souls?" I put my hands on my hips. "Lull them into a false sense of trust?"

"What?" he asks loudly.

"Bathe them."

"I dïdnae bathe ye. My house fae ran ye a bath, and ye go' into it, unassisted."

"And then—"

"And then!" He cuts me off. "Ye left. Went back thonder to yer fucking house in a tree with the wee man and stayed there till he daen the next fucked-up thing to ye." Jamison shakes his head, angry. "Daen ye think I'm over here waiting for ye?"

My head pulls back, offended. "No."*

"Good." He gives me a look. "'Acause I'm no'."

"Yes, I know. I saw that."

---

* A girl may hope though.

He scoffs. "Aye, yer head is cut."

"What?" I blink.

"Yer angry at me for laying with someone else when yer thonner sleeping with him every night."

"I'm not angry at you," I tell him, sidestepping the very big hole in the conclusion he just made.

"Aye, y'are. Ye dae this thing with yer eyes when yer angry, where yer nose pinches but yer mouth goes heavy at the bottom, like yer frowning but yer no'."

I blink at him a few times; my cheeks go hot. "How do you know that?"

"Because I see ye, Daphne!" he yells. "Yer annoying and yer thran[†] and yer a pain in the fucking arse. Ye think you ken everything, but actually ye dinnae know a single thing, and yer fucking daft 'acause ye spend all yer heart's time thinking about some flying man-child who I ken, for a fact, daesnae give a fuck about you."

I glare at him, shaking my head a bit, worried it's all true. "You don't know what you're talking about."

"Aye, Bow, I do, because I give a fuck about ye." His eyes settle on me, steady, and his jaw tightens as he says this. "And y'are all-consuming."

He stares at me for a couple of seconds, then brushes past me, trekking up the steepening mountain.

A couple of minutes pass, and it's a different kind of silence now. One where I know he's angry at me, and I don't know how to fix it, which is a feeling I don't love.

He's about twenty paces ahead of me when I jog after him.

"I don't sleep with him." I call. "Not that way."

Jem stops walking for a second, goes still in his tracks, then he keeps going. "How then?" he asks without looking back.

"Just sleeping," I call, and he pauses. "Asleep. I sleep next to him." I keep going with a shrug.

Jamison looks back at me, and I give him a look.

"I'm certainly not bending him over tables."

He squashes a smile and shakes his head. "A'm sorry ye saw that."

---

† Which means "stubborn."

"Why?" I ask, feeling a bit sad about it all over again.

He shrugs. "Just am."

We walk next to each other now, and the mountain is starting to get snowy, though it's not cold yet.

Jamison's mindlessly picking plants as we climb on up, looking over at me every now and then, and I last only a few minutes before I ask the next question.

"Are you together?"

He looks over at me, and my lips are pursed as I wait for the answer, not looking at him.

He looks back straight ahead and shakes his head. "No."

We stare at each other for a few seconds before he looks around.

"Snow." He shakes his head and takes off his jacket.

"Oh, I'm fine," I tell him, but he drapes it over my shoulders anyway.

"Nae, take it." He gives me a look. "My fragile masculinity cudnae handle thon wee fairy coming back and tearing me up because yer fucking founthered."

I hug his jacket to my body, not because I'm that cold but just because I like how it feels on me, and I eye him. "What if you catch a cold?"

He shrugs. "Then I s'pose ye'll hae to come and bathe me."

I bite back a laugh and so does he, looking off and away.

"We're nearly there," he tells me.

"Nearly where?" I look around. We're sort of near the top, but I'd say to the peak is another couple of hours. "Do you even know where you're going, or are you lost?"

"Dae I seem lost?" He looks at me over his shoulder.

I inspect my nails. "Perhaps morally."

"Sure, what's yer dad like then?" he asks rather suddenly, frowning over at me.

"Sorry." I blink. "What?"

He glances over at me. "What does yer relationship with yer father look like?"

I don't know why this completely catches me off guard, but it does, and I stop in my tracks. "What are you asking me that for?"

He scratches the back of his neck. "Dinnae ken. Ye just sort o' strike me as someone with a complicated relationship with their father." He grimaces.

I stare at him, wide-eyed. I don't even think I'm offended—though maybe I am a small bit? I just shake my head, barely.

"I don't know him."*

Jamison nods slowly, thinking to himself, squashing a bit of a smile away. It's a knowing smile, a bit as though he knew it all along, and now—now, I am offended.

"You think that's funny?" I ask him, hands on my hips and ready for another fight.

Jamison walks right over to me so we're toe-to-toe and tugs on the lapel of his jacket I'm wearing, adjusting it to my body and pulling it snug against me.

"No, I dinnae." He shakes his head, eyes falling down me. "Who the fuck is leaving ye behind if they have a choice?"

His head moves in towards mine. He's still holding on to the jacket, pulling me into him, and I'm acutely aware of my own breathing and that I haven't yet closed my eyes. I'm staring at him getting closer and closer, and I know I should shut them because that's what you do before a kiss, which I think this is about to be, but then I shouldn't like to because his face is so lovely and I might cut myself on his jaw if I don't watch it closely, and actually, honestly, I'd really like to watch it closely.

His eyes aren't moving from mine as he leans in closer, and from the top of the mountain, this cool, soft air blows down around us and through us, dancing over our noses, and it's the kind of wind that you feel to your core, but it doesn't hurt like those awful winter chills we get in England. An ache does set up camp in my bones though, that's true—a new imbalance in me that I won't recognize or understand for quite some time. And I feel nervous, but I think it's the good kind? And I don't dislike it; maybe, honestly, I rather love it? His hands are on me, and his eyes still aren't moving, and I think it's starting to snow. I can feel it on my face—these tiny, cold drops that make me blink every time one lands on me—and they're landing on him too. One falls on his cheek under his eye, melting away into him how I suspect I will too in a minute, and if I could frame this moment, I would—take a picture, stare at it every morning to start my day off spectacularly right. And right as his lips hover over mine, the feeling of his

* He died before I was born. My mother met him on a dig.

breath on my face is a kick all over me, and I don't want it to stop. The breeze is moving around our ears like a whisper, and he's moving in towards me slowly, slowly, so slowly that right as I think our top lips graze, he pulls back.

"Thirty-one days," he breathes out, nodding to himself as he stares at the ground.

"What?" I stare at him, hurt and confused that he just dashed the moment completely.

"He's steeling himself," says a voice I've never heard before.

A woman's.

I look past Jamison, and my eyes land on her.

Lean, pretty but sharp featured, sparkly eyes. I can't completely place her age, but she's young. She's youthful looking.

"For what?" I frown over at her.

She raises her eyebrows. "For you."

Jamison catches my eye, then rolls his before he turns and claps his hand over her mouth.

"Thon's enough out o' ye." And then he kisses her on the cheek.

She looks up at him, annoyed. "Why would you bring her to me?"

British accent. Quite proper.

I stand there feeling self-conscious and stupid, wondering who he's brought me to. Another non-girlfriend of his? Fucking pirates! Fucking men, actually—I hate them all. They're all scoundrels.

He shrugs. "I wanted to see ye, and she was so doonhairtit,* asleep in a wee canoe all by herself."

The woman looks over at me, impatient. "Why were you in a canoe?"

"On land, what's more," Jamison butts in, looking over at me.

"Oh." The woman grimaces. "The saddest of canoes."

Jamison nods his head towards me.

"She came t' see me last night. I wasn't expecting company. I was…entertaining someone else"—he catches my eye, and I throw him a disparaging look—"and so struck with sorra,† she wallowed in a canoe."

---

* Which means "sad."

† Which means "sadness."

I glare over at him for a moment before flicking the woman a look. "He took many liberties in that tale."

"I'm sure he did." She nods. "Nevertheless, who are you?"

"Daphne," I tell her, but for whatever reason, that doesn't quite seem sufficient, so I glance at Jamison quickly before I compulsively offer her my surname for no reason. "Beaumont-Darling."

She looks me up and down and then, rather suddenly, without asking or warning, she grabs my hand. She flips it over in hers and inspects my palm, squinting at it. I look back over at Jem, my eyes wide with a mild concern, but he just gives me a half a smile.

Then the woman drops my hand and grabs Jamison's. She runs her hands over his palm twice,[‡] stretches it out, and peers down at it. Then she grabs mine again. Holds both our hands, lined up next to each other, and moves them around to catch the light she's looking for.

"Hm," she says. "Interesting."

And that's all she says before she drops both our hands and looks from him to me.

"She has the kiss." She points to my mouth.

Jem nods. "I ken. I quite like it there."

She glances at me. "Pan hasn't taken it?"

I flash her a quick smile. "He's tried."

Jamison shifts a little uneasily next to me.

"I'm Itheelia," the woman tells me.

My mouth falls open.

"Le Faye?" I blink at her. Of course! From the book! I thought she looked familiar. "The founder?" I clarify.

"Ah." She sighs. "If you believe certain history books…"

"I've read all about you. You came here with your brother and—"

"And my best friends." She nods.

"You traveled across six galaxies!"

"So have you." She gives me a look. "Well, actually, Earth is perhaps just two stops from here, but nevertheless, quite a trip, wouldn't you say?"

---

‡ And I'm not even at all remotely jealous.

"Quite, yes." I nod, staring over at her in awe before I find myself shaking my head. "I'm so sorry, I just—how are you alive still?"

She throws Jamison a look, as though I'm the rudest girl in all the world.

"It was a long time ago, wasn't it?" I add quickly when she doesn't answer me.

She nods, and a look I can't quite place rests on her face. "Aye, it was a long time ago." Then she clears her throat. "Why were you in a canoe, Daphne Beaumont-Darling?"

I cross my arms over my chest proudly. "I didn't have anywhere else to go."

"I see." She nods and then her eyes pinch. "Now, when you say entertaining…" She eyes Jamison suspiciously, and I wonder if they're going to have a lovers' quarrel.

I would be fairly gutted if indeed he had brought me up a mountain to dangle his potential other lover in my face, and if she's the reason he didn't kiss me, even though it was snowing and the breeze was begging us to and everything, I suppose I should cause a lovers' quarrel between them for just some small slice of justice.

Jamison smiles uncomfortably and I—already annoyed at him, both for indisputably ruining our (almost) kiss and for hypothetically being romantically involved with yet another person—clear my throat.

"It was entertainment of the sexual variety," I tell her merrily as I toss him under the bus.

The woman rolls her eyes and growls, "Jammie."

"Mum, listen—"

"Mum!" I interrupt, looking back and forth between them like a Ping-Pong match.

"Oh." He gestures at her vaguely as a son might. "This here is my mother."

"Oh!" I extend my hand to her again. "Oh, it's such a pleasure!"

His mother shakes my hand with both of hers, smiling. "You know, he's never brought me a girl before."

Jamison shakes his head. "I'm no' bringing her t'ye. She's—"

"Is she a girl?" she asks her son, impatiently.

Jamison glances at me. "Aye."

Her eyebrow lifts. "And she is here, is she not?"

Jem rolls his eyes and looks away, and I get the distinct impression that she is a woman who oft gets her way.

His mother shakes her head and holds up a hand to silence him. "Was it that Morrigan girl he was with last night?"

"I don't know. I didn't quite catch her name." I look at Jamison, eyebrows up, asking without asking, even though I know it was.

He rolls his eyes and nods all at once.

"Jammie."

"Unfortunately," I say to reinsert myself into the conversation, "I saw it all. She was bent over a table and everything."

Itheelia grimaces. "That is unfortunate."

"All right, listen." Jamison groans. "She wusnae too hard done by, ye ken."

Itheelia gives him a tight smile, patting him on the arm. "Then, darling, that doesn't sound like a job very well done, does it?"

He drops his head backwards towards the sky, defeated.

"Where's your coat?" his mother asks. "It's Baltic up here."

"She's wearing it." He points to me, I think just a little bit eager to get the focus off himself.

"Why didn't you bring a jacket?" she asks me, appalled. "Making my son freeze for you."

Jamison flashes me a smug smile.

I clap my hand on my chest in self-defense. "I didn't know I was going to the mountains today, and my fairy didn't want to make me a jacket."

She blinks. "You have a fairy?"

"Well—" I tilt my head. "No?"

"Maybe?" Jamison considers. "Sor' of."

"No." I shake my head. "She's my friend. She made me these boots." I flash them to her.

Itheelia stares at them, frowning a bit. "What's this fairy's name?"

"Rune," I tell her. "Why?"

She shakes her head, thinking. "Just, strange. Fairies don't tend to take to little earthlings all that often."

I'm not entirely sure that that's an insult, but I'm also not *not* sure either.

"Well, she certainly didn't care for it when Jamison asked her to make me a coat so he didn't have to give me his."

He breathes out loudly again as his mother gasps, smacking him on the arm. He throws me an unimpressed look, and I don't know what I've done but I grin at him, pleased he's back in trouble again.

"You asked a fairy to make you something?"

"*Her* something!"

"What did she say?"

I jump back in. "Mostly she just yelled at him and told him to give me his."

Her eyes pinch at me. "You speak Stjär?"

"Well too." Jamison nods, staring over at me, and for some reason, I blush.

"Interesting." She nods to herself and then turns away. She snaps her fingers and slides her hand to the right, and the rocks move with her, revealing a home built within the wall of the cave.

My jaw falls to the floor, and I grab Jem's arm with both my hands as I stare up at him. "She's magic?"

He smiles down at me and walks inside, and somehow, for some reason, I don't let go of him. My grip moves down a little so I'm holding on to his wrist now, almost hugging his arm as we walk into his mother's home.

I lean in towards him and whisper, "Why is she magic and you're not?"

"I could be." He shrugs. "Probably am. Just daen practice."

"Oh." I frown. "Why?"

He shrugs again with the indifference that a person only can if they've grown up around magic. "Who has the time?"

"You—" I stare at him. "What do you even do in a day?"

"Oh, you know." He sighs but catches my eye playfully. "Rescue women that fall from the sky, buy wayward souls dresses—"

I (unsuccessfully) bite back a smile.

Itheelia Le Faye is rummaging around in a wardrobe, and when she turns back around to us, she's holding a beautiful fur coat in her arms.

Her eyes land on my hands, holding her son how I am, and she stares for a few seconds. Then, ever so faintly, as though tugged by an invisible string, I see a hint of a smile.

"Put this on." She shoves the coat into my hands.

Somewhat reluctantly, I unfurl myself from Jamison's arm, and he gently tugs his coat off my body.

"First time I'm undressing ye and it's in front of my marm," he sighs, and I roll my eyes at him.

He pulls his coat back on himself and blows air out of his mouth like he's been freezing this whole time (though he's not said a word about it), then he takes the coat from my arms and holds it open for me. I slip inside it, and maybe his hands hover on my arms a second longer than they need to, I'm not sure.

I look over at his mother. "He's very well-mannered."

"He is." She nods, proud, before she looks at her son, struck as though she's just remembered something. "I've something for you."

She darts out the room, and as she does, I notice some stones in a bowl with carvings on them. I pick one up to inspect it, then glance at Jem. "What are these?"

"Truth runes," he says.

"What?" I blink.

"You throw them in the air and ask a yes or no question, and the way the stones land tells you the answer."

I stare over at him, incredulous. "How?"

Jem pulls a face, as though he thinks I'm silly. "Magic."

"Oh." I flash him an embarrassed smile.

"Here, I'll show ye." Jem grabs the stones and tosses them into the air. "Is Daphne attracted to me?"

In a panicked rush, not knowing quite what to do, I dive to cover the pirate's eyes and quickly scramble the stones as they land.

Jem peels his hands off me and gives me a look.

I shrug demurely. "You wouldn't have liked the answer."

He flicks me a look. "Aye, but I already ken the answer, so…"

"I know you think you know the ans—"

"Oh." He cuts me off. "I know the answer."

My eyes pinch because I feel like I'm losing and I'm see-through, and clearly, I am, but then his eyes pinch back at me, and for some reason, it makes me feel better.

"Well." I cross my arms over my chest. "You think I'm attractive."

"Sure." He gives me a look. "Ye didnae need the stones to tell ye that though."

My cheeks go pink, and then his mother walks back in with what looks like a little gold compass in hand. She offers it to Jem.

He looks down at it. "What's this?"

"A compass," she tells him with a look, and he flips it open, looking down at it.

"It's broken." He tells her.

She leans over and peers down, and I can't see it, but she looks from the compass to me and then says, "No, it's not."

And then she waves her hand and starts rearranging the flowers that are on her dining table.

Jamison frowns down at it in his hand. "North's that way." He points north, apparently.

She glances back at him. "Who said anything about north?"

And then they seem to have a mother-son conversation with their eyes, and he pockets the compass and says no more about it.

I stare over at Itheelia, whizzing flowers through the air, and I try to do the maths. "How old are you?"

She gasps dramatically, but there's a twinkle in her eye. "The nerve."

I look over at Jamison instead, who's moved to an armchair by a fireplace that isn't lit.

"Mum." He nods his head at the empty fireplace.

"Can't my son build a fire with his own two hands?" She scowls.

"Cannae my mother no' just"—he snaps his fingers—"with her magical powers?" He gives her an impatient look.

"Lazy, impatient, slothful—"

"Cold." He interrupts her.

Itheelia rolls her eyes. With about four flicks of her wrist, the fire is ablaze.

Jem gets up from the chair and crouches down in front of it, warming his hands, and I stare over at him and swallow.

I like how he looks when he's lit up by flames, the shadows they cast over his face. I could possibly just actually like his face in general though.

Jem looks over his shoulder at me and nods his chin towards the chair he was in.

This floors me a little in a way that I know it shouldn't. To be surprised he wants me by him? To be happy that the boy I've spent the day with hasn't forgotten my name once? What is Peter Pan doing to me?

I go and sit in it, then watch him till he looks at me again.

"Are ye warm?" he asks.

I nod, not saying anything, and he nods back.

"How old are you, Daphne?" his mother calls.

"Eighteen," I fib, and Jamison gives me a tall look, so I add, "Almost."

She looks over at us with pinched eyes as she makes a pot of tea from scratch. "In thirty-one days, I'll bet."

I look at Jem, eyes wide and pleased. "Am I eighteen in thirty-one days?"

He nods once, smile all subdued, and I sit up taller at the thrill of it.

"Start of November?" she asks.

"Yes," I say and smile.

She nods her head at Jem. "End of November."

"Really!" I beam up at him, and he says nothing, doesn't even look at me, just sort of smiles at the fire.

"Born in 1948?" Itheelia asks me.

I shake my head. "Forty-nine."

She waves her hand, and the teapot lifts itself in the air and starts pouring into the teacups.

"How old were you when you had Jem?"

"Jem?" She blinks but I suspect she's perhaps at least a bit pleased, and I notice that, rather intentionally, her son doesn't look away from the fire; he just stares at it, waiting for his mother's comment to drift by.

I couldn't tell you why exactly, but this feels the same to me as when he put his coat around me. Sort of weighted. More than just keeping me warm, it's a heavy thing that feels like an anchor being laid on the seabed of who I am. Just settling in, making itself at home.

As though me having a name for him that's just mine needs no explanation.

"I stopped counting my age at five hundred," Itheelia tells me with a pleasant smile.

"And how did you meet Captain Hook?" I tuck my feet under myself, and Jem sits on the arm of the chair.

I like the feeling of him hovering over me. It's safe. And it's then I realize that actually, I haven't felt safe in quite some time.

She rolls her eyes again, as though she's annoyed to have to talk about it, but you know the look women get in their eyes when they're asked to regale stories of their youth? She's not too displeased, even if she's pretending to be.

"Here." She nods. "On the island."

"Were you married?"

Jamison scowls, shaking his head.

"But together for quite some time though." She nods.

"Longer than they should hae been," Jem adds, eyeing his mother.

"He wasn't a founder though?" I say, but mostly I'm asking.

"No." She shakes her head. "Neither were we though, really." She gives me a pleasant smile. "Can't find something that's already been founded."

"So where are the rest of you?" I ask her brightly, but immediately her face pulls in discomfort.

"Day—my dear friend Day—lives on Alabaster Island now. And Aanya, she's—I don't know—somewhere. She moves around a lot. Hard to pin down."

"There were five of you, weren't there?" I ask, thinking back to my book.

She nods. "The other two are dead."

"Oh," I sigh, sorry.

"Ban was Mum's brother." Jem nudges me.

"And Vee"—she forces a smile—"was my best friend."

I look between them, then ask cautiously,* "What happened?"

Itheelia takes a big breath.

"Ban killed her. Accidentally," she offers as an afterthought.

"Oh my god." I blink.

"They were a wee couple, were they no'?" Jem squints at his mother.

"Sort of." She tilts her head. "No, but yes. Ban and I come from a very old line of magic. Old lines"—she looks at me—"they're dangerous, like money in your world. Magic is power in ours. Ban was, since we were small, obsessed with power. And Vee…" She tosses me another look. "All those stories on your planet about Aphrodite and Venus, Inanna, Minerva, they're all based on

---

* Read nosily.

Vee. She's not quite a god; she's just…beautiful and persuasive and magically charming." Itheelia shrugs hopelessly but still smiles as she thinks about her friend. "People just adored her. Ban adored her. Obsessed with her, he was."

They were a complicated couple, apparently. Itheelia says they were on and off and on and off, and then one day, they were on and they found out she was pregnant. And everything was good. They were good. And then rumors started swirling around Ban and his motives. He'd been trying to gain power and favor with the fairies with relationships and bribes and blackmail, and when he couldn't get it those ways, he turned violent.

"And that's when we found out about the prophecy." Itheelia sighs.

Jamison makes an "achk" sound with his throat. "It's just a story."

I look between them, wondering if it's the same one Rye mentioned.

"What prophecy?"

Itheelia gives her son a long-suffering look. "When two founders meet under an oxblood moon, the true heir will rise and sit on the throne once again, and the island will be restored."

Jamison stares at his hands, looking bored, but I frown at her.

"Restored?" I look at her like she's crazy. "Is the island in disrepair?"

Itheelia tilts her head. "You mightn't think so from looking at it, but then neither does your Earth look unwell, but trust me"—she gives me a solemn look—"it is dying."

"Of what?" I frown.

She frowns over at me a little before she says it. "Hope."

"Or lack thereof," Jamison adds.

"Hope?" I repeat.

"Our world daesnae operate by the same rules and laws yours does," Jamison tells me like I hadn't noticed.

"Hopes are currency here; they're a weighted substance. They fuel it."

"And hope is…dying?" I ask, not quite sure I believe it.

"Not dying." She shakes her head. "But disappearing."

"What would that mean?"

"For us?" Itheelia squints. "Our world will rot and crumble away, and for yours—"

"For mine?" I stare over at her, a bit alarmed for my family.

Itheelia gives me a strange look.

"Hope is our biggest export," Jamison tells me. "It's made here but used universally."

"Really?" I blink.

"We're all connected." Itheelia shrugs. "If we run out of hope here, for your world, it's probably just another Great Depression, but forever."

"Oh." I scrunch my face up. "Is that all?"

Itheelia breathes out her nose, looking flummoxed. "We can't tell why the wells are so low."

"There are wells?" I look between them.

Jamison's mother gives him a long-suffering look. "How do you stomach her incessant questioning?"

Jamison looks down at me for a few seconds, then he says, "Her face," before he crosses his arms over his chest.

The way we're sitting now, we're sort of pressed up against each other, and I'm shamefully aware of my breathing and how benignly his arm is touching mine. Some sort of wonderful, splintering pain rolls through me that I don't understand. My face!

"So Ban was trying to make the prophecy come true?" he asks.

His mother nods. "Vee had the baby. She tried to smuggle it away, and we tried to help her get it off planet, somewhere away from him, you know, once we knew what his motives were, but he got to her. He tried to stop her. They had a fight, and she injured him badly. So he did a spell to save himself, killed both of them in the process."

Her face looks strained, and I make a note to myself to remember that time doesn't heal all things.

"What spell?" Jem asks with a curious frown.

"Soul tether," she says with a solemn nod.

Jamison tilts his head. "I've never heard of—"

Itheelia shakes her head. "It's old magic," she tells him. "Finicky. Dangerous." She breathes out her nose and looks between us. "It only works if you're soulmates."

"What only works if you're soulmates?" I ask, trying to glean as much from this woman as I can.

"The spell," she says, as though I'm an idiot.

I lift my eyebrows. "Which does what?"

Itheelia gives me another impatient look. "It's a complicated one. It can give you life when you're losing it and powers when you had none before even, but it's costly. You become one. It can kill you if you're not fated."

"How do you know if you're fated?" I ask her quietly, not looking anywhere remotely near her son's eyes.

"You don't die when you do the spell," she tells me unceremoniously.

Jem rolls his eyes. "There are other ways."

I lift my brows. "And they are…?"

Jem opens his mouth to say something, but his mother cuts him off. "A shortcut to something you should just figure out in due time," she says sagely, and though I can't be entirely sure because I was still avoiding his gaze, I suspect that his eyes and mine both rolled. "Souls aren't to be trifled with." She gives us warning eyes. "They're too delicate and impossible to untangle."

"How do they get tangled?" I frown and then pause. "Do you mean literally tangled as though they're a literal thing?"

She eyes me like I'm some sort of terrible dope. "They are of course, a literal thing."

"Inside us!" I stare at her. "Like an organ we don't know about on Earth yet?"

And then she erupts in laughter.

Jamison tosses her a look. "Mum—"

"Sorry." She shakes her head and gets a hold of herself, trying to make her face look actually sorry and not just amused. "No, darling, not like an organ inside you."

I give her a tiny glare for laughing at me but only a tiny one because she's magic and I don't want her to hex me, and also I think I love her.

"Where then?"

"The Cave of Souls," she says like it's the most obvious thing on the planet. "It's remarkable down there, but"—she pauses thoughtfully—"souls themselves are remarkable. Delicate but amenable. I've never had the chance to see one be tied, but my mother did long ago, and she said it kind of smells of strawberries when it does."

"And that's what Ban did?" Jem asks. "Tried to tie their souls together?"

Itheelia nods.

"And they weren't fated?" I ask.

"Evidently not." She shrugs. "See, Ban needed to be linked to Vee, needed the tether to control her, but soul magic is a different kind of magic. It's pure, doesn't like to be manipulated. It just won't be."

Jem blinks a few times, shaking his head. "Fuck."

"And the baby?" I ask quietly. "You said they had a baby."

"The baby." Itheelia looks from her son and over to me, where her eyes settle. "Well, he grew up. Handsome little thing, charming, just like his mother. I think he's a friend of yours."

"Oh my god." I blink.

She nods. "The fairies found him, raised him."

My mouth gapes.

"What the fuck, Mum?" Jamison pulls back. "How long have ye been sitting on thon one for?"

Itheelia's mouth pinches. "A while."

Jamison's on his feet now, shaking his head, pacing. "Why dïdnae y'take him in?"

"I didn't want a child." She shrugs, then adds quickly as an afterthought, "At the time! That and I didn't think the legend was true." She lifts her shoulders like she's innocent. "And then Peter grew a little, and I began to become afraid that it was." She looks over at me. "You know how the land behaves around him."

"Is it true," I start, and I feel guilty as I do, as though the question I'm about to ask is a sign of me doubting him, "that he doesn't age because of the fountain of youth?"

Itheelia nods. "It was the fairies at first; they used to give him water from it. They thought if they kept him small, they could control him more easily."

I frown. "Could they?"

"Well." Itheelia gives me a delicate, albeit long look. "He's not a normal boy."

"Does he ken?" Hook asks, looking from me to his mum.

I shake my head, and Itheelia gives me a pointed look.

"Nor should he."

I shake my head at her a bit. "He has no idea where he's come from."

She nods. "For good reason."

"He thinks his mother abandoned him—that no one wants him—"

Jamison shifts uncomfortably on his feet, but my mind is reeling, and I think you can see it on my face because Itheelia looks at me and then at the clock on her wall. "Time to go, I think." She gives me a look—maternal, eyebrows up. "You won't tell him?"

I swallow and sigh. "Do you not think that—"

"More than think, I know," she says, eyes firm, "that the boy knowing would bring no good. Not to him, not to you, not to the land." She pauses, lets it all hang there heavy. "You mustn't tell him, Daphne."

"Okay," I say, eyes on the floor, voice quiet. I thank her for telling me her stories and for my tea, and when I try to give her back the coat, she insists she bought it for me without knowing she bought it for me.

Jem kisses his mother on the cheek and gives her a hug that makes me a tiny bit jealous, because I think I should quite like it if he were to hug me like that. Or even in any way at all.

Itheelia seals herself in the cave as soon as we're outside it, and the snow's picked up quite a lot.

Jamison stops in front of me and tugs my jacket closed, fastening it, staring at me as he does it.

A part of me feels crushed. I don't know why.

It was a heavy story, I suppose, that involves someone I care a great deal about.

Jem's eyes are zeroed in on me. "Ye okay?" he asks.

I nod without saying anything.

He pulls my hood up over my head, and then he turns, starting to walk down the mountain.

"Are ye going to tell him?" he says, looking back at me.

"That you're related?" I stare over at him like he's mad. "I should think not. Peter is so temporarily focused. He's interested in exclusively shooting the messenger."

Jamison snorts a laugh—or maybe it was a scoff?

"Do you think it's bad to not tell him?" I ask. "Is it dishonest?"

He considers this in an actual way. "Maybe."

"What if he's the heir?" I say quietly.

"He might be." He shrugs. "Is thon why ye like him then?"

I give him a cross look and stop walking. "I didn't know he might have been it until today!"

He pauses. "Then what is it then?"

That question puts me on the spot, and my cheeks go so hot that as soon as the snow hits them, they melt.

"I don't know." Then I say in a stupid voice, "Fate or something?" I think. I roll my eyes like I think it's silly.

Jamison's eyes pinch. "Says who?"

"Everyone." I shrug like it's beyond me. "All my family, all my life—"

Jem's mouth pulls tight as he nods once. "Aye, the Darling girl family legacy o' loving the same boy. That is well fucked."

I cross my arms over my chest defensively. "To be fair to me, he's more of a man-child now."

"Sexy." Hook tosses me a look. He walks down the mountain a bit more, his pace picking up. "Ye could buck it, ye ken?" he calls back, not turning around. "Love someone else."

I stop walking. "You, do you mean?"

"No," he says quickly, and then he stops walking. He turns around. "Maybe."

I stare over at him, my breathing quickening as my mouth falls open a bit. I don't even know what to say. I don't even—I—

I shake my head ever so slightly. "But we're not in the stars."

Jem rolls his eyes, annoyed. "Aye, and who gives a fuck about stars."

I stare over at him again, feeling lost. "Well, they've brought me this far."

"I s'pose they have." He nods coolly. "Ye ken there's more to yer family's story than riding the wind and loving the Pan."

I roll my eyes at him, like he knows what he's talking about. "And what's that then?"

"They all left here broke," he says, and he speaks the truth.

It is the truth, I know it. I can see it in everyone's eyes; they just don't want to talk about it. Some families pass on red hair, some families pass on a cancer gene. Mine—we're generationally brokenhearted.

Jamison catches my eye and holds it to deliver this next part. "But, Bow, you dïnnae have to."

Something akin to a small little hope, like a budded-up rose, begins to bloom in me. "Do you really think that?"

He nods. "I ken y'are fully capable of fucking the stars and forging a new path."

"With you?" I ask softly.

He shrugs a shy shrug as he moves towards me, tugging me in again by the coat. "Would it be so bad?"

I think for a moment that maybe he's going to kiss me, or at the very least, I'll finally get that bloody hug from him, and then before I know it, I'm yanked backwards and away from him.

"Daphne!" Peter yells and hurls me behind him into some snow. He lands on his feet, positioning himself between Jem and me. "Get back! You stay away from her, you filthy pirate!"

Peter's eyes are wild and afraid. I've not seen him afraid before—? This is new.

I jump back to my feet and run over. "Peter, stop!"

Peter shakes his head, eyes locked on his enemy. But me, I'm staring over at Jem, my eyes all wide, already filled with sorry's that I don't know why but I feel sure I'm about to owe him. And then I feel that stupid kite heart of mine blow all the way over into a tree, rattling around, twisting, and getting tangled on itself.

"Girl, stay there," Peter signals me. "He's not safe."

"Peter." I shake my head at him, impatient. "I'm fine!"

"He took you from me." Peter shakes his head, and I shake mine back. "No, he didn't."

Peter turns to face me. "But don't worry. You're safe now."

Jamison's jaw goes tight. "She wusnae unsafe before."

I stare over at Jem, my eyes heavy but not as heavy as his.

Peter draws his favorite new dagger. "Don't you speak to me."

Jamison rolls his eyes at him. "And dïnnae ye wave that wee fucking knife in my face."

"Or what?" Peter asks with high eyebrows.

Without thinking twice, Jamison draws his sword. "Or this."

"Stop!" I yell urgently, shaking my head at him. "Please, Peter." I pull on his arm. "Stop."

And then Peter spins on his heel, grabs my face with both his hands, and kisses me.

It happens so quickly and with such a peculiar force that stretches beyond me. Was it physical? Was it gravity? Was it his hands? I honestly couldn't tell you, only that I don't stop it. I don't even think to stop it till it's already naturally stopped.

A bit because it feels counterintuitive to stop Peter Pan from kissing you, and I wonder if that's maybe his mother's fault. Magically charming, is that what Itheelia said? In this moment, that makes a good deal of sense to me, actually, and over time, I suspect I will dull to what that quietly implies.

When Peter's near me I feel like I forget why sometimes, truthfully, I like it better when he's not.

It's hard to remember things around him at the best of times, but when he's touching you—it's hard for that fog to fully lift.

Then the kiss is over and the fog lifts to a haze, and I see that Jamison's gone.

And here is the terrible thing and the part that frightens me: Was that kiss three seconds? Was it three hours? I couldn't tell you—I have no idea.

I didn't even get the chance to tell Jamison that if I could figure it out, no, I don't think that would be even sort of bad at all.

CHAPTER
TEN

OVER THE NEXT DAY OR SO, PETER REGALES SO MANY PEOPLE SO MANY TIMES with how he saved me from Hook. That I was in danger and Hook was grabbing me, about to kill me or worse, and then Peter came—swooped in, crowing, to save me.

I don't like it when Peter calls him Hook either. He says it like it's a dirty word, and it's not. I'm rather fond of his name.

I'm rather fond of all of him, actually, I think.

Two nighttime's have passed since I saw Jamison last, and every second I've had to myself, I've spent in my mind trying to get back to the moment before Peter came for me as though it's a puzzle that I'm missing a piece to. Was he about to kiss me? I wanted him to so badly.—I didn't even realize how badly until it didn't happen.

And before that, before we went inside the mountain. The air on my face and the snow that fell on our noses—I go over it again and again in my mind because I'm scared it might slip away as all memories do here.

How angry I was with Peter—for what happened with him and Marin and him and Calla—since being around him again, has dissipated how I worried it would.

It began to feel less bad; time can do that—lessen things, make them more bearable, dull the sharpness of truth till it's something you can swallow.

It doesn't hurt me like it did before. I'm not angry like I was; it's all muted now.

And we haven't spoken about it or anything.

In Peter's version of the story where he saved me, he doesn't mention that

I ran away from him. He doesn't mention that he didn't care that I was gone for nearly two days. He doesn't mention that it was a reaction to him kissing other girls. There are facets to the story Peter leaves out entirely, and the more he says it, the more believable it becomes except for the part that floats to the top of my consciousness every single time: when my face and Jem's face were close, and the wind was against us and pushing me towards him, and the snow was dusting us lightly like we were a dessert and it was the icing sugar. It felt like tiny kisses even though they weren't, and I remember how I felt in that moment in the freezing cold freshness. It was the first time since being here that I actually felt free.

So even as everything else around that moment starts to dim, for some reason, that particular thought remains illuminated in my mind.

I've started notching it under the dining room table, every morning that I wake up, to count how many days are passing. Jamison said two days ago it was thirty-one days till my birthday, which means twenty-seven days from now is November 1, which makes today October 3.

I shouldn't like to miss my eighteenth birthday; that's my main incentive for tracking the time here, but then also a part of me feels maybe it's wise to do anyway.

"I turn eighteen soon," I tell Peter, and he looks over at me, eyes wide in horror.

"I'm so sorry."

"Oh." I shake my head, a bit flustered by his response. "No. I—I'm happy to—"

"Eighteen is old," Peter tells me tonelessly.

"You're about eighteen or nineteen," I tell him.

He looks down at himself, bothered by it. "Any older and I'd be gross." He moves over towards me and lowers his voice. "I don't do this for the others. Don't tell them, okay?"

"Okay?" I frown.

"I can bring you the fountain water. You can drink it, and you'll stay seventeen."

I stare over at him. Stay seventeen?

Oh my god.

Something about that sounds nearly like a dream come true—to be young forever?

I stare over at him, frowning a little.

"Don't you want to be young forever?" he asks, grinning down at me. He touches my face.

"Maybe?" I eye him nervously.

He beams at the thought, lifts me up, and spins me around in the air, and we free-fall onto the nets behind us.

We land so he catches me, breaking my fall, then he rolls on top of me, pushing some hair from my face.

"Think of the adventures, girl!" He crows to the ceiling. "Stay seventeen with me," he tells me, eager.

"You mightn't even be seventeen," I remind him gently, rather positive he's definitely not. Seventeen-year-olds don't have shoulders like he does, no matter how much regatta or rugby they play.

Peter ignores me. "Nothing good happens once you're eighteen."

I give him a look. "How do you know?"

He shrugs. "What good things happen when you grow up? You're just old. You have to work, and it's stupid." He shakes his head. "There are responsibilities. You have to look after things and people and—"

"Those aren't bad things, Peter," I tell him a bit sternly.

"I just want to look after you," he tells me and kisses the tip of my nose.

"And I'd be seventeen forever?"

He laughs and shrugs. "Age is just a number. Take the water, and if you keep taking it, you'll be young forever. You'll just always look like you."

I look down at myself.

"I take it every week," he tells me with a shrug. "Sometimes twice."

"Oh." I nod.

Then he sits up. "If I bring you some, will you drink it?"

I frown a little. "Let me think about it."

He makes a sort of *pfft* sound.

"Stupid." He stands up and shrugs. I can't tell if his dismissiveness is from a lack of care or because he's offended. "Be back later."

"Where are you going?" I stare after him.

"I got stuff to do," he says without looking at me.

And then he flies away.

The truth? I wouldn't mind staying young forever, staying how I look right now forever. That might be quite lovely, wouldn't it? To be forever young?

But there's one thing hanging over it in my mind that's reason enough for me not to. He's got eyes like a fire and a hang-up about the number seventeen, and I don't know that something's going to happen when I turn eighteen—maybe nothing at all will—but I don't want to know for certain that nothing could.

I need to speak to him.

I put on my favorite one of the dresses he bought for me—a little red-and-blue tartan dress that sits just above my knees and has a big white Claudine collar.

I don't wear shoes because I only have the boots, and actually, since being here, I've decided I don't much care for footwear anyway.

I think I don't? Is that a me thing or a Peter thing?

He bleeds into your thinking a bit.

After about ten minutes of giving Peter what I think is enough time to have cleared the area, I take off for town. Quick as I can.

It's barely past lunch, the sun is out and bright, and the day feels promising. There's a blueness to the sky that I shouldn't have trusted, and I don't feel a lick of wind.

I make my way towards Jamison's boat, finding a couple of men on it, scrubbing and cleaning.

Orson Calhoun's standing on the bridge, bossing them around and commentating on how well they are (or are not) doing.

I stand there till he sees me, and then I wave uncomfortably.

"Hello," I call to him.

He nods his chin at me, walking down towards me. "You again."

I nod my chin towards Jamison's cabin. "Is he in there?"

Calhoun shakes his head, squinting.

"Oh." I frown. "Do you know where he is?"

Orson nods suspiciously.

"Hey!" says a familiar voice, and I spin around.

"Rye!" I look over at him, surprised.

"Daph!" He smiles, eyebrows up. "There you are!"

"Were you looking for me?" I go over and give him a hug.

"Yeah, of course." He nods. "Just wanted to see how you are."

I pull a curious face. "How did you know I was here?"

"Oh, saw you on your way over."

"Oh." I nod.

"She's looking for Jam," Orson tells him.

Rye rolls his eyes. "Course she is."

"He's at the Dirty Bird," Calhoun tells us both.

Rye pulls a face. "It's two in the afternoon."

Orson shrugs and I look between them, confused.

"What's the Dirty Bird?"

"Have ye ever been so drunk that ye fall asleep under the table at a pub and ye wake up with peanuts on yer face and just one shoe?" Orson offers.

I shake my head, flicking my eyes between them. "No."

Orson shrugs. "Well, that's the Dirty Bird."

Orson leads us there, and on the way, Rye bends down and whispers in my ear, "Are you sure you want to go there?"

I roll my eyes at him. "It's a bar, Rye."

"Here, it's a tavern." He gives me a look. "And it won't be like anything you've been to before." He looks me up and down before he pushes a dark, heavy door open.

He's right.

It's dark, windows all boarded up. It's lit by candles—candles everywhere, actually, the floor, the tables, the wall—and the wax from them is pooling everywhere. Aside from the wax, the floor (I think) is made exclusively of peanut shells. It's filthy. It's the back end of human civilization. This is where the plague started, I'm sure of it. Which plague? Oh, just all of them, probably.

It's all shadows and shady people, women with theater makeup on and men with busy hands.

It's not the kind of place you want to find the person you like to tug on your coat.

I spot him quickly—a bit because he sticks out here, as though there's a spotlight on him, partially because everything here is so ugly and he's so magnanimous, but also because…just because. Your eyes drift in a room, you know? Mine drift to him.

It is worse than I expected. Before I even reach him, I know that to be true. He's with two girls. One of them's Morrigan,* and the other has raven-dark hair. There are empty pints tipped all around them, and the girls are laughing, fawning, touching all over him. And then right as I look over, he claps the arm of the bartender merrily, who hands him a dark-green bottle. Morrigan leans over and bites down on the cork, pulling it out and grinning up at Jamison mischievously.

My mouth goes dry, and I instantly feel a tiny bit sick.

Rye nudges me. "Let's go," he whispers.

I shake my head.

"Daph—" Rye calls for me, but I'm already walking on over. I stand directly in front of Jamison, hands crossed over my chest.

"Wow." I eye him up and down.

Jamison looks over at me, completely unfazed. "Are ye talking to me?"

"Yes." I stare at him, daring.

"Okay." He pushes up from his stool so he's standing. He burps and sways but catches himself. "Care t' expound?"

I squint up at him. "How drunk are you?"

"How"—he gets very close to my face—"is that any o' yer business?"

I sigh. "Jem—"

"Fuck you." He points right in my face, and I shift backward.

"Excuse me?" I gape at him.

"Fuck ye and go," he spits, looking me up and down. "What're ye doing here? Why dae ye keep coming to me?" He lifts his shoulders dismissively and stares me down. "I dinnae want you about. Ye keep fucking everything up."

"We're friends," I say quietly and hold my breath so I don't start crying.

"I dinnae want to be yer friend!" he yells loud enough that the whole tavern goes quiet for a minute.

He glances around, self-conscious for half a second, and then he shakes his

---

* The table girl.

head as he looks at me. His top lip, which I have had a particular fascination with over these last few days—the shape of it, how it curves and is perfectly defined by his facial hair, the color of it, how it sits when he's thinking—it's usually the most splendid thing, and here, now, it's curled up all ugly and spiteful.

He gives me a tight smile. "Ye ken it's easy to forget sometimes when yer with ye, because yer English and ye read books and ye think yer smart—"

"I am smart."

"Yeah, okay, if ye say so." He scoffs, and that one winds me up a bit.

I've always known I'm clever. I've never cared before if people didn't think I was clever because I knew that I was, but him scoffing at that—I feel like an ant.

Jamison waves his hand around my face. "It's all just to distract from what ye really are," he slurs.

I stare at him defiantly. "And what am I?"

He gives a thoughtless shrug. "Yer just a girl."

"Okay?" I frown over at him and shrug back. "I'm a girl, and you're a boy, and what's your poi—"

"No." He cuts me off. "I'm a man."

I roll my eyes. "Okay."

He lifts his eyebrow, catching my eye to deliver this next one. "And I'm interested in actual women." He nods his head towards Morrigan.

I take a couple of breaths to steady myself, and he uses the moment to drink half of that bottle he's holding in one go.

I wouldn't like to cry in front of him, or maybe I wouldn't mind doing it under any other circumstance but this one in particular, with that girl watching on, sneering over at me. I glare back for a few seconds, and Jamison notices, so he turns to her and kisses her for three incredibly smutty seconds, and then he turns back to me, eyebrows up like he's proved his point.

I shake my head at him. "Are you trying to hurt me?"

"Aye." He nods coolly. "Is that no' what yer into?"

"No!" I shove him. "You can't treat me like that! Sometimes Peter hurts me but he's like a kid. He's just selfish; he doesn't know he's doing it. But you're doing it on purpose!"

Jamison steps towards me and gets right in my face. "He daesnae ken he's doing it 'acause unless yer right in front of him, he's never thinking of ye."

"That's not true." I shake my head.

"Aye sure, it is." He nods, glaring at me. "Ye know it is."

"That's just how he is! It's not his fault!"

"O' course it's his fault!" Jamison growls, and it's a proper growl. Like an animal. "He could choose t' be better. He could choose t' evolve. He just won't!" Hook shakes his head. "The fountain daesnae stunt ye emotionally, Daphne. It just means ye dïnnae look older." He shoves his hands through his hair all impatient. "My mum's looked thirty fer about seven hundred years, but she's no' running about behaving like a fecking prat."

I stare over at him, trying to work out if it's true or whether he's just being unkind for the sake of being unkind. It sort of makes sense—? But then, I wouldn't put it past him because I don't really know Jamison all that well. Sometimes it feels like I do, in this stupid, transcendent way, in the way that I had a pathetic, fleeting thought this morning where I wondered if perhaps I'd flown all the way across the universe not to be with Peter but to find Jem, and do you know what? I thought that was a stupid thought at the time when I thought it, and I think it even more so now, because as I look over at him, bleary-eyed and unaware of the woman's hand reaching down his shirt, I realize I don't actually know him. Not at all.

Jamison's head falls to the side, heavy with drink.

"Yer man chooses no' to act like an adult…chooses t' forget ya, chooses to—" He takes a big breath, and somehow it makes it all feel sadder. "Let ye plummet to yer death, leave ye t' drown."

"Stop it," I tell him, my eyes startling to prickle.

Jamison gives me a look. "Aye, but it's true." He throws back the rest of the bottle, finishing it in one go.

"Slow down, maybe, Jam?" Orson suggests.

"Nah." Jamison scrunches his face. "Dïnnae think I will." Then he turns to the other girl with the dark hair and kisses her.

I look away for that one, over my shoulder to Rye, who's standing there, watching me, eyes all big and sorry for me.

He nods his head towards the door, telling me without words that we should leave, but I look back at Jamison, who's still kissing that girl while also aggressively feeling her up.

I clear my throat, and he pulls back from her, looking over at me, annoyed.

"What?" He shrugs. "Just taking a leaf out o' the wee man's playbook." He gives me a shitty smile.

"What are you doing?" I ask loudly and obviously hurt.

"Right now?" Jamison clarifies, eyebrows up. "Right now, a'm doing this, and then in a wee bit, I'm going to take her home"—he points to Morrigan—"take her clothes off—"

"Jem—"

"And fuck 'er in a bath just t' piss you off," he tells me, staring me dead in the eye.

I take a breath, but it's staggered. "Jamison, I didn't come here to fight with you."

"Then what did ye come here fer? Because I dinnae want ye here." He shrugs his shoulders, and he's back to yelling in my face now. He points far away. "I want ye the fuck away from me and fer ye to stay on yer side of the island." He swallows. "Go Rudyard Kipling with the man-cub thonder to yer fucking heart's content, but sure ye stay away from me."

I turn on my heel to leave, and I go quickly. And were I to have the sort of ears that could hear unsaid things, as soon as I'm leaving, I would hear that he regrets it—that it hits him quickly and immediately and feels like a thousand arrows that pierce down to his bones. Regret can do that. So can pride. Right now, Jamison has both, and I am the biggest fool on the planet.

A pirate? I actually thought a pirate and myself...

I don't even know what I thought. I can't think straight. I need to get out of here.

Everything they said, it's true. You can't trust a pirate; they're sneaky and bad, and they get into your head and make you doubt good things, things you've wanted, and maybe you even have them and they're right in front of you, right there for you to have, and you just haven't been paying attention to them because of some stupid pirate with eyes that look like your home planet and because some snow fell on your stupid face—?

I hate Jamison Hook. I completely hate him.

"Daphne," Rye calls as I scurry out of the tavern, definitely not crying, because why would I be crying? Rye reaches over and wipes my face. He looks sorry for me. "Not your week."

I sniff a laugh that sounds a bit like a cry, but to reiterate, I'm definitely not crying.

"Want me to walk you back?" He nods his head to my side of the island.

I nod once, but I can't meet his eyes. "Please."

When I get home, it's getting dark, and I take a few moments to myself, breathe in the cool, damp air, feel the ground beneath my feet, tell myself I am exactly where I'm supposed to be.

This is what I came here for. Peter is who I came here for.

I might have lost sight of that for a second—tricked, let's call it, actually. I was tricked, and it'll be my secret, and I won't think about fires and snow the same way ever again.

I take a big breath to steady myself and wipe away the last dregs of tears that don't belong here anymore when Rune zips in, hovering in front of me.

She chimes.

"I'm fine." I shake my head. "I'm just going to head inside."

She chimes and I stare at her, confused. Then she grabs my hair and pulls it away from the tree house.

"Ow!" I stare at her. "What are you doing? No, it wasn't Peter. No. No, truly, it wasn't. Well, if you must know, it was Jamison."

She chimes again.

"No!" I shake my head at her. "Nothing happened I don't li—" I give her a tight smile. "I—" I breathe out and swallow. I won't keep crying over him. "I can't talk about this, Rune. I—please let me just go inside."

I move past her and walk into the house, and the boys are sitting around the table.

Peter grins up at me happily and walks over, kissing me a lot and more than I deserve, considering things I shall no longer be considering.

"Girl." He smiles. "I was wondering where you were."

"Were you?" I smile, relieved and delighted.

"I have a new boy for us."

I look at him, confused. "What?"

Peter points to a child I've never seen before. "This is…" Peter trails off, trying to remember, and I backflip over and around everything Jamison fucking Hook said about Peter.

"Holden." Kinley smiles, proud of himself for remembering.

He's young. About ten, maybe? Eleven at very best. Really golden hair, big brown eyes. He gives me a hopeful, nervous smile.

"Hi." I smile at him as surely as I can. "Holden, I'm Daphne."

When he doesn't say anything immediately, Percival elbows him.

"I know." He nods a lot. "And you are not my mother."

I flash him an uncertain smile. "Right."

"Nor my girlfriend," he adds.

I nod again. "Also true."

"She is my girlfriend though," Peter announces, and I look over at him, surprised.

"Really?"

"Yeah." He shrugs. "I wouldn't like you to be anyone else's girlfriend, so you have to be mine."

"Okay." I nod, squashing away a smile.

And then I notice something. I look around over my shoulder.

"Where's Brodie?"

"Hm?" Peter asks, shoveling food into his mouth, and Kinley and Percival look over at Peter, waiting.

"Where is Brodie?" I sit on my hands, feeling a little bit concerned.

"Oh." Peter shrugs. "He got lost at sea today."

"What?" I yell.

Peter throws his head back, laughing, but I'm just staring at him, worried.

"I'm joking, Wendy." He grins.

I don't correct him.

"Where is he, Peter?" I ask clearly. "Really."

Peter takes a drink and then has a bite of his bread roll.

"He found his brother." Peter flashes me a quick smile. "And they lived happily ever after."

CHAPTER ELEVEN

THOUGHTS ARE LIKE HELIUM BALLOONS—SOMEONE SAID THAT TO ME ONCE. They drift into your mind, and you can choose to grab the string—hold on to the thought tightly, think of it, dwell on it, mull it over—or you can let it go.

Neverland, in general, is a place where balloons of thought drift by frequently and easily, but were I to be entirely forthcoming, I'd be remiss not to admit that anytime the Jamison balloon drifts into my consciousness, I not only grab it by its string, but sometimes I leap into the air to reach for it and yank it down close to my face so I can look at it properly.

"Peter." I sit down next to him, his brown legs dangling over one of the balcony nets, hands cupped together with a little blue bird sitting in them, staring at it intensely.

"Yes, girl?" he says without looking at me.

"You know that place in the sky where you can go—" I pause, trying to think how to say it without arousing potential suspicion. "The place…with the baggage?"

He nods, still not looking away from the bird, who's staring back at him just as intensely.

"Can you go there anytime?"

"Yes," he says, bored.

"Can I?"

"I suppose," he says indifferently.

"I have some thoughts I should like to put away," I tell him, and he looks over at me curiously, and then the bird makes a little tweet and flies away.

He gives me a frustrated look. "You just made me lose."

"Lose what?" I frown, confused.

"Staring contest," Peter says, wiping his hands on his trousers. "Now she'll tell all her friends that she's better than I am."

I look after the bird and shake my head. "I can't imagine she would do that."

He stares after her too. "She better not," he says, and were the sun not hitting the exact angle of his cheek how it is, lighting him all up like a glorious statue we'd pray to if we're lucky enough to sit at its feet, I feel I may have feared for that small bird. But I don't, because I'm at the statue's feet, and it really is terribly golden. "What thoughts?" Peter asks, squinting at me in the sun.

"Terrible ones I shouldn't like to bore you with," I tell him politely.

"Are they about blood and guts?"

"Nothing so thrilling." I give him a quick smile. "Just grown-up things."

He pulls a revolted face.* "Yeah, let's get rid of those then."

"Please." I nod, eager, and he offers me his hand. He can be sweet, I tell myself. Beg myself, actually, to remember that. "I'm desperate to."

He pulls me to my feet and watches me with a curious face. Mindlessly, he pushes some hair behind my ear. "I'll protect you from grown-up things."

I swallow as I let myself be swallowed by his eyes.

"Thank you," I tell him quietly as he takes my hand and floats me into the air.

That is a lovely feeling, the floating with him, up and high and away; it feels in these moments how I imagine it's always meant to when you're here. When you aren't bogged down with thoughts about where a certain Lost Boy might be or whether that bird will really be okay in the end or pirates with warm hands and bad intentions.

Peter drops me to the shack in the sky and tells me he'll be back soon—that he'd heard of a star coming loose in the sky and he has to go and convince it to tighten up.

I walk over to baggage claim a bit gingerly and flash the old man a smile—John, was it? He stands, setting down his fishing rod.

"Was wondering when I'd see you again."

I nod at his bucket. "Do you ever catch anything up here?"

---

* I knew that would put him off.

"Flying fish, mostly." He shrugs. "Sometimes a meteor."

"Oh." I nod, impressed even though I don't sound it.

"Dropping off some thoughts?" He nods his head towards the shack.

"Yes please."

"You've been here awhile." He gives me a look.

"Have I?" I ask, genuinely curious.

He nods a bit. "A couple of months."

"Right." I frown, thinking back, trying to puzzle out where all the time went.

"Have you enjoyed it?" he asks pleasantly, and I wish it didn't roll over my face, the briefest of pauses, but it does.

Have I enjoyed it? Maybe? Time's flown, and they do say that about fun. I suppose I just always imagined Neverland to be a wistful, mindless experience with long days and warm nights and swashbuckling adventures with an adoring, me-focused Peter Pan, but so far, it's been a rather heady, multi-seasonal marathon of the heart where Peter adores everyone with breasts, and until (I think, possibly) yesterday (was it?), my attention was the tiniest bit divided between him and the other one.

But still, I answer with, "Yes. Very much so."

He gives me a small smile, but I feel as though he mightn't believe me all the way. I don't think that bothers me though, because I don't know if I believe me all the way either.

I stare over at him, and while I don't mean to, I do find myself frowning at him.

"You do really look ever so familiar," I tell him.

He gives me a fond smile and a shrug. "One of those faces."

I nod and point to the door as I step towards it, then I spin on my heel, hands behind my back.

"No one can see these, can they?"

"Just me," he says, and I must look affronted because he quickly adds, "When I take them out to polish them."

"Oh." I purse my lips, thinking about anyone but me seeing what I put in there.

"You have to polish your thoughts. Otherwise, they get messy."

"Of course." I nod as though I knew that already.

"It's a sacred honor. I don't take it lightly." His eyebrows lift. "I don't pry or judge. Just polish."

I reach for the door handle, then pause again, looking back. "Do many people bring their thoughts up here?"

He nods and I nod back, working my way around to what I'm really asking. "Lots of people?"

"Yes." He scratches his neck, waiting for me to just spit it out.

"Pirates, even?"

He nods again. "Yes."

I purse my lips, thinking. "And if he wanted to, could he—I mean, they!" I clear my throat and flash him a quick smile. "Could they—or anyone, really, if they wanted to—could they ransack my thoughts? Or someone else's?" I add at the end as though the caveat makes it less obvious.

He sniffs an amused little laugh. "They'd have to get past me first."

I give him a smile that feels a bit like a grimace.

"I'm so sorry if this comes off rudely, but I worry that that mightn't the feat you might imagine it to be,"

And then erupts from him a hearty chuckle. "I'm stronger than I look."

I breathe out apologetically. "Well, sir, you'd have to be."

John keeps laughing as he sits back down in his little chair in the clouds; he waves at the door. "You go on in now."

When I step in, it doesn't take me long to notice this time that the baggage is alphabetized. Surname first, then given name. Many names I don't recognize, but some I do.

Beaumont, Alfred.[*] Darling, John. Darling, Michael. Darling, Wendy. Hook, James. Hook, Jamison. And my eyes snag on a bag on one of Jem's shelves—he has many. Not as many as Peter, mind you, but there's this one particular bag, and it's beautiful. Quilted leather, gold chain, white—I won't go around naming names, but the bag's a brand that we've all heard of, and I have the strangest but most distinct impression that actually, that bag is mine. Or rather, that bag is his baggage of me.

---

[*] I didn't know till this moment that my grandfather had visited Neverland.

It's a good bit smaller than I'd have hoped—that's disheartening—but honestly, the bag is lovely still all the same.

I think about it—about picking it up, peeking inside. I could do it. No one would know. And then I think of him looking at the thoughts I'm about to put away and decide that being in this room is a trust system and one I must honor.

I stand in front of the great mirror and find myself more weighed down than I realized.

I should explain how the baggage system works, I suppose. Because now that I've been here a minute, it's easy enough to understand.

When you check in a piece of baggage, you mustn't think it's gone forever nor that it no longer has any bearing to you.

Imagine this: You're carrying around a disastrously heavy duffel bag, you wear it on your shoulder, and it weighs enough that it makes you walk funny while you're holding it.

But then you put it down. The bag is still there. Even if you were to leave the room, even if you were to leave the house, the bag is still there. And of course, you could think of the duffel bag at any given moment, think of how you felt when you held it, how heavy it was, why it was heavy, what was inside it—but it's so much easier to not think about the bag when you don't have to hold it. And as time goes on, the harder it becomes to remember the contents of a bag. If you check a bag every day, it's quite easy to remember what you're carrying around in it, but if you put it away, it sort of fades away into a blurry memory of a thousand things that could be crammed into a bag.

The thoughts I put away when I arrived, I don't not ever think of them; they're just a balloon floating by with a string I don't grab. What my mother is doing in El Salvador or Honduras or wherever she is*—it's balloon with a string so high up in the sky, I'd have to climb something tall to remember it.†

You pick up so much from just living, I think. Some of the bags are draped

---

* Much to my own point, I honestly can't remember.

† Or be reminded with something horribly abrupt. Rye tells me that can happen too. For better and for worse. He told me a story about a missing man from his village, and his wife was so distressed for so many years that she eventually put the memory of him away so it wouldn't haunt her all the time, and after many years, he finally returned, and it all came hurtling back. He said she went crazy, that she left the village (and him) soon after.

over me, backpacks and handbags and shoulder bags—all things that are relatively easy to shrug off, which I do. There are some in my hands though, and I'm holding on to them tightly.

My mother. Where Brodie is. Why do we take medicine every day? Is there really something in the water? Did that fish die? Is that bird okay? Jamison's face when he saved me and I was drowning—that pops into my mind once an hour easily. How his brows dipped with what I thought was concern but maybe now I'll conclude to be just a nosy curiosity. His eyes falling down my body that day when he fished me out of the water and I wondered if I'd ever felt so seen. What Itheelia meant when she looked at our palms and made that "hmm" sound. That's the first one I put down today, and as soon as I drop it, it feels stupid to have held on to all this time. Nothing—she meant nothing by it.

Why Rune doesn't like Peter—I let go of that next. Now, I've said before that it's slander what they say about fairies and how because they're small, they can only feel one thing at a time—that's a lie—but it is true is that they can hold a grudge, and Rune has one against Peter. It's not a big deal is what I think the second I lay it down. People don't always get along. It doesn't mean anything and certainly doesn't mean anything sinister.

I cannot put down fast enough the thought about Peter and Jamison being related. Glad to be rid of it, but I've found that one difficult to drop on my own. Cousins—first cousins? Peter would find betrayal in the mere fact of it, but for me to know it and not to have told him—that's a different sort of betrayal, I suppose. I don't know why it feels like putting down this thought will make it less true, but that's how it feels, so I brush my hands clean of it.

Then there's Peter and the mermaid. I've held on tightly to that since it happened—pored over it, studied where he touched her body versus mine—and I'll be relieved to not have to think of it anymore. Though I do wonder briefly, for a moment, if it's something that I should think about, that maybe, as far as concerns go, it's a valid one—? It seems as though there's a tiny bit of sense in that thinking, but I don't want sense; you don't come here for sense, do you? So I let it go, watch that shell-shaped clutch purse clatter to the ground and bounce around my ankles, and I feel so light all of a sudden, so quietly reassured of Peter's affections for me, I have no idea why it's taken me this long to lay all this down.

I laugh at the silliness of myself because a kiss is a kiss, do you know what I mean? And quietly, I know in myself, that were the other to have tried to kiss me any moment up until now, I'd have let him. But I don't want to let him anymore, even though I maybe do.

Which leads me to by far the prettiest bag I'm holding. It's all sterling silver, solid. More of a clutch than a bag, I suppose. The front is covered in repoussé flowers, and the back of the case has something engraved on it that I dare not read. It all hangs on a silver chain link I'm gripping too tightly, and I know without opening it that it's his hands on me, how he tugged his jacket tight around me. I would bask in this moment all the time, lie under it like it's a sun I'm bathing in, but I know now that having feelings for a pirate isn't a good idea. He isn't who I thought he was, and I'm not what he wants, so I drop it. I hate how it feels on the way down—the letting go feels more like a ripping—but once it hits the ground, the great weight lifts from me, the one where I was worried that I was starting to love him.

What a silly thought! I can be so stupid sometimes. Peter's right.

There's just one bag left in my hand now. It's the one I'm holding on to tightest. Small, leather. A pouch. The kind that looks unassuming but might have jewels in it or gold.

I peek inside it, not because I don't know what's inside but because I do.

The snow on our noses when we almost kissed and the breeze that felt like more than a breeze. I close my eyes, let myself remember it one last time before I pack it away forever—breathe it in, smell the crispness of the air, remember how he smells like leather and rum and tobacco and promises and fa—

No. I shake my head at myself. It doesn't smell like that. It can't. It couldn't. He couldn't. Even though a small voice inside me somewhere (who sounds older and wiser than I) tells me that I shouldn't, I use my free hand to pry the pouch from my other one. It clatters and falls heavily, and I instantly want to pick it back up, but I fight the urge and kick it away instead.

And then, right as I'm about to leave, I spot it. Under a pile of the shoulder bags. A backpack. Ugly, cheap, scratchy material. It must have fallen off by itself. I didn't want to remember it, but in light of it all, I feel I perhaps should—remember him how he deserves to be remembered…how he wants me to remember him. So I pick it up and put it back on. Make myself remember Hook in that bar, with those girls, his hands as eager as his mouth to tell me stay away from him, nothing about his words softened now by any of the lovelier things I'd clung to before. I stare at myself in the mirror. From the side, the leather pouch calls to me, and I ignore it, then I clip the backpack around my chest and walk away.

I squint up in the light of about eight suns when I walk out.

Peter frowns at me. "Took long enough."

I flash him a light smile. "Just being spectacularly thorough."

Peter bats those dangerously green eyes at me. "You are spectacular, girl. Come." He takes my hand. "There's a place I want to show you."

"Where is it?"

"Somewhere." He shrugs.

"What is it?"

He leans in close to me and says with a smile, "It's where all the big things come from."

Then he grabs me by the waist and tosses me into the air, grinning as he zooms after me, takes my hand, and pulls me higher, higher into the sky.

I stare over at him with a fresh kind of fondness. It's easier now. Now that the bags I was holding are hidden away and also now that we're up in the sky. Peter Pan is something else in the sky. He ripples his finger through the air like water, dives through clouds like a dolphin, all the while being lit up from behind like a Greek god of sorts.

He beams at me. "Never taken anyone else here before."

"Never!" I'm delighted. "Not even Calla?"

He pauses to think.

"Maybe her," he says, then shrugs and keeps flying. "But I made her close her eyes." I purse my lips, fractionally less thrilled till he zips over to me, nose to nose. "But you get to keep your eyes open."

I roll them. "How lucky."

He smooshes his nose into mine and gives me a smile, and I get butterflies so big they could fly me into a whole different sky, but then Peter grabs my hand and starts bringing me down.

"Almost there." He looks back at me. "You're going to love it, Wendy."

That stings for a second, but then I spot something from afar that I cannot possibly be seeing.

I stop dead in the tracks of the sky.

I squint. "Is that—"

Peter hovers in front of me, hands on his hips, proud and tall like he built this place himself.

"A dinosaur," he announces, then he grabs my hand, flying us down towards it.

A brontosaurus, to be exact. Blue. On the greenest grass I've ever seen, that's covered in—

I look at Peter.

"Are those mushrooms?"

He holds both my hands as our feet touch the ground.

"Giant ones." He nods.

I look around us. Flowers as tall as trees. Trees as tall as skyscrapers. Eagles overhead the size of a light aircraft.

"Is everything giant here?" I ask him as a lady beetle the size of a cat crawls by us.

Peter gives me a big grin. "Welcome to La Vie En Grande."

"This place is amazing," I tell him as I stare up at the sky. He's lying next to me; we're on a huge lily pad, the size of a pontoon.

"Do you think?" Peter asks, rolling onto his stomach, looking down at me.

I give him a look. "Are you crazy?"

Underneath us swim koi fish the size of orcas and blue whales their regular size, because Peter said the ones on Earth are the giant kind; they just escaped one day to our world, and we shouldn't like them to be any bigger or else who knows what might happen.

"I love it," I tell him sincerely.

And then all the fish beneath us scatter, and a shadow spreads in the water about the size of a lorry.

"Peter," I say as I sit up slowly, tucking my legs under myself. "Something's here."

He looks around, unaffected. "Oh!" He sits up. "That's just my kraken."

I stare over at him. "Your what?"

He shrugs, dangling his feet in the water. "My kraken," he says, looking back over his shoulder at me before he slips into the water, and I let out a little scream as I scramble after him.

"Peter!" I call for him, reaching into the water. Nothing for a long few seconds, then he pops up on the other side of the lily pad, elbows resting up on it.

"I'd stay away from the edge if I were you." He gives me a look. "The kraken likes me, but he doesn't like you."

I scurry back into the center, and Peter lets out a little laugh as he climbs back onto the leaf, lying back down on his stomach, warm under the sun.

He has a beautiful back. So brown, so broad, sprinkled freckles on it from all the suns here, a gift of a tiny constellation all mapped out on him.

I lie down on my side and blink over at him.

He watches me. He smiles a small bit before he rolls on his side, head resting in his hand.

And then he leans in towards me, eyes dashingly sure, and his mouth falls open as his eyes drop to my mouth. We're close enough now that I can feel his breath on me, and it feels heavy. It hits me like that tired wave you get late at night to carry you off to the place where the dream lives. It makes me dizzy. Peter is like that though; he's a free fall. Being with him can be scary and uncomfortable, but god, the view on the way down, the rush you get when he remembers you—it's intoxicating.

And there are worse things than being forgotten accidentally.

Say, someone choosing to forget you, someone choosing to hurt you because you accidentally hurt them? That's worse. Peter isn't the villain. He might be occasionally misguided, and he might need a little bit of refining—he is inarguably in dire need of a mother—but he isn't the villain.

He brushes his mouth over mine, lightly at first—it feels like butterfly wings and nervous feet—and then he rolls on top of me, kisses me heavily, and it spreads through me like flooding water. I feel it in every part of me. He's like a dip in the ocean. You know when you're in the water and you're fully immersed, and you walk into a cold spot and you feel it everywhere, and it's fresh and it makes you feel alive and startles you all at once?

That's what it feels like to kiss him. Like that and a rip. Like with him on my body like this, it feels as though I'm being pulled by a current, far out to sea. The sea is impossibly blue and the sky is unimaginably clear, and I am incredibly alone in the ocean besides him.

It's him and me in the cold patch in the deep, and I think it's good that kissing him feels like a cold patch in the ocean, don't you? Because it's refreshing. That's a good thing. Refreshing is good. Not everything needs to feel warm and like a fire, and besides, fires can really hurt you if you get too close to one, can't they? I got too close to one before, I think. Did I? Was I too close, or was I not close enough? What am I thinking of him for anyway? I don't want to think of the pirate now.

I want to think about Peter and where his fingers are running along my body. I want his fingers on my body like this, don't I? It's lovely to be wanted, don't you think? It's a great way to feel alive, which I am, and I'm increasingly aware of what it means to be human: how good it feels to be seen and touched and how sweet it is to be gazed upon by the eyes of a boy who likes you, to have your shoulders kissed by seven suns but also kissed with the strange and quiet awareness of mortality… That I'm here and I'm breathing and there's air in my lungs, and I'm with Peter and I've waited so long for his attention to just be on me and me alone, and finally it is—his attention and his eyes and his hands. Are his hands on my throat? I don't think they are. Maybe, are they though? I don't open my eyes just in case, because I love being here, I think, and I love being with him, and it's where I'm meant to be, right here, all alone with him.

And then it scurries through my mind—this quick, terrible thought that I don't want in there, like a mouse scurrying through the house in the middle of the night with the lights off—because it is just him and I alone in the middle of the sea that this great and tremendous kiss has pulled us out into, and the kiss is just that—it is great, I promise, it's great; I can feel it in my fingers and crawling up my spine, which is great—and I wonder, quietly, maybe, just for a second, whether he might drown me, and then my eyes spring open.

I sit up a little bit on the lily pad, breathless, face flushed.

"What?" He props himself up, frowning a bit.

"Nothing." I shake my head, flashing him a smile that the pirate would never buy. "I just lost my breath."

He nods. "I do that to girls."

I stare past him at the sky, let that comment slip off me like silk on skin, but it lands less lovely than that sounds.

"Girl," he says, staring at me very intently.

I look over at him, waiting.

"Is there more?"

I frown at him a little, curiously mostly. "What do you mean?"

"To this." He nods at me, glancing at his hand on my waist. "I feel like there's more to do than just this, what we keep doing."

"I mean, yes." I scratch my neck. "Technically," I add as an afterthought.

Peter perks up quite a bit. "More to kissing than kissing?"

"Well, yes." I frown. "But then it becomes—do you remember when we spoke about sex?"

"Of course I do," he says unconvincingly.

"Right, then do you remember what sex is?"

He scowls at me, face darkening even though he's sitting in a sunbeam. "Course I remember. But remind me so I know you know too."

I shake my head politely. "Actually, I would rather not if I don't need to."

"You need to," he tells me without skipping a beat.

I sit up, tuck my feet under me, and hug my knees, then I give him a look. It's gently reprimanding, softened both by how my frustration towards him dissipates when he blinks at me as well as by the giant poppies and tulips on the edge of the bank that hang over us like willows.

Peter moves in towards me, one of his eyebrows up. He touches my face. "You could show me?"

I breathe in. It takes me off guard. Why has this taken me off guard?

"Show me," he tells me, his hand on my leg now. It's casually demanding. It's not a threat, more an expectation.

I shake my head at him. "I'm not ready to show you."

He takes his hand back and rolls his eyes. "Do you not know how?"

"I do know how, but I'm not—" I shake my head. "I don't want to."

He stands up, proud and annoyed. "Why don't you want to show me?"

And his name flashes through my mind like a burn.

Jem.

It shouldn't though. So I grab a cold compress and smother it away.

I stand so we're toe-to-toe. He has two freckles on his chest, on his right pectoral muscle, and when I put my head on his chest, they align perfectly with my chin and my nose, and sometimes I think it's a sign. If I was looking for a sign, that might be one.

But my head isn't on his chest, and I stare up at him with big eyes that feel small.

"Because I've never done it before," I tell him, and then he laughs, and for some reason, it sounds mean.

"So you don't know then."

"Well, I suppose I don't." I give a small shrug.

Peter tilts his head, not letting go of my eyes. "Then how do you know you don't want to?"

I stand up straighter and say to him rather clearly, "Because I know I don't want to."

He reaches for me, slips his hand around my waist how I always want him to, but in this very moment, I don't want him to, and I don't like it.

He tilts his head the other way. "But how would you know?"

"Because I know!" I say quickly and hotter than I mean to. "I've never been punched in the face before, and I know I don't want to be."

He rolls his eyes, a smirk on his mouth now. "We aren't talking about punches, girl."

He's right. We aren't. We're talking about you shoving cake down my throat, forcing me to swallow it.

I stare up at him, breathing in and out to counts of four so I don't look as upset as I feel. He doesn't like it when people are upset.

Peter watches my face, looking for a crack in the door of my resolve, but it's all sealed shut with nerves and a faraway memory of some snow dancing on my cheek or something.

"You really don't want to find out about the more?" Peter presses.

I shake my head. "No."

"One day?"

"Maybe." I shrug.

"With me?" he says.

I say nothing, and till I die, I will swear that no other name sailed through my mind.

Peter eyes me. "I wouldn't like you to find out with anyone else…"

I nod. "Okay."

"I would kill them," he says with a perfectly straight face.

I breathe in and out to the count of four before I give him an easy smile. "You're being hyperbolic, of course."

He shrugs as he looks away. "Of course."

I stare at my hands for a couple of seconds, out of things to say.

Peter ducks down so our eyes have to catch. "Are you sure you're not the smallest bit curious about this now, here with me?"

"Peter," I sigh.

He shakes his head, tired. "If I bought Calla here, she would wonder with me."

"I'm sure she would." I cross my arms and turn my head away from him to let him know I'm a tiny bit piqued, and then I glare at him from the corner of my eye. "But you're not seeing her anymore, you said."

"Hm." Peter frowns. "Did I say that?"

"Yes."

"I remember saying it, obviously." He flicks his eyes, and I breathe out my nose loud enough for him to hear, and it's too much emotion for him. "Let's go then," he says, wiping his hands on his pants.

"We could stay?" I offer, stepping towards him. "Walk under the giant flowers again?"

"No." He shakes his head. "They don't have what I was looking for here."

Those words hit me like a smack in the face,

It's by the wrist, not my hand, when he takes me, pulling me into the air, and then he flies ahead. Hard to keep up with. He only looks back a few times on the way back. He talks to the stars, not to me. About halfway home, I think he forgets why exactly it was he's angry at me and instead becomes vaguely indignant.

En route, he stops at baggage again, drops something off, and then I go in again after him and drop off the parts of the day I shouldn't like to remember.

CHAPTER TWELVE

THE MORNING OF MY BIRTHDAY, I DON'T INITIALLY REMEMBER IT'S THE DAY that it is until I feel the notches I've been making under the table and do the maths in my head.

I'd hoped he'd remember, see? All my birthdays till I was twelve were incredibly celebrated, and then every year after my twelfth marked another year where the boy in the window hadn't come back. I'd watched my birthdays wear away my grandmothers' hopes, watched me getting older as my age frightened them into wondering what happened to the boy they love(d) so very much. So I have mixed feelings about birthdays as it is. Around age fourteen, I started taking myself out on my birthday. I'd tell Wendy and Mary I had something I had to do for school, and then I'd make my own way to someplace I wanted to go.

Last year, I took myself to the white cliffs of Dover. That took some planning and lying and roping in Charlotte and her older cousin* to drive us there, but it was worth it not to see the worried looks on my grandmothers' faces all day.

They never meant to say it. They didn't say it actually. It was always tacit, never aloud, but their faces told me that getting older was a terrible thing, and it was never a conviction I've shared. Still don't, I don't think.

I did love that day too. My friends humored me the entire day, prattling on about the formation of the cliffs, how between one hundred and sixty-six million years ago, Great Britain and really most of Europe

---

* Oliver was his name.

was actually submerged under the sea, and this sea's floor was covered in this white mud that was made from the skeletons of this very, very small algae called a coccolith, which combined with the microscopic remains of other bottom-dwelling creatures to create this white, muddy sediment. It wasn't until the Cenozoic era during the Alpine orogeny that it was raised above sea level.

We stayed out the whole day, and when I got home, they were sitting around our dining room table with a cake and candles, and I felt guilty for not spending the day with them, but I wasn't even two bites into my birthday cake when Mary's face twisted like something was hurting her. She looked at me.

"Where is he?" The question—even then, even before I knew him—was asked with such a genuine agony.

All I could do was shrug.

"Did something happen to him?" she asked Wendy, both their faces old by then yet still rimmed with an old pain they had each acquired in their youth.

Nothing happened to him, so it would turn out.

He forgets what he wants to forget, remembers what he wants to remember. I think I believe that to be true now. I might drop that revelation off up in the sky later.

Peter walks into the dining area about ten minutes after me, his face tired from a heavy sleep. He sleeps through everything; I sleep through nothing. Every sound, every creak, every time he moves in the bed,[†] [‡] my eyes spring open. Never his. Not a care in the world. He sleeps so loudly too, sometimes it keeps me awake. I've tried sleeping elsewhere around the place, but there are no spare blankets, and now I'm used to the sound he makes, his loud breathing that isn't quite committed enough to be a snore but certainly not soft enough to be able to ignore either. I always end up wandering back to him.

"Where'd you go?" he asks me, sleepy every time.

---

† Which, I'll remind you, is actually a nest.

‡ Also, can you please imagine with me how kicky a sleeper Peter Pan is? The most effervescent boy in the world.

"Nowhere," I always say as I cuddle into him but still feel cold anyway.

"Morning." Peter grabs the top of my head and kisses it gruffly, sitting down next to me, arm slung around my shoulders.

He bangs the table twice—a demanding thing he does that I don't care for—and then a plate appears in front of him, and an orange squeezes itself into a goblet.

Brownie magic is very strong, Rye told me; it's not to be trifled with. But I suspect Peter trifles with it often all the same.

"Thank you!" I call out to the brownie for good measure, and Peter rolls his eyes.

Peter starts eating his breakfast—three different kinds of eggs and a lot of bacon.

"Do you know what day it is?" I ask him pleasantly.

He ducks his head a bit to peer out the window. "A sunny one."

"Yes." I nod once and lift my eyebrows. "And?"

"And—" Peter looks out the window again before glancing at me with a confusion he masks with annoyance. "Breezy?"

"Sure." I offer him a little smile. "Also, it's my birthday."

His face falters. This displeases him. "Oh."

I shift a little next to him.

"How old are you?" he asks, looking at me out of the corner of his eye.

"Eighteen," I say, and I sort of hate myself for it, but I swallow as though I'm nervous about it.

He pulls a face I don't know if I'm supposed to see or not. "Kind of old."

I cross my arms. "Still younger than you."

He shrugs. "Barely."

"You're at least three hundred years ol—" I start to say just to spite him, but he clamps his hand tight over my mouth to stop me from talking, and if I were in the business of being completely honest with myself,* I'd quietly have to admit that, actually, it hurt.

"Don't you say that around here," he says in a low, serious voice, eyes pinched.

---

* I'm not.

I nod as quick as I can—remind myself never to say that again, make sure he can see on my face that I won't—and I tell myself I'm not nervous. I'm not. Why would I be?

He moves his arm from around me, bites down on his thumbnail. "Did the boys take their medicine?" he asks.

I nod.

"Did you?"

I nod. "Mm-hmm."

"Good." He picks up a blueberry, eyeing it closely before squishing it between his fingers for no reason I can tell.

I clear my throat. "Do you have any plans today?" I ask, trying not to sound too hopeful.

He looks over at me, nods as he sucks something from his teeth with his tongue.

"Oh?" I inquire, eyebrows up.

"Marin told me about a shipwreck by the Mistica Cornucopia." He shrugs. "She's going to show it to me. Probably find some treasure or something amazing like that."

"Oh." I nod once. "Is that all?"

"I don't know." He shrugs again. "Maybe kill a pirate or something—if there are any leftover ones that survived the wreck."

I frown, and he doesn't notice.[†] He moves towards the door and then pauses, looking back at me.

"Oh." He shakes his head. "You said it was your birthday."

My balled-up paper bag face uncrunches a bit. "Yes."

He nods. "Do you want me to bring you some water from the fountain of youth so you don't get any older than now?"

My face falters. I shake my head a tiny bit. "No," is all I say quietly.

Peter shrugs. "Your funeral."

And then he leaves.

I give him about a half hour to see if he comes back, changes his mind. He doesn't. He never would.

---

† Or if he does, he cares not.

I go upstairs to find my boots because I know what I'm going to do today anyway. I'm going to do what I always do. When I finally find the fortitude to grow up and can figure out how to leave this beautiful, awful place,* I do still want to be a geologist. The volcano will feel like an old friend to me at this point.

Upstairs by the little shelf I built for myself with branches where I keep the few belongings I have here, I find a pair of sandals with straps made of crawling vines and a parcel wrapped in a bow made of flowers. I tug it open, and the flowers and fairy dust fall to the side as I pick up the most beautiful, magical dress. White, tied at the waist with rope, flowers growing up it and making almost a cloak at the back.

I look around the room for Rune to thank her, but she's gone. I wonder if she heard what Peter said to me—? For a moment, I feel embarrassed, but then I suspect she already knows about his ways.

I head down to the water's edge in my new dress. I don't want to take the long way; I have places to be. I just don't quite know how to get there. A quick stop into town for a map, and I should be on my way.

There's a rowboat tied to the dock by the tree house. Peter doesn't use it, but sometimes I see the other boys take it out fishing.

I slip into the boat, row it over the harbor to the town. I'm about to heave the boat onto the shore, but luckily the tide washes it up for me, which was helpful. Everything around here's awfully helpful if you're a friend of Peter. I shouldn't like to find out how they treat you if you aren't his friend.

I wander into the town center, and I don't really know where I'm going. I don't know where I go to find a map of the island. That woman who made me clothes seems like as good a place to start as any.

I loosely know the way to her shop, so I make my way there, being sure to keep my head down as much as possible. I don't make eye contact with anyone. He doesn't want me here, that's what Jamison said, and in case he is actually the mayor of pirates,† I shouldn't like to walk a plank for defying him.

I didn't come here to see him, by the way, even if a small part of me hopes that I might. What part of myself would I have to let go of for that to stop

---

* That I love increasingly more and more each passing day, even if I also sometimes hate it.

† Or something.

living inside me? I wonder. I think back to when I last saw him—I don't know how much time has passed. Weeks maybe, could be days? Fifteen of them if I remembered the notches, but I don't in this very moment. Instead, I dwell intensely on his hands on those other girls and how he told me to stay away from him. I will. I plan to.

The only thing is, I'm not overly paying attention to my surroundings. Finding my way to a shop I've only been to once while staring at the ground is problematic on a purely navigational level, and that's not yet even touching on the complexities!

Right as I glance up, ready to acknowledge that I am a little bit lost in this little town square, it's then that I walk—bang!—right into someone.

"What are ye doing here?" Hook asks, frowning at me.

I cross my arms over my chest, suddenly self-conscious of the dress I'm wearing. I'm wearing it for me, not him.[‡] [§]

"I'm just collecting something. I know you said to stay on that side of the island, but I just—"

He shakes his head. "I shudnae hae said that."

That disarms me for a bit, but just for a second. I straighten up again. "But you did."

He shrugs. "Aye, but I didnae mean it."

I step around him as though I know where I'm going. "Do you make a habit of saying things you don't mean?"

He walks after me. "It's a habit a'm trying t'break."

I turn around to face him, and my eyes pinch.

"Why are ye here?" he asks, gentler.

"I told you." I look past him like I have some other place to be. I do, actually. "I needed something."

He nods. "Where's the wee man?"

"I don't know." I shrug mindlessly. "Off somewhere."

His face falters. "It's November first."

[‡] Mostly for me.

[§] A bit for him in the imaginary hope that we would bump into one another, but not in the actual reality of us really bumping into one another, where he then frowns at me.

"I know," I tell him, rather dignified.

He waits a few seconds, lifts an eyebrow. "It's yer birthday."

I don't know why, but my face falls to a pout. "How do you know that?"

He cocks an eyebrow. "'Acause ye told me and I'm no' a piece o' shit."

I say nothing, because what could I even say?

"Is this what yer doing fer yer birthday?" Jamison looks around a bit confused. "Daphne, where's Peter?" he asks, looking up in the sky for a second as though he might be circling us from above. He then looks back at me, and I suppose my face gives away that I have absolutely no idea.

Hook angles his jaw and gives me a look. "Yer joking me."

I sigh and look away, fold my arms over my chest.

Jamison nods his chin at me. "What do ye need?"

"A map."

He nods. "To where?

"Mount Carnealian."

"Yer going t' the volcano?" he asks, an eyebrow up.

I nod.

"By yerself?"

I nod again, nose in the air this time.

Jamison scratches his chin. "Aye, I've got a map. Come on." He nods his head in the direction of his ship.

I follow him wordlessly. He weaves through people, me weaving after him. I don't mind the feeling of it, me following him instead of him following me. For a moment, I catch myself thinking he might be someone worthy of following, but I look to my hand, feel the memory I'm holding that I can't see: "Take her clothes off. Fuck her in a bath."

Just because someone's giving you a map doesn't mean they're good all of a sudden. It might just mean they want you off their part of the island and handing you a map is the fastest way to do so.

I follow him into the cabin of his ship. He starts rummaging around, pulling things from drawers, tossing them on his bed. He's talking to himself. Everything he's looking at looks nothing like a map.

"Come on then." I put my hands on my hips. "What are you doing? Where's this map of yours?"

Jamison looks over at me, flashes me a curt smile. "Yer looking at it."

"What?" I frown.

He points to himself.

My head pulls back. "You?"

He nods. "As I live and breathe."

My eyes pinch. "You hate me."

Another nod. "I dïnnae."

I fold my arms over my chest. "I annoy you."

"Aye," he nods. "Very much so."

I shake my head at him. "You don't have to do this."

He stares over at me for a few seconds, then turns away. "I ken I dïnnae hae to." He starts putting the things on his bed into a rucksack and says without looking at me, "I want to."

"Are you sure?" I stare over at him, nervous.

He looks back at me and doesn't speak for a moment or three. "Aye."

"Okay."

He ties his pack, then walks over to me and maybe stands closer to me than he needs to. "It's about a day's hike there and back."

I feel dizzy being close to him again. Stupid girl. I swallow. Nod. "Okay."

His eyes flicker over my face. "If it goes dark, we'll hae t' set up camp—stay the night."

Please god, let it go dark, I think to myself, but instead, I just say, "Okay."

He tilts his head. "The wee man winnae mind?"

I give him a grim smile. "It's ever so likely that the wee man won't even notice."

He runs his tongue over his teeth and nods once. "Let's go then."

We walk out to the edge of town, mostly in silence. I don't mind silences with Jamison though. And maybe we're better if we don't talk? I walk on his left-hand side, a few steps behind him, and I could pretend that it's by chance but it's not, it's on purpose. Jamison Hook is spectacular from every angle you'd turn him in, but the most striking one of all is his profile. It highlights all his edges, and of those, there are many—I believe I saw a couple new ones at the Dirty Bird—but this angle in particular, his left side, sun facing—his features are so sharp. It is worth noting though, there's a gentleness to him that I don't think he wants me to see, that I don't want me to see anymore either, I don't think.* That's why I put those thoughts down.

He looks back at me and smirks a tiny bit. "That's a grand hiking dress ye've got there."

I give him a look. "Rune gave it to me. For my birthday."

"Very athletic," he tells me wryly, and I push past him grumpily.

He chuckles to himself, jogs a few steps so we're walking side by side, and he clocks my top lip.

"He dïdnae get it."

I frown, confused. "Get what?"

On his own mouth, he points to the part of my lips where my kiss lives. I feel for it, touch it, swallow, relieved.

"No, he didn't."

Jamison gives me a single nod, and a smile I think he wouldn't want me to see breezes over him, because he looks away.

"Ye've been here some months now," he says to me. "Are ye liking it?"

"Sometimes." I nod.

"Just sometimes?" He watches me.

I nod back. "Just sometimes."

"Ye've had a good run."

I give him a look. "I have?"

"Aye." He nods. "No rogue magical villains hae floated through or anything. That's good fortune."

"What do you mean?" I frown.

"It's Neverland." He gives me a wry look. "It's no' all good. A lot o' it's fucked."

"How?"

"It goes both ways." He shrugs. "Has to. If it can be wonder-filled, then it has to be terrible too."

I lift my eyebrows, waiting for more, and he rolls his eyes at me.

"Last year, a hellhound got loose on the isle—tore a bunch o' people t' pieces. The year afore that, there was an oilliphéist that would come out and terrorize everyone. The queen of hearts—"

---

* Even if it's maybe actually all I want to see.

I roll my eyes. "She's not real."

"Sure, not in the way ye ken her to be, no."

I cross my arms, waiting for more.

"She's a witch." He gives me a look. "The man she loved dïdnae love her back. Now she takes the hearts of men in love and eats them. Feels full for a moment, then it empties her more."

I stare over at him, eyes wide. "That's a legend."†

"No." Jem shakes his head. "I saw her with me own eyes."

I feel sick as I blink over at him. "But she didn't eat your heart?"

He shakes his head. "I was no' in love at the time."

Our eyes catch—I don't know why?—and then he gives me a quick smile and clears his throat.

"Hae y'seen a volcano before?" he asks, looking at me out of the corner of his eye.

I nod. "I have."

"Where?"

I purse my lips, and he looks at them as I do. "I've seen Vesuvius in Pompeii and Mauna Loa in Hawaii."

"Hawaii?" He looks over at me all interested. "I've always wanted to visit thonder." He smiles in this far-off way that I don't understand because he comes from Neverland, and how could you long for any place else? "What's it like?"

"Well, parts of it are quite like here, actually—not too dissimilar from Cannibal Cove. Bigger waves. No mermaids."

He gives me a look. "That's a plus."

"Not for Peter."

He watches me for a second, says nothing, then says, "How dae ye get there?"

I give him a funny look. "Airplane?"

"Flying tin in the sky?" His head pulls back. "I dïnnae think so."

I roll my eyes at him. "Don't you captain a flying boat?"

He chuckles. "Nae. My dad did." He shrugs. "My ship's just a ship."

---

† A horrible, awful legend. Isn't it?

"Oh." I look up at him. "What did happen to the Jolly Roger?"

"I dïnnae ken." He shakes his head. "It's just gone—disappeared." He shrugs. "It disappeared before he died, actually. Bit o' a sad demise." He looks far away when he says that, and I want to reach over and touch his hand, and then I wonder who that hand has touched and how many times since I saw him last, so I do nothing.

We're around the back of summer now, the edge of the island. It's a sharp drop-off into the bluest, clearest water I've ever seen. More so than on our side of the island. There's an honesty to this shade of blue—a trueness to it that makes my heart spark in a funny way.

"I heard yer his girlfriend," Jamison says a bit suddenly, and I look over at him.

I frown. "How did you hear that?"

He shrugs. "Word travels."

"Yes." I nod. "It does. And I think his are empty."

His face pulls a little. "So y'are?"

I purse my mouth. "So he says."

He nods a few times and doesn't look at me when he asks, "What does that look like?"

I glance at him, confused (or, in the very least, thrown) by the question.

"Ye…what?" he fishes. "Ye share a bed?"

I lift my shoulders mindlessly. "We always have."

His eyebrows dip in the center, a quiet frustration present. "Yer fucking him now then?"

I stare over at him. My mouth falls open, and I say nothing.

I hated hearing him say that. It was awful, that word in his mouth in that particular way. About me, no less? I don't want to hear him say that about me. The back of my neck goes immediately hot.

Jamison takes my silence as a yes, and he breathes out in a way that makes me wonder for a second if the thought hurt him.

"No," I tell him quickly.

"No?" he repeats. "Why no'?"

I stare at him for a good couple of seconds—any seconds spent looking at Jamison are good seconds, I think, maybe?—and then I look back down at the water.

"Why is the water so blue here?" I nod at it.

His eyes don't immediately move from me. They stay a couple seconds more than they probably should before he speaks again.

"Compared to yer planet, do ye mean?" He sniffs. "We dïnnae throw our shit in it."

"No, I mean"—I give him a look—"it is exceptionally blue."

"Aye." He nods mostly with his chin, watching me closely. "Sometimes things are just extraordinarily beautiful fer no reason at all."

A breeze dances over my face that reminds me of a thing I think I forgot, and I frown trying to remember exactly what it was, because I feel as though perhaps it's a thing I should know—?

Jamison takes that to mean I found his answer unsatisfactory. However, the truth is I find nothing about him unsatisfactory, at least what I am beginning to remember.

"They say this is where the color blue comes from." He nods at it. "That this here is the original deposit from the start o' the universe, and then the fae carry it out to the other places." A little shrug. "Thon's why it's so concentrated here."

"Oh," I say, because what else can you say to that? I clear my throat, nodding at him. "I like your coat. Is it new?"

His brows tug. "No?"

"Oh." I keep walking.

"Ye've worn it before," he calls after me, and I stop, turning to face him.

"Have I?" I ask.

He stares at me a few seconds, and then he blinks in this funny way, as though he's annoyed or tired. "Ye went to the place in the sky."

I nod. "Yes."

He nods slowly. "Ye put things away o' me?"

"I guess," I say quietly.

His mouth turns down at the edges, like a shrug, and then he moves past me, walking ahead.

"You go up there," I tell him.

"Everyone does." He shakes his head, not looking back. "But I'd never put away a thought about you."

I stop walking.

"Liar," I say with some authority.

He turns back to look at me, eyebrows up. "What?"

"I know you have," I tell him, brows daring.

Jamison walks back quickly and right up into my face. "Ye went through my baggage?"

I shake my head quickly.

"Then how do ye ken?"

"I could tell." I stare up at him, my eyes big and kind of afraid. I don't think he'd hurt me, but I sort of feel as though I'm going toe-to-toe with a storm.

"By the shape." I swallow. "How it looked—I don't know." I shake my head. "It felt like it called me."

He glares at me for this, like I already know too much. "Ye dïnnae know what I put away," he tells me as he shakes his head, right up in my face. "Whatever ye put away o' me and what I did, it's no' the same thing." His eyes drag over my face. "There's nothing about ye I want to forget," he says before he turns and keeps walking.

"That's evidently not true," I call after him.

"Ye dïnnae ken o' what ye speak," he calls back, and I frown even though he's not looking at me to even care.

We walk in a prickly silence after that. Mostly just dotted with "careful's" and "it's slippery here's" and "dïnnae touch that, it's poison's," things like that. That's all it is for hours between us, but I don't mind because I'm using the time to remember what's in those bags that I put away. Something about a coat, obviously. I remember that now. He put a coat on me. But why did I care about it? And snow or something? And there was another? Something about family? His family? And one more that escapes me—

I feel I'm on the cusp of remembering it right as we get to the mouth of a cave.

Jamison looks back at me. He still looks a bit cross with me, if I'm honest.

"The Carnealian Mouth," he tells me as he trots down a few rocks on a beach at low tide.

He offers me his hand to help me down, and I'll be honest with you—I do think about not taking his hand. Maybe that's what I should have done.

It's easier if I don't remember things with him. And I think, perhaps, if I didn't take his hand, he'd have stayed angry with me the whole time we were in the volcano, and it might have made for an overall wiser trip.

But I'm eighteen, and it's not wisdom that I want for my birthday, so I take it. A wave crashes loudly on the face of the cliff right by us, and my hand stays in his a few seconds longer than it needs to before we each snatch our respective hands away.

I gesture at the entrance. "After you."

He nods, and I follow him in.

It's dark instantly and humid and rather difficult to see—though not impossible—and then I trip on something.

"Ouch!" I cry, looking over my shoulder, glaring at the nothing I tripped on.

"Watch yerself." Jem frowns at me, and then I move in closer towards him. Without looking back at me and without a word, Jem's hand reaches for mine and takes it again, and somewhere behind us, a steam vent blows. He holds it tightly in a mindless way, and I remember properly what was in that silver bag—the one about the coat and how he pulled me close in to him, how it felt when he tugged it around me. And something about a breeze? There's something about a breeze in another bag, but I feel nervous to remember what's in that one, so I don't.

Rather a terrible thing to remember if it wasn't one of my favorite thoughts to wear in the world.

"Have you been here before?" I ask him.

"Many times," he says. "My mum likes it. There's magic here, she says."

"Where are we going?"

He looks back at me. "Ye'll see."

We walk deeper and deeper into the cave, and it gets hotter and hotter. The flowers on my dress fold themselves back into buds. He stops for a second, peels off his coat, and throws it over a boulder.

"Don't you lose that." I nod my chin at it, some worry in my voice.

A pleased little smile spreads over his face. "Aye, look who's been doing some remembering." He flicks me a look as he takes my hand again and keeps walking for a bit. "What did I say to ye at the Bird?" he asks, staring straight again. I peer over at him, and he looks at me. "Or did ye check thon in too?"

"No." I shake my head carefully. "I kept that."

He gives me a measured nod. "Orson said it wusnae good."

I look up at him. "Did you drop it off?"

"Nah," He shakes his head. "Was just steamin'."

"Ah." I nod, and the air feels thicker now, like we're wading through it.

"Is that why ye dropped off the thoughts? Because I hurt ye?" he asks as he unbuttons his shirt so it falls wide open.

My eyes snag on his chest, and I swallow heavy, nod.

He stops, turns to face me, and tilts his head as he watches me. He pushes some hair behind my ears. "Will ye go collect them now then?"

I stare over at him and feel a new boldness rise up from within myself that I believe comes to you exclusively upon turning eighteen, and then I* reach up and shift some hair from his eyes.

"We shall see."

He looks at my hand in his, smiles a tiny bit, then nods.

Just when the air is at the consistency of custard and I think I'm about to run out of it, that's when Jamison says, "Here we are."

There's an opening into another chamber off the main one. He pulls me through it, and I gasp.

Ground-to-ceiling crystal, growing out every which way, and at the center of the room, a natural mantelpiece filled to its brim with every kind of gem and crystal you could imagine.

I look around in disbelief. "What is this?"

"A crystal chamber." He shrugs as he goes over and picks up some of the crystals. "Do ye no' hae these on Earth?"

"No, not really." I shake my head.

"What about these?" He flashes me that dagger of his I've seen before. "Ye have these on Earth?"

I gasp again at the sight of it, and he offers it to me. I take it in my hands, roll it around in them. "Oh, it's beautiful."

"Golden blade, ruby inlays."

"It really is so gorgeous." I can't take my eyes off it.

---

* Very bravely, I might add.

"It's yers," he says, and I look up at him, surprised.

"What?"

"It's fer you." He shrugs and gives me a quick smile. "Happy birthday."

I shake my head at him. "I can't take this."

"Well, a'm giving it t' ye, so—"

"Jem."

"Daph." He lifts his eyebrow as he wraps my hands around it. "Keep it hidden. Use it only when ye need to."

I nod obediently. "Okay."

"I hope ye never need to."

"I hope I do!"

He gives me a look as though he's tired of me, but I don't think he is.

He picks up a big selenite, inspecting it, and I take the time to inspect him. How broad he is, how strong he looks, how sweaty he is in this room, and then, regrettably, Jamison catches me staring at his chest for the fortieth time in the last thirty minutes.

My eyes shoot to the roof. "It's so very hot"—I clear my throat—"in here."[†]

He sniffs a laugh and doesn't say what he could in that moment because he's a gentleman. Or maybe just because it's my birthday.

In my defense, it does feel like a steam room—a beautiful steam room, filled with sapphires and emeralds and diamonds and rubies.

"We're right by a magma vent," he tells me, and I give him a sharp look that he laughs at. He walks over towards me. "I'm no' going to let anything happen to ye, Bow."

He gives me a steadying look, and I match it with folded arms over my chest.

"You can control volcanic eruptions now, can you?"

"Maybe." He smirks, and I stare at his mouth. That top lip of his looks like trouble, but I'd really like to know that empirically.

It's foggy all around us now, thick and hazy and dreamy. The crystals catch on lights that aren't even present, and my head feels spinny. It could be the air or probably it's just him.

---

† Which it is, but it's not really what I meant.

His hand's on my waist, and I remember the feeling, remember why I must have put it away. There's a weight to his touch that grounds me, sinks me right where I am, and I'm thrilled to be here, and then…I remember.

"Peter can," I say quite quietly.*

He looks over at me, brows furrowing deep on his face. He's considering it, I can tell. Actually, not just considering it but worrying about it.

His eyes hold mine for a second before there's a deep rumbling from a part of the cave we're not in. Then a steam vent pops, and he grabs my hand, pulling me out of there before I even suggest that maybe it's time we leave.

Back the way we came, the air getting easier and easier to breathe in the farther we get from the center. He grabs his coat with his other hand. Doesn't have time to put it on.

I can see the mouth out of the cave, but it's dark out now. The only light we have is the one the moon's reflections on the ocean are giving us.

I don't hear him breathe easy till we're out, and I want to tell him that Peter would never, but I have a feeling that maybe he might?

He breathes out and gives me a long look. "We're going t' have t' wait till the scraigh o' dawn."

I nod as though it's a solemn thing to me, not my very birthday wish. "Okay."

It's cold now. Freezing, almost. We're both soaked through from the steam we were in before. I start shivering so he builds a fire and puts me near it. Finds food, feeds me. I'm waiting for him to do more, but more doesn't come.

He just sits by me, staring at the fire, holding his hands out to keep himself warm how I'd hold my hands to him for the same reason.

"He did try the other day," I say, looking at the flames, not him.

Jem looks over at me. "To what?"

I give him a look.

"Oh," he says, eyes straight ahead. A singular nod. "And ye—"

"I said no."

Now I have his attention.

"Oh." He frowns a bit, thinking. "Why?"

---

* And I feel nervous and cross at once.

"I didn't want to."

"And what did he say t' that?"

I consider this. "Not much to it, so much as he lay upon my decline some reasons as to why we in fact…should."

His eyes pinch. "What were they?"

I sniff. "Primarily that he wanted to."

Jamison breathes out. "He's such a fucking prick."

"Sometimes, yes," I concede.

"But ye dïdnae?" he asks, looking over at me all earnest.

I shake my head.

He stares over at me. "Why dïdnae ye?"

I can't quite remember, more than that I just didn't want to. I think I put that thought away too? I think it had to do with Jem. I think he might have run through my mind when he shouldn't have, when I was lying there with Peter—with Peter's hands on me, with Peter trying to do more. I think my mind might have kept falling through some trapdoor back to Jamison. That frightened me, wanting him so viscerally even after I'd banished him the best way I knew how at the time.

How can I say that though? I put away what I did for a reason. I must have had a reason. But it is hard to remember what that might have been with him here in front of me, lit up by the flickering amber light, backed by a million stars.

"I don't know" is the weak and flimsy answer I give him instead of the truth that I'm afraid of.

And still, my eyes fall down him like they shouldn't.

Why didn't I? It was Peter Pan with his hands on my body how I'd thought I wanted them to be, and then when I had them there and on me, I just thought about Jem. I wondered: How does a nose get so perfect? And where does he get the nerve to have that rose-petal mouth?

I think he knows why. His face is searching mine for clues to crack my hard-shell exterior.

He gives me a quarter of a smile. "Just didn't?"

I shake my head, cheeks on fire.

He lies back on the ground, rolling in to face me. "And now?" His eyes find mine.

"Now." I lie down, copying him. "Now, I'm eighteen," I tell him very bravely and extremely kicked.

"Y'are," he says quietly and just watches me.

It's a slow kind of watching, a drinking me in, an inspection of my whole face, with a particular focus and fascination with the corner of my upper right-hand lip.

"Are you going to do anything about it?" I ask him.

Jamison breathes out slow and measured; that frown of his that's always sort of there is very much present now. This brilliant spattering of consternation and frustration, and I wonder how much is too much when it comes to staring at another person's face.

"No' today," he says, and I can't hide it; that barrels me over. It's not what I was expecting—not at all. I thought he'd grab me and kiss me up against the palm tree over there. Slip those hands of his under the dress the fairies made me, and I'd let him how I didn't let Peter.

Why didn't I let Peter? I wanted to want to. At the time, I felt as though I should. I didn't want to say no; I wanted to say yes. But that wasn't reflective of my actual wants—I just don't like to say no to Peter. Does that make sense? Is that strange?

There is this pull towards Peter. How many deals with gravity does he have, I wonder. Pulls can be good, but they can also be bad.

A black hole has a gravitational pull; it sucks in everything near it into its darkness, never to be seen again. My affection for Peter sometimes feels without my permission, as though I can't help but like Peter. I guess that's the fate talking.

There is something about Jamison though. If Peter is gravity, Jamison might be the earth the apple falls to. And I might be a slave to gravity, but Jamison might be the place I prefer to land.

However, judging by his polite decline, I'm not his preferred landing site. Eighteen and still not an actual woman.

I stiffen up as I remember what I should have all along.

He sighs. "Dinnae go like that."

"Why shouldn't I?" I ask, more emotion in my throat than I want him to know exists in me for him. "It's not a big deal to you! You do it with Morrigan all the time."

He pulls a face. "Sure, yeah, no' all the time—"

I cut him off. "And then you did it with her and that awful girl from that stupid tavern."

He tilts his head. "Aye."

"And others, I'm sure!"

"Are ye sure then?" he asks, eyebrows up and annoyed at me for that.

"Well, have you?" I ask, sitting up again.

He licks his bottom lip. "Aye."

I shake my head at him, and it's full of hurt. "But you won't do that with me?"

Jem's face suddenly goes solemn. "Bow, I winnae ever do what I did with them wi' ye."

"Oh." My head pulls back, and my eyes well up. My cheeks go hot, and my mind starts to sink in a million questions of how I could have gotten this so wrong. Have I been wrong all along? I must have been. "Okay." I nod. "Perfect. That's…good to know."

Jem stares over at me, and I can't pick his face anymore. I thought I could but obviously I can't.

"It's no' the same, Bow." He sounds tired now.

"What's not the same?"

"You and me."

"Why?" I demand, hands on my hips, and he frowns as he watches me, confused. "Because I'm not an actual woman?"

He licks his lips. "Did I say thon t' ye?"

I nod.

"To yer face?" he clarifies.

I nod again, and he sighs.

"Fuck." He breathes out, and I don't understand a thing in the world.

Jamison shakes his head, eyes still not quite on me.

"Sorry." He sighs, watching me for a brief moment before he looks down, pressing his hand into his mouth. "That's no' it."

I frown.

"Is it because we're friends?

He gives me a long-suffering look. "We're no' friends."

And that guts me—more than a little—if were to be honest.* I'm offended again, and I shake my head, refusing to believe that and hoping that he can't see on my face how much that hurt me.

"Yes, we are! Of course we are," I tell him. Actually, truthfully, he's probably my best friend here.

"Daph." He gives me a look. "We're no' friends."

I roll over because otherwise my eyes will give me away, all stupid and watery.

"Hey." He rolls me back so I'm facing him, and I think his face might soften at the sight of me. "Listen, I dïnnae think about my friends how I think about ye. I dïnnae want t' be around them how I want to be around ye. I dïnnae want t' touch my friends how I want to touch you, Daphne."

I take a shallow breath and wonder if he's saying what I think he's saying, but he's hurt my feelings a few too many times in the last few minutes, so I cross my arms and glare over at him proudly. "And how, might I ask, do you want to touch me?"

He breathes out his nose. "One day, yer going to ask me to show ye exactly how wi'out that defiance in yer eye, and on that day, I will very gladly show ye."

I swallow heavy. "But not now?"

He gives me a sliver of a smile, but it's a new kind of his that I don't know about yet. To be entirely honest with you, I'm getting rather well versed in all Jamison's different faces. There's something melancholy caught in his eyes, and he mashes his mouth together, thinking before he talks.

"I dïnnae remember"—he peeks at me out of the corner of his eye—"the first time I did that."

"Oh." I frown.

"I ken who it was with and all." He shrugs. "My dad took me on a voyage to another isle. There was a princess—"

"You lost your virginity to a princess?" I cry, a bit distraught, and he huffs a laugh as he looks at my face.

"Aye, I did." He shrugs. "And I liked her, sure, and she me, but she haed done it before, and I was so fecking nervous. I just got steaming drunk, and we did it. And I dïnnae really remember. Flashes, just…"

---

* Which I shan't be.

I stare over at him, frowning.

"But it would be nice to remember the way the sky looked or how she felt when I held her or how the light was on her face or—" He looks up at me like I've caught him doing something embarrassing, and he flashes me a quick, apologetic smile. "I dïnnae feel bad about it. It happened. I did it to myself, but I dïnnae remember, and I wish I did. It's important, ye ken? Yer first time, it's important."

I stare over at him in a new kind of awe. He's terribly thoughtful and, perhaps in this specific moment, frustratingly considerate and sweet.

"Okay." I nod a few times. "But to clarify, do you think I'm drunk right now?"

Jem lets out this barrel laugh; it's big and deep and has the warmth of twelve thousand bonfires to it, his hands on his stomach as he properly laughs at the sky.

"No, I dïnnae think yer drunk." He gives me a long-suffering look. "But, Daph, yer figuring yer shit out. Yer mind's all over the place." He breathes out his nose. "I just want it on me."

"It is on you!" I protest, and my foot stomps in my heart.

"Now"—he shrugs like he's already conceded to it—"for bye, when we do that, we're no' doing it because some wee footer forgot yer birthday."

"Why will we do it?" I ask him very quietly.

Jem stares over at me a few seconds. "Because we cannae no' anymore."

Our eyes catch, and I swallow heavy. He moves in closer towards me so there's just a few inches between our faces. The fire flickers beside us, and his eyes come alive next to it. All the sapphires in the world appears to be stock-piled in his eyes. But then I wonder if maybe he just himself is all the sapphires and all the diamonds and all the gold in the world. In all worlds, perhaps.

He gives me a half smile. "Good night, Bow."

"Good night, Jem."

CHAPTER THIRTEEN

HE DIDN'T NOTICE, BY THE WAY—PETER—THAT I WAS MISSING THAT NIGHT. Or if he did, he didn't care. He didn't say anything about it when I just showed up at the tree house at around lunchtime the next day.

He didn't ask me where I'd been or what I'd been doing or even if I was okay. He just wrapped his arms around my waist, lifted me off the ground, and gave me a kiss that I didn't understand.

There was a sort of roughness to it that I couldn't tell you even now whether I cared for or not. A bit of me did, a bit of me didn't…but if that isn't just my entire relationship with Peter…

"You take your medicine this morning?"

"Hmm? Oh." I look back at him, shake my head. "No."

He goes inside to get me some, and I stay there, watching the younger boys.

Peter's back after a minute, hands me the tonic in the flower like always. I don't even mind the taste now. I think I used to not like to drink this, but now I can't remember why.

My eyes fall onto Holden, the Lost Boy who arrived however many days ago he arrived—I can't remember. He's playing in the sun with the others. He looks so small.

I nod my head at him. "Has he been okay?"

Peter frowns. "Course he has. Why wouldn't he be?"

"He might miss his parents." I shrug. "That can happen when a child is lost."

Peter shakes his head as though he knows of such things, though I suppose of all the boys present in one way or another, he is the lost-est. "He has us."

I give him a tall look. "We are hardly parental figures."

He stands up taller, slips both his arms around me. "I think we're okay."

"You disappear on adventures for days at a time." And you'd best believe that I absolutely sidestep the fact that I just did that also. Peter's not brought it up, so I won't either. "You're not very safety conscious."

"A father's job is to instill in his sons a drive to have fun and to never grow up."

I press my finger into my top lip as I stare at the boys and say nothing.

Peter rests his chin on top of my head, and for a quick minute, I feel like we are together—properly together—and I feel a dash of guilt for how I spent the day prior to this one. I think it was the day before? Right? Wasn't it? It could have been a week before. It feels cloudy all of a sudden, and then I see some love bites on the nape of Peter's neck and some ink smudges on his chest, and I know without knowing how he spent my birthday. And maybe in light of Jamison by the fire, I'm not really entitled to feel sad, but I do.

"What are we doing today?" I turn in his arms to face him.

"We?" he repeats. "Nothing." He grimaces a bit. "I've got boy stuff to do."

I frown a bit. "What's boy stuff?"

"Secret boy stuff." He shrugs. "I'll take you to the Indians on my way."

"I don't think they're Indi—"

"Rye wants to see you," he says over me before his eyes pinch. "Do you think he has romance inside him for you?"

I shake my head reflexively, even though sometimes I do wonder. "No."

Peter doesn't buy it. "It would make me angry if he did."

"I know." I nod, feeling tired all of a sudden.

He nods his head. "Let's go."

We fly, of course. Peter only ever flies, I think a bit because no one else can ever seem to do it very well if they aren't with him, which he likes, and also (obviously) convenience.

He drops me off by the river. Calla's lying on the edge of it, barely wearing anything. She props herself up when she sees him, gives him a wave. Peter just nods his chin at her and flies off.

The way it crushes her—he's crushed me like that before too—I feel guilty that he's doing it for me. Not guilty enough to ask him to stop but enough that what I asked of Jem yesterday burns hot in my mind like a fever, and I feel like a traitor somehow to both of them.

Rye and I go for a walk past Cannibal Cove, past Moon Crescent Cove, and then a bit into the rainforest.

There are submerged caves he thinks I'll like, and I can tell even before we get there that he's going to be right.

Rune flies in and joins us on the way.

She tinkles in my face.

"It was wonderful, thank you!" And then I give her a grateful look. "I loved my dress."

"Oh, I forgot it was your birthday!" Rye says, looking back at me. "Sorry! Was it good?"

"Yes." I flash him a grateful smile. "I had a really happy day."

"What did you do for it?" he asks.

"I went to the volcano," I tell him, choosing my words carefully.

"Oh!" Rye sings, pleased for me. "Peter took you to the volcano? Did you like it as much as you thought you would?"

I pause, thinking how best to proceed.

"Someone"—I give Rye and Rune a delicate smile—"took me to the volcano, and yes"—another quick smile—"I liked it very much."

The fairy stops flying, and the Stjärna boy turns around, eyes pinched.

"Daphne," he says at the same time as Rune jingles something.

"What?" I frown at Rye before turning to look at Rune. "Yes, he did," I tell her. She replies something I won't be telling you, and I gasp, "No, he did not!" She chimes, and I whisper to her, "Though not entirely without trying on my behalf." And she winks at me.

"Where was Peter?" Rye asks, walking backwards, watching me.

"With your sister." I shrug, like I don't care. "It wasn't on purpose by the way, and I didn't ask Jem to take me. He just—"

"Jem?" Rye repeats with a smirk, and Rune flies over to him and clangs around his ear, angry. She honestly might have even given him a tiny kick.

I roll my eyes at him. "I didn't ask Jamison to take me. We bumped into each other. I was looking for a map."

"Did he say sorry?"

"Who?" I ask.

"Hook." Rye eyes me. "For what he said to you."

"Oh." I shake my head, frowning. "I think so. I quite can't…"

"Remember." Rye nods once and then turns around and walks on, hitting the grass, not saying anything.

Rune bells quickly in my ear, and I give her a little look.

"He mightn't have a problem," I whisper. "He's Peter's friend. Maybe he thinks I'm doing wrong by him."

She chimes louder, and I roll my eyes.

"Yes, well, we all know how you feel about him."

She flies around by my foot, circling the ankle. I have the dagger Jem gave me hidden in my boot. Not because I think I'll need it but because I like having something he gave me with me. It feels a bit like a talisman, but for what, I don't know.

She flies back up to me, ringing.

"Yes," I tell her, feeling pleased with myself. "He did, for my birthday. Would you like to see it?"

She chimes and I frown.

"What do you mean 'you've seen it before'?"

And then she zooms in front of my face, hovering, jingling curiously, changing the subject to something that's rather uncouth.

"Why do you always ask about that?" I roll my eyes, putting my hands on my hips. "It's such a busybody question."

She chimes hotly.

"I know it is! No, I know. I've seen it."

She jingles excitedly.

"No! You know not like that. It's just…very hot in those caves down there."

She gives me a look.

"Rune." I give her one back.

She shrugs and says it's my loss in Stjär before flying off ahead.

"Do you have feelings for him?" Rye calls back to me without turning around.

I think about denying it. I've never said it out loud before. I've just thought it in my head a billion times.

"Yes," I say defiantly, though I can't be entirely sure who it is I'm defying.

Rye sighs. "Daphne—"

"No." I walk up to him and grab his arm, shaking my head at him. "You don't understand. You don't know him."

"Yeah, I do." Rye gives me a look. "He's great."

"Oh." I frown.

His eyebrow lifts. "But Peter…"

Rune flies back, chiming loudly.

"But Peter!" I sigh, ignoring her. "What is it about him?" I ask hopelessly.

Rye shrugs. "He's the dream boy."

I roll my eyes and so does Rune, but Rye shakes his head.

"He's a literal legend. Most people find it hard to say no to him or not to fall for his charms and shit, but you and your family—" He gives me a look that makes me feel hopeless. "It's in the blood."

I ask the question I don't know I want anyone else's answer to. "Do you think we're fated?"

"Yeah." Rye shrugs, and his face looks bleak.

Rune's chiming away angrily, she's swearing, I think. She's saying words I don't know. They sound like words one's grandmother mightn't teach them.

"Yeah, I do." Rye keeps nodding. "I kind of hate that." He laughs dryly, then looks over at me like he's sorry. "Probably rather you'd be with Hook, honestly, but yeah, there's something about how Peter is with…you."

I look at him, eyebrows up, and Rune jangles loudly for my attention.

"Stop it, Rune," I tell her, stomping my foot. "I know that you don't like him, but this is complicated for me."

Rye catches Rune's eye and nods his head at me.

"He grew up for her."

"Well," I clarify, "not for me."

But Rye shakes his head. "I don't know. Something made him grow up after all these years, so many years of being a kid, and then—" He gives me a look. "He grew to your age. What are the chances?"

I purse my lips. "Slim, I suppose."

Rye flicks his eyebrow. "Fate, I think."

You'd think this might make me feel better, but it doesn't because it's binding. To belong to Peter Pan is, in so many ways, a dream come true, isn't it? But perhaps not my dream come true, just someone else's dream that I'm living. Maybe it could be mine? And maybe it's just that—that I didn't know it at the time, or did I? It's so difficult to be sure of anything before whichever present moment you're currently in here, but I think that's what I came here for? To be with Peter? And then there's that pull towards him…that gravity, that thing that sucks me in, and it's impossible to ignore, and I feel it in me even when I'm happier lying next to someone else, even if I'm growing increasingly sure that the someone else in question is who I think I'd quite like to be next to in general. Peter is the idea that trickles into my heart like a leaky window in a storm. He's this creeping vine of a thought that wraps its way around everything, chokes everything to death but him. He colors everything. The other day with Jem was my favorite day maybe of my entire life, and then as soon as I was back in the tree house, all I wondered was what Peter would do if he knew.

It worried me, what might happen if he did. And maybe it would have been nothing, but the way the volcano rumbled instilled in me a quiet fear that perhaps Peter wouldn't even have to lift a finger and there'd still be hell to pay.

"Does he like you?" Rye asks.

"Jamison?" I clarify, because I suppose I have a few balls in the air at the moment, and I wouldn't be entirely offended if someone were to wonder whether Peter actually does.

"Yes, Jamison." Rye rolls his eyes.

"Oh, um—" I purse my mouth. "I think so?"

Rune rolls her eyes.

He lifts an eyebrow. "You think so?"

I nod. "Mm-hmm."

Rye's eyes pinch. "Did he say he did, or—"

"Well, we mostly really spoke around it?"

"Okay?" He nods, unsure.

"Um—" I frown as I try to word it. "I think it was topically inferred."

Rye pulls a face.

I breathe out loudly. "We talked about having sex."

"Whoa!" Rye pulls back, and Rune starts chiming like a maniac, practically bouncing off invisible walls.

I gasp and point at Rune firmly. "You honestly have a terribly filthy mind for a fairy, I do mean it."

"No, that one's on you." Rye shakes his head. "You nearly had sex with Hook?"

"No." I shake my head. But maybe. "We talked about it. We haven't even kissed. Nothing happened, but—"

"But you wanted it to?"

I straight up look at him down my nose. "Maybe."

Rune throws a tiny fairy firecracker at my shoulder that looks like someone popped a water balloon made of glitter. I give her a look as I dust my shoulder off.

"Peter tried to have sex with me the other day," I tell them.

Rune starts saying the bad words under her breath again, and Rye looks far away in his thinking.

"I have a headache," he says mostly to himself before he looks up at me, frowning. "What happened?"

"Well, he tried, and I said no."

"Why did you say no?" he asks.

There is an answer; it's plain as day on my face. I don't say a word. I don't need to. I think it just lives there. An affection and a fondness that aren't safe on the outside of me, but I don't know how to keep them in anymore, and I hate to tuck them away.

"Wow," Rye says as he watches me quietly. He nods at the mouth of the cave. "This is it."

We walk in past some columns five times as tall as the tallest man I know.* The cave itself is spectacular. Rimstone dams and flowstones galore. It gets dark quickly in here, though it's okay because Rune is a light in and of herself. We move through the hallway and into a different room that's darker and dryer than the others.

Rye gives the wall a solemn nod, and it takes a moment for my eyes to adjust, but then I see it. The prophecy. Or at least I think that's what it is. It's mostly written in some kind of hieroglyph that I don't understand, but I feel quite certain my mother could.

---

* Not to name names, but Jamison.

"The true heir," Rye says, staring at the glyphs in front of us before he looks back at me. "And you don't even know if you like him." He laughs dryly.

"I do too like him." I frown, and Rune trills in discontent, and I don't know whether I can look either of them in the eye at the minute so I look at the wall instead, running my hands over some Latin engraved into the wall also. "What's this?"

"Praecepta vivimus," Rye says with a tight smile.

I purse my lips, trying my best to translate it. "The rules we live by?"

He nods, then shrugs dismissively. "They're not real, just something the founders wrote on the wall when they found this here."

There are a few things written down: sanguis pro sanguine, in somnis veritas, in scientia et virtute, semper fortunas iuventutis, and a few more that are harder to read in the lack of light.

"Ad pacem, ad lucem, ad magicam, ad naturam, ad omnium bonam ac libertatem," I read aloud to no one in particular before I look between the two of them. "Were they true to it?"

Rye purses his mouth and shrugs. "Some."

Rune jingles in agreement, and I hope to myself that Itheelia falls under the banner of that some.

"Come on," Rye says, leading us back out to the main cave. "That's not even the best part."

And he's right.

A great deal of this cave is at least partially submerged. It's impossibly dark in parts, but then there's holes in the roof where the light pierces through in a way that almost looks like shooting stars, and the water—it glows.

I stare at it in wonder only for a half a second before I dive in, unable to help myself.

"They're Noctiluca scintillans," Rye says, smiling down at me.

"They're what?"

He laughs, then jumps in too. "Bioluminescent plankton."

I let out a small laugh. "I thought you were going to say it was mermaid dust or something magical."

"No." He shakes his head. "Just phosphorescence. Still magic though," he says, looking straight at me.

Rune coughs to break the tension in the room that I don't understand.

"Hey, Daph." Rye catches my eye. "Hook's a really good man, you know."

"I know." I frown defensively and duck under the water for a second. I think he's maybe the best man. And then I sigh at the same part I do every time—the part that doesn't make sense. I pop my head back up. "He can't be my fate though."

"Says who?" Rye asks.

"Well—" I roll my shoulders back. "You. Everyone. Anyone whose paying attention to myself and Peter and everything that's happened with my family till now."

Rune chimes in my ear, kicking up some water into my face with her tiny foot, and I roll my eyes at her because she's really hung up about that breeze.

"Would it matter if Hook wasn't?" Rye asks, swimming into a beam of light.

"Well." I swim after him. "I should think so?"

"But why?"

I shrug, hopeless. "Because it's fate."

"Right." He looks sad for me. "Maybe fate's not all it's cracked up to be."

The fairy tinkles again about the snow, but I think she's putting too much stock in the weather.

"There wasn't a great anything to it, Rune." I give her a look. "He just put his coat on me is all."

She sighs, belling again.

"No, maybe she's right," Rye says with a shrug. "Maybe there are different kinds of fate. Maybe everything's fate." He gives me a long look. "Maybe we all are."

And then he ducks under the water.

CHAPTER
FOURTEEN

"Wake up, girl," Peter says, his nose pressed against mine. "We're going to play."

I rub my eyes, tired. "Play what?"

He beams down at me. "Make-believe." Then he pulls me out of bed. "Let's go."

He shakes me by the shoulders excitedly, and I give him a look. "Peter, I'm not dressed."

He growls under his breath. "Fine. Hurry then," he says, and then he walks away.

"I should like to have breakfast first," I call after him.

"No time!" he calls back. "You have five minutes!"

☽

"Where are we going?" I ask mid-flight.

"It's a surprise." He beams, holding my hand tighter. He looks at me in my fairy birthday dress. "Where'd you get that from?"

"Rune." I give him a proud smile. "Do you like it?"

He shrugs. "It's okay."

I'm wearing her boots again today. I've been wearing her boots a lot lately, mostly because it means I can hide the dagger in them.

I give his hand a squeeze. "I am hungry though."

Peter looks over at me with a long-suffering face.

"Sorry." I grimace. "You didn't let me have breakfast."

"You should have been up earlier!" He rolls his eyes.

"I didn't know we were going somewhere!" I tell him, and he groans, rolling like a barrel in the air. "I would ever so love even just a small bite to eat," I say, hopeful.

He breathes out exaggeratedly. "We're almost there, girl. Can you just hold on?"

"Almost where?" I look around.

All I can see is blue. Blue every which way. Blue skies, blue seas, and they melt together on the horizon, making you feel like you're in some sort of aqua prism. Which is funny because we haven't been flying that long. It's just... Neverland, I suppose.

And then I see it. An island, sort of just there suddenly. It's tropical, but there's a big monument or something in the center. Big enough for me to be able to see it from far away.

He starts flying us down towards it.

"What are we doing here again?"

"Playing make-believe."

"Right." I nod, ignoring the rumble in my stomach. "And how do you play that?"

He gives me a smile. "You'll see."

"Well, what are we make-believing?"

He gives me a more impatient look this time. "I said, you'll see." We make ground after about ten minutes, and he stands there facing me, his hands on his hips. "Are you just dying to eat something now?"

I half smile, half frown. "I suppose so?"

"Okay, good." He nods and sits me down on the sand. "Wait here."

I nod.

"Don't move," he tells me.

I give him a look to let him know I think he's being weird and silly but oblige him anyway.

I lie back on the sandbank and stare up at the clouds.

They're performative here, the clouds I mean. I think they learned to do it for Peter when he was a boy. They dance, put on shows. It's all silent of course, but in a narrative sense, they're very easy to follow. Definitely easier to follow than *Invasion of the Body Snatchers*.

Peter sits down next to me about twenty minutes later.

"What are they putting on today?"

"I'm not quite sure." I shake my head. "I think it's some sort of Greek tragedy?"

He looks up at it, his eyes pinching. He looks almost annoyed. "It's the one about Theseus."

"Ah," I say, my eyes pinching too, trying to see what he does.

Peter holds out his hand, offering me a bunch of berries.

I take them from him, pleased. "Thank you!"

"He's not real, you know," Peter says, watching me.

I look over at him. "Who's not?"

"Theseus."

"Oh." I nod, indifferent. "No, I hadn't thought he was. He's a legend."

Peter gives me a look. "Some legends are true."

It's then I realize I've eaten half the berries before I've even offered him one.

I hold my open hand out to him. He looks down at them, shakes his head, and his face goes funny—right as my head does.

"Peter?" I say, as the sand starts to slip beneath me. "What's happening?"

The edges of my vision start going black, but he looks down on me, fallen in the sand, beaming.

"Let the games begin!"

Crowing. That's what I hear first. My eyes aren't open yet. They feel heavy, like feet stuck in sand. Is that Peter, or is it birds?

My face feels sticky. I'm sweating. Why am I sweating? It's hot. Am I outside? Where am I? This feels like a dream. Not a good one. There are these few seconds hovering before me before I lean in to being fully conscious, and I hold them dear because I don't know what I'm about to find next.

In those few seconds, I could be still asleep with Jamison by the fire. In those few seconds, I could be curled up next to Peter in the nest.

Both thoughts are thought in vain, but I give myself the courtesy of hope anyway.

When my eyes peel open, he's right there in my face. Am I relieved? Am I afraid? For better and for worse, I suppose I'm both.

His head flops to the side once our eyes meet.

"Took you long enough."

"What did you give me?" I frown, looking around. I can't really see for the four suns are at noontime, beating down on us.

"Well, I didn't want you to say no and me to get angry at you, so I just gave you some sömaberry's." He shrugs with a pleasant smile.

"Peter—" I stare at him, a nervous pit growing in my stomach. "Say no to what?"

He thumbs to the clouds. "Those sneaks were trying to give my surprise away because they think they're the only ones who can do surprises because they're in the sky, but they didn't realize you were stupid and didn't know that you don't know your Apollodorus very well."

I look around quickly, because unbeknownst to him, I actually do know my Apollodorus rather well. I just didn't realize I was being shown a precursor for my day.

I'm tied to some sort of monument or an altar. There are hedges every which way. Bones scatter the ground.

"Are we in a labyrinth?" I ask him at the same time as I realize another terrible thing. "Peter, am I tied up?"

He beams at me, pleased.

My hands are bound behind my back, ankles tied in front of me.

"Peter," I say nervously as he stands, and that's when I see it charging at us from about a hundred meters away. A minotaur.

The minotaur, I presume, actually.

Peter takes flight and looks down at me. "We're going to have the best day."

He soars through the air, knocking the minotaur backwards.

It's only down for a second before it's back on its feet, and my view of it is now completely unimpeded, though I wish it still were.

The head of a bull, white and brown fur, crazy eyes. You know how cows have so much white around their eyes? This has that. A giant ring through its nose. Horns the length of my forearm, and then the most unsettling part: the body of a normal man. The biggest, strongest man you've ever seen—ever—times infinity. He's Goliath. Pitifully white and alarmingly scarred, wielding a double-headed axe that catches the light of one of the suns no matter which way he swings it, and he's running towards me, fast as I've ever seen anything move.

I reckon with it quickly that I'm very likely about to die, and it bothers me that the last sound I'll hear is an axe grinding as the minotaur drags it behind him and the grunting it's making that sounds quite like a bull. To be expected, I suppose, but then he is part human, so I suppose you never know what to expect in a situation like this one.

The minotaur gets about two meters from me before Peter soars through the air feetfirst, kicking him backwards.

"Don't worry, girl!" He looks back at me valiantly. "I'll save you."

The minotaur lets out a furious, frustrated growl and beats his chest before thundering towards me, swinging that axe around like a helicopter blade.

Peter rushes him, but the minotaur dodges him, axe swirling above his head, and I can tell he's coming for me. I can see it in his eyes. I've never seen that before— a decision that you will die. The minotaur has decided that, at his hands, I will die.

He takes an almighty swing, and I throw myself to the side and onto the ground, missing it but barely.

The axe grazes my cheek right as Peter shoves the creature back with a strength that I find surprising, impressive, and unsettling all at once.

Peter lands next to me on his knees, pressing his fingers into my cheek.

"Quick!" I tell him. "Untie me."

"Girl." He stares at me. "There's blood on you." He looks over his shoulder at the beast. "You made her bleed."

Peter stands, and I cry at him. "Untie me, please!" I beg, and he ignores me anyway.

"For that, you will die."

The minotaur is up on his feet again, running back towards us, and Peter's back in the air, but this time when he swoops him, he grabs the minotaur by the horns.

The minotaur flails about in the sky as Peter lifts it higher and higher, flying it above the labyrinth, and I'm watching him, sort of furious, sort of in awe-filled disbelief.

And then Peter's face changes. His gaze goes from the minotaur in his hands to someplace far away, off in the distance.

"Hey, what's that?" he calls to no one in particular.

"Peter!" I call to him cautiously.

He barely looks at me as he says, "Be right back!"

He drops the minotaur. He plummets, releasing this petrified, grunting wail as he falls somewhere in the labyrinth.

And then Peter flies off.

I stare at the sky, watching him in disbelief, and I'm convinced for probably twenty seconds that this is part of it—part of the game, part of the ruse that I wanted no part of to begin with. But it's not. It's just Peter, seeing a shinier thing on the horizon and leaving me to die for it.

The minotaur will be back soon if the fall didn't kill him, and I don't suspect that much really could. I wonder for a moment what it will be like to die, and as I'm lying here wondering how he'll do it, I notice all the skulls tossed away from skeletons around here. Does he chop off heads or pull them off? Both, probably. I'd prefer the chopping, I decide. Not that I suspect that the minotaur will oblige me my preferences, but you've got to take control where you can. I think about how I shouldn't have put away whatever was in the little leather pouch of Jamison. I know it was the snow, but I have a feeling there's more to it that I'm not remembering at this very moment, but whatever it is, I feel very sure that I shouldn't have put it away. I think it was important.

And that's when I remember my boot—or, more importantly, what's in there.

I manage to bring my arms forward by sitting between them and squirming through—it takes a minute. I might have popped my shoulder in and out of the socket,* but it works. I use my tied hands to reach into my boot and fish out the knife. I cut my ankles free first, then hold the knife between my feet to

---

* I only suspect as much because for a brief moment, I'm in a kind of agony that makes my eyes go funny, and I fall to the ground, and I think the fall may have knocked it back in.

cut through binds at my wrists, and as the last bit of rope snaps, the minotaur appears—bloodied. His leg looks like it might be broken. He doesn't seem to care as he runs towards me anyway.

I grab my dagger and dart right into the labyrinth.

It's huge. The hedges are double my height easily. I run around aimlessly for probably five minutes, and I can feel myself getting somehow closer and closer to the edge of it but farther and farther from the way out.

I hear him getting closer and closer. He thumps his chest, deep and hollow, and grunts, panting.

My body starts to tremble even though I don't feel that afraid in my mind, which is weird, don't you think? Trauma is weird.

I back up into the hedge, and he rounds the corner towards me, but as he does, suddenly the hedge grows around me, shielding me.

The minotaur's looking all over for me—he's confused. I think he knows I'm here, or at least that I was just a moment ago.

It's getting closer, head looking left and right. I grip my dagger…wait till he's right in front of me, standing in front of the part of the hedge that just grew around me, and then he turns his head a bit, and I have a clear shot, so I reach through and stab him in the eye.

I've never stabbed anything in the eye before. Actually, I've never stabbed anything anywhere before.

There are layers of sounds—all of them grotesque—when I do it. The most obvious one being the sound that he makes, less a groan, more a cry.

As well the sound of a blade piercing an eye and grinding bone as I drive the dagger through. These are sounds I've never wanted to know.

The sound of someone crying (I think it's me) as he tears through the hedges to get to me, and then the hedges wilt back, revealing me to him.

And right when I think I'm definitely, absolutely about to die, even though he only has one eye, the layers of hedges behind me pull back like curtains at the same time as the minotaur falls on his knees in pain.

He stares up at me, my dagger still in his eye.

Then he does something strange.

He pulls it from his own eye, wipes it on his chest, then offers it to me.

I stare at it. It feels like a trick.

When I don't take it from him, he lays it at my feet.

I stare at it, confused. He kneels there, unmoving, head bowed towards the ground, and it still feels like a trick? Maybe he's just giving me a head start. Maybe it's not fun to kill someone when they're easy to kill. Whatever it is, I take the chance presented to me. I grab the dagger and run through the path the hedges made for me. They close behind me like gates slamming shut, and I fall to the ground when I'm finally out of it.

My breath is jagged. I'm crying, I think? I yell for Peter, but he doesn't come. I yell for Jamison and Rune, but I'm too far away, I think. I don't think they'd hear me if I was even on Neverland proper, and I'm somewhere much farther than that.

I make my way back to the beach where Peter gave me the berries. I know it's the same spot because the berries I didn't eat still rest on the sand.

I can just barely spot Neverland Island from here. It's not close. A couple hours' swim at least. I look back at the island I've just escaped from and then back at the ocean. I fancy my chances with the sea.

I wade in, hold the dagger under the water, and the red washes away. I put it back in my boot—boots are not great to swim in, by the way—and then I start swimming.

Swimming and swimming for maybe an hour—two possibly, even—and my arms are getting tired, but I'm so far out, and I've nowhere to go.

I stop for a minute and tread water.

I don't know how to summon fairies or even if you can, but being able to right now would be fantastic. Maybe there's such a thing as water fairies.

I suppose there are mermaids.

That makes me feel uneasy, now that I'm thinking of it. I'm quite sure, given the chance, Marin would let me drown, if not swim on over and drown me herself.

I look beneath me at the clear and crazy blue waters below.

You know how the water can wreak havoc in your mind with benign shadows?

Immediately I am positive that I'm going to die. Again.

I'm sure of it, that something's there, circling me. It's not dark, it's light, but it's something, and I'm spinning around, splashing as I look everywhere for it—seems dangerous. Splashing attracts sharks, doesn't it? I go still instead, stare down at whatever's beneath me.

And then a tiny wave knocks my chin up.

I stare back down at the water.

It does it again.

Then from behind me, a wave scoops me up like I'm in an armchair and propels me forwards. Forward and forwards and through fields and kilometers of water.

The wave carries me home.

It washes me up on the shore next to the dock by the tree house, and I turn to say thank you to it, and I think it laps at my ankles extra to say that I'm welcome.

I empty my boots of ocean water, make sure my dagger's still tucked away, and then I walk towards the tree house.

I'm out for blood. Ready completely to kill Peter for this, I am.

Part of me hopes he's not in—that something happened to him, that he's detained somewhere, or that there's been an emergency. That's a horrible thing to hope for someone you care about, but if he's not detained and if there's nothing wrong, then it means he just left me to die, and I think that might be worse.

When I walk into the room, the boys are playing football in the house across all the different stories of nets.

It's Percival who spots me first, and he pulls a face when he does. "What happened to you?"

Kinley flies over to me. "Are you okay?"

"I'll get you a towel," says little Holden before darting out of the room.

And it's then—then, when his game is interrupted—that Peter looks up and over at me.

"Whoa." Peter laughs. "I totally forgot about you!"

I glare over at him. "I know." I stand there, hands on my hips, chin low.

Percival gives Kinley a look, nodding away from us, and then scurries out.

Peter watches them go before he looks back at me. "Sorry." He shrugs.

I shake my head at him. "Peter, I could have died."

"Yeah, but"—he rolls his eyes like I'm crazy—"dying would be an awfully big adventure though."

"I don't want to die," I tell him very clearly, and he rolls his eyes again.

"Well, then it's good that you didn't."

"Peter." I frown.

He flies over to me, takes less than three seconds for him to get from one side of the tree house to the other. How quickly he could have saved me if he tried.

He looks at me suspiciously. "How'd you get here?"

"I swam." I gesture to my saturated self.

"The whole way?"

I shrug. "The waves carried me."

His face pulls, and his brows knit together. "That's weird."

"Why?" I frown. "I would have thought you told them to."

He pauses. "I did."

"Right, so?" I lift my shoulders a bit, waiting for his point.

Peter eyes me curiously. "You're way braver than I thought."

I blink twice. "Than you thought?"

He nods, but he doesn't look pleased. "And stronger, I guess?"

My head pulls back. "You guess?"

He crosses his arms, head tilted to the side. "How'd you get out of the maze anyway?"

"What do you mean? It was easy." I shake my head, and his face flickers. "I stabbed the minotaur in the eye, and then he fell down, and he opened the maze for me."

Peter says nothing.

"That's the game, isn't it?" I stare at him. "I won."

"Right." Peter nods, walking past me, and then he pauses, looking back. "You stabbed him in the eye?"

"Yes." I nod. "He even gave my dagger back."

"What dagger?"

I pause and my mouth forms a rather conspicuous O shape. I squash my lips together. "Hook gave me a dagger. For my birthday." I say it lightly like it's nothing. Tack on a smile at the end, just to keep it breezy, but it doesn't work.

"You were with him on your birthday?" Peter yells, standing over me.

I scoff a laugh. "Well, I certainly wasn't with you."

"Yeah." He rolls his eyes. "And whose fault is that?"

I wave my hands at him in disbelief. "Yours!"

"Mine?" He pulls back.

"Yes!" I yell, stomping my foot, but it does nothing because I'm on a net. "You went with Marin and Calla to find some stupid treasure."

"It wasn't stupid," he interrupts. "You're stupid."

I look away, shaking my head, but Peter ducks, taking my eye.

"Did he touch you?"

"No," I say quickly, and it's mostly the truth. Right? It's mostly true. He held my hand, and he pushed some hair from my face, but is that even really touching?

"Not how you touched Calla anyway," I say mostly under my breath, but he hears me and gets up right into my face.

"What was that?" he asks, eyebrows up.

"Nothing." I shake my head.

"No, say it." He juts his chin a bit. "Say it."

I say nothing. My eye doesn't even flicker to the love bite on him that's still there now. Or maybe that's new? Is that in a different spot than before?

Peter sniffs and eyes me down. "You're disgusting. I can smell him on you." He takes a step from me.

"Nothing happened." I reach for him, I don't know why. Compulsion, maybe? "He was just being kind. It's lucky he gave it to me!"

"Lucky?" Peter says in disbelief.

"Yes!" I nod. "Otherwise, I might have died!"

Peter shakes his head. "Honorably, at least."

I breathe out quietly. "You'd rather me dead than use something Hook gave me to live?"

"He is my enemy!" Peter yells loudly.

"No, he isn't!" I insist. "That's all just crazy talk. It's all in your head!"

"When was he with you?" Peter grabs me by both my wrists, moving me backwards. "Did he take you? How? When? Right out from under my nose?"

"He didn't take me. I went with him," I say clearly. "Happily, because for the fourteen millionth time, you went away with the mermaids or Calla or whoever you go to when you aren't with me, and you forgot about me!"

He shakes his head, stubborn. "I never forget."

"You just forgot me!" I yell. "You left me!"

He shrugs. "I knew you'd be fine. I never forget."

"You always forget!" I yell. "Always! And if you don't, then that's worse."

"Why?"

"Because, Peter! We're either together or we're not, and if we're not, than you can't give a fuck when I'm with him."

His eyes pinch. "What's a fuck?"

And I don't mean to. I shouldn't have done it. But I sniff a laugh.

He grabs me by the shoulders, his face darkening in an instant. "Don't you laugh at me."

"I'm not laughing at you." I sigh. "I'm just…tired of you."

Peter breathes out loudly from his nose. "No friend of mine likes a pirate."

I straighten myself out a little as I peer up at him. "Are we back to just friends?"

Peter pulls a face. "What else would we be?"

I let out a hollow laugh.

"I told you not to laugh at me," he growls.

I wonder if he's truly forgotten what we were before, what he called me before. It feels too embarrassing to have to remind him, so I refuse to do it and simply let the weight of this rejection be distinctly lessened by the fact that however many nights ago,[*] I would have given everything I had on my body and in my bank to be with Jamison Hook.

"What else would you and me be, girl?" Peter asks, impatient. "I asked you a question."

"Well." I clear my throat demurely. "I don't tend to share my bed—"

"My bed," he cuts in to remind me.

I ignore him. "—with other boy…friends of mine."

Peter's face clouds over instantly. "You have other boy friends?"

"Male friends," I clarify with an eye roll. And when he still looks equally horrified, I offer him a shrug. "Back in London?"

"Who are they?" Peter asks sharply, jumping straight to his feet. "How tall are they?"

---

* I don't know how many, to be precise with time here, you know?

"Well, one of them is quite tall." I think to myself. Jasper was a tower.

"Which one?" Perter scowls. "What's his window street?"

I look over at him confused and give him a little shrug. "I'm…not sure."

Peter squints at me annoyed for a few seconds before he shakes his head like I'm an idiot. "He's not taller than me."

"Jamison is taller than you," I say without thinking, I suppose. Just rolls off the tongue. I don't know why.

His face clouds over. "Who's Jamison?"

I swallow, a bit nervous, because I mean, if anything was going to send him—and I really don't like to send him—fuck. I could have said no one. Probably I should have, really, but I don't because it wouldn't have been a lie I liked to tell. He is taller than him, in every single possible way.

I swallow before I say it.

"Hook," I tell him with a shrug like I'm not nervous, like I'm not wincing already.

Peter just stares over at me, incredulous, as though I've grown a whole other head. "Jamison?" He blinks.

I feel nervous suddenly, so I just shrug a bit. "Well, that's his name."

Peter glares at me. "You know his name?"

I shrug again, trying to play it down. "It's just his name. I didn't give it to him. It's just what you call him."[†]

Peter stares over at me, brows low and his eyes dark as he shakes his head. He nods his chin in a direction away from him. "Go stay in Jamison's bed tonight."

---

† I mean, it's technically not what I call him, but Peter need not know that.

CHAPTER FIFTEEN

I DIDN'T GO AND SLEEP IN JAMISON'S BED, THOUGH PERHAPS I SHOULD HAVE.

However, I did leave. I went into the woods and walked till I got lost and confused in the dark.

Some fairies found me—friends of Rune's, I presume. They made me a bed of clover and a patchwork quilt made of leaves.

It was a lovely sleep, actually.

Probably one of the better ones I've had since being here. Rather peaceful.

I'm woken with a sigh, and the clover tickles me awake.

I peer up at Peter Pan, arms folded over his chest, eyebrow up.

"There you are." He rolls his eyes. "Wondered where you wandered off to."

I sit up, frowning already. Why am I always frowning with him? "You sent me away."

"You left," he tells me.

I stand up quickly. "Because you told me to!"

Peter makes a sound at the back of his throat. "Girls take everything so seriously…"

"Yes." I give him a look. "This is so obviously me just blowing this right out of proportion. It's not as though you kicked me out of our house* after leaving me on an island with a fucking centaur to die."

He shrugs and gives me a condescending look. "It was a minotaur."

I let out a little cry of frustration and stomp off.

"Where are you going?" He flies after me.

---

* "My house," he interrupts me with.

"Away from you," I tell him.

"You don't know these woods," he tells me in a voice I don't like. I wouldn't say it was entirely a threat, nor would I necessarily say that it wasn't.

I give him a look. "I know them better than you think."

"Yeah?" He lands in front of me. "How?"

"Rye," I tell him defiantly, and Peter looks away, annoyed.

"You can't make it to the Old Valley from here by yourself."

"Yes, I can." I glare at him. "I've done it a million times."

"Go then." He nods his head in its direction.

"I will." I shrug.

"I'm not coming for you if you get lost," he tells me. "Or if a bear attacks you or something, you're on your own."

"Yes, Peter." I give him a look. "It appears I have been all along."

He frowns at me, confused, and I walk away.

I don't go to the Old Valley though. I want to be farther away from him than that. There's a breeze that tugs me through Preterra, through Haustland, and I know where I'm going now. I know where it's taking me.

It's taking me to her.

I've only been the one time with Jem. I don't know the way, but the breeze leads me. I don't know why it's being nice to me when Peter and I are at odds. Maybe this is his way of making sure I don't die. He won't keep me safe himself, but he'll have nature do it. It seems as lazy as it does lovely.

It's a bit of a walk.

A few hours.

I don't have a coat again, and I already feel as though I'll cop an earful for that.

It's worth saying, the breeze is a good guide; she keeps me right. Nudging me gently if I stray from the path up the mountain.

Rune joins me a bit of the way up. She tinkles hotly, and I give her a wry look.

"Oh, heard about that, did you?"

She jingles louder.

"I didn't know how to call you! I would have if I knew."

She clangs loudly.

"He didn't leave me. He forgot about me."

Rune's whole face goes red, and she pokes me in the forehead.

"No, I know." I sigh. "No, it really isn't much better."

She gives me a look, and her little eyebrows go up.

"I do like Jamison." I tell her with a frown.

She tinkles.

"Yes, that way."

There's some exuberant jingles, and I give her a look.

"I don't think that means anything though."

She chimes gently.

"Sometimes I think he does, then…" I shrug. "He's quick with his words."

Then that mouthy fairy tells me that Peter is quick to forget, and I give her a look, but I wonder if she has a point.

I like the walk up to this mountain; there's something cleansing about it. The higher I climb and the deeper into the altitude that I get, the better I feel, and I decide I should do this more often. Walks alone, the breeze and me—and a fairy who yells at me for things I'd imagine a mother might too.

When the ground starts to get snowy and my teeth start chattering, Rune lands on my shoulder and stomps impatiently before, from completely out of nowhere, a white feathered cloak cascades down from my shoulders.

"You're very good to me," I tell her with a fond smile.

And she says something along the lines of "someone ought to be."

When we get to the top of the mountain, Itheelia is standing there waiting for us.

She looks at me, eyebrows up and intrigued. "Hello."

"Hi," I say a bit quieter than I feel she'd like, but I've gone shy. I don't know why I've walked up a mountain to see the mother of the boy I'm very rather sure I have feelings for.

"What are you doing here?" she asks, and it's neither annoyed nor delighted by my presence.

"The wind blew me," I tell her a bit sarcastically, but also, I'm being a bit literal.

"Did it just?" She peeks around me like she might see it standing there beside me, then she nods at the fairy. "And who's this?"

"Rune," I say as she flits over to her, extending her hand.

"Ah." Itheelia nods. "I've heard good things." Rune chimes, pleased, as Itheelia looks over at me, gesturing to the cut on my cheek. "What happened here?"

Rune trills angrily, and Itheelia gives me a tall look, nodding for us to come inside.

"I fought a minotaur and won."

She stops still for a moment before she looks back at me. "What?"

"Oh." I give her a quick smile. "You know, the minotaur on the island with the labyrinth?"

"Yes." She stares at me.

"Well, Peter wanted to play a game—"

"What kind of game?" she interrupts.

Rune tinkles loudly, and I sigh. "A stupid one."

Itheelia stares over at me. "What kind of game?" she asks louder and clearer.

"I think it was a sort of rescue scenario he invented in his mind, where he'd put me in danger and then he'd save me, and then—"

Rune jingles hotly, and Itheelia—who obviously speaks Stjär—stares at her in disbelief.

"Well, what then happened was that Peter—very true to himself," I add to appease Rune, "became distracted and…left me."

Itheelia presses her lips together. "With the minotaur?"

"Yes."

"And you survived?"

"Yes."

"I'm glad you did." She touches my arm gently. "But how?"

"I just won the game." I shrug, and she looks confused. "You know. I got into the maze, and then the hedge grew around me, and then I was able to stab him in the eye, and then he sort of…fell over in pain, I suppose? And then he gave the dagger back, and the hedges opened up and let me out."

Itheelia stares at me for about four seconds, and I can't read her face.

"Right." She blinks five times and then nods. "Tea?"

"Oh." I pause. "Sure, thank you."

She moves over to the stove and puts the kettle on. She looks over her shoulder at me. "In the eye." She lifts a brow, sort of impressed. "I didn't think you'd have it in you."

I lift my shoulders like the whole thing was out of my hands. "I was just trying to survive."

"Aren't we all." She gives me a look as she hands me my tea and Rune a tiny one. Itheelia sits down opposite me. "How is my boy?"

I frown at her, defensively. "How should I know?"

"Ahh." Itheelia lets out a big, dramatic sigh. "Still beating that drum, are we?"

"I don't know to what you refer," I tell her with my nose in the air, and she and the fairy trade looks.

"She's a bit exhausting," Itheelia says to Rune, and she jingles in agreement. Itheelia eyes me. "A mother just wants to know about her son, Daphne. Do you think I drink all this tea because I like the taste?"

I shrug. "Perhaps."

She looks at me like I'm an idiot. "It takes like grass."

I look at the teacup she just handed me. "I suppose it does," I concede,* and Itheelia gives me a stern, maternal look.

"And you will drink it anyway."

I take another sip, and so does she.

"Did you say the minotaur gave the dagger back?" she asks as she blows into her tea. Steam rolls off of it.

I nod.

"Which dagger was it?" she asks.

"Oh." I smile at her. "It was one Jamison gave me for my birthday, so I was pleased the minotaur returned it, actuall—"

"Gold and rubies?" she asks.

I nod. "I love it very much."

"So does he." She gives me a careful look. "I gave him that dagger."

"Oh." I frown. "Should he not have given it to me? Was it—"

"It's his." She flashes me a smile that looks a kind of tender I don't know about. "To do with what he pleases."

---

* Because it really does.

Rune flits ups and whispers something to Itheelia, who gives her a look, and I don't know what they're talking about.

"Finish that." Itheelia points to my teacup before her eyes pinch curiously at me. "He hasn't said anything to you?"

I look over at her curiously. "About what?"

"About…anything?" She shrugs like she meant nothing by it, but her eyes flicker over my hand. I glance at it confused before I look back up at her.

"No?"

She nods, thinking whatever it is she's thinking all the way through.

"What?" I frown, not liking the feeling that she knows something about Jamison that I don't, though I'm quite sure there is plenty.

His mother gives me a sympathetic look. "He keeps his cards close to his chest, doesn't he?"

My shoulders slump a bit. "Impossibly so."

"You had a spat," she says to me.

"Just a tiny one a while back," I lie. "But not anymore. It's fine now."

She nods.

"Did he tell you?" I ask her, but she just shakes her head as she walks over, picks up my empty teacup, and peers into it. Rune flies over, lands on her shoulder, and squints into it as well, both of them for a moment, then Itheelia looks over at me, back to the teacup.

"Hmm," she says to herself and then takes it away, and right as she does, Rune flies over to me, and with her tiny little hands, she pinches my right cheek a million times.

"Ow!" I try to swat her away, but she just moves to my other cheek and does the same thing again. "Rune!" I growl, and she ignores me, flying behind me and tugging at my hair. "What are you—"

Then—

"Mum?" calls maybe the best voice in all the worlds, and I sit up straighter immediately and toss Rune a grateful look. She's a better friend than she is a fairy, and she's a phenomenal fairy.

I look over my shoulder only to catch sight of him as he walks into his mother's house.

"Mum," he calls again, and then his eyes land on me. "Oh." He looks confused but not displeased. "What are y'doing here?"

I say nothing for a few seconds. I don't know why? Because he's so lovely to look at, sometimes words escape you.

"I had a fight with Peter."

"Surprise, surprise," he says, though he looks pleased.

I give him a look. "I just went for a walk."

Jamison's face falters. "And ye came here?"

I purse my lips before I nod.

He frowns a bit, and I like very much the shape his face goes when he goes like this. "No' to town?"

I shake my head, not too sure what to say.

Itheelia appears behind me. "Just to your mother's house, darling, so don't be too vexed." She gives him a look.

Jamison rolls his eyes at her before they snag on me.

In two steps, he crosses the distance between us, a hand on each of my cheeks as he pulls me into the light.

"What the fuck happened to yer face?" He frowns, but my heart skips a beat.

I shake my head a little bit but not too much, because I don't want to shake him off.

"It's fine," I tell him. "I'm fine."

He doesn't let go, stares at me so intensely I swallow heavy, and something starts to pool in my belly.

Jamison breathes heavily through his nose. "Did he do this?"

"No," I say as Rune trills away unhelpfully.

Jamison looks over at her, and I feel relieved that he doesn't speak Stjär too well.

"Who did this?"

I shake my head at him like he's being silly. "It's a long story."

He spins me around to face Itheelia, his hands still on me. "Mum, fix it," he tells her.[*]

---

[*] Much more sternly than I would ever dare speak to her, that much is for certain.

"Darling." She rolls her eyes. "Jammie, it's a scratch."

"It needs a stitch," he says, impatient now.

"I don't want a stitch in my face!" I look back at him.

"It's deep, Daph," he says, voice serious. "Ye sleep in a fucking tree. It could get infected." Then he looks back at his mother, face all serious. "Make it, Mum, now."

Itheelia walks over to her son, unbothered by how demanding[†] he's being. She lifts an eyebrow. "I will make it if you drink a tea."

He rolls his eyes and waves his hands impatiently. "Nosy witch," he says under his breath.

"I heard that," his mother calls back to him.

"Said it so ye would," he tells her before he gives me a look, moving me away from his mum and Rune. His face goes back to serious. "Bo, why dïdnae ye come to me?"

Itheelia walks over with the tea, hands it to Jamison, and then just stands there, smiling pleasantly.

He gives her a curt look that makes me feel like he's either brave or stupid[‡] to be so capricious towards her. "You dïnnae need to stand here while I drink it. I said to ye I will."

Itheelia rolls her eyes. "This is my house, you know," she tells him as she retreats.

He stares at me, tongue pressed into his cheek, mostly annoyed (but with the smallest hint of amusement present as well) as he waits for her to move out of earshot.

He lifts his eyebrow, waiting for me to answer.

"Jem," I sigh. "I—I don't—"

I stare up at him. I don't know when his hand made its way to my waist, but it has and he's holding it.

I sigh. Why didn't I go to him? I don't know. Because I didn't want to go to Jamison's boat and find him with Morrigan on the table again and have him see it crush me on my face in front of him? I didn't want any kind of confirmation

---

† And arguably rude.

‡ Or perhaps just her very brazen son.

that Hook is exactly who I worry he might be, that he's not as good as I think he is, as I so desperately want him to be.* Because I already don't really know what I am to one boy, except something between nothing and everything depending on the day, the hour, and the moment. I don't want to be that to Jamison too. And I can't actually figure out what I am to him.

I open my mouth to say something, but nothing comes out, so I just wave my hands between us once vaguely with a confused look on my face.

Jamison shakes his head, looking genuinely annoyed.

"How?" he asks, sounding a bit desperate.

Then Itheelia pops up beside us again, an impatient smile on her face.

Her son swears under his breath and rolls his eyes. He swigs the tea back in one gulp and thrusts her the teacup.

"Thank you." She gives him a tight smile and then watches him for a moment afterwards with pinched eyes. "Did that burn your esophagus on the way down?"

"Aye." He nods once, wincing a little, and our eyes catch.

I sniff a laugh, and so does he.

He turns to his mother, the moment before now broken.

"What dae they say?"

She holds it to her chest. "Oh, now you want to know?"

Jem gives her a look. "They're mine."

"No longer," she tells him politely (but she does flash the leaves to Rune).

Jamison throws me the kind of look a boy who loves his mother but is annoyed at her might make, and it makes me smile at him, but he just frowns at me, runs his finger over the cut on my cheek.

"Sure, who would do that to a face like this?"

All of me goes soft, and my eyes go heavy as I stare up at him.

"Ahem." Itheelia clears her throat, and we both snap our heads over at her, like we've been caught in a moment. She's holding a little mortar and pestle that's full of a crushed-up lilac paste. She scoops some up on her finger and eyes me. "This will sting for a moment, and then it'll be gone."

I nod once, then she smears it on me.

---

* Need him to be, even.

Now, I must say, "sting" was an understatement. My eyes go wide and Jamison grimaces, looking sorry for me like he knows it's worse than she made it sound.

It's skin cells regenerating on the spot—growing and creeping back towards one another to make my skin close again. It feels like a burn, this pulling, boring kind of pain, and Jem holds my gaze as I frown through it all.

After about a minute, it stops hurting, and Itheelia looks over at me rather indifferently. "It's done."

Jamison reaches over and wipes the paste off my face. "Perfect," he says, watching me, and I swallow heavy.

I reach up and touch my cheek where the wound was before. "Oh my god." I look over at Itheelia, wide-eyed. "That's magic!"

"Literally, yes." She nods, wiping her hands on her dress.

I stare over at Jem a bit dumbstruck, and he gives me a little wink.

"I think we are done here," Itheelia announces, Rune sitting on her shoulder.

Jamison frowns. "But I just got here."

His mother nods. "And now you will walk this girl back down the mountain."

He tosses me an unimpressed look, but I give him a big, hopeful grin. I liked the walk up here by myself, but I will like it more with him. He rolls his eyes at me and moves towards the door.

"I love you," his mother calls.

He gives her a long-suffering look. "Love you. Thanks for—" He gestures to his cheek and nods his head towards me.

"Yes." I look over at her. "Really, thank you. And sorry for just dropping in."

"Anytime." She shakes her head. "Well, not anytime, but you know, within reason."

I nod at her, pleased because I feel as though I've made a friend, and I don't think I have that many here.

The first few minutes down the mountain are spent in silence, but I love silence with him. Our shoulders keep brushing against one another, and I become acutely aware of where my shoulder sits in correlation to his. His shoulder and my nose are about the same height. I like him from down here—I have such a prime view of the angle of his jaw, the way his facial hair shades him. He has a freckle on his neck that I think is calling my name, and I swallow heavy again.

"Jamison—"

He looks at me out of the corner of his eye. "Yes?"

"Do you remember that I'm eighteen now?"

He stares straight ahead but smiles a little. It's only for a second before it's replaced with frustration.

"Daph, ye can come to me." He looks over at me. "Always."

I give him a nod because I don't know what I am to him, and I don't know whether I believe him.

"I like your mum," I tell him to change the subject.

He looks down at me. "She likes you."

I purse my lips. "Does she?"

Jamison laughs. "She's a bit of a closed book, hard to read, but aye." He nods a few times before he eyes me. "Are we going to talk about what happened?"

"No." I look straight ahead.

"Wusnae a question, Daph." He knocks me with his shoulder gently. "Tell me."

I squint at a tree that's nowhere near him. "I don't think I should," I say eventually.

He asks, a few paces behind me now, "Why no'?"

I take a breath before I turn to face him. "I don't suspect it'll thrill you."

"Nor do I, but I want ye to tell me anyway."

But it feels like an invitation to trouble, and it's already been a big couple of days, so I shake my head. "No."

Jem grabs my wrist and stands me still as he adjusts the clasp on the feather cloak Rune just made me.

His eyes hold mine, and the breeze all of a sudden blows so cold I huddle in towards him without thinking.

"Tell me," he says, and neither of us notice the way the wind is moving around us.

I stare up at him a few seconds, frown as I think about saying it. I breathe out my nose. "He took me to the labyrinth."

Jem eyes me. "No."

I shrug like it's not a big deal, but it is a big deal, I think. I don't know why I'm acting like it's not. "He wanted to play a game."

He gives me a look. "No, he dïdnae."

"With the minotaur," I tell him matter-of-factly.

Jamison's mouth twitches in an angry way.

"And then"—I clear my throat demurely—"he got distracted and left me."

Jem nods his head a few times, then starts walking down the mountain a lot faster. "A'm going t' kill him."

"Jem!" I scurry after him.

"No." He shakes his head. "Enough's enough."

"Jamison, wait." I reach for him, and he spins again, grabbing me by the shoulders, holding me tightly as he ducks so we're eye to eye.

"You could hae died," he tells me.

"I know." I shrug. "But I—"

"Didn't?" he cuts in, shaking his head madly. "That daesnae make it okay."

"It was an accident, I think."

His face pulls. "Ye think?"

We stare at each other crossly before he breathes out, shakes his head, and starts walking again.

"He's just so forgetful," I call after him. "Where are you going? You're going the wrong way."

Jamison stops dead in his tracks and stares over at me. "Yer having a laugh, right?"

"What?" I frown.

He stares at me wide-eyed. "Are ye really going back t' him?"

"Well." I breathe out, annoyed. "Where else can I go?"

He presses his tongue into his bottom lip. "Really?" he asks, and I don't like his tone.

"Yes, really." I put my hands on my hips. "The last time I came to you, your hands were very full."

He starts to shake his head again. "Thon was before—"

"Before what?"

"Afore—" He stops short. "It daesnae matter. It's—" He scoffs and keeps walking. "What the fuck is it with you and him?" He looks over his shoulder at me. "Yer smarter than this. Yer better than him."

"I think it's fate," I say, and I sound worried. I think I look it too, my brows all knitted together. I want Jamison to tell me I'm wrong, but he doesn't, and for some reason, it looks like I've slapped him.

He takes a moment to recompose himself. He steadies himself, giving me a long look. "Do ye no' think you choose yer fate?"

I shrug as though I'm helpless to it all. I think I am. "I don't know that you can control it."

"Dinnae like that." He scrunches his face up. "Sounds…awful."

"Not awful. Just inevitable."

"And you're sure you and him are inevitable?" Jamison asks, eyebrows tall and waiting. "All meant t' be?"

Actually, Jamison, less so by the second, I think to myself as I stare over at him.

"Well, who else might I be meant to be with?" I say, hoping he'll say something like "me, you idiot" and finally kiss me stupid and maybe more right now—I think I'd quite like to do that with him on the side of a mountain—but Jamison doesn't say that. He doesn't do it either. There's no kiss, no wandering hands, no wonderful more where he's pressed up against me how I think about all the time when I'm sure Peter's not looking. There's no protest from him, just eyes that look a bit ragged, and I suddenly feel nervous.

He nods slowly. "All right."

Jamison clears his throat, pushes his hands through his hair. I don't like it when he does that. I like it when it falls over his face. He's less buttoned up. I think I can see him clearer, and sometimes, I don't know why, but often I find myself worrying with Jamison that I'm not seeing him clearly at all.

"So how was yer man after yer birthday?" he asks without looking at me.

"He didn't mention it," I say, definitely looking at him.

"Right." He nods.

"Hickeys and jagua smudged all over him though." I eye him carefully for his response, half expecting him to fly off the handle and thunder down the hill again, yelling that Peter's gone too far and I'm an idiot, and I'll run after him to calm him down and maybe I'll get to hold his arm—

But then Jamison just gives a quick, indifferent shrug.

"Well, when opportunity knocks," he says mostly to himself, but he catches my eye quickly at the end before he glances back away. "Or, ye ken, knowing her, when opportunity throws itself at ye."

I let out this sound that is all air escaping my lungs. Less of a breathing out as much as the sensation of someone invisible coming up behind me and squeezing all the air I have in me right out.

"Oh, come on." Hook tosses me a look. "Ye know I think he's a fucking twat o' a boy, but you can scarcely blame him fer that."

I stare over at him, and I feel like it shows on my face, my little sunken heart all on display for him to see. "Can I not?"

He shrugs big, and I can't be sure but I feel its intention was to hurt me. "She is gorgeous."

My mouth tugs downwards but I nod. "Okay."

"Honestly." Jamison eyes me. "I'd probably hae a crack if I could."

I take a quick short breath, ignore the stinging in my chest that's worse than when his mother closed the gash in my face, and give him a defiant look. "And why can't you?"

"Besides the fact that she's a fucking nut, I cannae imagine that would go down particularly well wi' ye." He eyes me.

"With me?" I say and stare at him as though I've no idea what he's talking about.

"Aye," he eyes me. "You."

I scoff. "I can assure you, I wouldn't care," I lie, and it's an obvious lie, I think. To me, it's an obvious lie—my eyes are glassy, my cheeks are hot, we're in each other's faces, and I feel like he should know that actually, I'm full of shit, but whether he does or he doesn't, it doesn't seem to dull the sharpness of his pride.

"Is thon so?"

I put my nose in the air. "It is so."

"Right then," His jaw juts out as he nods. "Maybe I will."

"Marvelous." I shrug breezily. "I hope she likes tables."

He gives me a ragged look. "I hope she likes baths."

"Do you know what?" I glare at him. "You're not very mature for a twenty-two-year-old."

"Actually, a'm twenty-three."

"Since when?" I frown.

"Since two days ago."

"Oh." I pout. I don't know why. "Happy birthday."

He rolls his eyes a bit. "Thanks."

"What did you do for it?" I ask, trying to keep the conversation light and pleasant.

"Nothing," He shrugs. "I had some drinks at the Dirty Bird."

"With who?" I ask lightly, and I don't let it show on my face that it hurts my feelings that he didn't tell me. Why didn't he tell me?

"Just some friends." His eyes graze over the trees we're passing, but mine fall to their stumps. Am I not his friend?

I suck in my left cheek, try to ask it like it's any old question, completely unloaded, just asked for the sake of asking—"With Morrigan?"

He flicks his eyes over at me briefly, then away again, and I get the feeling that he's reluctant to answer. "Among others."

I let out a puff of air, walking ahead of him as I study the horizon intently for no reason at all.

"Are ye jealous?" he calls to me.

I spin around, eyebrows up. "No more than you are of me when I'm with Peter."

I'm glaring at him, and I don't say a word, but I'm begging for him to tell me that he's a madman when it comes to me and Peter, that his jealousy is insatiable when it comes to me, that he hates it more than he can wrap words around, and he's glaring back at me, and I wonder for a brief moment if it all could be true. And then his eyes pinch.

"I just dïnnae get jealous."

I think my face falls. That or you can see physically on my face the whiplash I get from the merry-go-round he and I are on.

Hook eyes me. "Does thon bother ye?"

"No, it wouldn't bother me at all if you weren't a complete and rotten liar," I tell him bravely.

"I'm no' lying." He shrugs, completely indifferent.

"You lied again!" I stomp my foot, trying to get off this stupid ride.

"No, Daph. I dïnnae get jealous." He shakes his head, then eyes me, and there's a mean look in there. "Especially no' of boys who live in trees with girls who dïnnae ken what they want."

"Take that back," I tell him quickly.

He puts his face up close to mine. "Which part?"

I scowl at him. "You know which part."

"I winnae take it back." He shakes his head. "It's true. Ye are a girl, and you dïnnae ken what you want."

My eyes go round. "You don't like girls," I remind him, and it's obvious that I'm hurt.

"No," he tells me as he looks me square in the eye. "I dïnnae."

"And I am one?" I ask, eyebrows up.

He waves his hand towards me dismissively. "Evidently."

"Fuck you," I tell him angrily, but actually, I think I just sound sad.

"All right." He nods, unfazed, and walks ahead.

I walk after him, head down, and he groans as he shakes his head.

"When did we start fighting?"

"We're always fighting," I tell him with a sigh.

He faces me. "Aye, and whose fault is that?"

"Yours!" I yell at him, poking him in the chest. "Why are you such a prick about everything?"

And then Jamison gets right in my face and yells, "Because ye make me so fucking angry."

"So?" I yell back. "You make me angry all the time, and I never hurt you!"

"Ye nev—" He chuckles dryly. Pauses. Breathes out. "Sure, okay, if ye say so."

"Do I?" My face falters. "Hurt you?"

And then I don't know what's happened, but he looks winded. Just innately winded. Like everything about me right now is deflating him on the spot.

"Jamison," I press. "Answer me. Have I?"

He says nothing, so I keep going.

"When?"

He rolls his eyes and brushes past me again and trots farther down the hill. "Yer a fucking eejit," he says mostly under his breath but definitely loud enough for me to hear.

"Stop talking to me like that!" I yell down at him.

"Then stop being a fucking eejit!" he yells back.

And then there's a ripple through the trees and the smell of summer in the air as Peter Pan lands next to me.

"Girl." He peers at me. "Is this scoundrel bothering you?"

I stare at Hook I've got daggers for eyes now. "Yes, actually."

Peter flies over to Hook and glares at him. "I should cut your throat for this."

Hook gives him a disparaging look. "For what?"

It flickers over Peter's face that he doesn't know for what he'd be cutting his throat. Can't imagine that would matter too much to him. I think he'd like to cut it either way.

"For that—for—what you did to her," Peter says like he knows, and he moves back over towards me.

Hook rolls his eyes at Peter and then looks past him back to me. "What dae I do to ye? Hurt yer feelings? Call ye a girl? Make ye jealous?"

"Oh." I shake my head at him, pretending my heart isn't a splattered can of tomatoes on a tiled floor. "But you don't get jealous, so how the fuck would you even know?"

Peter looks from me to Hook, brows low and confused, and Hook just says nothing. His nostrils are a bit flared.

I grab Peter's hand, and he lifts me into the air.

"Come on, Peter. Let's go," I say to him, but I'm staring at Jem.

"Give Calla my regards, would you?" he calls after me, and I pretend something gets in my eye when the tear spills from it.

"He is scum, Daphne," Peter tells me once we're back in the house, lying down in his bed. "Pay no mind to him."

"No." I stare straight up at the ceiling. "I shan't."

Peter elbows me gently. "I won't send you away again."

I look over at him. "Promise?"

"I promise." He nods, and his mouth looks very pink. He brushes it over mine, and it makes me feel sad and happy in the same strange moment. "I came for you because the trees told me that you needed me."

"I did," I tell him.

"Did I save you?" he asks with a frown.

"I suppose." I flash him a quick smile, and Peter doesn't notice the edges of it are turned down.

"Ah." He sighs, putting his hands behind his head. "The cleverness of me." I say nothing when he says that, and Peter notices, frowning as he perceives my sadness. "Should I fly over the way and gut him later?"

"No," I say quickly. "No." I shake my head.

"Are you sure?" he asks pleasantly. "It wouldn't be a bother."

But I fear he is wrong. I would be quite terribly bothered, and therein lies the problem.

"Peter?" I roll in towards him.

"Mm?" he says with his eyes closed.

"When you call me a girl, do you mean it nicely or cruelly?"

Peter's eyes spring open, upset by the question. "A girl is the nicest thing you could ever call someone."

That pleases me a bit. "Do you think?"

Peter gives me a confused look.

"Hook called me a girl, but I don't think he meant it as a compliment," I try to explain.

He shakes his head as he stares at the ceiling. "You don't want compliments from pirates anyway."

"No, you're right." I close my eyes. "I don't."

He kisses my cheek. "Good night."

"Good night," I tell him, but I can feel him watching me in the dim lighting of the tree house.

"Girl?" he says after a few seconds.

"Mm?" I say with my eyes shut still.

"Do you know what beautiful means?" Peter asks.

I look over at him with a confused look. "Yes?"

He nods solemnly. "You are it."

CHAPTER
SIXTEEN

I'm going to tell Jem, I decided. That I'm sorry and that before, I was scared and stupid, but actually, I'd like to be together, and if he'd like that too, then I'd like to find a way to make it work.

Because I want it to work. I want him, really. And actually, there's a word that I've never really said before about a boy, but I think I might—I could?—I feel as though I do.

I couldn't sleep all night because of it.

A bit because it felt funny to sleep in a bed with Peter knowing that I want to be with someone else and also just because I really wanted to tell Jamison.

I'm up before the sun, which I never am. It also means I'm up before Peter, which somehow casts the world in a curious light I don't know much about.

I think he wakes everything up around here. As I creep out of the tree house, not just the boys are sleeping, but so are the flowers and the woodland creatures. The suns are still tucked away, cozy beneath the horizon.

I creep down to the dock and untie the rowboat.

The water is still, mist hovering above it. It's not entirely dark because of the four moons, but it mostly is. I'm not trying to beat the light. You can't anyway. It always wins. Peter will wake soon, he either will or will not notice my absence, and whichever way that goes, it won't affect what I'm about to do. I'm going to do it regardless.

I'm about halfway across the harbor when I hear him.

"Hello down there," he calls, a little confused.

I look back and up, and there he is, Jamison Hook, sailing the Golden Folly, staring down at me with a confused smile.

"Oh." I blink up at him. "Hi."

He looks so handsome. Brows low, hair falling over his eyes and blowing in the barely there wind, his cheeks flushed, mouth sun-kissed, which I love. I don't remember his mouth looking this color yesterday, but it makes him look all the dreamier, so I'm pleased for it.

He gives me a confused smile. "I was just on my way to ye."

I give him a proper one. "Me too."

He nods his head at his ship. "Want t' come aboard?"

I gesture to my little rowboat. "Do you want to come aboard?"

His face pulls, and I smile up at him playfully.

"I'm joking. Throw me down a rope."

He sniffs a laugh and tosses me down a rope. I stand on top of the big knot at the bottom of it, and he pulls me up to him with an ease that makes me swallow heavy and my heart fall down a flight of stairs. He offers me his hand as my feet find their place on the deck, and our hands linger a few moments longer than they need to in one another's.

I glance up at him, feeling shy. I pinch my bottom lip nervously. "You look nice," I tell him.

His face falters. "Dae I?"

I nod, not looking away from him. "Fresh or well rested or something."

He laughs. Sort of a weird laugh, I suppose. A bit bewildered, or something.

Either way, he doesn't return the compliment. I'm hardly offended though, as I don't suppose he could in good conscience. I damn well didn't sleep a wink last night and am quite sure my face lives to tell that puffy, tired little tale.

"I wanted to talk to ye," he tells me, face looking serious, and my eyes skip a beat as I nod.

"And I you." I blink over at him, my eyes blooming like the flowers that are doing so right now on the mainland as Peter strokes their chins awake. "You go first."

I shouldn't care to tell him I have feelings for him first needlessly, not when he's about to tell me himself.

"Right." Jamison gives me a tender smile and sniffs, amused, nodding to himself. And then he shrugs. "We're a fucking mess, you an' me."

Have you ever been caught in an emotion? Where you've been feeling something so heavily and so intensely, and then there's a sudden change in the emotional atmosphere, and you feel your face, feel the way you're holding yourself change, feel the smile fall off you like old fruit on a tree that's past its picking day?

I let out an unsure laugh. "Are we?"

Jamison gives me a wry look. "I like getting in yer head. I like making ye jealous. I like riling you up."

"Why?" I ask, and I hold my breath to puff myself up so he can't see me deflating on the spot.

"I dïnnae ken." He shrugs like it's a puzzle he's trying to figure out. "I think we just bring out the worst in each other… dïnnae ye think?"

"Oh." I stare at him blankly for a few seconds, then I look down at my feet to make sure they're not actually sinking into the ground, that I'm not really draining away between the cracks in the floorboards of his ship, that it's just how I feel inside my body. I clear my throat. "I suppose. Maybe."

"It's fun getting a rise out o'ye." He gives me a weak shrug. "It feels good t' annoy ye, have ye chasing after me."

I give him a despondent look. "Charming."

He smirks a little. "Sorry. But forbye"—another lift of the shoulders—"yer a pretty girl, and it's good to have yer attention—it feels good—but I ken yer not here for me."

The breeze picks up, and it blows around us. This time yesterday, it would have blown me into him, had me huddling in to have him keep me warm, but today it just cuts me through like a knife.

"Right," I say, and there's no air in my words.

"Aye?" he asks, eyebrows up and maybe a little hopeful, and I wonder if he's waiting for me to correct him, but how could I?

"Um." I stare at him and swallow. "I—right." I can't correct him. I can't even hold my hand steady right now.

Jamison nods and gives me an easy smile. "It's just a game, you an' me."

I swallow. "Okay."

His face falters, and I shake my head.

"I mean—" I clear my throat. "Yes." I nod instead. I'm not making sense.

"Good then," he says, but I can't tell if he means it.

I stare over at him and wonder in this sinking way whether he ever actually knew me how I felt he may have or whether that was a stupid hope I fastened myself to because I'm just a girl. He can't have known me how I thought, because if he did, he would have seen it—it's right here on the surface. None of this is good.

He lifts his eyebrows again, a bit hopeful. "Because we can be friends now."

"Right." I nod, smiling tightly. "Friends."

He nods back and gives me a pleasant look. "Is that what ye were coming here t' say?"

There's a fraction of a second reaction delay to my response, and I wonder if it's obvious and he knows I'm lying.

"Yes." I do one emphatic nod. "Exactly. Yes."

"Good then."

"And also, sorry." I flash him a smile. "For being a brat yesterday."

He gives me a quarter of a smile. "Yer a wee brat every day, so…"

I give him a weak, empty laugh. It sounds like a few pennies rattling around in a tin can. Something innately pitiful about it, although you can't quite put your finger on exactly what.

"Jam?" says a girl's voice from behind us.

I look past him to a girl standing outside his bedchamber.

"Oh, hey," he says reflexively.

She's quite beautiful. Dark, curly hair. Rather olive skin. Pink lips, and I realize his lips I'd been admiring just before—it wasn't the sun that had kissed them, it was her. Her legs are bare, so are her feet. Her hair's all disheveled, and they've obviously—obviously—just had sex.

But do you know what? That's not even the worst part. The worst part? She's wrapped up in his coat. The one I love. The one that I think means something to me and I thought to him, and as soon as he sees she's in it, he looks over at me, but my eyes aren't his anymore. They belong to the sea now.

For me, want feels like being kicked in the stomach, but anguish feels like pain shooting through my fingers down into my nerve endings. I feel it in my bones, where he feels want—which I think he must have never truly felt for me. I feel that now.

The girl eyes me carefully for a moment before she looks over at him. "Where are we?"

He gives her a smile. "I just needed t'catch up with a friend about something."

She stares over at me again, and I raise my hand awkwardly.

"A friend."

"Go back t'bed." He nods his chin at her. "I'll be ri' there."

My mouth falls open, and I shut it quickly, absentmindedly pinch my lip between my fingers until I taste something salty.

Jamison looks back at me, and his face falters. "Ye hurt yer lip." He reaches for me, and I dodge his touch. Something like hurt or offense rolls over him, and I'm glad for it. He clears his throat, looking uncomfortable now. "Can I give ye a ride back?"

"Oh no." I shake my head. "I've got the boat."

"A tow then?" he offers, eyebrows up.

"Nope." I shake my head as I walk back towards the rope. "The water will take me." I flash him a quick smile. I need to get out of here before he sees me crying.

He offers me his hand. I pretend I don't see it and dive off into the ocean, beg the water to wash how my heart's stinging away, but it doesn't. Not as I climb into my little dinghy and stare up at him. We say something to each other with our eyes, but I don't know what it is because we don't know how to talk to each other, and I don't think we've ever been on the same page.

I'm just a game.

I put the paddles in the water and make one big stroke, and the water and the wind do the rest for me. They carry me the whole way back to the home I thought I left this morning.

It's a pirate thing, I think—he gets into my head sometimes, that's all. Being around Jamison pulls the rug from under me; everything I'm sure of when he's not around becomes so uncertain the second he's in a room, but that doesn't mean anything other than he's good at making me feel uncertain about myself, which isn't even a good thing! Why did I think that was a good thing? It's actually a terrible thing. Jamison is a terrible thing.

I'm not ready to go inside when the boat pulls up at the dock. I don't know how to yet face the boys I just tried to leave, one of them in particular.

I sit at the end of the dock, my legs dangling in the water, staring at the blue that still feels like a miracle no matter how many days in a row I see it.

I take a deep breath, look up at the sky, and as I do, I see one of the suns rise between two of the moons, and I have this deep revelation that there's no going back.

If it can't be Jamison—and it can't be—then it must be Peter. What can Jasper England do for me now that I've known this life? These boys? The wind in my hair, the ocean giving me rides home, secrets that live inside a volcano. Anything else now would feel like half a life, and I don't want half a life. I just want one here. Whatever that might look like.

I take another staggered breath and wipe my face.

"Girl?" Peter says quietly from behind me.

I look back at him, and he's frozen there, eyes wide with nerves.

He creeps towards me the way you might move towards a frightened animal. "Girl, why are you crying?"

I give him my bravest smile. "It's the grown-up things, Peter. They keep coming for me."

He sits down next to me, eyes heavy and sorry for me. "Okay." He takes his sleeve and wipes my nose with it. "Want to go up to the cloud? You could put them away."

I shake my head, my eyes filling up again. "Not this time."

"I don't understand." He pulls back. "You'd rather be sad?"

I bite down on my bottom lip. "I just need to feel them for a moment." I flash him my bravest smile. I need to remember them so I don't go back to him.

A moment, I tell myself. And then I'll put them away forever.

CHAPTER SEVENTEEN

"GIRL," SAYS PETER, FLOATING OVER ME AS I LIE ON THE DOCK, SUNNING.

I peer up at him through one eye.

The width of his shoulders takes up half my view of the sky, blocking two of the suns. I can't imagine that he's actually getting bigger in real life because he drinks from the fountain every few days, but still to me, he looks to have grown.

Maybe just in my mind's eye.

A couple of weeks have passed since Jamison definitively categorized our relationship as "friends," and they've both dragged and slipped by.

Sort of how it feels to be pulled under a wave and tossed around.

Once you get past the feeling that you can't breathe and maybe you're dying, the rolling about's not so bad. Almost like a ride.

Peter Pan is a ride and a half and the most beautiful distraction from the ache in my chest that I could have ever daydreamed.

He took me to Aqueria the other day. I met the Poseidon, who Peter told me isn't a god but is king of the sea. Not just this one but all the seas.

He was quite firm, but I get the feeling that were you to be on his good side, he might be quite nice. I suspect I'm not on his good side though. I don't think the mermaids care for me much, not now that most of Peter's attention is on me.

Still, he said he wanted me to meet them. Actually, he said he wanted them to meet me.

He wasn't unkind, the king, just stern. Bowed his head in a little nod and spoke mostly in hushed tones to Peter.

It was still impossibly beautiful though; Aqueria is beyond imagination. An underwater city and palace that's made of coral and limestone and sandstone, with underwater plants you've never seen before, crystals I've never heard of, and streams of light pouring through windows that never close, because why would they? We're so far down that it doesn't make sense for the light to still reach, but it does, and I suppose it makes sense here, because magic.

Peter gave me this little thing that you hold in your mouth. It's almost like a tiny harmonica, and it lets you breathe underwater.

Speaking's still hard. Kissing harder still.

But breathing is easy.

We also went back to La Vie En Grande. We found buried treasure on an island off the coast of the mainland. We saved a baby whale that was beached on the shore of Buccaneers Cove.

He taught me how to paint the sky.

The days have been good, how I think I imagined they'd be in Neverland all along. I make a habit of going to the cloud every day to drop off the parts of the day that I don't think I should like to remember. I drop off my thoughts of the medicine now—it's just medicine after all. I drop off the thoughts about where Peter goes when he thinks I'm sleeping or when I'm with Rune or Rye. I have my own friends; why shouldn't he?

There are a few specific things I feel it would be wiser for me to keep so I don't fall back into bad habits with pirates, but I definitely did drop off that terrible thought Rye seeded in me that there are different kinds of fate, and I'm glad I did too. That kept me up at night before I put it away—wondering what he meant, what it might mean—and now that it's sitting on a shelf in the clouds, when I think of it (and I hardly ever do), I don't even know what the fuss in my head was about. Different kinds of fate? Who cares? I don't even know what that means. Nothing about a mountain and a breeze whistles through my mind, and there's no snow on our noses. The only fate I've ever heard of is the kind about Peter and I, that he'd come for me, and he has.

He floats in front of me now, waiting for my attention.

"Yes, Peter?"

"There is a ball tonight."

I sit up. "A ball?"

He floats over to land on one of the dock's wooden columns. He balances on one foot. "Yeah. Do you know what balls are?"

I cross my arms. "Yes."

"Not a throwing ball, a—"

"I know what balls are, Peter," I interrupt.

He nods. "And dates? Do you know about them?"

I swallow, sitting up straighter. "Do you know about dates?"

"Course I do." He rolls his eyes, annoyed. "You're mine to this."

I stand up. "When is it?"

"Soon." He shrugs.

"Soon as in, in a few days?"

Peter shakes his head like I'm the silly one. "Soon like now." He jumps off the column to the dock, hands on his hips. "Go get dressed." He walks back towards the tree house.

"Into what?" I call after him.

He ignores me. "And be quick about it. You're looking a bit heavy."

My mouth falls open at his rudeness.

"I can tell you've got things on your mind." He tells me with a shrug. "We'll drop them off on the way."

I didn't drop them off.

It's Jamison. That's what's heavy on me—what I feel for him.

I see it every time I stand in front of the mirror in the baggage claim.

It's not even a bag; it's a yoke around my neck.

I stare at it, feel it weighing down on my shoulders, imagine how much nicer it would feel, how much easier my days would seem if I were to take this particular thought off—but like every time lately when I've stood here and seen it, I don't.

I stare at my reflection. I'm in a gown Rune made for me.

"She's really annoying, that fairy, but she's good at making you those dresses" is what Peter said before Rune kicked him in the temple and he yelled "ow" and said sorry.

I straighten my dress out. As best as I can tell, it's made entirely out of flowers and vines. They climb up one shoulder and cascade into a giant skirt at the back, and while it is rather covered, it's still rather breezy.

I do look lovely, though it looks strange in my reflection when paired with the yoke. At least no one can see it but me.

I head back out to the cloud where Peter's waiting, and I stare over at him.

Light linen trousers (clean ones) and a white linen shirt that was ironed when we left the house but is all scrunched up again, and I think he did it on purpose.

No shoes, because he insisted he would "rather die" and "what do we need shoes for anyway? We fly everywhere." He has a point, I suppose.

"All dropped off?" John says with a smile as he casts off into another cloud.

"Yes." I flash him a liar's smile.

I didn't. And I think he can tell.

Peter can't. He doesn't have the kind of eyes that could see the true weight another person is carrying. But John does.

He knows I didn't.

I couldn't.

It felt like a betrayal for some reason.

Jamison hasn't done anything wrong. All he's said is he wants to be my friend, and I'd wash away my feelings for him because of it?

How childish.

I'll let it run its course, like a fever. And one day, the fever will break, and I will wake up cured.

I don't need the island magic.

I am my own island magic.

"Come." Peter flies over to me, taking my hand. "It's a long flight to Alabaster Island."

He's not taken me here before. We've been near it but not on it. Alabaster Island is the main island. It's big. More of a city than a small seaside village like we have on Neverland.

But it's a funny kind of city. Like a melting pot. Not of different cultures but of different times. It could as easily be ancient Egypt as it could be the year 2000.

"Whose ball is it?" I ask Peter as we fly over the city, swerving through the streets.

Peter shrugs. "Just this man's."

"Just this man's?" I repeat, staring back at him, but he doesn't notice and keeps flying towards a castle that's nestled up against the mountains.

Alabaster Island mostly looks like Cape Breton Island. Dramatic and beautiful and calm and fascinating but not in a way that makes you overly eager to discover it. There's no great urgency to peer around every corner, but a nice walk to a place you don't yet know about sounds like a lovely idea.

We land on a balcony, and it's quite the entrance. Not because we crash or anything, but it appears Peter and I are the only two to have arrived by flight.

I'm immediately relieved to see Rye and fractionally disheartened that Calla's right there beside him.

Peter spots her quickly and glides over to her. He puts his hands on her waist, smiles at her like I wish he wouldn't.*

She looks beautiful—much how you'd expect. Her dress is made from some kind of animal skin, fur. It's got no sleeves and ties off at her neck like a halter.

She looks sexy in a way that makes me in my flowers feel like a stupid schoolgirl.

Rye touches a bud on my dress. "This is incredible."

I flash him a smile. "Rune."

He nods and I take his wrist, feeling grateful for him.

"I didn't know you'd be here. I'm so glad you are." I look around, and it's decorated like Christmas. "What is this?"

He stares up at the ceiling that's glistening away like real stars. "The hibernal solstice."

"How is that possible?" I give him a look. "There are four suns here."

Rye laughs. "It was Day's favorite holiday on Constanopia."

---

* Even though I don't technically have a leg to stand on.

"Day?" I frown, thinking on the name. It sounds familiar.

I think I know about a Day in a part of my brain I haven't used in a while, and I flick through the pages of my memory, looking for the thought I know is in there about who this Day man might be, when a hand slips around my waist.

I know whose it is immediately—there's no question. Only one person takes me by the waist these days, and only one person does it with something akin to force. Peter pulls me back tight against him, and he doesn't notice when his grip knocks off one of my flowers. It tumbles down the rest of my dress, and I watch it skitter across the floor, landing at the feet of a man whose face I can't see but whose back I should know.

He stares at the flower for a moment before looking back over his shoulder, and our eyes catch like my heart does in my throat at the sight of him.

I tell myself to smile at him—quickly! Like a friend would!—but I don't, and he swallows heavy, crouches down, picks up the flower, and then looks the other way.

Peter digs a finger under my rib to get my attention, and I spin around to him, smiling with the face I've practiced a thousand times for when he catches me thinking about the other.

But it's not just Peter. It's another man also.

Tall, broad, dark skinned, regal looking. He stares at Peter with a heavy brow.

"The Never Prince."

Peter nods at him curtly. "Old Man."

The man doesn't look too old, really. Not much past middle-aged.

He flicks Peter an unimpressed look. "It takes one to know one," he says before he smiles at Rye and Calla, calling them each by name. And then his eyes land on me. "And who's this?"

Rye gently pushes me towards him, and Peter's grip on me tightens, but I don't think anyone can see it.

"Lady Never," Rye tells him.

And the man's eyebrows go up, intrigued. "Ah." He nods once. "He's taken a lady."

I give him a wry look. "I'm afraid he's taken many."

That delights him. He chuckles as he extends his hand. "I'm Day."

I shake it. "Daphne."

"Daphne." He nods once in a knowing way, and I feel myself frown a little. He notices, I think, because he smiles quickly and gestures to the room around us. "Do enjoy. And welcome! I'm very glad you've arrived." And then he walks away.

"Girl." Peter tugs at my wrist, turning me around to face him. "Calla says there are mermaids at the dock. Should we go and say hello?"

I give him an uncomfortable smile. "The mermaids don't much care for me."

"She's right." Calla shrugs, indifferent. "They don't."

Peter gives her a sharp look. "Why not?"

Calla shrugs again, this time like she's innocent, but I think I see it skitter across her face that she's worried that he's cross at her.

Peter turns back to me and gives me a valiant look. "I'll get to the bottom of this."

"You don't have to!" I tell him, but he's already marching off. "Peter, it's fine," I call to him.

He ignores me and instead calls back, "Calla, come."

She walks after him, her face all pinched with worry, and I feel sorry for her how I used to feel sorry for me.

Rye sighs. "I need a drink." He nods his head towards a table filled with them.

"Did you bring a date?" I ask him with a light smile.

"No." He shakes his head. "The person I wanted to come with came with someone else."

"Ah." My eyes fall to the drink he just handed me.

He stares over at me and says nothing, and I don't know what to do so I do nothing.

"That's my friend over there." He points to a boy who looks about our age. "I'm going to say hi."

I nod.

"You'll be okay?"

I nod again.

Our eyes catch, and his face looks serious—angry, almost?—and then he moves away.

I throw back my drink and pluck another before moving out onto the balcony.

I don't need some air—my entire life is air nowadays—but it feels more acceptable to be on a balcony by yourself. As though I'm perhaps being decidedly pensive, not just accidentally alone.

The air smells different here. On Neverland, it's sweet. Like dew on fruit. Here it's like pine and maple pecans.

And then a flower appears in front of me, offered on the hand I like best in the world. I know it before I even look up to see that it's him. I know his hands impossibly well because it's always felt so scandalous to think of his face when I'm lying next to Peter, but to think of Jamison's hands? What's in a hand? Nothing at all. Least of all me these days.

"I believe this belongs t' ye," he says, offering it to me.

"Keep it," I tell him, flashing him a smile that I hope looks less threadbare than it feels on my mouth. "One's grown in its place already."

"Ah," he concedes. "Ye love an enchanted dress, dinnae ye?"

I give him a demure shrug. "I wear what's given to me."

Jamison's eyes fall down me before they drag back up to meet mine. "This dress—"

I swallow, my eyebrows bending in the middle. "You don't care for it?"

"Aye, sure, I care for it." He gives me a playful look. "That fairy missed her wee calling there."

I breathe out a small laugh. "I suppose she has."

Jem holds the flower out to me again. "Put it on me." He taps the lapel on his jacket.

I take a breath, but it's shallow because I tend to lose mine when he's around me.

I find the buttonhole in his jacket and poke the flower through it. I'm sure it's going to fall immediately, but then quite on its own and rather magically, a little stem grows and fastens itself onto him.

He stares at it, confounded. "Did ye do that?"

I shake my head, and he looks up at me.

"Magic," he says, staring at me.

I say nothing and drop my eyes but give him a smile before I turn back towards the balcony. I lean over it, looking down, and I hope he'll stand next to me.

I don't want to not be beside him. I'm just afraid he'll see something in my eyes that tells him what I should have just put away. How stupid of me to hold on to it. Let it run its course? Pish. Give me the aspirin.

He sidles up next to me, arms on the balcony, leaning over it. His shoulders feel like a shield even though they aren't around me.

"Y'are here wi' Peter," he says.

"Yes," I say as I stare at Peter down on the dock with another girl. I hope Hook doesn't notice; he will if I keep staring at them, so I look up at him instead. "Who are you here with?"

He gives me a long look, and I realize that's a question I probably don't really want answered. Morrigan, I think he's about to say, but he flicks me a little look.

"Me marm."

"Oh." I laugh once, and I hope it doesn't sound relieved. I give him a little shrug. "Most beautiful woman here then."

He tilts his head in consideration. His mouth pulls, and he stares right at me. "Sure, I dinnae ken if I agree."

And somewhere far away, that bag I threw to the floor rattles around, begging to be remembered, but I can't hear it, and even though it excites me, it incenses me also that he'd say that to me after what he's put me through.

Of course, he doesn't know he's put me through anything, but it's my right as a woman to hold him in contempt for that which he's done without his knowledge. Of that I feel quite sure in this moment.

I square my shoulders and stare over at him coolly. "Friends don't say things like that to one another."

He swallows and clears his throat. "No." He clears his throat again. "I s'pose they dinnae."

I cross my arms over my chest. "What, then, are you doing?"

Jamison presses his lips together, like there's something he'd like to say but he's not saying it.

"Old habits" is what he tells me.

Something about that deflates me, flattens me all the way back down to a pancake.

Old habits. That's all I am.

"How's the girl from your ship?" I ask him with a smile that tries its best to be bright, but it's wilting.

Jamison juts his chin out and shakes his head, disinterested by the question. "I've no' seen her since."

"Ah." I nod, clearing my throat as I glance away. "She sounds special."

My voice is dripping with sarcasm, but it's all I could muster that wouldn't lead to tears. Something about that makes it worse.

He shrugs and tosses back his whole drink. Rum. Full glass. Neat.

"A wee bit heavy-handed coming from the girl whose boyfriend is a womanizing toddler."

I roll my eyes at him and give him a dark look. "There you go again, calling me a girl."

"And there ye go, being one," he shoots back, and it crushes me.

"Well then." I lift my shoulders like his words mean nothing to me, like that yoke around my neck I feel all the time whether I'm with him or not isn't now just choking the life out of me. I flash him a quick smile. "Don't let me keep you. So many people here...so many women"—I give him a pointed look—"for you to choose from."

"Aye." He nods once. "Dïnnae mind if I do."

He saunters away and I stare after him. My neck is prickly, and my eyes are burning, and I feel like I'm drowning, so I look around quickly for something to grab on to, but everyone I know has left me.

Without the distraction of Peter immediately in front of me, that thing that I should have dropped off that lives inside my rib cage—the thing that's like a wild animal trapped inside my chest—it starts to howl again. Trying to claw its way out and find a way to tell Jamison what I didn't get a chance to the day on his boat.

When Peter's with me, it feels embarrassing and like a thought I used to think about. Something I could have done in another life, but I don't have that life anymore. Which is true, I suppose. I suppose that I don't, but it feels less stupid when I'm alone, the idea of telling him. When I'm alone, I can convince myself it might be something Jamison would like to hear.

Maybe he'd like to hear it?

That I think of him, of his hands to fall asleep. And something more about snow?

Maybe he knows about what the snow means.

I walk back inside to find him.

The ballroom is full of people, and it's dark, even though it's not entirely dark outside.

And right as I'm about to round a corner, I hear his voice.

"This dress," he says to someone who isn't me, and my heart crashes like a ship sailing right into a cliff.

"Do you like it?" the girl says. She sounds pleased.

"Aye," he says back.

They can't see me.

I lean against the wall that's hiding me and listen with a macabre sort of hunger.

"Who was that you were with before?" she asks.

"Just some wee girl from my island," Hook says.

I swallow heavily and wipe my nose.

"You seemed to be fighting with her?" the girl inquires.

"You ken how some people just rub ye the wrong way?"

"Yes."

He pauses and it hangs there. "She rubs me the worst."

The girl snorts a laugh at what he just said.

"No' like that," Hook says wryly before his voice changes to serious. "Never like that."

Piano.

That's enough soul crushing for me this evening, I decide, and I push off from the wall as quick as I can.

My chest is going tight. I think I'm going to be sick.

Air.

I need air.

Peter Pan has ruined me. Once upon a time, if my heart was breaking, I didn't need air; I needed earth. Rocks. Stones. Soil composition. Dirt under my nails or my eye in a microscope, those were the things that would have made me feel better before, and now, it's air.

As though how I feel about Jamison is choking it all from my body.

I don't mean to, but I gasp a little once I'm outside.

I lean over the balcony and gulp it back.

"You're not enjoying yourself," says the deep, warm voice of Day.

I look back at him and smile as much as I can muster. "Don't take it personally."

"Oh, I'd never." He shakes his head. "This place has a way of…undoing people."

I nod once. "Consider me undone."

"Is it Pan who's upset you?"

There's something so dignified about him that I find myself folding my hands in front of myself and squaring my shoulders, and that's when I place him.

Day.

The founder.

"Do you know with whom you're here?" he asks gently.

"I do know." I nod. "And just now, I've placed you also."

He gives me a small smile before his head falls to the side curiously. "Do you really know who he is?"

I frown at him, trying to remember.

This is a bag I put away, I think. Something I've tried very, very hard to forget.

Think, Daphne, think.

What was in the bag? And why would it be relevant to founders? What was in that bag? A brown leather suitcase. Tattered with patches. What was in it?

Oh.

Fuck.

It drops like a penny in my mind. A stone on a tin roof. A loud clang that sort of jolts me.

Peter's parents were founders.

Day flicks me a little look. "There it is."

I shake my head at him. "That's not a good one for me to remember."

"I understand," he says sagely. "But you should remember who you are with."

I roll my eyes a little. "I know who I am with."

He gives me a tall look.

"Some of him is Vee," I remind him. "Some of him is good."

"And some," he says, "is pure evil."

I sigh. "Do you not think that the sum total of our existence must amount to more than who our parents were?" I fold my arms over my chest. "Or are."

I tack that on at the end because the insinuation of otherwise feels oddly personal.

Day gives me a peculiar smile that seems loaded with things I don't know about.

"Family weighs much on this island," he tells me right as Itheelia drifts over to us.

"I see you've met the Never Girl." She gives me a tight smile.

"Indeed." Day nods. "She's quite charming."

"So I've heard," Itheelia says as she eyes me, and I get the feeling that I'm about to be in trouble.

Day's face grows a bit more serious as he gives Itheelia a look. "We must speak before you leave."

She frowns. "Of what?"

Day's eyes flicker around the room before he speaks quietly. "Terrible stories have been reaching my shores."

She looks at him impatiently. "They could be old."

"There have been sightings." Day gives her an ominous look. "A black flag flying."

Itheelia sighs. "But has anything actually been corroborated?"

"No." Day gives her a sharp look. "And we'd best hope for it to stay that way."

Itheelia's mouth purses. "I'll find you later."

Day nods at her and then turns back to me, squeezing my arm. "Chin up."

I stare over at Itheelia, trying not to frown but still frowning a bit. "What was that about?"

She shakes her head. "None of your concern." She peers around us, making sure no one around us can hear us before her eyes settle on me. "What is your concern is why are you here?"

I frown at her rudeness. "I was invited."

"I meant with him." She gives me a look.

I give her a long, measured look. "Itheelia, your son has made very clear his feelings for me."

"Yes." She nods once, giving me an exasperated look. "I do agree."

I don't know what she's doing? Either she doesn't know or she's just being unkind to me. It could be either. There's an edge to Itheelia. You wouldn't like to cross her. If she thinks I've hurt her son, if she thinks I've wronged him, she could just be toying with me.

I breathe out and stare over at her. "He wants only to be my friend."

His mother rolls her eyes, and I shake my head at her, insistent.

"Itheelia, he told me—to my face!"

"Told you what?" she asks, brows low.

"That that's all he wants from me! And"—I pause for dramatic effect and hope he gets in trouble from her for this part in particular—"that I bring out the worst in him, and—"

She interrupts me. "So you're here with the other?"

I stare over at her. "What would you have me do?"

"Listen," she says, eyes wide and speaking with her hands, "with more than your ears."

I let out a sigh and shake my head at her. "Itheelia, I don't know what that means."

"Yes, you do." She stares at me sternly. "The universe is alive, and she is speaking all the time."

I keep shaking my head. "To whom?"

Her head rolls back, exasperated. "To you! I know you know."

I blink twice. "Know what?"

She grabs me by the wrist and pulls me farther away from the party. "What did the wind say to you on the mountain that day?"

"What day?" I blink at her. "The wind doesn't speak to me."

Does it? Did it?

She stares at me, defiant and nodding. How sure she is makes me wonder.

Is that what's in the leather pouch?

"No." I shake my head, but I'm less sure. "It never has."

"It did when you were with Jam." She folds her arms over her chest, searching my face. "What do you remember about that day on the mountain with my son?"

"Nothing, really. Nothing happened." I shrug. "We came and I met you. That's all it was. There was no more." Something blows around in the back of my mind, and I squint as I try to think of it. Except I think there was more.

"Oh." She nods once as she looks me up and down. "You put it away."

My chin drops to my chest, and I feel like I could cry. "Not everything."

"What, just enough to hate him?" she asks, eyebrows up, and I shake my head defensively.

"I don't hate him."

"Not yet," she tells me. "But spoiled lo—"

"Don't say it." I glare at her, shaking my head. "Don't say that word."

"Hey," Peter says, grabbing me from behind. "Are you okay?"

"I'm fine," I say, staring at Itheelia, my eyes begging her to say nothing. Peter nods his chin over at her. "Witch."

"Pan." She gives him a curt smile.

Peter spins me around to face him. "Girl, is she bothering you?"

I shake my head. "I'm fine."

Peter searches over my face, and he goes serious as he does sometimes and almost exclusively about me. He touches my face with his thumb, presses into my cheek a tear that I didn't know was there.

"Are you sure?" He frowns, glaring up at Itheelia.

I nod quickly, always wanting Peter at his most defused self.

"She's my friend," I tell him, even though I'm not really sure she is.

"Oh. All right then." Peter shrugs, indifferent but relaxing. "Itheelia." He nods.

She nods back. "Peter."

He hooks his arm around my neck and pulls me away from her. "Let's go now anyway." He nods his head in the other direction. "There's a mountain peak I want to show you."

And thank goodness, because I want to be shown a mountain peak. I want to be distracted—desperately—from whatever it was she was trying to make me remember.

It's a short flight up there, and it's freezing once we land, but it's worth it because it's beautiful. That and I have a feeling that I'm ever so fond of the cold? What a strange thing to have an affinity for. Is there something cold in that pouch? I wonder as a few snowflakes rustle by my ear, but I brush them away because they're distracting me from what I'm trying to remember. Except do I even want to remember, I wonder now that I'm with Peter. To what end does remembering take me to?

There's a little clearing on the tippiest-top of the mountain the castle's nestled up against, and you can see as far as the eye will let you.

Peter stands behind me, ducks, then rests his head on my shoulder. He points to a distant light. "See that?"

I nod.

"That's our island."

I turn my head to look at him, and our noses brush, and through me cracks an interesting whip. Some sort of strangled wistfulness for Jamison, some kind of relief and fragile hope that I've Peter here all the same. "Our?"

He gives me a half smile. "My."

I look away, rolling my eyes, but I don't move away from him. A bit because I'm cold, a lot because he's being the Peter that I think I came here for.

Peter slips his arms around me from behind. "Are you happy here?"

I stare out at all of it. "Sometimes."

"Just sometimes?" He sounds bothered.

I don't look at him. "Yes."

Peter turns me around. "I want you to be happy here." His eyes dance over my face like he's looking for clues. "Is there something I could do to make you happier?"

I lift my brows playfully. "You could…remember my name…"

He rolls his eyes. "I know your name."

"You could…" My voice trails as my eyes fall down his arms that are holding both of mine. I pick off a shiny scale. "You could not make out with mermaids."

"I kiss mermaids," Peter says, pulling a face. "I don't know what make out is. It sounds stupid."

"It's the same thing."

He shrugs. "I knew that."

"You could not be weird when it's my birthday." I give him a look.

Peter scoffs. "I don't even care that you turned old. I've been good about that." He gives me a defiant look. "I haven't brought it up once. You don't look old. You just look the same, so that's good." He gives me a little shrug.

I poke him in the ribs. "You could…not leave me to die with a minotaur."

And then something peculiar happens. Peter's countenance changes. Something rolls over him that I haven't seen in him before. Guilt, I think? Remorse, maybe? Regret, as though he feels actually bad for what he did. Peter's eyes drop from mine, and his face pulls uncomfortably.

"I would never let you die."

I nod because I believe that he believes that.

"Perhaps not on purpose."

That makes him frown more. He licks his bottom lip and stares at me. "You are my favorite one, do you know?"

I tilt my head patiently. "Your favorite what, Peter?"

"Girl." He shrugs. "Ever."

I stare over at him, surprised. "Really?"

He nods, sure.

"Why?" I ask, genuinely curious.

"I don't know." He shakes his head. "There's something—" He grabs my hand and puts it over his heart, places his hand over mine. "Do you feel it? Like strings?" He looks for my eyes. "From me to you?"

I nod. "The Darling girl and the Pan."

"Yes, but no." He sighs as though I'm misunderstanding him. "It's more than that. It's…you." Peter shrugs like it's hopeless. "You are more beautiful than the others. And better, I think. I like your face." He touches it with his big paw hands. "I think about it all the time. Sometimes I get angry at it because I'll be doing important things like painting the sky or fighting a monster and your face just—bang!—pops into my head and distracts me from what I'm doing." Peter looks truly bothered by this, and he swats his hand through the air. "It's annoying," he tells the smile on my face.

"Sorry," I tell him, but I don't mean it.

He stares at my mouth. "You kiss better than the other ones too."

I square my shoulders and take my hand back from his chest, instead unbuttoning one of the buttons of his shirt.

"Are you kissing lots of people then?" I ask, not looking him in the eye.

He knocks my chin up with his finger so I'm looking at him. "What's lots?"

I give him a defiant look. "You tell me."

Peter shrugs again. "The mermaids are good, but usually it's slippery and kind of salty."

I grimace. "Right."

"Marin is okay at it," he goes on. "The best one out of them. Calla is good too, actually."

I give him a long look. "This doesn't make me happy here, Peter."

His brows cross. "Why?"

"Because." I turn away, indignant he'd have me explain it.

He stands in front of me. "Because why?"

I cross my arms over my chest. "Would you like it if I talked about other people I was kissing?"

And then he grabs me, a hand on each of my arms, grips me tightly. It hurts me a little, but I know it wouldn't be on purpose. He just gets swept up in moments. He shakes me twice. "Who are you kissing?" he yells.

"No one." I shake my head quickly, thankful I can say it and mean it. Grateful Jamison never did because I'm worried of what Peter might have done if he had.

"Who!" he yells more. "I'll kill them. Give me their names."

I stare up at him and I tell myself that I'm not afraid, but my voice comes out small.

"No one, Peter."

And then he hugs me.

It's a strange hug—desperately tight. He wraps his whole self around me as much as he possibly can.

"I would kill them," he tells me.

"Okay." I nod.

Peter shakes his head. "I won't share you, Daph."

"Okay." I pause, glancing up at him. "Well then, I'd prefer not to share you also."

Peter looks confused. "With who?"

"With anyone." I give him a funny look. "Not with Marin, not with Calla—"

And then Peter laughs. "You don't have to worry about mermaids."

"And Calla?"

He lifts his giant shoulders like she's a beetle on them. "Or Calla."

"Do I not?" I blink. "She's with you every chance she gets."

Peter sniffs, amused. "Yeah, but everyone is."

"Peter." I fold my arms. "She likes you very much. Maybe even more than that."

He frowns a bit. "She more than likes me?"

I nod.

"Like on the lily pad?"

I scratch my cheek before I fold my arms again. "I'm sure if you wanted."

"Oh." He thinks for a few seconds, brows low, and then the thought's gone. Flies away, right off his face. "If she makes you jealous, I won't see her anymore."

I stare over at him, surprised. "Really?"

Peter nods. "Yeah."

"Do you promise?" I ask cautiously.

He bows dramatically. "On my honor."

I stare at him for a couple of seconds, then nod. "Thank you," I tell him.

"Daphne, girl." Peter hooks his arm back around my neck. "Of all the things I have, you're my favorite one."

CHAPTER
EIGHTEEN

I'M IN FRONT OF THE SHACK LIKE I HAVE BEEN EVERY DAY THIS PAST WEEK. Weeks, actually. I've been like this awhile. Since before the ball, and the ball was fifteen notches under the table ago.

And I shouldn't be like this. I should be unfastening this bloody yoke from around my neck and leaving it for dead, but I'm not.

I'm swinging my arms back and forth as I pace, trying to convince myself it's the right thing to do.

"You're going to burn a hole in that cloud," John calls to me as he reels his line in.

I stare over at him, my eyes wide and wild in a way that I think only happens when I'm feeling exponentially crushed by Jamison.

I put my hands on my hips and sigh. "Do you see it?" I call to him. He's rather far away. Maybe seven or so yards. "What's on me?"

The man shakes his head, staring out at the sea of clouds. "It's not my place to judge."

I walk over towards him. "I'm not asking if you're judging me. I'm asking whether you can see it?"

He flicks his eyes over at me, and they catch on the yoke—so yes—then he looks away again, casts another line out.

"I don't have anybody!" I tell him urgently, now suddenly at his side, whether he wants me to be or not. "I have no one to talk to about this, except a hotheaded fairy whose opinion is extremely slanted."

He shrugs as he tips his bucket hat that he's always in. "For a reason, perhaps?"

"Perhaps! I don't know." I shrug wildly. I think there is a reason. I think I used to wonder about it. I think I put it away, didn't I?

I stare over at the sweet old man whose eyes look as familiar as they do sorry for me. I plop myself down on the cloud next to him, cross my legs, and drop my head in my hands.

"I don't know! But I'm exploding inside." I look up at him. "So I need to know, sir. Do you see it?"

His face softens. "Yes." He nods gently. "I see it."

I nod back at him, wipe a rogue, treacherous tear from my eye. "And you know what it is?"

"I think so, yes."

"I don't know what to do," I tell him, and it comes out like a muffled cry.

He touches my shoulder gently, and I take a staggered breath.

"Because I—I think I…" My voice trails and I look over at him, my eyes going how they do about Jem. I swallow heavily, try to push it down. "You know?" I shrug hopelessly. "And I didn't come here for—well—I didn't come here to—"

I wonder how many ways there are to not say you love a person?

I sniff, wiping my nose with the hem of the dress he bought me. I stare back up at John.

"I came for Peter, I think." I frown. "Didn't I?" I stare over at him, shake my head like it's a kaleidoscope, like moving my brain around might help me to see. I press my hands into my temples and squint at nothing. "It feels so fuzzy now, but why else would I have come here?"

He nods, reeling his line in again. "I suppose that makes sense."

"And it's Peter." I look up at him with a shrug. "That's my fate, isn't it? He's my fate. Who I'm meant to—" I sigh and drum my fingers on my lips for a few seconds, working up the courage to say it. "Love?"

John pulls the line up from a cloud and scowls at the shimmering star he's caught. He unhooks it and throws it back, tossing me an annoyed look. "Just a baby star."

I watch it shimmer away, then look over at him, waiting for him to say something.

He stares out over the clouds and watches as a comet sails by. He tips his hat at it before he looks down at me. "In a way, he's all your fate. You all come here for him." He shrugs. "None of the ones before you remained with him though. That ought to count for something."

"Well, how could they?" I give him a scowl. "They were mere children."

He lifts his eyebrow. "And you are—"

"A woman," I tell him, offended.

"Of course." He nods. "My apologies."

I shake my head, staring at my hands. "Jamison doesn't want me."

John tosses me an unsure glance. "Are you sure about that?"

"Quite." I nod.

"Really?" His face falters. "Quite?"

I stand up quickly, decidedly. I brush rogue bits of cloud off my dress. "I should just put it away," I say, moving back towards the shack.

"That doesn't work how you think it might," he calls to me, and I pause. "Who we love, how we love them—it shapes us."

I fold my arms over my chest. "Well, I don't know what shape I am anymore."

He gives me a look like he thinks I'm silly. "You're a fine shape."

"Do you have any ancient wisdom?"

He gives me a look. "How old do you think I am?"

"Just tell me what to do," I plead.

He sighs, scratching his chin. "Both of them make you happy. Both—" He gives me a knowing look. "Both make you sad. Both of them make you feel free but in different ways. Both hurt you but"—his face strains—"differently also." He breathes out his nose and stares at the darkening sky.

I think I've been up here for hours.

Peter and I went diving for pearls this morning, but then a hurricane blew in, and Peter wanted to play in it. I said I needed to come up here anyway, and he didn't say anything about it. I've come up so many times lately, he got me a cloud that floats me up and down on his command. You can access the shack through the mountain and a lot of stairs, but it's about a day's hike from the tree.

"One of them makes you peaceful," he goes on. "Sometimes," he adds as a caveat, then his eyes pinch. "The other makes you feel a peace, but it's not real. It's just a numbness."

And I know which one he's talking about, but I don't even know if that matters because—

"Only one of them wants me though."

"So you say." The old man sighs.

"So he says!" I tell him, indignant.

And then he does something that throws me off a little. He shrugs. "If you believe him, then you have your answer."

I stare at him, frowning, admittedly unhappy with the conclusion but too proud to tell him why.

"I suppose I do." I arch an eyebrow. "Fine." I shrug as I turn on my heel. "Cumbersome, antiquated thing that is it, I'll just take it off—"

"No!" he calls, hobbling after me, and I stop.

It's rather rude to make an old person hobble after you, don't you think? I think my grandmothers would be cross at me for it.

"No?" I turn back, my eyebrows arched.

The old man shakes his head. "Can't."

"I can't?" I repeat, indignant.

He shrugs. "I'm closed."

I cross my arms over my chest and give him a dubious look. "Since when?"

Shrugs again. "Since now."

My eyes go to slits. "Until?"

His face pulls as he thinks about it. "Morning."

"And for what reason are you suddenly closed?" I ask him, tapping my foot impatiently, but it loses its effectiveness in the clouds. Cumulus. Very fluffy. Too fluffy for irritable feet.

He stares over at me. "Family emergency."

And I'm seconds away from unleashing on this old man a tirade about unprofessionalism, about lying, about how he doesn't have a family because he's a man on a cloud, and then a thought sails into my mind, and I stare over at him.

Terribly blue eyes. Quite like...

"My grandmother had a brother," I tell him.

He stares over at me for a few seconds before he nods once. "Yes, she did."

"His name was John."

He nods again. "Yes, it was."

I take a step closer towards him. "No one's seen him since the Second World War."

His face goes rather solemn. "No, they haven't."

I'm standing. "They say he went missing somewhere over the Indian Ocean."

His face flickers. "Somewhere over it, yes."

"What happened?" I ask him, my voice quiet.

He knocks my chin playfully with his hand. "Another day."

I sniff, nose in the air, indignant once again. "I shall be back in the morning."

"All right then." He sighs as he sits back down in his chair. "Bring me a cuppa, would you?"

I roll my eyes at him but am quietly delighted by the request.

"What kind?"

He looks offended by the question. "English breakfast." Then he casts another line, muttering under his breath, "What kind? What other kind is there? British—the nerve of—"

I catch my cloud home, and I love my little cloud. Of all the things Peter's given me—and there's been a few things now (jewels, a crown, the water breathing thing, a map, a baby bird that I insisted we give back to its mother)—the cloud is by and large my favorite (aside, perhaps, from the bird).

Neverland is so beautiful from the sky, especially at dusk and dawn. When all the fires are lit and the lights start turning on and the fairy dust starts to twinkle, the entire island looks like a Christmas tree.

The cloud drops me off at the net balcony of the top floor of the tree house, where Peter and I sleep.

The boys aren't home. That's the first thing I notice.

It's quiet. It's never quiet here.

I wonder where they are? They know I like them to be home by dark. I peer around and nothing.

Nothing, and then—

I hear a moan.

Did I? Did I hear that, or am I imagining things?

I take a step deeper into the tree house.

And then I hear it again. Unmistakable and rather close by, a deep groan.

"Peter?" I call, feeling nervous, and I worry quickly that something's happened, that someone's hurt or maybe worse. Maybe someone (not naming names) hurt someone smaller by accident, and I swear at myself in my own mind for wondering it, and I tell myself it's wrong, that it couldn't be true. He loves them. He'd never—

And then, from under a blanket, Calla's head pops up, shortly followed by Peter's.

"Oh" is what I say as I stare at them.

She's straddling him, naked, I think? Or mostly so. His hands are on her—on her, you know. He keeps them on her as he looks over at me.

"Daphne!" He looks surprised but not entirely inconvenienced by the interruption. He gives me a big smile.

Me? I stare over at him in disbelief. "What are you doing?"

He stands up and climbs out of the bed we share. His bed, not ours. He is always very specific about that.

He is, in case you were wondering, fully naked.

I've never seen him fully naked before. Partially naked, many times, of course. The boy lives his whole life partially naked. But here he stands, entirely nude, and I feel strangely light-headed.

"We figured out what the more was!" he tells me with a lazy smile.

I'm definitely going to be sick.

I blink at him. That's all I do.

"It's so good," he tells me, stretching his arms up in the air before extending his hand to me. "Come join us."

Calla's head rolls back, sullen. "No, Peter."

Peter gives her a look like she's silly. "She can play too."

"Are you mad?" I shake my head at him a tiny bit. I feel like I'm in a dream. "You said you wouldn't see her again."

Pan looks over at Calla and rolls his eyes, scrunches his face up, and nods his head back at me. "I wouldn't say that."

"You said that!" I yell at him. "Thirteen days ago, you said that."

His face folds to a scowl. "How do you know about days?"

I ignore that strange question and instead counter it with a different one. "What are you doing with her?"

"This." Peter shrugs, then nods his head towards the bed. "You'll like it. Come! Lie down here with me."

"No!" I yell, shaking my head.

"Why are you upset?" Peter frowns for a second before his face fractures into a strange laugh. "Your face goes funny when you're sad."

"I'm not sad." I glare over at him. "I'm revolted."

Peter shrugs and sits on the edge of the nest. "Maybe you wouldn't be if you would have just done it with me when I told you to."

I put my hand on my cheek and nod a lot, my mind racing, thinking about what I'm to do from here. I flick my eyes over at him. "How long have you been doing this?"

He scratches his neck, then shrugs. "The mermaids showed me at the ball, so just all the time since then."

I press my lips together and let the mental imagine of Peter doing this with Calla and the mermaids in every spare moment he had without me soak through every good memory and feeling he gave me since then also.

I nod my head to the side. "Get up," I tell him, and do you know what he does?

He just laughs.

So Calla laughs.

And my neck goes hot, and my eyes start to sting, but I grit my teeth and glare over at him.

"Now, Peter."

He scoffs. "You're not the boss of me."

"Get up now!" I demand and he stands, then floats over to the other side of the room, eyeing me like he does an animal before he tries to catch it.

"You don't talk to me like that." He shakes his head, hovering high above me. "I'm the king of these woods."

And then I grab his wrist and yank him down to the ground. "And I am its queen, and you treat me like shit!"

"Yeah?" He stares at me. "You're a bad queen, so you're fired."

"Fine." I turn on my heel and start racing around the room, grabbing anything I can see that belongs to me.

Which isn't much, really. I don't have many belongings here.

My dresses, my shoes, the dagger that I keep in my boot at all times anyway. The book from Hook.

I find a blanket and start tossing them into it, looking over at Peter as I do. "So which one is it?" I call to him.

Peter glances over at me, disinterested. "Wendy, I don't even know what you're talking about."

He catches eyes with Calla, who laughs and stretches her arms up over her head without a word, inviting Peter back to her.

He swallows heavily, then looks back at me.

"Well?" I blink.

He frowns. "Well, what?"

"Are you a liar, or are you a cheat?"

Peter rolls his eyes. "What are you talking about?"

Calla laughs again, and I decide that she really is quite intolerable, rather an awful person.

"You said I'm your favorite. You said I was the most beautiful. You said you wouldn't see her if it made me uncomfortable. You called me your girlfriend, said that we had a string. So were you a liar then, or are you a cheater now?"

Peter's shoulders square, and his eyes go defensively dark.

"I don't like your questions," he tells me, shaking his head, and even though both his feet are on the ground, he towers over me. "This is my tree, in my forest, on my island. You're here at my pleasure."

"Oh, well!" I roll my eyes. "It's all about your pleasure tonight."

"Yep." He nods. "And it always will be."

I tie the edges of the blanket together and make a little sack, heaving it up as I glare at him. "You know, they were right about you."

Peter's eyes pinch. "What about me?"

"Oh, you know." I shrug, baiting him. "Just what they call you."

His eyes cloud over, and so does the sky behind him.

"What do they call me, girl?" he growls, and thunder cracks, but I don't flinch for a second.

"They call you deficient."

His face pulls tight, and the little muscles around his mouth start twitching.

"How am I deficient?" he asks in a whisper that might have frightened me on my weaker days.

I look him square in the eye and deliver him the blow Hook's been delivering to me all this time. "You're just a boy."

Peter makes a sound like a bark, snatches my makeshift rucksack from me, and shoves his hands through his hair angrily.

"What more do you want from me?" he asks, and it starts streaming outside.

"Nothing, actually." I shake my head at him, and I completely, entirely mean it. "I don't want anything from you." I snatch my things back from him. "We're finished."

Peter shakes his head. "We aren't finished till I say we are."

I roll my eyes at him and turn to leave.

"Don't walk away from me!" he yells after me, and thunder claps.

I ignore him and pick my pace up, heading for the door.

He flies after me and grabs my sack. "I said, don't walk away!" he shouts. "Daphne! I'm not finished with you yet." He drops my things and grabs me instead by the wrist, yanking me back in towards him.

I shove him off me, but he grips me tight.

"You are mine," he tells me, eyes undaunted, and slams me into a wall behind me.

"Get off me!" I squirm, trying to shove him off.

He presses me harder into the wall, and I am aware of his hand placement on my body—how with every shove, his grip gets closer and closer to my throat.

He shoves me again. "You'll stay here till I'm finished with you."

And then I reach with my free hand, down into my boot. It's difficult. I can scarcely reach it, his grip on me is so tight, but then I feel it on the tip of my fingers, and I reach harder and I grasp it, drawing it up and holding it in his face with a trembling hand.

"No, I won't!" I bellow, and the entire island seems to fall quiet for a second before the whole sky lights up with a crack of lightning and the loudest thunder I've ever heard in my life.

Peter's face crumbles in a funny way. Like I'm betraying him?

Calla's sitting there, frozen. She's wrapped in a blanket now. She finally looks something other than smarmy. Now she looks afraid.

"Leave," Peter says, nodding his head towards the door. "Now."

I nod once, backing away from him. "Happily."

"And don't come back." He spits. Literally spits. "You're banished."

"Good." I nod, wiping my leaky face.

"Good." He nods back, insolent. "Go back to England."

"Can't wait." I glower at him.

He rolls his eyes. "Good luck getting home without me, you stupid girl."

"Oh, I'll be all right." I nod coolly, though on the inside, I'm jelly. "I've figured out everything else around here without you."

His eyes fall down me like I'm now a thing he hates. "You're not as smart as you think you are."

"Yes, I am." I glare at him. "And when I get home, I'm nailing that window shut."

CHAPTER NINETEEN

I LEFT WITH NOTHING. JUST WHAT I'M WEARING AND THE DAGGER. I WALKED to the door as calm as I could because I didn't want him to see that I was afraid, and once I felt sure I was out of his line of sight, I ran.

Straight to the dock, where waves like tsunamis were beating up against it. I threw myself into the little fishing boat, and I started to paddle.

Crazy in a storm like this, like trying to blow a bubble inside a tornado.

I thought the waves would stop me, actually—that they'd be upset that I left him and pull me back to the shore in front of the house, but they're propelling me, this great current that I can't see, water traveling in a different direction from the way the wind is blowing it, and I suppose that's it, isn't it? He's literally pushing me away, across an ocean. I guess now I really am free. And if I'm free now, then what was I before? That question feels like a sinkhole that opens up inside my mind that I'll skirt around for the rest of my life.

I think Peter keeps the storm on full blast so I might catch my death.

I wash up to shore eventually. The ocean sort of tosses me from the boat, and I fall onto the wet sand like a dead body in a bag, and before I'm even sure I'm fully out of it, the current snatches the boat away.

I watch the little boat get beaten and pounded as it drifts back to where it took me from, and I feel a grave gratefulness for it before my mind turns to wonder how it is I'll get back to where I'm truly from. Or perhaps most pertinently, where I can even go now at all in the meantime.

I can't go to Rye because I don't want to see Calla.

I don't know how to find Rune; Rune finds me.

In no uncertain terms could I climb Neverpeak in this weather. Maybe in the morning once the storm dies down, I could get to Itheelia or John.

And I know I'm kidding myself, avoiding acknowledging what I already know to be true. There's a reason that I ran to the harbor without a second thought.

There's one person on this stupid island who I trust to help me, and I don't want to see him, even if I always do.

He's not home when I get there.

I'm unreasonably cross about it too,* as though he were to know I was coming. If we were meant to be, he would is a lie I tell myself to keep me indignant and proud in a moment that would otherwise be terribly cold and humbling.

I bunch my legs up as I sit by his door. I'm under cover, and somehow, the rain is still slamming right into my face. It feels personal, and it probably is.

I'm not just fighting with Peter but the entire island, it would seem.

I wait for a long time. That feels personal too, or in the very least, it feels long. Shivering away in this terrible cold because Jamison decided not to be home when I need him to be.

Better than him being home with someone else, I suppose.

Considerably worse though would be if he were to arrive home now with another woman,† and why wouldn't he?

He very well might. We're not together. We never have been. He has every right to arrive home with other women. He probably will.

I feel sick again.

Seeing Peter with Calla was like stumbling upon a reality I'd been trying to avoid seeing, but seeing Jamison bring home someone else might push me over the edge of a cliff, and this time when I fall, there'll be no catching me.

There's no golden-haired boy to break my fall, no giant paw hands to brush away my tears and distract me by whispering to flowers and making them blush.

When Hook comes home soon with a girl on his arm and his hand up her

---

* The bleeding prick.

† Or, more aptly, just a woman, as we all know, to him, I am not one.

dress, I will be forced to admit that the reason I'm crushed is because I have feelings for him that are so big and so heavy and so impossible for me to deny without also denying some great part of myself that my only option is to be crushed by them.

Or to leave.

I pick the second one.

I'll figure out another way home. Or I'll come back in the morning. I'll find Orson, have him check that the coast is clear, and then I'll ask for Jamison to find me a way home. That's what I'll do, I nod to myself, standing up and going to gather my things. And then I realize I don't have things, so I roll my eyes at myself, wonder if it would be dangerous to sleep under the dock in this weather or where else I might be able to wait out this horrible storm.

I turn to leave and—

"Daphne?" Hook says, standing in the rain, frowning. I can scarcely tell he's frowning, what with the monsoon and the lack of light, but I can feel it on him—the frown. "What are ye doing here?"

"I didn't know where else to go." I shake my head. I can't even look at him, I feel so embarrassed. "I need to go home."

"Aye." He takes a step towards me. "We cannae go across till the storm passes, but once it—"

"No." I shake my head. "I need to back to England."

His brows go low as he stares at me for a few seconds, then he nods his head towards his quarters. "Come inside."

"No, I want to go home," I tell him, my voice starting to break a little. It's because he's here, and he undoes me.

"Daph, it's wild out here. Just come inside," he says again, ushering me in. He closes the door behind us, then turns to face me, and I notice immediately that he doesn't close the distance between us. "Now, what's come about?"

"I told you." I cross my arms over my chest. "I need to go home."

Jamison shakes his head, brows low, voice firm. "Daphne, what happened?"

I roll my eyes. "I'm banished."

"Yer what?" His head pulls back. "For why?"

I sigh. "Because he wills it."

Hook tilts his head, watching me. "Why does he will it?"

I breathe out, frustrated. "He was getting sexual favors from…" My voice trails, and Jamison's eyebrows go up. I give him a look. "Your favorite girl."

His face tugs in confusion. "You?"

I roll my eyes. "Calla."

"Fuck." His face falls for me. "Shit. I'm sorry."

I cross my arms over my chest tightly and breathe out of my mouth because I'm cold.

"Yeah," I say to the other side of the room before I glance over at him. "It's okay."

His brows flicker. "Is it?"

I nod. "I think that it should have crushed me, but it just made me cross."

He says nothing for a few seconds, just watches me. "Why?" he asks eventually.

"I don't know?" I shrug. "I'm indignant or something, that he has all these rules and expectations and he's a hypocrite and a liar and—"

"But yer no' sad?" Jamison clarifies, holding my eyes with his.

And I can feel it happening as his gaze is on me. The kink in my brow, the scowl that's been on my face since I saw Peter starts to melt off me, and my face starts to soften to a bloom just because he's watching me.

I shake my head, but barely. "Not sad."

His eyes don't move from me, but he nods before he notices my trembling hands.

My whole trembling self, actually.

"Shit." He moves towards me. "Ye must be founthered." He crosses that space that separates me from him and unhooks the cloak that's around my neck, and it falls heavy and soaked to the floor with a slosh. "We need t' get ye out o' these." He starts undoing the buttons at the front of my dress, and I freeze still because his hands are on me. He gets about midway down my chest before his hand hovers at the button. "Do ye hae anything on underneath that?" he asks that specific button.

I swallow, shake my head.

He nods his head, then he turns, grabs a coat that's thrown over a chair that's by him, and holds it up, shielding me from his line of sight.

I undo the rest of the buttons myself, fractionally disheartened, but when am I not with him? Then I peel the wet clothes off my body. They make another loud slap on his floor, and then he brings his coat around my shoulders, and I slip my arms inside.

He turns me around so I'm facing him, and he tugs the jacket closed over me like a robe. "Better?"

I nod, still shivering.

He puts a hand on each of my arms and starts trying to warm me up.

My teeth are chattering away, and Hook frowns at me.

He moves me back into the light. "Yer lips are blue."

I frown a bit defensively. "I'm cold."

"Broonie!" Jamison calls out to him. "Now, please. Quickly, come."

His house fairy appears, looking about as grumpy as he did the last time I saw him.

"Yes, sir?" The brownie looks up at him.

Jamison clears his throat. "Please would ye run her a bath?"

"Yes, sir." The brownie nods as he walks over towards the bath behind the partition. "Always baths here. No baths at home, filthy girl," he mutters under his breath, and I catch Jem's eye and, through my chattering, smile, rather amused.

Jem's eyes go wide with embarrassment. "Broonie!" he calls after him.

"Sorry, sir," the brownie calls back but doesn't sound all that sorry at all.

Jamison breathes out a laugh and then wraps his arms around me, holding me tightly against him, and within seconds, the shivering stops.

"Th-thank you," I whisper, my voice a bit raspy.

He nods, slowly lowering his chin to rest on top of my head. "O' course."

I've had his hands on my waist and his hands on my face, but not this. It's my favorite feeling I've ever had in the world, his arms all the way around me.

"You're a very good friend," I say, all muffled into his chest.

It comes out more wry than I mean it to, and a hot worry flashes through me that it gives me away, that being his friend isn't what I want.

He presses his mouth into the top of my head. "Or a shite one."

I shift in his arms and look up at him.

Our eyes catch.

"Bath's ready," says the brownie.

Jamison breathes out, and it sounds dangerously close to a sigh.

His hold on me lags for a few seconds before he releases me, and I follow the brownie over to the bath behind the screen.

I slip into it, and the brownie carries away the coat, giving me an impatient look as he does.

"Better?" Jamison calls after a minute.

"Yes, thank you."

"Good," he says, and I hear him pull out a seat at his table.

"I saw your mother at the ball," I tell him, just to make conversation.

"Aye, she told me," he says back.

"Oh." I sink lower into the bath and swallow nervously. "Did she tell you anything else?"

"Aye." He sniffs. "She said a great many things."

"I see." I frown at my fingernails.

It hangs there for a minute, a peculiar awkwardness.

"Did my ma say anything to ye?"

I clear my throat. "What about?"

"About…anything?" he says casually, drumming his hands on something. "About me?"

I purse my lips. "Not with her words."

He sniffs a laugh, and I swallow heavy.

"Jem?"

"Aye?"

"Will you come and sit with me?" I ask.

He says nothing for about two seconds, which mightn't sound like much, but in context of the question asked, it really does feel like a tiny little eternity.

"There are bubbles," I add quickly to save what stupid face I have left. "You can't see anything."

Again, there's a pause, and I wonder whether he'd notice if I just drowned myself in his bathtub.

"Would ye min' clearing off the bubbles then?"

I freeze and my eyes go wide, and without meaning to, I say nothing.

"A'm joking."

I breathe out, which somehow, miraculously, sounds like a small laugh, but really, I'm just breathing. Barely.

I hear him approaching. He stops on the other side of the divide.

"Decent?"

I look down at myself, fully naked in his bath.

Not remotely. Always not remotely with him apparently.

"Yes," I say all the same.

He rounds the partition, and our eyes catch and a smile whispers over his face.

"Decent." He scoffs as he rolls his eyes before sitting down right next to me on the floor. Back against the tub, facing away from me.

He says nothing for what feels like five minutes. He just stares straight ahead, gripping his own wrist.

I look over at him, feeling embarrassed again. "Are you okay?"

He nods. "Aye."

I nod back even though he isn't looking at me. "You seem strange."

"I'm no'," he says strangely.

I swallow, then sigh. "Should I not have come here?"

At that, he turns to face me with a little frown. "I told ye, you can always come t' me."

Our eyes hold for a second, and then he turns away again.

His grip on his own wrist tightens. "Sure anyway, I wanted t' talk to ye."

I go a bit stiff. "Oh?"

He nods to himself. "I lied t' ye before."

"Oh." I frown. I shift in the bath a little and sigh.

"What I said to ye the other day, it was shite. You dïnnae bring out the worst in me. I might bring it out in ye but—"

"You don't," I interrupt him.

Jamison looks over his shoulder at me again, and his eyes flicker down to my mouth, then he swallows heavy and looks away again. He breathes out.

"I heard you," I tell him quietly.

He looks back again, frowning.

"What you told that girl—that I rub you the worst?"

His mouth pulls tight.

I stare straight ahead.

"'Not like that,'" I quote him. "'Never like that.'"

"We haenae," he reminds me, and I toss him a stern look.

"That's not how you meant it."

He looks annoyed. "Oh, and ye ken I meant it, do ye?"

"I know how you meant for her to hear it."

He looks away again, staring at his hands. "Aye, well, I was full of shite thon night too."

I sigh, pick up some water in my hands, and drip it slowly back into the tub. The drips drip louder than you'd think they might. That, or it's just quieter in here than you'd think possible.

"Did you bring her back here?" I don't know why I ask that for. Because I already feel sad? To make myself sadder? To fight with him?

"No' here," he tells me.

A sneaky clarification.

I inhale sharply, and I think he hears it.

"But somewhere?"

He's quiet for a moment, and then his head falls back against the side of the tub. "Aye."

I nod once, feel my heart sink at the thought of his hands on someone else.

"So—" I drag my finger around the edge of the bath. "How many girls have you had sex with in this bath?"

He scoffs.

I stare at the back of his head, frowning. "That many?"

He turns over his shoulder again, scowling. "No' that many."

"How many then?" I ask, and our noses are so close they're almost touching.

His eyes fall down my face, and then he turns away from me again, lets it hang there.

"None," he says after a moment.

"What?" I stare at him. "You said—"

"Yeah." He shrugs, telling the wall in front of him. "Forbye, this girl frae England bathed in it once and ruined it."

"How?" I ask, mortified, my cheeks on fire.

He shrugs again, back to holding his wrist and staring at it. "Just felt sick thinking about anybody else being in it after her."

Hold on. What?

I blink a few times, then look over at him.

Is he—?

My heart starts going absolutely mental on the spot.

I tap-tap on his shoulder, and he turns back around, and then I just take his cheek in my hand and brush my mouth over his.

It is, in the scheme of kisses, a tiny one.

My lips barely part his open. It's shy and nervous, but it does the trick, because as soon as our lips touch, his body turns the whole way around and he takes over. He slips his hand behind my head and kisses me as he kneels over me. I curl my arms around his neck, and he lifts me out of the water, drenching himself in the process.

This doesn't stop him, doesn't slow him down. I don't even know whether he noticed.

He carries me backwards towards his bed and then lays me down on it. His eyes brush over my body, and then his hand touches my face. This sweet frown appears.

"I dïnnae want t' force anything. I ken that ye haven't, and yer not—"

"I lied to you before too," I tell him, and the frown on him shifts a little.

"Aye?"

"On my birthday, when you asked me why I didn't want to…" I trail off. "With Peter, and I said I didn't know. I did know."

Jem licks his bottom lip. "Why dïdnae you do it?"

I give him a look. "Please don't make me say it." I roll my eyes. "I already don't have clothes on."

He pulls a face. "Bow, that's mostly how this thing here goes."

"Jem." I cross my arms over my chest, covering myself as best I can.

He keeps going, eyebrow up and playful. "Sure, it's an important component to it, so it is." He reaches down and pushes some hair behind my ear.

"Please." I give him my best pleading eyes.

He smiles down at me, uncrosses my arms from over my chest, swallows heavy. "Just say it, Daph."

I sigh and glance away from him as I do. "It wasn't what I wanted."

Jamison crawls over me, takes my chin between his finger and his thumb, and angles my head so I'm back to looking at him. "Aye, and what do ye want?"

My cheeks have turned into full-bloom roses, and I poke him in the ribs.

Jem gives me another look. "Say it."

I swallow nervously and take a few deep breaths that come out shallow. "I'd like you, please."

A smile breaks over his face, and he drops his body on top of mine, my face still in his hand. "Then ye shall hae me."

He pulls his own shirt off, and I stare up at him wide-eyed, and he smirks for a second before he grabs me by the waist and throws me farther up the bed, crawling up after me.

"Take your trousers off," I tell him, because I'm nervous.

"Easy." He sniffs. "Settle down."

I gesture to myself. "I don't like just lying here, naked."

He clicks his tongue and gives me a playful look. "Well, I like it."

"Jamison."

He laughs, kicks off his trousers, and glances down at himself. "Is that a wee bit better then?"

I stare at it, and my eyes go wide and my face bursts into flames. "Does wee mean something different to you than it does to me?"

He beams over at me, chuffed, tosses me a little wink, and chuckles. Then he clocks my face, and his goes a bit serious. "Are ye nervous?"

I nod quickly, swallowing.

"Well, fuck." He rolls his head back. "Now a'm nervous too."

I flash him a look. "Don't be mean to me." I shake my head. "You've done it a thousand times."

He pulls a face. "No' a thousand."

I roll my eyes. "Many, many times."

Jamison pulls another face. "Ye cud just say many? Ye daen need to say 'many, many.'"

I let out a sigh and look up at him with heavy eyes. "What if I'm bad at it?"

He holds my chin between his thumb and his index finger. "You cudnae be."

"I'm sure I could be." I tilt my head, considering it. "After all, we had such a good kiss just now, and what if—"

His face pulls. "Sure, are ye going to blether on the whole time then?"

I give him an indignant look. "Perhaps."

A little smile escapes his lips, and he plays with some of my hair between his fingers. "Okay." He nods, watching me.

"Okay?" I give him a proud look.

"Aye." He nods. "Works fer me." That makes me happy, and he rests his chin on my bare chest, looking over at me. "Will I talk ye though it?"

"Oh!" I nod quickly. "Please, if you wouldn't mind."

He licks his bottom lip and sits up, staring down at me. It's a funny kind of stare; it would have been awfully intimidating if his mouth wasn't so pink and his eyes hadn't gone all tender at the edges.

"Ri', well first." He cocks an eyebrow. "I'll lie down on top o' ye."

And then he does. You know when you're cold on a winter's night and someone throws an extra quilt on you, and you settle in happily under the heaviness of it? That's how it feels when he lies down on me.

"Okay." I nod, waiting for more.

"Then a'm going t' reach up and touch yer face." He does. "Push some hair from it, sure, but I won't need to really. I'll just want to."

He brushes hair that isn't there behind my ear.

"Then I might just look at ye fer a minute." He stares down at me, nodding. "Because I've thought about this since ye fell from the sky."

I smile a tiny bit.

He nudges my nose with his. "And a wee bit of me cannae believe this is happening."

I brush my lips over his quickly, still shy. He smiles, does it back.

"Next—" He gives me a look and flashes me his other hand that isn't behind my head. "I'll take this hand and run it down yer body,"

I nod once. "Okay."

He does. My skin is so on edge, his lightest touch almost hurts.

He finds my waist, keeps it there.

"And then, I'll probably start kissing yer neck." He knocks my head to the side with his forehead and kisses down, from the base of my ears and down my neck and lower and lower—

How much he wants me is the sun, and I am a cone, and he's the ice cream melting over and down and around my body.

The "more" that Peter asked about, that feeling you get that's like a strange new hunger that I've never had for anyone till now, I get it.

It feels a bit like being famished, like you've not eaten for days and days on end, like you're dying for a drop of water. Everything starts to feel urgent, and I feel less worried about what my hands are doing. They're just on him.

His mouth drags over my body, and every now and then, he'll pull back and smile at me with these stormy-wild, perfect eyes all clouded at the moment by want for me before I pull him back down towards me.

"Okay." He looks down at me eventually. "Could be time fer the main event?"

I nod solemnly.

He pushes some hair behind my ear, then keeps his hand on my face. "Are ye ready?"

I nod again.

"Are ye sure?"

Another nod.

"It may hurt ye."

I take a deep breath. "Endeavor to survive, I will."

He nods a couple of times, then brushes his mouth over mine again, holding my eyes with his. "Tell me if ye want me t' stop."

"Jem." I shake my head at him. "I'm not going to want you to stop."

He nods once more.

When he pushes inside me, the whole boat rocks with the wave that hits it. Funny timing that, don't you think?

There's this moment when you're flying through the galaxy and you've taken a shortcut through a black hole, where once you're on the other side of it, once you've pushed through, it's just light and color and every good feeling and everything warm, everything happy—and this. I feel this.

Jem is what I came for.

And suddenly I remember the snow on our noses and what the breeze told me—it did tell me something!—that day that I tried to forget about. It was a whisper, barely audible, and it was confusing at the time, but it isn't anymore, because all the stars, all the planets, the moons, the galaxies, if I were looking at them (and believe me, I wasn't, but if I were), I'd have seen they're in a row—perfect alignment. I wish I knew. It would be handy to know because it's easy to forget the things we know in an abstract way, and I do know it now in that abstract way, but it's harder to argue with space and time aligning for you, though one day eventually, I'd try to anyway.

Jamison takes one of my hands in his, stretches it up over my head, and kisses down my arm, back up my neck, and whispers, "How are we faring?"

I can't speak. My voice is lost somewhere inside me.

I give him a wide-eyed nod.

He cracks a smile that's half a laugh, but it doesn't make me feel self-conscious. Actually it just makes me feel safe.

The best way I can describe sex is this.

You know when you're lying in the sun at the edge of the water, and you're quite close to where the tide laps on the sand but not close enough that the waves will get you every time?

It feels like you're lying there, eyes closed, the sun is warming your whole body from the inside out, and you're getting hotter and hotter, and you're feeling it through you more and more, thirstier and thirstier, and you know a wave is coming. Soon something is going to crash into you and cool you down and balance will be restored, but until the wave comes, you're this sweaty, breathing, grippy mess of a girl.

Jem starts to pick up pace. He's in the sun too, both of us dying for water only the other one can give us.

His chest starts rising and falling, faster and faster against mine. My toes pinch to a ballerina point, and Jem's whole body goes taut as he watches me and then—wave.*

The crash is huge, everything I could have daydreamed it would be. I feel it from the soles of my feet to the tips of my fingers. Every single part of me—cheeks, mouth, heart—is pulsing.

---

* Literal and metaphorical.

Jem falls back down on me, tired, his face in my neck, and I realize that the storm's stopped, both in me and out there. Me in his bed, him on top of me, his hand holding mine, the weight of him anchoring me to the moment and maybe even the earth—god, I love the earth. He makes me think of it.

He lies there, breathing heavily for a minute, then he pulls back, looking at me.

He is the most beautiful man I've ever seen in my life.

The way his hair's all rugged, bridge of his nose pink, those eyes that look like the water planet I was born on, look like the closest thing I've seen to home since I left it.

He gives me a tired smile. "I feel it like a flu."

CHAPTER TWENTY

WE DO IT AGAIN ONCE MORE AFTER, AND THEN I FALL ASLEEP IN HIS ARMS.

Such a cliché, I know.

I've never slept in a boy's arms before. Peter sleeps stretched out, both arms behind his head. If I grew cold in the night, sometimes I'd curl myself around Peter. If he was cold, sometimes he'd hold me back, but he scarcely needed to because Peter runs warm. He flies so close to the sun, there's a residual warmth in him. That sounds sweet, doesn't it? Maybe it is. It did mean he never needed me to stay warm though, and I have a sneaking suspicion that even if Jamison were warm, he'd hold me all the same.

I wake up before him and shift myself ever so slightly so I can watch him.

As I do, one of the suns starts to rise up through the window behind us and casts over him this perfect, blushy light.

I've never had the privilege of looking at his face this close up for this long, entirely uninterrupted.

Sometime in the last decade in Berkeley, California, a man invented a kind of coffee drink called a latte. The coffee and the milk combined make this beautiful, milky brown color, and that's how his skin looks. His hair's all a scruffy mess from my hands being in it, and I fight the urge to touch it while he sleeps. It's brown, mostly, flecks of honey through it.

He has facial hair too—more than a five-o'clock shadow, less than a proper beard. More golden than the rest of his hair, and it runs along his immaculate jawline as though it's been painted on. Two pronounced freckles. One on his right cheek, one to the left of his nose.

And his nose. I think I already told you that it's the best one I've ever seen, but up close, it's a work of art. Michelangelo himself couldn't have sculpted it better. Light pink lips that are perfectly balanced, top to bottom, and still they part in the center anyway, as though something's weighing them down. Soon it will be me, I'll weigh down his lips with my own, but for now they rest, parted anyway, and they feel like an invitation. My thumb traces over them without my consent, and Jamison's eyes blink open.

The eyes. I said they remind me of the earth, which I mean as the highest of compliments, but somehow, it still undersells them. The calmest sea in the world, on the prettiest part of the planet. A tidal wave of blues, flecks of it that I'm sure come directly from those fabled Neverland deposits. They're like gemstones. Sapphires are too obvious, and his eyes deserve more. Aventurine and lapis lazuli and chryso-colla and dark blue opal—how many kinds of blue is that? Too many. Calling them blue dishonors them. Though staring into them right now, I've not got a single clue what else to call them. Whatever color they are, whatever it is I should be calling them, it's a question you'd want to spend your whole life trying to answer.

Jamison smiles at me, tired. His eyes look over my face how I was just doing with his. They drift over my mouth, and then his eyes catch and he jerks up a bit.

"Did I get it?"

"What?" I frown.

"Yer kiss." He stares at my mouth, wide-eyed.

"Oh!" My hand flies to my mouth. "You tell me. Can you see it?"

He squints at my mouth.

"Is it gone?" I press where it used to live.

He pulls back, looking at me all bewildered.

"I think it's gone," he says, barely keeping his smile in check.

My eyes go wide. "You got it?"

He nods, bright-eyed.

"Wow." I laugh, shaking my head. "Congratulations."

He stretches his arms up behind his head, looking pleased with himself, and I roll my eyes at him.

"I wonder where it went." I look around for it.

"It must be somewhere around here." He glances around too, then shrugs, nodding his head over at me. "How do ye feel?"

"I'm starving," I tell him, and he starts laughing, pushes his hand through my hair.

"Aye, it'll do that to ye." He nods. "Briggs!" he calls out. When the house fairy doesn't appear after a few seconds, he calls again. "Broonie!"

Briggs appears. "Sir?"

"Would ye mind getting us some breakfast, please?"

"Yes, sir." He nods, backing away. "No baths this morning?"

Jamison points at him. "Watch it."

Briggs nods once at me. "Apologies," he says with absolutely no eye contact.

Jem looks back at me, squashing a smile. "God, he's no' yer biggest fan."

I flop my head into his chest and start laughing.

He plays with my hair mindlessly.

"Hunger," he says, tugging my hair back so I face him again. "Is that the prevailing feeling of the hour?"

I give him a look. "What would you prefer me to say?"

He gives me a gentle look. "You can say anything ye want t' me."

I press my lips together, watching him. "I like you more now than before we did that."

He squashes a smile, nodding.

"You're really good at that," I tell him.

He nods confidently. "I am."

"Why?" I ask delicately.

"Why am I good?"

"Yes." I nod, then give him a little look. "Is it because...'many, many'..."

Jamison pinches the bridge of his nose and squints over at me. "I dïnnae know how many girls you think I've bedded, but it's nothin' outrageous."

"How many then?" I ask curiously, my chin in my hand on his chest.

"I dïnnae ken." He shrugs. "Seven? Eight?"

"Including me?"

"Aye."

Unconsciously, my lips pout as I think of him being like this with anyone but me.

He lifts me up, pulling me on top of him, and he holds my face with his hand. "Believe it or no', before ye got here, no one else quite pissed me off so much that they drove me into the arms of another woman."

I frown at him. "So you started having sex with other people because I arrived here?"

"Aye." He nods.

I pull a face. "Is that a compliment?"

"I dïnnae know." He laughs, pulling a face back. "But it's a commentary on something, sure."

"Are you good though, because of the practice?" I rephrase my question to be more delicate.

"That cannae hurt." He shrugs. "But sex is better when ye do it with someone you care about."

"So last night was terrible for you then?" I ask him with pinched eyes.

"No." His thumb runs back and forth over my cheekbone. "Thon's the best it's ever been fer me."

I stare over at him, eyes wide, cheeks pink, stomach all in knots for wanting him.

"Oh" is all I say.

Jamison sniffs a laugh and pulls me farther up him so we're nose to nose, slips his hand to the back of my head, and then kisses me quickly.

Light and perfect, like a sea mist that graces you with its presence on a hot day.

Then he pulls back a bit, hand still behind my head. "Do ye still want me t' take you back to England?"

"Mmm." I purse my lips, pretending to think about it. "I think I've found a compelling reason to stay."

"Sex?" he asks with a grin.

"Jamison." I toss him a look and he laughs, rolling me over. Me under, him over.

"Stay," he tells me, the top right corner of his mouth tugging away to be a smile. "Please stay an' annoy me."

"Annoy you!" I say back, wide-eyed and laughing.

"Sure, but aye." He nods. "Stay and annoy me. Stay in my bed." He shrugs. "Stay in my bath, I dïnnae care. Just stay."

It feels as though there's some gravity to what he's saying that neither of us was anticipating, but suddenly the room sounds terribly quiet, and the tide switches to serious. None of it's bad; all of it's just weighted.

I swallow nervously and toss him a smile to break the tension. "Well, I don't have anywhere to live so I might have to."

He doesn't smile back but nods once. "Fine by me."

That old brownie is a real grump, but gee, can he cook a good breakfast.

The spread is incredible—croissants, Danish, muffins, berries (some I've never seen before), bacon, every style of egg, mushrooms…

I eat some of everything and then keep on picking still because I've never been so hungry in my whole entire life.

I pluck a strawberry and then get up from the table, looking around his cabin.

Jem follows after me, shirtless because I'm in his shirt. He tugs on it as he wraps his arms around me from behind.

And then these gold things catch my eyes on an otherwise empty shelf.

"What are these?"

I reach up and pluck one down, rolling it over in my hand.

It's a trophy.

"That's from the Blood Tide." He nods at it.

I look back at him, blinking. "The what?"

He smiles. "They're wee games here. Every four years."

"Oh." I perk up, understanding. "Like the Olympics?"

Jamison shrugs. "Sure, but people dinnae really die at the Olympics."

I frown up at him. "But in these, they do?"

"Aye." He nods.

"Why?" I ask nervously.

"They're fighting beasts."

I give him a dubious look. "Like what?"

"This from a lass who fought a minotaur." He gives me a tall look. "This is another world, here. Last games, I fought a typhon."

"And you lived?" I stare up at him.

He gives me a proud smile. "Aye, I won."

The Blood Tide, Jamison tells me, happens every four years. Anyone over the age of sixteen can enter, but barely anyone does, just a handful of people each time.

Jamison says it's for glory and for nothing else.

There are four tournaments, one after each of the elements.

In each game, there's a creature they battle. For example, in the last games, Jamison and the others had to battle a Midgard serpent for the water challenge, and the fire beast was a salamander. No one or nothing has to die for there to be a winner, but often, Jamison says, people (and beasts) do. There's a totem hidden somewhere—first to find it wins. Each player also has a personal talisman that they have to collect to qualify into the next round. You can play the next round even if you didn't win it, but you can't if you don't collect your talisman.

At the end, the person with the most totems is the victor.

"You have so many." I peer at them. There's six.

"I've won the tournament twice," he tells me with a shrug, and he tacks on a smile at the end. "If I win next year, I'll have won more than anyone else has before."

"There's one next year?" I blink.

He nods. "You'll like it," he tells me.

"If it's dangerous, I'm not sure I will."

Jamison rolls his eyes and puts his totem back up on the shelf.

"You're dangerous," he says, backing me up into the bookshelf with a thump, and he starts kissing my neck.

I flick him a look.

"Ye are." He nods, resolute. "Look at that face."

I roll my eyes.

"I'd fight fer that face," he tells me with a nod, and then his face goes solemn almost. "Sure, but I'd die for that face."

Then he kisses me and carries me back to bed.

We don't leave his cabin the entire day.

Not because we're animals but because I love it here.

It's so nice to be in a room with walls and a ceiling. It's so nice being in any old room with him.

In the afternoon, we sit in his bed and read next to one another.

That evening, we take a ridiculously squashy bath. Briggs isn't pleased with the water spillage, but I enjoy myself, Jamison behind me, me leaning back into him.

I'm the happiest I've been since I got here, and I feel silly that it took me so long to realize it.

We do go outside the next day, and I feel like the cat who got the cream being on Jamison's arm.

He holds my hand, fingers interlocked, as we wander through his little village.

He greets people, smiles at them, kisses me in corners.

We wander towards the edge of town, where the village starts to fade into the jungle. There are a couple of boys fixing a rowboat under a palm tree.

Orson's snoozing away, loosely overseeing the project, when I spot someone I think I recognize—

I blink a few times.

That can't be…

"Brodie?" I stop in my tracks.

He looks over his shoulder and stands up, dropping his hammer.

"Daphne!" His face lights up, then he shakes his head as he walks towards me, arms open for a hug. "You remember me."

"Of course I remember you." I frown at his silliness, then I look from him to Hook, gesturing between them. "Sorry, Jem, this is Brodie. He was—"

"A Lost Boy," Hook tells me.

Brodie gives a strangely solemn nod.

And I stare at him, bright eyed and confused. "What are you doing here? Peter said you found your brother."

Brodie's face pulls, and he looks over at Hook, eyebrows up.

Jem puts his hand on my waist and starts guiding me away. "Aye, we should have a wee talk."

"Okay." I frown up at him, hands on my hips. "What?"

"For some time now, I've ken thon when the lads age out—"

I shake my head. "What does 'age out' mean?"

Jamison gives me a sobering look. "When they get too old."

I stare over at him, shaking my head. "Too old for what?"

"When they turn sixteen, Bow, Peter leaves them on an island t' die."

"No." I shake my head.

He doesn't. No. There's no way.

"Yes." Jamison stares at me.

"No!" I shake my head, moving away from him. "No, he said he found Brodie's brother and they—"

"He left Brodie." He speaks over me. "On an island, the same as he left Orson—his brother—five years prior." Jamison lifts his eyebrows. "When Peter found them on a sinking ship off the coast of Alabaster Island."

I keep shaking my head. "That can't be true."

Jem crosses over the small distance I put between us, places a hand on my face. "It is, my love," he tells me gently, and I stare over at him.

I swallow, and it hangs there for a couple of seconds.

I stare up at him, my face still in a residual strain from what he just said before.

"You've never called me that before."

"I ken." He nods, his cheeks going a bit pink. He gives me a little shrug. "Thought I'd try it out."

"And?" I ask, eyebrows up and waiting.

He nods. "I like it."

I smile a little bit. "I like it too."

He presses his lips into mine for a few seconds before he pulls back. "He's bad, Daph."

"Jem," I sigh. "Sometimes he plays and he forgets, and I'm sure it was an accident." I stare up at him because I am sure.

He wouldn't do that.

"Peter probably thought his brother really was there on the island still. Peter's thoughtless. He's not—he's not murderous."

"Why did he leave Orson on an island in the first place?"

"I don't know." I shrug, desperate to believe it's not true. It can't be. "Maybe he didn't realize, or—"

Jem shakes his head and turns away from me. "Forbye, heed what you need to then."

"I'm not trying to fight with you." I walk after him, grabbing his arm.

He turns back around and gives me a solemn look. "Nor I you." He touches my face. "It's just half my crew are men I found about marooned on islands by yer boy."

I dig my chin into his chest and give him a look. "He is not my boy."

"Then why are ye defending him like he is?"

I breathe out my nose. "I just think there's some kind of misunderstanding."

Jem cups my face in both his hands. "I hope, my love." Then he kisses my forehead before he nods his head another direction. "Care to take a dander up the mountain?"

"No, I'm happy enough in town." I shrug.

Jamison's face pulls. "We dïnnae want it getting back to him, sure we don't."

"Oh!" I blink. "Do we not?"

Then he rolls his eyes, big and exaggerated. "Bow, let me have a fucking day afore all hell breaks loose." He sighs dramatically. "I just want ye a day."

I purse my lips, supposing that's a reasonable enough request. "Fine."

Jem extends me his hand, but before I take it, I dart over to Brodie, throwing my arms around him.

"I'm sure there's been a misunderstanding, but I'm so glad to see you. I'm so glad you're here."

Brodie nods. "I'll see you around, Daph."

I wave to Orson and then run back over to Hook. "Have you seen Rune around lately?" I ask Jamison.

"No." He gives me a smile. It's breezy, unworried. "She's probably just giving us space."

"Yes, but I haven't told her there is an us."

He gives me a look. "Sure, as though she daesnae know herself anyway?" He rolls his eyes, and up the mountain we trek.

The walk up is spent learning about each other, more than we already know.

Jamison's dad died five years ago,* at the hand of Peter, but Jem doesn't hold that over him. He said his dad deserved it.

---

* So when Jamison was seventeen but not far off eighteen.

He's close with his mother, obviously. Raised by a Scottish nanny. Controversially, he did not attend Eton like his father; instead he went to boarding school in Armagh, Ireland, because the principal there was an old friend of his mother's. I asked "How old?" and he laughed and said, "Very." After, he attended Oxford to study literature, which is probably why he's so romantic and beautiful.

To the best of his knowledge, he's inherited none of his mother's magic, but he says she says if he tried, it'd be in him. His favorite food is a Sunday dinner. His first kiss was a girl from the village called Claire. His best kiss is me. He likes winter best; it reminds him of his mum. He didn't want to be a pirate, but it was the family trade. He's killed more people than he's slept with, which was a fact that elicited quite the look from me. He insists it's not as severe a crime here as it is back on Earth but that he's "trying to cut back." He said that as though he was talking about smoking.

We kiss our way up the mountain, against trees, against boulders, in fields of wildflowers, in the snow—

I pause, looking around us, then back at him.

"Do you know what this place is?"

"I might do." He nods, a small smile spreading over his face. "Do ye ken what this place is?"

"Aye." I nod, imitating him with a big smile.

"Aye." He laughs, hand around my waist. "Didnae ye put it away?"

"I remembered," I tell him, cheeks going hot.

He nudges my nose with his, then kisses it. "Did ye?"

I nod.

"When?"

I do my best to squash away a smile, but it doesn't work, and I just start laughing.

"Ah!" He nods knowingly. "I ken bedding ye would be a good idea."

I keep laughing, and his arms slip all the way around me before his mouth brushes over mine.

"Why do ye like this memory so much?" he asks, looking around us.

"You don't know?" I pull back a little, surprised. "The wind didn't speak to you?"

"Nae?" Now he pulls back. "Daen it speak to ye?"

"No!" I shake my head quickly, laugh once like he's being silly. "No! Of course not."

Jem ducks so we're eye to eye, and he squints at me. "Does the wind speak to ye, Bow?"

"No!" I laugh airily. "Don't be crazy!"

He grabs me by the waist, a hand on each side. His eyes are wide and fascinated. "Aye, it did, dïdnae it?"

"No."

He has this confused smile. "What did it say?"

"Nothing."

"Tell me." He smiles, his hands moving up towards under my arms, as though he might be able to tickle it out of me.

My cheeks are iron hot now. "No!"

He grabs my chin and kisses me, that cheat. "Say!"

"She'll tell you if you tell her what's in your cute little bag up in the cloud," says Itheelia Le Faye from behind us.

"Mum," Jamison says, tone warning her quiet.

"Oh yeah." I pull back, looking up at him. "What is up there?"

"Nae. No." Jem shakes his head, letting go of me to walk over to his mother, pointing at her. "Dïnnae."

"But—" I start, and he looks over at me.

"You, stop. Quiet now," he tells me. "Conversation's done. You and me irnae* talking about the same thing."

"Or are you?" Itheelia says, peering between us.

I go rather still as I glance over at Jem and our eyes catch.

I feel nervous suddenly, that weighty feeling he has to him—a bit like I could cry, a lot like he'd be worth it if I did. He gives me a tiny wink, and all the butterflies living in my stomach fly away, freed now.

He looks at his mum. "Pot-stirrer," he says as he kisses her on the cheek.

She flashes him a quick smile, and I follow them farther up the mountain, past her house.

I don't know where we're going.

---

* Which means "aren't."

She glances back at us. "And to what do I owe the pleasure?"

Jem tosses his arm around me proudly, and his mum gives us a quarter of a smile.

For Itheelia, I'm gathering, that's practically a parade thrown.

"Very good." She nods.

Jem rests his chin on top of my head.

"When?" she asks.

"Just recently." I shrug demurely.

"Last night," her son tells her uncouthly.

She rolls her eyes. "Jammie." She then shuffles me over towards her, not letting me go.

"I go' her kiss, Mum."

"Did you?" She looks up at him quickly before searching my face for it, but it's gone. She tilts her head. "You know, there's a legend about that."

"Is there?" Hook looks between us.

"Do you know it, Daphne?" Itheelia asks me, her gaze sitting on me, heavy.

There's that weight again, thick in the air around us.

I swallow, nodding quickly.

"Anybody going to tell me what it is?"

I don't look away from his mother but shake my head all the same, and Jem rolls his eyes.

"Go on." He nudges me.

"Don't pry, darling," Itheelia scolds him. "It's unbecoming."

Thank you, I mouth to Itheelia.

She nods back, then motions her head towards something up ahead.

"What's that?" I squint at it. It looks like a—

"A well," Jem tells me with a smile. He takes my hand, leading me over to it.

Whatever's in the bottom, it's glowing, swirling, moving around like mercury.

Jem reels up a bucket and dips his finger in it, then holds his finger out to me. "Try it."

I frown at it, confused, but he lifts his eyebrows, waiting.

I lick it quickly and barely, and then my eyes go wide.

It tastes like—

"Hope." Jem nods. "The island runs on it, remember?"

I look over at Itheelia. "Like a fuel?"

"It runs all under the island, like a current, feeding everything."

I look between them. "But where does it come from?"

Itheelia tilts her head as she tries to explain it. "Your atmosphere is made of oxygen and nitrogen. Ours is made of hope and wonder and also a little bit of oxygen and nitrogen and another chemical called Luxithogen that your lot don't know about—"

"Mum." Hook interrupts her and gives her a look.

"Hope is a universal property," she goes on. "And we are the only exporters of it."

"Okay?"

"Our island needs it to survive, but it's also the only place it can be made."

I eye her curiously. "How do you make it?"

"Similar to how oxygen is made on your planet." She shrugs. "We breathe in trepidation, and somehow amidst the human experience, we breathe out hope."

"No' all the time," Hook adds as a caveat.

"And only on this planet." His mother nods. "It's why the Pan's important," Itheelia says carefully. Her eyes flicker between me and Jem. "The heir should bring hope." She frowns, looking a bit confused. "Instead, it's in decline."

"Hope is?" I look down into the well.

"I monitor its levels closely." Itheelia sighs, lowering the bucket back down. "It's been in decline the last few hundred years."

"Really?" I stare over at her.

"Extra lately." She eyes Jem. "Have you heard the rumors?"

He nods. "Are they true?"

His mum licks her lips and frowns. "I'm afraid so."

I look between them. "What are you talking about?"

Itheelia breathes out her nose, and Jem nods his chin at me.

"We have t' tell her."

"Tell me what?" I frown.

"She's gon'to hear about it," he continues over me. "I want her to hear it from us."

"Fine." Itheelia waves her hand dismissively. "But speaking of him only summons him faster."

"Who are you talking about?" I look between them.

Jem sighs, shoving his hands through his hair. "My uncle."

"Oh." I purse my lips.

"James's brother,"* Itheelia says.

"Give ear till,"† Hook says, holding my shoulder. "If ye see a black flag flying on a ship with an upside-down flower on it, ye run."

"What?" I sniff a laugh. "A flower?"

Jem shakes his head at me. "I mean it, Daph. You run."

I frown at him. "Why would he hurt me if he's your uncle?"

Itheelia thinks on this. "He's a funny kind of uncle."

I toss her a look. "Are any of the uncles in your family good?"

She snorts a laugh. "Apparently not." Then she nods her head away from the well, back towards her house.

Jem puts his arm around my shoulders, but he looks sad and tense.

I take his hand and squeeze it. "I don't think he'd hurt me if he knows that you care about me."

He stares down at me, and the worry in his face doesn't dissipate how I hoped it would, but he forces a smile anyway. "Aye." He grabs my head, kissing the top of it. "What kind o' monster would dae that?"

---

* As in, Captain James Hook.

† Which means, "listen to me."

CHAPTER TWENTY-ONE

"Mornin'," Hook says, sitting at the other end of the bed, watching me.

It's been nearly a fortnight of this. It's funny how time is easier to track here. The days slip by just as quickly as they did on the other side of the island—quicker, depending on how we spend them—but they're not a blur, and I can count them. Today's number twelve of these dreamy days that don't really feel real. Cups of tea in bed, his hands in my hair, my hands under his shirt. A thousand kisses and counting.

I prop myself up with some pillows. "Good morning." I rub my eyes. "You're up early," I tell him with a frown. "What are you doing?"

"Daph." He runs his hand over his chin. "We need t' talk."

My heart sinks into a panic immediately.

I stare over at him, sort of in disbelief that he's doing this to me—whatever it is he's about to do. And it strikes me like a bolt of lightning that I was right all along: you can't ever trust a pirate. And it's so like a pirate to make me lo—well, I shan't even say what he made me do. I won't give him the dignity of it.

I sit up straighter and eye him. "Go on then." I brace myself for the inevitable blow that's coming.

"There's a wee thing on Neverland we call the council," he starts, and I frown, confused.

Hold on.

I might have gotten ahead of myself.

"It's representatives o' the people as well as the founders who are still alive, like my mum and Day and, well, no one's seen Aanya fer years, but her if she's about."

"Okay?" I frown at him.

"I'm on it, and the chief's on it. Rye and Calla's dad comes wi' him." He licks his bottom lip and squints. "And Peter's on it."

"Why would you put a child on a council?" I frown over at him.

Jamison throws me a look that implies he's asked that question himself. "Because he's the heir."

I cross my arms over my chest

"So, well." I shrug impatiently. "Go on."

I wait for him to break my heart.

"We only ever meet when there's something t' organize. Or a threat."

"What are you organizing?" I ask.

He frowns. "Nothing."

I blink a couple of times. "So there's a threat?"

He nods. "My uncle, Daph. I told ye, he's bad news." Jamison sighs, rubs his eyes, looking stressed. "Council's been called. I'll have t' go. We'll make a plan."

"Okay." I lift my shoulders, not getting it. "Is it far away?"

He shakes his head. "In the forest."

I stare over at him, not really understanding his distress about anything he's saying.

He stands and pushes his hands through his hair. "So get up. Get ready."

"I'm not going," I tell him with a laugh, lying back down in his bed.

Now he frowns. "You hae t' come."

I give him a quizzical look. "Why?"

"A'm no' leaving ye until my uncle's out of these waters."

"Orson will stay with me," I tell him with a shrug.

He sniffs, amused. "Orson's coming with me."

"Fine." I shrug. "Brodie—"

"—is a child," Hook tells me gently. "Ye have t' come. I cannae leave ye right now." He crawls up the bed and lies down on top of me, eyes roaming my face. "It's no' safe."

My eyes pinch at him. "I feel as though you're being dramatic."

"Aye." Jem kisses my nose and gives me a tender smile. "If only."

He pulls something out of his pocket. Two identical necklaces. No chain, just yarn or something like it, with some small netted crystals at the bottom.

He slips one over my neck, and I pick it up to look at it.

Black tourmaline, clear quartz, and amethyst.

I give him a confused look. "What's this?"

He shrugs like it's nothing, but there's something on his face. "Ye like rocks."

"I do." I nod.

He shrugs again. "An' we can wear the same ones." He slips his over his neck and tucks it in under his shirt before reaching over and doing the same to mine. "Dinnae take it off," he tells me, tacking on a smile at the end. "Okay?"

My mouth pulls, confused, but I shrug. "Okay."

He kisses me, then keeps his face close to mine for no real reason I can tell.

I give him a sheepish smile. "Can I tell you something?"

He nods, eyebrows up.

"I thought you were going to end things with me."

His face pulls, amused. "When?"

"Just now." I shrug.

Jem's face unravels to entirely bemused. "Why would ye think that?"

"Just…felt ominous." I shrug again, feeling stupid now. "Over there at the end of the bed, something to tell me…"

"I see." His face pinches into a smile.

"I'm glad you didn't?" I offer.

"Aye, sure." Jem sniffs. "Me too."

I sit on my hands, feeling embarrassed as I purse my lips. "I said mean things about you in my head," I blurt out.

He laughs now, a big one. Barrel-y and deep.

"Did ye?" He sits up, shaking his head. "Like what?"

"Oh." I shrug airily. "Just, you know, pirate this, pirate that, serves me right for falling in l—"

I stop myself short. My face freezes, eyes wide in a mortified horror. Not him though. His smile is cracked wide, eyes delighted.

"In what?" he asks, mouth open, waiting.

"Nothing." I shake my head quickly.

"No." He shakes his head back. "Go on."

I inspect my hands thoroughly. "No, it was nothing. I didn't say anything else. I said it serves me right for falling in…your…vicinity. Because I fell." I nod at him. "Near you." I nod again. "Remember?"

"Aye." He nods back. "I remember."

I throw myself out of bed and scurry over to where my new dresses he had made for me hang. I love them. They look like the kind of dresses someone who lives with a pirate might wear.

I pull the shirt on over my head—big billowy sleeves that fall off my shoulders—and then I tug on the big, pillowy, white linen skirt with an embarrassingly high slit up the side.

Jem walks over towards me as I wrap the black leather underbust waist corset around myself, and he takes the lacing from me, threading and tugging it together, and I don't know why having him put clothes on my body is equally thrilling as him taking them off me.

He ducks down so our eyes catch.

"You dïnnae want to say it first?"

I put my nose in the air. "I don't know to what you're even referring."

Jem sniffs a laugh, holds my waist in one of his hands, and pulls me in towards him, brushing his mouth over mine.

"Fer what it's worth." He gives me a look that makes me turn to a puddle. "I fell a long time ago."

"This is nice," Orson says, nodding his chin at Jamison and me as we stroll through the summer rainforest hand in hand towards where the council is held.

Jem rolls his eyes but lifts my hand to his mouth, kissing it all the same.

"Haven't seen Jam this happy in…" Orson thinks to himself. "Ever."

Jem rolls his eyes again.

"You two have been friends for how long?" I look between them.

Jem glances at me and says nothing, but Orson juts his chin in Jem's direction.

"Jam found me when I was seventeen."

"On the island that Peter left you on?"

"No." He shakes his head. "Peter left me for dead on a sinking ship because I was seventeen. Took Brodie because he was eleven."

I feel the need to protest because that can't be right, but Jem squeezes my hand, and I feel it isn't the time.

Orson tosses Jem a tender, grateful smile before he looks over at me. "Yer with a good man now," he tells me before walking up ahead.

Hook looks over at me. "Ye feeling okay about seeing him again?"

"Peter?" I purse my lips. "I'm a tiny bit nervous."

"Sure, aye." He nods. "I'll be with ye though."

I kiss his shoulder because it's what I can reach as we're walking.

I spot what I guess is the council meeting place a few kilometers away. A stone, open, outdoor rotunda that runs over the little river that splits the summer land from the spring. The summer side is all giant palm leaves, birds of paradise, and flowers as big as your head, and spring is wildflowers as far as the eye can see, with moss growing up oak trees that are so big and so magnificent, you get the distinct impression they predate any of this.

As we get closer, Jamison lets go of my hand, but he gives me a smile that I think is supposed to be reassuring.

When we walk in, Peter's not there yet, and I'm relieved.

But Ithcelia is; so are Day and Rye. Rye's with two older men I don't know and one who looks about our age.

Rye pushes back from the table he's seated at and walks straight over to me, throwing both arms around me.

"They said you left," he tells me as he pulls back.

I glance over at Jem, who's saying hello to his mother.

Rye's voice goes lower. "Calla told me what happened."

I'm not sure how accurate Calla's version of events will be, but I give him a quick smile.

"They didn't have sex," he tells me, and I give him a look, because for one, I'm not sure that it's true, and either way, I don't particularly think that it matters.

"They may as well have."

"They still haven't," Rye insists. "She won't. Our mother would kill her.

There's an old woman in our village who knows if you've done it or not, and she tells the person you're betrothed to."

I pull a face at him. "That seems invasive."

He gives me a look. "It is." He looks me up and down. "Are you dressed like a pirate?"

"What else am I going to wear?" I shrug, defensive. "Peter didn't let me take anything."

And then Jem comes up behind me and puts his hand on my back.

I see Rye see it, stare at it for a few seconds, before he looks over at me.

Jamison reaches over, extending his hand to Rye. He takes it; they shake. Then Jem sits down.

Rye looks over at me. "So you're okay then?"

I nod. "I'm okay."

I'm better than okay, but I suspect I shouldn't be too enthusiastic about it.

My friend leans over and kisses my cheek. "I'm glad."

Then he goes back and sits with his dad as I sit down next to Jamison.

Itheelia gives me a little wave as Day clears his throat.

"Should we start?"

"Is Aanya not coming?" asks one of the men with Rye, the sterner-looking one of the two.

Day shakes his head at him, and then the man's eyes fall to me. "Who are you?"

"That's Daphne, Dad," Rye says to him.* "I told you about her."

The other man nods. I think he's the chief.

"The new girl," he says, eyes settling on me, and I wonder if he does a fraction of a double take. What would you call that? A quarter take?

Jem tilts his head, considering this. "Sure, but she's been here fer some time now."

"And why is she sitting with you?" the old man asks.

"She's under my care, Sorrel," Jamison says, which I think to myself that that's a funny way of saying we're together.

Rye's father's eyes squeeze. "Why is she not under the boy's care?"

---

* I would later learn that Rye's father's name is Ash.

"Is anyone?" Orson asks with a glare.

"Because he banished me," I tell Rye's father, not enjoying being spoken for. I flash the old man a curt smile.

"For what?" he asks, looking at me a bit impatiently.

"Because your daughter was giving him a"—I think of how to word it—"treat." I flash him a smile, but both old men's eyes go wide. "And as it was particularly defiant of the relational boundaries I thought we were both operating under, I did protest, and I got myself banished."

I catch eyes with Itheelia, and she smothers a smile with her hand as the man turns to Rye and whispers something angrily. Rye shoots me a look across the table as though he's annoyed at me, but I shrug. For him to think that I owe his sister my discretion? The gall.

"Where is the boy anyway?" Day asks me, like I'd know.

I gesture to myself. "Banished, remember?"

Jamison squashes a smile.

"Where is he?" Day sighs, looking around the room, but ultimately his gaze lands on me again.

I sigh.

"With a mermaid? Finding treasure? Chasing a squirrel? How am I to know?"

"Shall we start without him?" Itheelia suggests.

Day sighs, and they do.

Everyone shares all the information they have about the uncle and his apparent impending arrival as I sit quietly and listen, and I become no more sure about this man than I was the day when Jamison and Itheelia first mentioned him.

Multiple sightings all across the realm. I didn't know we were in a realm; I don't know what I thought we were in. I suppose I thought we were on a planet, just. Probably a bit silly.

Anyway, sightings all over the realm, stories dripping in of people going missing, many of them young, so that's particularly sad and awful.

Roaming patrols will commence tonight. And killing him on sight is the plan of attack.

Harder than it sounds, I'm gathering.

I did suggest why don't they just take him to the police, and Jem said, "Oh, why daen we think of that? Oh, because there're no police here. It's Neverland."

Which then elicited a very unimpressed look from me.

"Can he be killed on sight?" Rye asks, eyebrows up.

"Kind of," Itheelia considers.

"A stab through the heart should do it," Rye's dad declares, but Itheelia doesn't look entirely sure.

"There are rumors that he's hidden his heart."

I look over at Jem, completely lost.

"He's…" Rye's voice trails. Magic is the word he doesn't say.

"He harnesses magic," Jem tells him. "He daesnae hae it innately himself."

Rye nods, sort of following along. "Any tips?"

"Aim true?" Jem offers with a shrug. "Wherever true is."

"I've heard," Itheelia starts, "that you can see the location of his heart, pulsing under the moonlight."

"Why does it have to be through the heart?" I ask, looking between them all.

Jamison looks strained as he thinks on how to explain. "He's collected some things over time that've made him powerful."

"Oh," I say, still not really sure what he means. I think that might be his intention.

"Will you see Pan?" Itheelia asks Rye. "Will you relay to him all th—"

"No need, witch," Peter says, waltzing in with all the Lost Boys in tow, new freckles on each of them.

I feel a funny twinge of relief to see the little ones. They spot me before he does.

"Daphne!" Kinley yells happily.

"Oh, Daphne!" Percival goes to run to me, but Peter puts out a hand and stops him.

"What are you doing here?" Peter asks, scowling at me as he takes a seat. "I banished you."

Under the table, Jamison's hand squeezes my knee, but on his face, he gives Peter a grimace.

"I know ye may find this hard to believe, mate, but thon actually means fuck all."

Peter doesn't look at Jamison; he doesn't take his eyes off me. "You shouldn't be here," he tells me.

I stare over at him. "Says who?"

"Me," Peter spits. "I want you off my island."

"It isn't your island, Peter," Itheelia tells him calmly, and he tosses her a dark look.

"Don't be stupid. We all know it is." Then his eyes go back on me. "And I want her off it. I'll drag you back to London myself."

Jamison stands. "And I will kill ye if ye try."

Peter matches him, jumping to his feet. "What are you even doing here?" He jumps onto the table and stares down at me as he walks over.

I push back from the table. The chair loudly scrapes over the stone as I move away from him, and Jamison stands between us.

Peter peers around Hook to me, eyebrows furrowed. "This is where you've been staying since you left me?"

"Since you banished me," I correct him.

Peter jumps off the table, eyes wide in a funny way—panicked, almost.

"You can come back now, girl," he tells me, nodding. "You can stay in my bed."

I shake my head at him. "I don't want to stay in your bed, Peter."

Peter pulls back. "But you'll stay in his?"

His eyes fall down me like I'm a traitor or a whore, and I open my mouth to defend myself, to say absolutely yes, that it's a decision I wish I made sooner, that it's something I'd do every day, again and again, when Jamison jumps in.

"Do ye really think so little o' her?" he says, and both his mother and I look at him, confused.

Hurt, actually. I don't understand.

Hook gestures towards me. "She's my guest."

"You can't have her," Peter spits at him.

"Neither can you," I tell Peter quickly.

Peter stares down at me in the seat I'm in. His eyes pinch. "You are mine."

I stand up and step around Hook. "I am banished," I remind him, and then Peter does a silly thing. Peter often does silly things, and though he wouldn't have known it at the time because Jamison didn't make the nature of our relationship known to him, this would prove to be one of the sillier ones.

He grabs me, Peter does. It's rough, by the arm, and he yanks me over to him.

Within that split second, Jamison's sword is drawn, Itheelia's wand (that I didn't know she had) is drawn, Orson runs in from outside, and Rye starts edging around the table.

"Ye let her go," Jem tells him, an edge in his eye that makes me feel uneasy.

"Don't think I will." Peter shrugs. "She is mine after all."

Hook pulls a face. "If ye hae to hold on to her thon tightly, is she really?"

Peter's grip on me loosens, and I snatch my arm away from him, going and standing behind Jem.

Peter nods his chin over at us. "Do you think she's yours?"

Jamison shrugs with his shoulders and his mouth. "Sure, I think she's her own, and I'll fight anybody who says otherwise."

Peter stands tall. "I say otherwise."

Jem nods a few times calmly, then gives him an indifferent smile. "Then draw."

I stare over at him, eyes wide.

Peter scoffs. "Are you challenging me to a duel?"

Jem blows air out of his mouth. "Mate, I'm just trying t' shut ye up."

Peter sniffs a little laugh. "Tomorrow. Cannibal Cove."

"Jem." I touch his arm, but he shrugs me off.

"When the second sun is a third down the left of the sky," Peter tells him.

Hook nods. "Okay."

"To the death," Peter tells him.

Itheelia's eyes go wide, but Jamison's don't. He just rolls them. "Everything's so dramatic wi' ye." Jem pulls a face, then offers an alternative. "First t' draw blood."

Peter shrugs, bored. "Fine." And then he gives me a glare. "When he bleeds, you'll come home with me."

I straighten my back and stare over at him. "There's no such thing as 'home with you,' Peter. You made sure of that."

Something whispers over his face like sadness, but it's just for a second and then it's gone.

Peter brushes past me before he flies off, the Lost Boys running after him.

Itheelia smacks Jamison in the arm. "What were you thinking?"

He scowls at his mother. "I was thinking he cannae talk t' her like that."

"He won't fight fair," she tells him, and I sidle up next to her.

"She's right, he won't."

Jamison scoffs, looking mildly offended. "I can take on the boy."

"You mustn't play fair if he doesn't," his mother tells him.

"Sure, but that'd just be poor form. My old man would be rolling in his grave."

Itheelia gives him a stern look. "Better than you in one alongside him."

Jem gives her a look before he kisses her cheek, then he hooks his arm around my neck and pulls me out of the rotunda.

"Are y'okay?" he asks after a moment.

I stare straight ahead, breathing out of my nose.

Do I care that Peter looked sad? Do I care that he said he'd drag me back to England himself? That he wants me off this island?

No. I don't care about any of that, not compared to the burning question I have in the center of me.

I look up at him, frowning already.

"Are you embarrassed of me?"

"No?" Jem's face pulls back, blinking a couple of times. "No, I'm in love wi' ye."

I stare at him, obstinate. "Then why didn't you tell him we're together?"

"Daphne." He sighs. "Do you nae remember when were in the volcano and I almost kissed ye? He was nae there, he daen see it, but the isle felt it for him. Acted on his behalf." Jamison gives me an exasperated look. "What dae ye think he'd do if he knew?"

I shrug. "He'll have to know eventually."

"Aye, he will." Jem nods. "And when thon day comes, I'll be there, and I'll get ye off the island for it."

Hands on my hips, I roll my eyes at him. He's as dramatic as Peter. "It won't be that bad."

Jamison blows some air out of his mouth and keeps walking. "How much ye underestimate him is wile dangerous," he calls back to me.

"Jem," I say, and he can hear the doubt in my voice.

He spins on his heel.

"Daphne, he thinks yer his." He gives me a long look that's weighed down with a lot of cute little things, like jealousy and concern. "When he finds out yer not, I dïnnae want to see what he'll do. I'll take ye away. We'll go back t' London. I'll—"

I look up at him, my eyes wide as I touch his face. I swallow. "You said something to me just now—"

"No." He shakes his head and turns around, back to walking. "Dïnnae say it now. It'll just feel like an afterthought after all this."

"No!" I run after him. "I was just distracted because of the nature of the conversation before, and it felt like you—"

He glances at me over his shoulder. "Moment's passed. Yer window's gone."

He gives me a half a smile and offers me his hand.

He's in love with me.

CHAPTER TWENTY-TWO

JAMISON SPENT THE WALK BACK REASSURING ME THAT HE WOULD BE FINE IN his duel against Peter, that he's been trained by the fiercest pirates in history, that he knew the way Peter would fight, that he's won harder duels for worse reasons, but as soon as we were back in his cabin, he gave me this look, chin low, eyes bright and pinched.

"Maybe I may die," he said.

"Jem." I rushed to him, his face in my hands.

He grimaced. "We should probably make the most o' tonight." And then he grinned.

I said probably really, we should head to bed early to make sure he was well rested for it.

He said that sounded like a different kind of death.

So I obliged him because he loves me.

And I love him.

I kept watch all throughout last night to find a time to tell him that I loved him, but none of them felt worthy of the moment.

I suspect he knows anyway, but I plan to tell him before he leaves this morning for the duel.

But when I wake, he's not in the bed.

My stomach goes to funny knots for a few seconds as I worry that he's left without me. I'm not meant to be going to the duel with him. I'm meant to be staying here and packing.

Packing because we're going to leave Neverland for a little while.

So we can be together without being afraid of being together.

But I woke up early so I could pack and watch on, just in case. In case Peter is a little bit as bad as they keep telling me he is. Which I don't think he is.

Though it's not beyond the realm of possibility that he goes too far or does something thoughtlessly dangerous. A child holding a pistol isn't necessarily a murderer by intent, though he might accidentally murder someone in the process.

Besides, Jamison is fighting for me. It would be awful of me not to be there.

When I get out of bed, I find a note on his table.

My love.

Practicing with Ors.

Home before I head.

Yours.

Mine. I smile down at it, and my heart swells like a big wave as I press the note to my chest, and the ocean jostles the ship around—funny timing. I smile out at the sea.

I get to packing.

I've never packed for a boy before?

He doesn't have that many clothes, so I pack them all.

I can only find one bag though, so I get dressed and then head out to find another. I know my way a little better through the town now, so I walk in the general direction towards Bets as a starting point.

I don't remember off the top of my head whether or not she makes bags, but she feels like a good place to start.

I pass a few people I'm a bit acquainted with by now; I pass Morrigan, who sneers at me. She hasn't enjoyed my arrival in town.

I overheard Orson telling Jamison that Morrigan's "dirt filthy" about me being here, that he heard her wish me dead. Jem scoffed and shook his head, muttered something under his breath I couldn't hear, but I could tell he was upset about it.

I wish I could go after her and tell her that Jamison and I are running away together, but it seems unnecessarily unkind, because I've got him and she doesn't.

Which then leads me down a rabbit hole of thoughts about what our lives might look like now that we're running away.

Where would we go?

How long would we be gone for?

Also, if you don't fly like Peter does, how do you even leave here?

Those are the things I'm wondering when I walk past a corner and hear my favorite laugh in the world.

"And I heard you've got a new bedfellow," says a voice I don't know. British. Rather proper.

I don't know why I don't make my presence known, but I don't. I probably should have. It's sort of dishonest that I don't, but something makes me not.

Instead, I hide behind it and listen.

Now, much can be said about eavesdropping—that one should never do it, that one must understand that if they do, they're only getting part of the conversation, that one should trust the man they love enough not to feel the need to eavesdrop—but I'm only human. And perhaps a mildly mistrustful one at that.

"Aye," Jamison says. "Who'd ye hear that from then?"

"That redhead you knock about with," says the other voice, "said she's your new obsession."

I peek around the corner and watch them from afar.

"Well." Jem shrugs. "A part o' her was. I got it now."

My blood turns cold.

The other man—white, shoulder-length hair, pointed nose, brown eyes so dark they're nearing on black. He has strange glasses on. The glass in them is colored.

"And what did you get from her?"

I swallow, waiting for him to say something that clears up this mess, makes it all go away.

But then Jamison just gives the man this look. His head pulls to the side, and a little smirk finds its way to his mouth, and I think my heart tumbles down a set of stairs.

The man laughs. He's kind of old but sort of ageless all at once. Mid-sixties? One hundred and twenty? I can't tell. His skin doesn't look old, but something in him looks worn away.

He gives Hook a grin. "How was it?"

"Shite." Jamison laughs.

Oh my days, I feel like I might faint.

He keeps going. "She dïdnae stop blethering the whole fucking time."

The man laughs again, and Hook shakes his head.

"You wud hae fucking hated it."

"I would have." The man nods.

"Sure, but I did get her kiss though," Hook tells him, tapping the corner of his mouth in the place where my kiss used to live.

The man looks up at him, interested all of a sudden.

Me? Oh, I just feel like I'm fading away.

"No?" The man stares at him. "Jam, those are a rare find."

"I ken."

"Had I known"—the man tucks his hair behind his ears—"I'd have come sooner."

"Had I known," Jamison counters, "I'd nae be the one t' take it. Would hae left it fer ye."

"Could I take it from you now?" the man asks, eyes looking greedy. "I'd love it for my collection."

My face balls up, confused.

"I'd say yes." Hook shrugs. "But I lost it the second she gave it to me."

I press my hand into my mouth, swallow heavily. Convince myself not to vomit.

The man rolls his eyes. "Highly valued, I see."

"She's nothing to me." Jem sniffs. "And I dïnnae think that kiss meant anything to her." Jamison scratches his neck. "The girl practically flung it me."

"Is she heartbroken?" the man inquires.

"No." Jamison shakes his head. "Maybe she will be, but she's no' just yet."

"Why don't you go now and break her heart, and then I'll—"

"Cannae." Hook shakes his head. "Gave her my word I'd take her back t' Blighty."

The man rolls his eyes. "You and your fucking word."

"It's about honor," Hook tells him.

The man rolls his eyes again. "Bit inconsistent there, son."

Hook shrugs. "A'm a pirate."

The man runs his tongue over his top lip. "Anything left for me?"

Hook gives him a dry laugh. "Not wi' what I've done t' her."

The man's eyes pinch. "I thought she was a virgin when you met her."

"Sure, well." Jamison shrugs. "Consider her defiled."

Piano.

I walk away from them, back the way I came.

There's this funny feeling of rushing water in my ears, and all my blood feels like it pools to the top of my skin, and I go hot and prickly.

My arms and legs feel like logs, and I find myself moving through the town without a conscious thought.

I don't know where I'm going.

Leave.

That's all I can hear inside my mind.

Leave and go home.

Leave this terrible, wonderful place and get back to London.

Marry Jasper England. *Marry no one! Marry your work like your mother. Never speak to another man again. Just leave.*

But how?

Without Hook, without Peter, without Rune—where is she even?—I don't know how to get home.

My heart's racing. I place my hand over my chest, tell myself to calm down, but then I feel the necklace Jamison gave me in the process.

I pull it off my neck, the string breaks, and I throw it on the ground.

"You right there, miss?" says a youngish-looking man, leaning up against the wall.

I've not seen him in town before.

He's got funny glasses on too. A different shape but colored lenses as well. Neverland is odd at the best of times though, so I don't think much of it.

"I need to get to England," I tell him. I don't know why. Because what could it hurt, I suppose?

"England, do you?" The man walks over to me, looking up and down. "Are you in some trouble?"

I shake my head and swallow. "No, no trouble." I might just be dying inside, that's all. "I just need to get home. My previous transportation has failed me."

"The gall. Anything failing you?" He eyes me, horrified. "The absolute gall."

I flash him a smile, pretend to be flattered by his pandering. It's a man's world.

"Do you know anyone with passage out of the realm?"

The man nods. "I do, yes."

"Really?" I look up at him, hopeful.

There is something awful about it, I think. How eager it is—how when we're hopeless, the smallest hope offered to us feels like a lifeline even if really it's a life sentence.

Hope clouds things like intuition, I think. If you're ever having to hope for something, it means you're having to ignore the flagrantly obvious to cling to something else.

Yesterday, this man in front of me would have been a man in whose presence I'd have reached for Hook's hand.

Now? He's an observant stranger willing to help a girl in distress.

"Really." The man nods. "Come."

He nods his head and I follow him through the town.

That makes me feel better too. We're walking through the town. No suspicious backstreets, nothing shady. We're in broad daylight.

People can see us.

I'm fine.

Though we are heading out of the main part of town. Away from the harbor. But I suppose I should be grateful.

I wouldn't much care to be in the harbor right now.

Actually, I never want to be in the harbor again.

My heart burns in my chest, and the fact that I'm not doubled over in pain right now is a testament to nothing except my pain threshold.

It's eating me alive, and all it's doing is telling me that I love him.

I love him, and I don't know him at all.

He isn't who I thought he was. I was right before.

He tricked me into loving him, made a fool out of me.

I should never have come here, and now I have to leave.

Leave. Even the thought of it makes me want to cry because it's not what I want either. Even though being here is hard, even though being here has blown my heart to pieces—even still, there feels something rather tragic about leaving it.

Both boys aside, I love it here. I feel a kinship with the land that I've only otherwise felt for England. To leave it feels devastating in its own separate way.

But how can I stay? Between being banished and being betrayed?

"Where are we going?" I eventually ask as we approach the edge of town.

There's not much out here, just a few boats; Hook said it's better for fishing. But that's all. It's just the water to the left, trees to the right.

"To my captain," he says, looking back over his shoulder at me. "He'll be wanting to meet you."

The wind picks up rather suddenly. This huge gust, out of nowhere, leaves swirling around my ankles like shackles, blowing me back towards town.

I pass by a shrub, and it shakes, its twiggy little arms scratching me as I do. My cue to leave, I suppose.

When nature turns on you or—more aptly—when Peter turns nature on you.

"Will he?" I call over the wind to the man. "Why's that?"

The man nods his head towards a big black boat. It's huge. Everything is black except its giant white sails, which are going ballistic in the wind. The island can't get rid of me fast enough.

The wind blows and the tree I'm passing under bends right over, smacking me in the face with her branches. I look back at it, give the same look I'd give a friend who just hit me.

Wounded, feelings hurt.

The tree does it again.

The man watches it happen and looks at me, confused.

"The weather here's mad," he says with a frown, but I shake my head.

"It's not the weather." I sigh. "It's me."

I untangle myself from all the branches that are for some reason around my chest, throw them off me with the same fever I now wish I'd thrown off Jamison's hands, and then step out from under it.

"Why will your captain want to meet me?" I ask him again.

"Well," says another voice from the boat, but I've heard it before. The man Jamison was with before appears at the top of the gangway.

Behind him, I see a black flag flying with an upside-down flower.

The man walks towards me with the worst smile I've ever seen.

"I've just heard so much about you."

CHAPTER TWENTY-THREE

I DID TRY TO RUN, IT'S WORTH SAYING.

I didn't board the ship willingly.

There was a chase scene. I was grabbed, taken back aboard—I won't bore you with the details because they are a bore.

I was taken. That's the real takeaway.

Honestly, I didn't put up much of a fight in the end. Perhaps I should have.

I don't know whether I froze or if I just already sort of felt as though I was dying and decided to roll with the punches.

None of this is the interesting part of the story.

The interesting part takes place in the captain's quarters where I find myself, and it's nothing like any captain's quarters I've ever been in before.

Now, granted, I've only been in the one, but it felt about what I'd imagined.

This though—it's a bed and a desk, and then every wall is lined with shelves and jars of things I can't make out.

Like a specimen library at a university or something.

Some things are glowing, other things pounding, some rattling, some lying limp, flinching occasionally.

One of his men—there are quite a few, all of them with the strange glasses—shoves me towards the captain, who's sitting on his bed.

He pats next to him, and I don't move.

The man who brought me in shoves me down.

"That's quite enough, Ian, thank you." The captain shoos him away.

The door closes, and he stares over at me.

"Hello."

"Who are you?" I ask, staring over at him. Then I shake my head at myself because I already know. "I know who you are, but I don't know what they call you."

He looks surprised by this. "You don't?"

"No one would say your name."

"Ah." He nods. "Wisdom."

I stare over at him, waiting.

His eyes are so dark. I think I said that before, but I mean it. Unnaturally dark, and I wonder to myself what a person has to do in order for darkness to fill them so much that it starts coloring their eyes.

"Some call me the Collector." He gestures around the room. "My friends would call me Charles."

"And what is it that you want from me, Charles?" I ask.

He peers over his glasses at me and squints, then pushes them up his nose. "There's so much more to you than I was told."

I look at him, confused.

"What's that I smell on ya?" He leans in towards me, breathing me in.

"What?" I pull away. "I'm not…wearing anything."

He shakes his head. "It's in you."

I blink. "Excuse me?"

"Ah." He sits back, pleased. "That's a nice broken heart you've got there. It's going to look perfect in my collection." Then he peers at me, eyes pinched as he leans in again.

Reflexively, I pull away, but he grabs my chin and holds me still.

His hands smell weird, like chemicals and rotting all at once. Then he laughs. "My nephew is a liar." His eyebrows lift in some sort of horrible delight. "Innocence, and—" Another big sniff. "My, old Jammie doesn't have a drop, but you are head-to-toe virtue, aren't you?"

He rubs his hands together, excited. He blows some air out of his mouth, and then I hear something.

A jangling? A chiming? It sounds like—

I look over my shoulder, then up, around the room.

"Where is she?" I ask him darkly.

Charles sniffs and nods. He stands and walks over to one of his shelves.

He picks up a jar, rattling it. Then he tosses it to me, and I catch it, holding it up to my face.

A battered little Rune gets to her feet. One of her wings look broken.

"Rune," I sigh, suddenly feeling the weight of the situation I appear to be in. I look over at him. "What do you want with her?"

"A fairy?" He pulls back, confused. "So hard to come by these days. They're so good at hiding."

I try to unscrew the lid of the jar but I can't.

He laughs at my attempt. "They can only be opened by the hands that sealed them."

He flashes his hands at me like he's on Broadway.

I offer it back to him. "Then I'm going to need you to open it."

He gives me a look. "In exchange for what?"

"Whatever you want." I shrug. "My virtue?"

I say it like it's a stupid thing.

He eyes me. "Do you know how one extracts virtue?"

"I don't," I tell him with a single nod. "But I suspect it's as horrible as your eager eyes imply."

"Drowning's the best way, usually," he tells me. "Then it just floats to the top. Like an oil."

I swallow. "Okay."

"Virtue's an essence. You'll die if I take it."

I point over to Rune in the jar. "But she'll live if I do."

He nods. "You have my word."

"Well, I'm quite sure you understand that that means literally nothing to me." I gesture to the jar again. "Release her."

"Not just yet." He shakes his head, peering over at me again. He lifts a colored magnifying glass. It's blue. "Let's see what else we've got in you."

I stare over at him, blinking tiredly a few times.

Not much. I don't think there's much else left in me. I feel as though I gave it all away.

I fell in love with a treacherous man, and I left my home for a boy who can't care about anything other than himself. Those are things that cost you more than you know you're giving away at the time.

Do you know about weathering?

Weathering is the geological process where rocks are dissolved or worn away or broken down into smaller and smaller pieces.

But lots of things, not just rocks, can be weathered.

Me, for example. Being here, being with Peter, loving Hook, it's worn me away.

What's left?

When I arrived, I felt like a whole person, and now that I'm here, there's this tiny part of me that would rather die than leave. Even though I want to leave, I want to leave only to escape how being here's made me feel, not because I don't want to be here.

As though being here is in some way the meaning of life itself.

As though here is my fate, actually, and I'd rather die than not have it.

"Heartbreak." Charles nods at me as he peers through the magnifying glass. "Lots of it. Innocence—a surprising amount!—considering what my nephew said of your time together."

I glare over at him.

"You're quite jaded. You doubt people quickly."

"Well, people quickly give me reasons to doubt them."

His eyes pinch. "Does the Pan love you?"

I roll my eyes. "Peter doesn't love anyone but himself."

"Are you sure?"

"Quite." I give him a firm, impatient look.

He lifts an eyebrow, and some nerves rattle in my belly. "Are you protecting him?"

"Peter?" I stare at him, confused. "I am nothing to Peter. I'm his enemy."

The Collector looks confused, and my brows bend as I stare over at him.

"Is that what you came here for?"

"To Neverland?" He tilts his head curiously before he shakes it. "No, my dear. I came here for you."

I stare over at him, my chin tucking in against my chest. I don't understand.

"The beauty the two princes are fighting for."

I scoff, shaking my head at this crazy old man. "Neither of them are princes."

His eyebrows go up. "Is that so?"

"That is so," I tell him, sure.

He sighs. "So you don't know the legend."

"Of course I know the legend." I scowl over at him.

Charles tucks some hair behind his ears and gives me a tall look. "Then you don't know it as well as you think you do."

I roll my eyes at him. "It's about Peter, if anyone. It's not about Jamison."

He gives me a long look. "Is it not?"

"Captain James Hook wasn't a founder," I remind him.

At this, he nods. "He wasn't one of the Founding Five, yes, but he was a founder."

I cross my arms, wanting to look impatient, but now I'm a tiny bit interested. "Of what?"

"Piracy."

At that, I roll my eyes, and he points over to me with a threatening finger.

"Don't roll your eyes at me for your own ignorance."

"There are no founders of piracy."

His head pulls back. "You've never heard of the Republic of Pirates? 1717. Nassau, Bahamas. You know the stories. Your grandmother wrote them." He arches an eyebrow and quotes a part of my grandma Wendy's book. "'If people knew who he really was, it would set the country ablaze.'"

My eyes pinch, undeniably interested now. "So who was he then?"

He lets it hang for a moment, and the suspense builds.

"Benjamin Hornigold," he announces, and I suspect he expects more fanfare from me, but I just stare over at him, unmoved and unreactive.

He looks disappointed.

"And they called you educated." He rolls his eyes. "He was one of the first, one of the greats, mentored Blackbeard. Loyal to his country as well, actually. He wouldn't attack a British flying flag, but his crew didn't much care for that, so they ousted him. He was pardoned by King George and became a pirate hunter."

I stare, now sort of (reluctantly) riveted by it all.

"Everyone hated him. He was a dead man walking…so what did he do?" he asks, brows high. "He found a fairy. Convinced her to take him to Neverland.

Faked his death—'hurricane.'" He uses air quotes for that. "No one was any the wiser. He started up again in Neverland, founded piracy here too." Charles shrugs.

Whoa.

"Piracy was all he was good for, really. And a poem," he adds as an afterthought.

Could it be true? Could Jamison actually be the heir?

"You don't believe me?" says Charles. He stands and walks to his desk, opening a drawer and pulling out a piece of paper. "November 30, 1944." He clears his throat. "'Brother. My son was born today to Itheelia Le Faye under a bloodred moon, if you can believe it. Quite the spectacle, the entire thing. He's a strapping young lad. He'll grow up to carry our name well.' Shall I go on?"

I shake my head. "Does he know?"

"Well…" Charles shrugs. "Wouldn't it explain how he treated you?"

I shake my head demurely. "Not really."

"Princes are entitled," he tells me.

"Some, perhaps," I correct him. "But not all."

He concedes with a sigh. "It would appear both of your princes are."

"Neither of them are princes," I tell him again. And then with a heavier heart, I say, "And neither of them are mine."

His eyebrows flick up. "We shall see."

"Please release the fairy." I nod to her. "You can drown me afterwards."

He gives me a pleasant smile. "In a rush to die, are we?"

I shake my head. "You just talk a lot."

"I heard you enjoy that sort of thing." He watches me closely as he says that, and I try my best not to let him see how that crushes me a little, but he sees it.

He sits back, pleased with himself.

Then he stands, walks over to his shelf, and plucks her jar off it.

He opens the lid slowly, carefully, assuring she can't escape on her own, and then he picks her up by her good wing, holding her out in front of him.

"Let her go," I tell him again, and he flicks his eyes over at me.

"In a minute."

Then he places a teeny, tiny cloth over her whole face and starts to smother her.

She squirms to breathe, and I jump to my feet, running over to him, but he kicks me back in a manic, violent way.

I lunge for him, but he kicks me again, harder.

"Courageous." He nods. "I'll take that too."

"We had a deal!"

Charles gives me a look. "I'm not killing her," he says, staring down at me on the floor.

I pick myself up, staring over at him suspiciously.

"I can't very well have her free and conscious now, can I?" He continues to cut off her air. "If I let her go and she's coherent, she'll help you." Rune eventually goes limp in his hands, and he lays her on the table. He nods at her little body. "Come see for yourself. There's a pulse still."

I walk over to her and rest my pinky on her chest.

He's right. She is still breathing.

I look at him and nod once. "Okay."

He gestures towards the door. "Shall we?"

I take a deep breath, and I don't even flinch when he takes my arm with his hand.

What's that thing my grandmother always used to say Peter said?

Something about dying.

Then—smash! From behind us. Glass flies everywhere.

And standing in the window with his hands on his hips is Peter Pan.

"Unhand that girl!" Peter tells him. "She's mine."

CHAPTER
TWENTY-FOUR

"WELL." CHARLES GRINS. "WHAT A TREAT!"

He pushes his glasses up his nose, eyeing Peter as best he can in the fading light.

"Oh, that wonder of yours will bottle nicely." He nods at Peter, who stares at him unfazed.

"Peter." I shake my head at him. "Go. He's awful. He—"

"He's no match for me, girl," Peter says with a big grin as he jumps down from the window and waltzes into the room.

Charles considers this briefly. "Potential heir," he says to himself. "I wonder what powers you possess?"

"More than you," Peter tells him coolly. He lifts his hand from his side, and then from behind him, water rises from the ocean that seems to be under Peter's control. I've never seen him do this before.

Peter thrusts his hand towards Charles, who's knocked clean off his feet, tumbling into his precious shelves.

Peter sniffs a laugh and walks over to him casually. He summons the water again, blasting him in the face for what feels like too long.

He's calm while he does it. Watching on as the man scrambles to try to get away from the water.

"Peter!" I call his name, shaking my head. "Stop!" I tell him, worrying he's enjoying it.

That gives Charles a chance. He reaches for a jar that's fallen to the ground—a shimmering, deep blue liquid.

He cracks it open, his eyes eager, and then he drinks it.

Peter looks over at me, confused. Our eyes catch, and honestly (surprisingly?), I feel relieved to see him.

And then something unexpected happens.

The blue shimmers through Charles. Down his throat, through his arms, down his body to his toes, and then he snaps his fingers, and Peter unwillingly flies through the air towards him.

Charles grabs him by the throat with one hand and rattles the empty jar in my face.

"The soul of a wizard." He gives me a pleasant smile. "A strong one too," he says before he squeezes Peter's throat.

Peter starts choking, and I lunge at Charles, but he knocks me back.

I fly across the room, falling onto some of the shelves.

Charles lifts Peter into the air, dragging him under a light, and then he adjusts his spectacles. He looks over at me, and his head pulls back.

"How wrong you were," he tells me, intrigued and annoyed. "Did you not know, or are you dishonest?"

I stand up with a frown, eyeing him carefully. "Did I not know what?" I ask quietly.

"That he loves you," the bad man says, and my wide eyes fall on Peter's.

His are wide too with this horrible fear. It's not just fear for his life, not fear that a madman is choking him. It's fear that I now know what was just spoken.

My eyes fall from Peter's and back to Charles.

"I didn't know," I say softly, weakly, maybe.

The man gives Peter's throat one last squeeze before he slams him to the floor.

Peter sputters a bit. It's just for a few seconds that he's down, and then he's back on his feet again.

"Daphne," Peter says to me, but he doesn't move his eyes off of Charles. "Go stand by the window."

"No, Daphne," Charles says, then he snaps his fingers, and blue, shimmering ropes spring forth from his hands and tie me to a mast in his room. "Don't."

Peter stares over at me, eyes wide and worried like I've never seen them before. He looks around, trying to figure out what to do next. He dives for the shelf, grabbing one of the jars, knocking them off, trying to smash them on purpose, and Charles just laughs.

Peter grabs another, trying to open the jar himself.

I shake my head at him. "Only his hands can open them!" I call to Peter, and Charles moves in towards him, smiling.

And then it happens rather quickly. A silver glint and a flash of a smile from Peter, and his sword's in his hand. With a swift flick of the wrist, he cuts Charles's hand right off. It falls to the ground with a thud, and Charles cries out in pain, falling to his knees.

Peter grabs the hand, maneuvers it to open the jar, and then pours it out.

"No!" cries Charles, trying to reach for it, but the shimmery gold spills onto the floor and evaporates.

Peter laughs, pleased he's found a way to hurt him, then he grabs another and another and another, opening them all.

Charles scrambles after him as he tries to nurse his wound where his hand was severed.

Peter grabs a jar that's dark green and swirling around. He opens it, tossing it at Charles, and for a moment, it seems he's swallowed by this cloud of green.

Peter flies over to me, trying to untie my magic ropes, but he can't.

"Are you okay?" He touches my face. "You're bleeding." He pulls out his knife and starts filing away at my binds. He frowns. "It's not working."

"Nor will it ever," Charles tells us with a sneaky grin. "Blood magic. Ties that bind."

I'm starting to hate magic, I think.

I look back at Peter, try to catch his busy eyes that are alive with the excitement of adventure. "Peter, you need to go. There are things he wants to take from you, really terrible things," I tell him.

Peter shakes his head. "He's not getting anything from me."

"Peter, please."

"Be quiet." He gives me a look. "I'm saving you." He pecks me on the lips, and I blink, stunned, then he flies back to the shelf. "Essence of lightning!" he reads from a jar out loud, beaming. He uses the hand to open it, then shakes the jar empty and onto the ground.

"No!" Charles yells but—

It feels like time and light crack open for a second. The sound of it is unparalleled. I've never heard a sound as loud as that. It feels warm. Like someone threw a cup of hot water at me.

When I can finally peel my eyes open, I see that the cabin's been blown apart.

I'm still tied to the mast, but it's fallen. One of the shelves fell in the explosion and is pinning me down.

"Peter!" I call for him.

I hear him crow. "Don't worry, girl. I'll kill them all and be back for you!"

Then—silence.

Well, not total silence, actually. I can hear something…

Rushing?

Something rushing.

Water?

Water. The ship's sinking.

I breathe out this sigh that's partly made of a cry and stare up at the ceiling that's not there anymore.

It's just a dark night sky and an impossibly bright moon.

A funny way to die, I suppose.

Magically tied to a sinking ship.

A bit of a metaphor for my last few months, I suppose.

The water's rising now, rather a lot. I'm still pinned under the shelf.

"Peter!" I call for him.

Perhaps this is stupid to do, alerting or reminding Charles of my presence, but also, it's my only chance.

Charles looks over at me, pinned with the water rising. He sniffs a little laugh. "I guess you're drowning either way tonight."

"Please, wait," I call after him.

Deep from within the belly of the ship, I hear groans and cracks, and then Charles runs, holding what he can, which isn't much.

He darts from the room, and I hear Peter crow a laugh from a distance.

The ship groans again and collapses in on itself a bit.

The shelf on top of me shifts but in a worse way, one of the shelves splintering off and driving through my arm.

I let out a cry of pain.

And then—a flash of shimmering light and the shelf flies off me, flung across to the other side of the room.

A tattered little Rune climbs up my chest and gives me a tired smile.

I sigh, relieved.

She jangles, annoyed.

"He's fighting the pirates."

She jangles more.

"Jem and I? No. We're not—we're done. I don't want to. Rune!" I yell, exasperated. "It's not the time!"

She stomps her foot and flies herself around the mast, moving it vertical again, but as she does, the ship makes a horrible lurch, and I fall through the floor I'm sitting on.

And I expect to be winded the second I hit the ground beneath me, but I don't hit ground. I hit water.

And then I'm sinking.

I see a dart of light shoot through the water as Rune tugs and heaves at the binds, but they don't budge. I see flashes of light—her throwing all the magic she has at it—but they never get any looser, and I'm going down with the ship.

She keeps trying, and I don't know how to tell her that there's nothing she can do.

I'm swallowing a lot of water, and I can feel my body filling up in places you don't want it to.

People say that drowning's not so bad, but actually, I can't say that I'd highly recommend it.

Then Rune shoots out of the water and away.

I don't know where she's going. Maybe she's saving herself. She should. That doesn't sound like her, but I hope it's what she's doing.

I can't help but wonder if Peter's forgotten about me. It feels like something he would do. Bedazzled by the potential victory in front of him rather than his drowning love in the water.

That's something though, isn't it? That he loved me? A feather in my hat. How many people can say that about Peter Pan? I might be the only one. The only person in the history of time who Peter Pan has loved, and I will pay the price for it as I lie here dying while he's off fighting to save me.

At least someone loved me here, I tell myself, trying to distract myself from the pain.

At least Peter loved me, and at least I'll be dead so I'll never have to admit to him that he was right all along about Jamison.

This is going through my head as the ship and I hit sand.

We've sunk. Hit the seabed floor.

We're not too far out from the shore, but I suppose that doesn't matter. You can drown in a few centimeters of water, and I think we can all agree I'm in much more than that.

My ears and my eyes are stabbing from the pressure of the water, and the pain feels almost unbearable. The water has risen also now over the head of my hope that I've any chance of being saved.

Hope is a terrible thing, isn't it? Poking its awful head out in the darkest places. I should be relieved when it's snuffed out once and for all.

My brain starts to feel floaty and strange.

Strange that the island lives off it, don't you think?

Maybe mine will leave my body and fill that well up a little bit higher.

Dying is so strange.

An awfully big adventure, that's what Wendy used to say Peter said.

Maybe he thinks he's doing me a favor.

Imagine.

I suppose he's not necessarily wrong. It probably isn't just eternal blackness and nothingness. There's probably more. Maybe it will be better.

I'm feeling foggy. Woozy. I feel like I'm drifting away someplace.

They said all children grow up, except one.

But maybe it's two now. This is it. I'm only eighteen.

Eighteen and I'm drowning. But then, I suppose I've been drowning ever since I arrived in Neverland. Literally, since the day I arrived, if you think about it.

But then also, in a worse way. I'd probably take water in my lungs over the feeling I felt when I heard Jem speak about me.

I hate him for that. I hate him more for still being the prevailing thought in my mind as I drift off here now.

His perfect nose, his bud pink lips, how they felt when they dragged over my skin. His accent that I could scarcely understand. How it felt to be held by him, even if it was all pretend, and I know it was. I suppose, at least, I was afforded the chance to love someone before I die.

And then, light.

I suppose this is it then.

Heading towards it and all.

You know the drill…

And that's when I feel water rushing around me. Something rushing to the surface.

Me?

I'm rushing to the surface. Something's dragging me there.

It must be Peter.

I'm looking for golden hair or the eyes of summertime.

But I feel confused, because I'm sure all I can see is a water planet.

I think we reach the surface, and I can feel my body shaking and convulsing as I vomit up water. I try to breathe, but I'm choking.

My lungs are aching like my heart is.

And then I black out.

CHAPTER
TWENTY-FIVE

I JERK AWAKE WITH A FRIGHT, SWINGING MY ARMS AT THE PERSON I FEEL near me.

"Yer okay. Yer fine," says a voice I used to love, and my eyes spring open. He holds his hands out gently, trying to placate me. "Yer okay. A'm here." Jamison shakes his head. "It's just me."

I sit up quickly, staring around the room. "What am I doing here?" I stare over at him.

"Ye passed out."

I cross my arms over my chest. "Why did you bring me here?"

His face pulls. "Where else would I hae brought ye?"

I look down at myself, then realize I'm not wearing what I had on before. "Where are my clothes?" I ask the dress I'm wearing, not him.

"Ye were soaked through." He shrugs. "I changed ye. I just—"

I swallow, glaring over at him. "You took my clothes off my unconscious body and—"

He scoffs, shaking his head. "Bow, I've seen ye wi'out clothes on before—"

"Yes, but that was before!" I yell.

"Before what?" He stares at me, and he looks—for whatever reason—genuinely confused.

And then his head drops.

He runs his tongue over his bottom lip and breathes out heavy.

"Ye heard us?" he says, his eyes not meeting mine.

I don't say anything, just look at him like the traitor he is. My eyes give me away, going all glassy and stupid.

Jamison's head tilts when he sees it, and he sighs. "He collects the abstract," he tells me.

I nod once. "Figured that out myself." I press my lips together. "How did you cut my binds? Rune couldn't do it. How did y—"

"Blood magic," he says, chin low. "We're of the same line." He swallows. "I can sever them."

I look down at my wrists that are all cut up and rope-burned from my trying to get out of them myself.

Jem wipes the corner of his eye. He sniffs as he nods over to me. "Ye took off yer necklace."

I give him a look. "Of course I took the necklace off."

"Aye, but I told ye to keep it fucking on," he yells now.

I jump to my feet. "Why would I keep it on?"

"'Acause it made everything ye are invisible t'him!" he shouts. He breathes in and out a couple of times. He quiets himself. "It was spelled."

I cross my arms again, chest heavy because I won't let it cry. "If that's true, when I took mine off, he should have seen that there's nothing left of me anyway."

He sighs again and looks sad in a way that hurts me. "Innocence, Daph." He swallows. "If he knew you were—"

My face flickers. "I'm not."

"Sure, yer no' a virgin anymore." Jamison gives me a look. "But y'are innocent." He rolls his eyes a little bit and looks annoyed. "It's a means to control women, that old trope. Virginity equates purity and innocence. Yer man's friend is a virgin, sure. But there's nothing pure about her."

I give him a wave of my hand and an impatient look.

"I was trying t'protect ye, Daph." He looks for my eyes. "I didn't mean it."

I suck on my bottom lip, staring over at him. My eyes go big and round. "You were very convincing."

He shrugs like he can't help it. "I'm a good liar."

"Oh." I force a smile. "Well, that's good to know."

"Daph." He drops his head into his hands. "You have to know I didnae mean it—"

"How would I know that?" I square my shoulders. "There have been too many times when I've seen you without you knowing I was there, and none of those times were you the person who you are when you're alone with me."

He shakes his head. "Because a'm better when I'm with ye," he says in a quiet voice.

I shrug as though I'm indifferent. "Or because you're lying when you're with me."

He rolls his eyes, impatient. "Why would I be lying when I'm wi' ye?"

I shrug again, as though it's a thought I'm just thinking now, as though it's not been the question torturing me since I began wondering about it. "Maybe you collect things too."

"Sure, yeah," He nods, properly annoyed now. "And what did I collect from ye?"

I glare over at him. "My kiss."

His face looks as though it falls a little bit, but maybe he's just good at pretending. He shakes his head, eyes on the other side of the room. "You gave that to me."

"Did I?" I move my head so I catch his eye again. "Or did you trick me so I'd throw it at you?"

That looks like it pricks him a little how I felt like I needed it to. His jaw goes tight, and he glares at me. "If ye think that's right, why are ye still here?"

I move towards the door, shaking my head. "I don't know anymore."

He grabs my arm and spins me around. "Yer here because we belong together, Daph."

"Another lie?"

His head falls back. "Come on!"

My eyes pinch as I shake my head at him. "How am I to trust a single word you say?"

His hands drop to my waist, both of them holding me how I want them to, and at first, his hands being on me relieves me, and then it hurts me because I realize how badly I want them there.

"Because I trust ye, and I love ye," he tells me, not letting go. "Even though yer a fucking punish sometimes and even though yer full o' shit."

I look at him darkly. "How am I full of shit?"

"Because ye trust me too!"

I shake my head, trying to brush past him. "Stop."

"You do!" He grabs me again. "It's me ye come to. It's me ye run to when shit starts happening. You dïnnae go t' Peter. Ye come t' me."

"And where has that ever gotten me?" I practically scream, and he pulls back, startled. My voice doesn't sound like mine anymore; it sounds wounded and mangled. I shake my head at him. "Peter would hurt me sometimes, sure, but you"—I stare at him, swallowing quickly—"are total destruction for me."

"Daph." He shakes his head, and I ignore him.

"You don't bring out the worst in me. You just flatten me. Dead."

"Dïnnae say that," he tells me softly.

He looks a bit war-torn now.

"When I was tied to that sinking ship"—I gesture someplace other than here and smack away the tears that are daring to show their face in this moment—"and it was all rising around me, and then I fell through the floor and I went under, it wasn't the water that was drowning me, it was you! What you said—"

He breathes out. "Daphne—"

"And I can't unhear it." I shake my head urgently. "It was so dismissive and so embarrassing and everything I've secretly worried about myself, and you said it. Out loud. To a man who wanted to hurt me!"

He reaches for my cheek, and I shove his hand away.

"And Peter might be selfish and childish and—"

He cuts in. "Controlling and manipulative and dangerous and a fucking prick and—"

"And even still!" I speak over him. "I've never heard him come close to speaking about me how you spoke of me."

Jem presses his tongue into his bottom lip and sighs. "I was trying t' protect ye."

I give him a big shrug, my eyes properly teary now. "I don't believe you."

Jamison presses his thumb into the corner of his eye again, sniffing. "How can ye no' believe me?"

"Because I don't!" I yell, taking a step back from him. "Because I don't know what's real with you!"

He scoffs and rolls his eyes. "Fuck off."

I pull back. "Excuse me?"

"I said fuck off, Daphne," he says loudly, then shakes his head. "That's horseshit. I love you an' ye love me and—"

"No," I tell him, shaking my head back. "Maybe I thought I did before but I—"

"Ye what?" He gives me a look. "Dinnae anymore?"

I stare over at him, him who I thought fate had called me to, and I think of what he said about me… I let my lovesick heart bathe in what I saw before, when he called me names and nothing. I drink deep from that cup, let the poison run down my throat, fill up my stomach, and push down and away the nagging feeling I have that he is good and steady and stable like the earth I love so much. I remember that under its beautiful surface is just fiery rocks and a molten core that would burn me alive the second I let it. I remind myself that the earth can crack and shake, spilt itself wide open and swallow you whole. So I let myself fall back into the crack in the ground that I fell through when I heard him and glare back up at him through that darkness his words pushed me into.

"Moment's over." I shrug "Window's gone."

He breathes out this staggered breath, then wipes his eyes gruffly. He nods slowly, then glares over at me.

"I should hae let him hae ye." He shakes his head. "I should hae let ye drown."

Piano.

Do you know, he doesn't even flinch as he says that, and it completely takes my breath away. Empties me of all air.

He doesn't renege, doesn't take it back, doesn't reach for me.

There might have been a ticking hand of a clock counting down the seconds when he could have taken it back, when he could have said sorry and he didn't mean it, but the hands spin out of control, and the clock breaks open. Kind of like how my heart feels now.

I back away from him and he lets me, and it feels like I'm fighting against invisible rubber bands, trying to snap me back into his arms, but I ignore them.

My eyes drop from his.

I walk out of his cabin, and those bands pull tighter still. I ignore the part where it feels like my circulation is being cut off.

I wave my arms around my body for good measure, in case there is something actually, literally tying me to him, but there isn't, even though there is. I just can't see it with my eyes. I can hear it in the mountains and on the wind and in the quiet fall of snow, and I don't want a bar of it.

I get myself off his ship that I'll never get on again and find a little rowboat that—with very little thought—I decide to take. I throw myself into it and start to paddle.

I feel rather the same as before when I was drowning. That strange, floaty, distant feeling, fuzzy in my mind and my thinking, and then there's this peculiar, dull ache in the middle of me. I wonder for a minute if the lightning essence Peter let loose struck me and I didn't know. Perhaps it tore me open a little or something, and it's too severe an injury for me to feel the full extent of the damages, and so I'm losing blood at an alarming rate and maybe actually, I'm dying? I feel a bit like I could be.

I check myself, just in case, but there's nothing I can see. I'm not bleeding out? Could have fooled me.

I suppose it's not on me. It's just in me.

I begin to row across the harbor towards the tree house, and it's the strangest thing. The wind picks up and tries to blow me back towards the town. The invisible ties that I'm fighting against to get away from Jamison pull tighter still, and I keep waiting to hear them snap and set me free, but they don't.

I row harder and stronger, and the wind blows more.

I focus on the strange pain I feel inside of myself. This smoldering kind of pain that feels dangerous in a way I don't yet really understand. It's a pain I think I'll fan into flame, drag it into a circle, and stand in the center of it. I'll make sure he can't get to me again.

There are different kinds of fate. I think someone said that to me once?

I thought that's what Jamison and I were, but we aren't.

We're done now, forever.

And forever really is an awfully long time.

CHAPTER TWENTY-SIX

IT'S NOT A COMPLETELY CONSCIOUS DECISION, ME GOING BACK TO THE TREE house. It's a decision I made off the cuff of the man I thought was my one true love telling me he should have let his uncle—to paraphrase rather indelicately—rape and kill me.

I found myself in a boat, rowing across a harbor that was pulling in the opposite direction. And I wasn't thinking about how it was only, what, a week or two ago that I fled this place, fled this boy, and here I am, rowing back to him.

I don't stand outside and stare up at it, deciding whether to walk in. I battle my way to the dock and climb out of the boat, and then I walk straight in through the secret entrance.

When I do, Peter's regaling the Lost Boys with his tale of how he killed "one hundred pirates" tonight, and they are watching on, enthralled.

He looks over at me, midsentence, his arms in the air, and then his face goes still, eyes wide.

"Hello," I say quietly.

Peter stares at me a few seconds, and then his hands drop to his sides, and he walks over to me in four big strides.

He grabs my face with both hands and kisses me in this big, wide-eyed, peculiarly sweet way.

"You're back," he tells me.

I shrug carefully. "Maybe I am?"

Peter looks around at the boys and nods his head for them to leave. "Can you give us the room please, gents?"

"Welcome back," says Percival.

"So glad you're home," says Kinley.

Percival gives me a little kiss on the cheek and Holden just waves.

They leave and Peter stares at me.

I swallow. "Was that true what he said?"

"What?" Peter frowns.

I cross my arms over myself, feeling stupid that I'm having to say it. "That you love me."

Peter shrugs like it's no big deal. "Yeah."

My heart surges in this strange way.

It's not pure excitement. I'm not happy that he loves me because he loves me; I'm happy he loves me like I'm shipwrecked out at sea and he is the first bit of land I've seen in weeks.

I'm excited not to drown anymore.

I lift my eyebrows with a cautious, choppy hope. "Do you really?"

Peter nods solemnly.

"And you'll stop with Calla properly? And the mermaids? You'll be mine, and I'll be yours, and that's all?"

He nods again, his eyes all big.

"Do you promise?" I stare up at him.

He reaches for my hand. "I promise, girl."

"Okay." I nod.

A smile spreads over his face, and he looks down at me, pleased with himself.

I stand on my tiptoes and press my lips into his cheeks. I pull back a tiny bit, hovering over his skin.

"Peter," I whisper.

He doesn't move a muscle. "Yeah?"

I stretch my body as tall as it'll go to reach his ear to tell him quietly, "There is so much more."

He pulls back a little bit, eyes busy all over my face. "Show me."

I look up at him with eyes that look heavy with lust, but actually, they're just heavy. "Gladly."

And then I throw myself into him, like a wave I'm trying to drown in.

I guess that's mostly true.

His kisses feel like he's starving, and I do my best to kiss him back the same way, even though I feel like I just ate.

My hands drop below his belt, which they've never done before, and it doesn't much feel like the kind of thing I'd do, but then, I don't much want to feel like the person I was when I loved Jamison Hook.

I want to feel different, rid of him, untethered from whatever it is that's tying me to him.

Peter grabs my hips and lifts me up around his waist, and for a moment, it feels like we're falling backwards but I realize we're actually just flying.

He floats me through the house and outside, where lays me down in a bed of clover, and then his hands run down my body and up the dress Jamison bought me.

That makes him pause—the dress I'm wearing. "Can we take this off?" He looks down at it, face scrunched. "I hate it."

I nod quickly. "I hate it too."

His eyes flicker over me again, and he looks troubled. "You look like you're his," Peter tells me as his brow bends in the middle, and I wonder if I hear a tiny bit of insecurity in his voice.

"But I'm just yours." I slip my arms around his neck.

He nods quickly and swallows. "Swear?"

I nod back. "I swear."

Speaking it into being, I suppose… I might not be yet, but I will be soon.

Soon I will rid myself of everything good I have ever thought or felt about Jamison Hook.

Peter breathes out a breath I didn't realize he was holding, then gives me a pleased smile and pulls out his knife.

It catches in the moonlight, and for the splittest of seconds, there's this stab of worry that pushes through me, and I feel the adrenaline rush to my fingers that maybe he's just going to gut me and I'll die tonight anyway, and in that same brief second, I decide it doesn't matter, really. Dying is dying. Kill me figuratively, kill me literally—there are so many ways to die. Maybe that's why it's an adventure? At the hands of Peter Pan, that's an okay way to go, I tell myself as I eye that knife hovering above me that he swooshes down towards me and—tear!—he slashes my dress in two. Just like he did my poster the night we met.

I sigh, relieved.

Peter stares down at my body, eyes wandering all fascinated.

His index finger grazes my stomach, and he tilts his head. "I'm the only one who's touched you, right?"

I nod, and I suppose I'm a liar now. "Right."

His eyes search over my face, and then they pinch a little bit. "I know you think I did more with Calla."

I start shaking my head. "I don't care—" I tell him.

"Some things we did," he says, speaking loudly over me. "I didn't do the most with her."

"You didn't have sex?"

He shakes his head.

I swallow. "This will be the first time?"

He nods, then pushes some hair behind my ears. "And your first time."

I nod back mechanically.

"But don't worry," Peter tells me with an encouraging smile. "I'll still know what I'm doing."

"Yeah?" I touch his face, trying to make this moment not feel like an absolute betrayal to my favorite night of my life.

I shake my head at myself. I can't think like that anymore.

"Yeah." Peter nods, and then he kisses me again.

I undress him as quickly as I can, desperate to get this over with.

I run my mouth over his shoulders; he tastes like sun and sweat. And then it gurgles in my mind, like the dying breath of a wild beast—

Salt and home. Smelled like snow, freshly fallen.

And I banish the thought quickly from my mind the same way Peter banished me from here, smack away as hard as I can my memories of Jamison that keep creeping in like an invasive species of vine, and I grab Peter, pulling him inside of me.

He makes a sound that should make me happy, but it doesn't, so I bury my face in the crevice between his neck and his shoulder and hope that he doesn't see how I know my face looks.

He swallows heavily and arches his neck back, crowing to the sky. "This is the best!" he tells no one in particular.

I just nod.

When I don't say anything, he looks down at me, face faltering a little. "Are you hurt, girl?"

I shake my head, sniffing a little.

"It was a good hurt," I tell him even though it wasn't.

He nods. "Will I good-hurt you again?"

I nod quickly, and he pushes into me deeper.

I let out a small cry, and he thinks it's because I like it, but actually I'm just tearing myself apart.

He does it again, and I close my eyes because if I don't, I'll start to cry.

I stretch my head back as far as it will go. Peter thinks it's because I want him to kiss me, but actually, I just don't want him to see my face, because I know it'll look like I'm broken.

He starts gaining speed. He's a lot quicker than Jamison—that's good, I suppose? I don't know how much longer I could do this.

I make the sounds I think I need to for him to think it's happening together, but it's not.

He goes. I don't.

The sky doesn't sparkle. There's no starry parade, no birds singing us home in the trees. The waves don't crash together triumphantly. The ground doesn't tremble. In fact, it's gone impossibly still, and all the bloomed flowers around us shrivel up and die, but he doesn't notice, and neither do I.

Peter lies on top of me, panting for a couple of seconds, and then he laughs, rolling off me, staring at the sky.

"Where'd all the stars go?"

I shrug.

"Weird." He stares at they sky. "Maybe they felt embarrassed to watch us do that so they hid."

I nod. "Maybe."

Peter elbows me. "That was the best, don't you think?"

I nod.

"Should we do it again?"

I flash him a quick smile. "I'm kind of tired."

"Really?" He frowns.

I shrug weakly. "Drowning, you know?"

He rolls his eyes, then he kisses me, smiling at me in a way that looks rather a lot like fondness. "I'm glad you're back."

I give him a quarter of a smile. "Are you?"

"Of course." He shrugs. "I love you."

I blink at him, and all I offer him is a weak smile.

"And you love me," he tells me.

I swallow. "Peter." I stare over at him. "Will you do something for me?"

He purses his lips. "Maybe?"

"Take me to the cloud," I tell him.

He frowns, looks almost offended.

"Why?"

"The Collector," I say quickly, then clear my throat. "I just…want to remember the good parts of Neverland, that's all." I flash him a quick smile.

"Okay." He yawns. "We'll go in the morning."

"Please." I shake my head, rolling back on top of him. "Please can we go now?"

"Daphne." Peter groans. "I'm so comfortable."

"Please?" I ask him, my eyes going teary. "I'm afraid that if I don't drop this thought off, it might haunt me forever."

He breathes out his nose and peers at me out of the corner of his eye. "If I take you, will you do that again with me after?"

"Yes." I nod quickly.

He sits up, stretching. "Okay then."

We find me something to wear that isn't piratey, a sheet that we tie around my body, and then it's up and away.

Neverland looks particularly monotone this evening.

I don't hear a single bird on the way up.

Usually it's victorious when Peter is—part of me was expecting a display akin to the northern lights—but up here looking down, it all looks kind of muted.

I can see Hook's ship as we rise higher and higher. It's easy to spot. The biggest ship in the harbor.

His lights aren't on.

A good sign or a bad one, depending on his disposition.

But judging by the state I left him in, my money's on a bad one.

The farther up we get, the more I feel the tugging back to the ground, back to that boat I won't ever run to again.

I dig my finger into the little wounds on my wrist from where I was tied to distract myself, but it doesn't work because fate is its own tie that binds, but the tie that binds Hook and me is a memory.

John's sitting at his seat in the cloud when we land, rod cast and a good little fire crackling away in front of him. He looks up like usual. He smiles, pleasant enough, and then he does a double take when he sees me and jumps to his feet.

"What happened to you?"

I flash him a quick smile. "Bad day."

He nods like he can see it. He can.

"It's unlocked." John gestures towards the door. "Go right in."

I walk in through that door rather calmly, close it calmly and with restraint, but once I know they can't see me, I all but run to the mirror.

I stare at my reflection and am completely horrified by what I see.

I'm littered in bags.

I haven't been here since I walked in on Peter and Calla.

That's the first one I toss to the ground and kick away.

Next is when he banished me.

After that is that sneaking suspicion I have that Peter forgot about me mid-rescue—that's not something I need to remember. I toss that to the ground and feel better about my choices already.

He was unreasonably outnumbered, after all. It was one against—what?—fifty? Of course his hands were full.

It just so happened that I began to drown, and he didn't know.

I take off that bad thought Jamison planted about what Peter does when the boys turn sixteen. I really hated that one. The moment it's off me, I feel better. Because I know he'd never do that! Whatever happened, it was definitely a misunderstanding and a salacious rumor.

The bags left on me now are all Hook.

I stare at myself, breathe in as the reflection staring back at me feels like a girl I used to know.

Time's so strange here, how it moves. I feel like I spent an age with Jamison, loved him for centuries, but it was just weeks. That could be a component of the fate I no longer want. Maybe souls exist outside of our bodies on a plane we can't otherwise see, and they know each other from this otherworld, so when they meet in this one, that's how they know. Why you can meet a stranger who feels like an old friend. Maybe you're just new friends in this life and old ones in all the others.

Or maybe, just maybe, I've been wrong about Jamison since the minute I met him. Maybe Peter was never the problem. It was that tricky pirate who found me when I first fell here.

Maybe I was a game to him this whole time. Maybe it was all pretend. He's a good liar—he told me.

So I take a big breath, and then I drop it. All of it. Every single good and kind and happy memory I have of him, I shed it.

When he pulled me from the water. How he looked at me when he made me reach into his pocket. Our first night together. Days with his mother. When he remembered my birthday. Standing with him in the cave. The first time he called me his love. Our first kiss in the bath. Reading in his bed all day. When he bought me those dresses so I wouldn't have to sell my earrings. Hope on his fingertips.

Him telling me he loves me.

Me loving him back.

I drop all of him to the floor with a clatter like it's nothing, not everything to me, and I sigh like it relieves me, not kills me to do it. I wait to hear those ties snap, but they don't. I can feel them still if I think of them, but I won't think of them again.

I stare down at the mess of us. My god, we really were a mess.

I feel lighter and more lost without it all at once—much less myself than I did a moment ago but also somehow less bound and perhaps even freer, because to love someone isn't freedom; it's to be a captive. And I was his.

But not anymore. I step over my piles of baggage and walk to my shelf. My eyes catch on a few bags way up high that I don't remember seeing before. *Strange*, I think to myself, but then, now's not the time for mysteries. I pluck off that leather pouch of ours that I love so much, that once felt so precious to me but now feels like acid on my hands and my heart. I walk back out to Peter.

He's sitting by John, who's back in his chair., and he watches as I walk over, his eyes pinching at me, seeing all the things I've shaken off myself. He nods his chin at me, eyeing the bag in my hands that only he can see.

"You look a good bit lighter," he tells me, but I don't think he means it as a compliment.

"I am," I tell him sternly to make a point.

John breathes out and looks away, like he feels sad for me, and I ignore him, going and standing with Peter instead.

The pouch feels impossibly solid in my hands. So strange, this invisible little thing that's hurting me so much, even though no one else can see it.

I feel the breeze from that day and the snow swirling all around in it, the memory alive and vibrating inside as I hold it tightly, and I count to three.

Fated, that's what the wind told me that day. And it scared me at first because of Peter. Because Peter was why I came here. Peter was who I thought I was supposed to be with. Because it was he and I, I thought, who were fated. Jamison felt like a threat to that, but actually, he was just a threat to me.

There are different kinds of fate in this world—someone said that to me once. I think I thought I was fated to love Jamison Hook. I think that's what the wind tried to tell me.

He should have let him have me? I blow air out of my mouth like I'm breathing through labor pains.

I'm not fated to love him; I'm fated to hate him.

I toss the bag Peter can't see onto the fire in front of us, and the flames swallow it with a shimmery, smoky lick.

Peter glances at me, frowning, confused. "What was that?"

I stretch my hands towards it, warm my shivering hands on my burning memory, and stare at the bag as the fire eats it, faster and faster, burning away like a piece of paper, and that day and how much I loved it begins to fade slowly from my mind the way it feels when you wake up and start to forget a dream.

And then it's gone.

I look over at Peter, confused myself.

"I—" I purse my lips. "I don't know."

He pulls a face but puts his arms around me anyway.

God, he's beautiful.

Rather statuesque, don't you think?

Impossibly golden, especially all lit up by this particularly beautiful fire in front of us.

"Peter?" I fold myself in towards him and then stare up at him, stars in my eyes.

"Mm?" He looks down at me lazily.

I rest my chin on his chest. "I love you."

ACKNOWLEDGMENTS

I have carried this story in my heart for maybe 15 or 16 years now. I can't believe that it's out (finally) and in your hands. Probably if you're here, reading this, it means you've likely read it*—or if you haven't read it and you're nevertheless here, you are maybe Ben or Aodhan†.

My very first thank you that will be slightly bigger than my second one‡ is for Emily Jane Averill. My sister-friend, ar*teest* extraordinaire, who has believed in me and this story since we met.

I am so grateful for how you have loved me and encouraged me, in all things but particularly this thing.

I am hugely confident that I would not be here—this would not be here without you.

Number two: Ben, you big fat two. You haven't even read this, I know you haven't. But that's okay, because despite this, you have been the most releasing, supportive, and selfless man. You worked so hard for such a long time so that I could write full-time and plant the seeds of all the books we've now gotten to share with the world. Thank you for never letting my own low expectations of myself be your expectations of me. You, along with Emmy, believed this book to life.

To Junes and Bellamy, I want to say a true and genuine, tenderhearted thank you. And also tell you that I am so proud of you, and so grateful for you, and so in awe of your resilience and adaptability. Our lives have changed so

---

* In which case, thank you.

† Annoying

‡ But don't worry Ben, my second one will still be very big.

much in the last year and you have been (for the most part) very patient and gracious with me as I learn to juggle.

Maddie, we were drowning and you saved us. I will be literally forever grateful for the joy and peace you bring to our family.

Abbey, Lindsey, Ash, Darion, and Cam, for all the ways you have help our family survive. I am so thankful for you presence in our lives.

Amanda and Madie, my daily sounding boards. I couldn't have done this without you.

To my wonderful team: Hellie, Caitlin, and Alyssa—thank you for obsessing over this story with me, for championing it, for fighting for it. Todd, for always busting balls and making me laugh. Thank you for being the wisest guy I know. Celia, a founding father in my little heart of hearts, I'll be grateful forever for you for DMing me on Instagram and becoming my editor. Emad and the rest of my Orion family, thank you for trusting me and hearing me and being open to trying out of the box things, I love doing this with you guys. And Christa, you have loved this story in an unwavering way since the minute you saw it. Thank you for loving it so much you moved mountains to get it, I'm so glad to be doing it with you.

And then lastly, to myself in 2008, who thought of this book in a nail salon in Maroubra, who tried for years and years to write this book, with infinity start-stop-starts that bore down on your consciousness and made you doubt that you could ever be what we've eventually become.

You did it. You stopped only writing when you felt like it. You learned to tap into old emotions, not just seek out new and terrible ways to feel things that were worth writing about. You developed a work ethic. You're not stupid or incapable (you just have ADHD) (SURPRISE!).

You would be both delighted at where we are and irritated that it took so long to happen (but also you are sometimes an idiot and have a tendency to be entitled; in 2023 we are still an idiot but hopefully a bit less entitled).

In 2023, I'm not totally sure if we believe in time as a linear thing, and so I say all this to you hoping that through the bending of light and time you somehow receive a vague sense of hopefulness that everything is going to be okay, because it is. It's really very okay.

ABOUT THE AUTHOR

Jessa Hastings is an Australian native who now lives in Southern California with her husband, two children, her beautiful, clingy dog, and two cats. She's quite a bad sleeper but hopes this won't be her lot in life forever. She has a busy brain, cannot do her hair to save her life (but this week bought one of those hot brushes, so is hopeful for the future), and is such a bad water drinker. *Magnolia Parks* was her debut novel, and she is grateful for and delighted by all the wonderful people who yell at her on the internet on a daily basis regarding her stories. She hopes they know they changed her life by loving her imaginary friends.

TikTok: @hijessahastings
Instagram: @jessa.hastings